I COULD WRITE A BOOK

Karen M Cox

KAREN M COX

To Sue ~
my dear friend

Happy Reading!

Kg

For my daughter, my own "darling Emma"
—and for all the Emmas of the world: young women who blaze new paths,
own their mistakes, do what needs doing, and love fiercely.

ACKNOWLEDGMENTS

Although the author's name is the one you see on the cover, there are many people who lend a hand in making a book a reality. It took me four years to write *I Could Write a Book*, and for a while I wondered if maybe I *couldn't* write this one! It's because of the people listed below that this book sits before you now.

First, I send truckloads of thanks to my editor, Christina Boyd of Quill, Ink, for her expertise and guidance, her insistence on always putting the reader first, and her gift for being a tireless cheerleader of insecure authors. Above and beyond seems to be her standard operating procedure, and this book is way better than it was before she saw it.

Claudine DiMuzio, the blog mistress of JustJane1813.com, was an amazing supporter of this project from the moment she learned of it. She organized reviews and blog tour stops, read advanced review copy and gave input, answered questions, and came up with ideas to let readers know that, as unusual as an *Emma* adaptation might be, it's a trip worth taking.

Shari J. Ryan of Madhat Books designed a beautiful book cover that reflects the story perfectly. Her patience and artistry gave *I Could Write a Book* a wide appeal out there in book world, and I'm grateful for her help.

I'd also like to thank my proofreaders, Janet Foster and Betty Jo Moss, for lending those extra pairs of eyes that help catch the oopsies. In addition, Karen Adams, Terry Jakober, and Jane Vivash read and gave input on this manuscript in its formative years, back when it went by the unimaginative name "Emmaesque." Thank you, ladies!

My family shows great patience with a wife/Mom/Nonna who's maybe just a little *different* from the other wives/moms/nonnas! I'm so grateful that they support me—writing on top of a full-time job means that they sometimes have to wait for my attention, although they always have the greatest share of my love.

Finally, I must thank Jane Austen, the genius, and her legions of readers, in whom she lives on into eternity.

"... an incredibly unique and riveting tale..." *Austenesque Reviews*

"...ranks on my list of all-time favorite *Pride and Prejudice* retellings. This novel will definitely make my Best of 2016 list!" *Diary of An Eccentric*

THE JOURNEY HOME

"...a beautifully written story about second chances..." *Just Jane 1813*

PROLOGUE

JULY 4, 1954

HIGHBURY, KENTUCKY

Barbara Taylor Woodhouse had occupied a place in George Knightley's life for as long as he could remember. In 1947, the year George was born, Barbara married John Woodhouse, his father's law partner. Mr. Woodhouse was the man for whom the second Knightley son, George's little brother, was named, and the two families were close friends. George's early memories of Barbara were of a beautiful, young woman with a classic Grace Kelly-look that exuded refinement and elegance, one who turned heads wherever she went. His mother often commented that Barbara Woodhouse was as "sharp as a tack," and if she had been willing and able to attend law school, she would have made a brilliant attorney. Instead, Mrs. Woodhouse assumed the Junior League, mistress of the estate role, spearheaded charity events, and lavishly entertained her husband's clients and associates. Although she was always busy, she was also a devoted mother to her girls, Isabel and Emma, after they came along.

George was seven years old when Emma was born, so he remembered the event well. His parents had dragged him over to the house on Hartfield Road to see her, and as he peered over the side of the crib at the sleeping baby, Mrs. Woodhouse put her hand on his shoulder, and the charm bracelet she always wore clunked against his arm. Looking pensive, she murmured in that musical alto of hers, "Isn't she just perfect, George?" He looked up at her, not sure what the correct answer was, but relatively certain it would not do to speak his real opinion on the matter. Baby Emma was red and wrinkly, and he thought even less of her when she let out a terrific squall in response to him touching her bald, little head. Barbara's joyful smile never wavered.

Even at age seven, George knew Baby Emma would never be as beloved in anyone's eyes as she was in her parents'.

1969-1973

"Nobody, who has not been in the interior of a family, can say what the difficulties of any individual of that family may be."

—Jane Austen, *Emma*, Volume 1, Chapter 18

ONE

JULY 20, 1969

HARTFIELD ROAD, HIGHBURY, KENTUCKY

I sat on the overstuffed sofa in my father's grand living room, staring without seeing at the television set. Daddy's business associates, their wives, and families were all outdoors, gathered poolside. Intermittently, shouts pealed through the air, and somewhere in the back of my mind, I registered the laughing and splashing of children, the rise and fall of conversations. But I, Emma Katherine Woodhouse, inhabited a different world, a world outside theirs.

To put it simply, I was in a foul mood.

Part of my melancholy stemmed from missing my aunt Nina, who had taken a much-deserved vacation to Florida for a couple of weeks. Caring for a teenaged niece all year long was a tall order, and I knew it was good for Nina to get away with her friends every once in a while. But why did Nina have to choose this particular week to go? Did she not remember what today was? Did she not want to remember?

The gray surface of the moon rolled across the TV set from top to bottom, almost too fast to see any of the craggy, pitted features covering the Earth's closest neighbor in space.

Funny how the moon looks so much prettier in the night sky, I thought with a stab of cynical irritation. *But that's always the way, isn't it? Things look nicer from far away; it's only when you're up close and personal that life gets ugly.*

My friend Carol Ann slid the glass door open and stepped inside, hair wet and tousled, a towel wrapped around her spindly frame.

"Hey girl. Whatcha doing in here? The party's outside."

"I know."

"You haven't been swimming at all today. What's the matter?"

"Don't feel like it, I suppose."

Carol Ann walked over and put her hand on my shoulder, dropping her voice to a confidential whisper. "Have you got your period this week?"

I looked up at her, startled, and then burst out laughing. "No, you silly goose. And that wouldn't matter anyway. I've been using Tampax since I was thirteen. You can swim if you use those."

Carol Ann's eyes widened. "You can?"

"Yup."

"You're so lucky you have your aunt to tell you these things. My mom's so old-fashioned, but Nina's modern and cool."

"Yup." I was a bit annoyed with Nina at the moment and didn't want to hear how great she was, although deep down inside I knew my aunt was about the best a girl could ask for.

Carol Ann plunked down on the gold, shag carpet beside my feet so she wouldn't get the sofa wet. "The Holloman twins are asking for you."

Rolling my eyes in contempt, I shot back, "Umm...no thank you."

"They are annoying, aren't they? All high school boys are annoying. They're only good for one thing."

Surely, she didn't mean...

"You know, going to school dances."

I breathed a sigh of relief, for Carol Ann's sake. I didn't think my friend was one of those fast and loose girls, but then again, who ever really knew about people? Sometimes, they weren't what they seemed to be.

"If I date, I wanna date a man—not a boy."

"Carol Ann, you are fifteen years old. You don't want to date some old man. Besides, any kind of *gentleman* worth his salt wouldn't date a fifteen-year-old anyway."

"True. I guess I'll just have to wait for him then."

"Wait for who?"

"George Knightley."

"George Knightley?" I scoffed. "What would you want him for? All he cares about is racquetball, and tennis, and politics, and books written by dead guys."

Carol Ann leaned back against the front of the sofa and let out a sickening little coo. "He's just so handsome—and worldly. And he just graduated from Berkeley. And he's so kind to me."

"Don't read too much into that. He's kind to you because he's a true gentleman—who is, by definition, a man who is kind to everyone."

I was used to my friends mooning over George; all of them seemed to have had a crush on him at some point. I couldn't really blame them for it. After all, I'd had a crush on him too before he went away to California four years ago. But it was nigh impossible to keep a steady infatuation going when I only saw the object of my affection at Thanksgiving and summer breaks. At least it was impossible for me. Carol Ann seemed to have no problem with it.

"That smile." Carol Ann shivered with pleasure, and I laughed at her. "Those blue eyes and that wavy brown hair. He's tall but not too tall. Athletic but not muscle-bound. Friendly but not obnoxious. He's ju-u-ust right."

As if we had summoned him with our conversation, George appeared at the sliding glass door. He opened it a few inches and knocked on the door frame.

"Come in," I called out, after narrowing my eyes and shushing my friend.

"Hello, ladies." Even his voice was smooth, with just a hint of bite, like the bourbon sauce Mrs. Davies served on bread pudding. "Am I interrupting anything?"

"Not at all!" Carol Ann's expression glowed as she leapt to her feet to greet him. "We were only chatting. You know, girl stuff." An uncontrolled giggle escaped her, and she put her hand over her mouth to staunch it.

George smiled, an indulgent grin that snuck around the corners of his mouth whenever *he thought* my friends and I were being silly.

In this case, though, he's right. At least about Carol Ann.

He shut the door behind him. "I was just coming in to get another iced tea. Hey, you're watching the moon landing. I wondered if they were about to touch down."

I stared at the TV set without replying. Carol Ann stared at George with a nervous smile.

He tried again. "I didn't know you were interested in space exploration, Emma."

"I'm not. It's the only thing on all three channels."

"Oh." A pause ensued, then an amused chuckle. "Ah, of course. No clothing shops on the moon."

I knew he was teasing. We often teased each other, almost the way siblings do, but today I wasn't in the mood for it.

After a closer look at me, he commented again. "You seem out of sorts today. What's wrong?"

"Nothing's wrong." All of a sudden, I felt like crying, and Emma Katherine Woodhouse *never* cried, never—and certainly not in front of houseguests. I stood and moved to leave the room. "If everyone's coming in here to watch the TV, I'm going to go fix a snack."

George looked in bewilderment at Carol Ann, and out of the corner of my eye, I saw my friend shrug her shoulders. The glass door slid open and party guests swarmed the television the way they had gathered around the pool earlier.

From my perch on the kitchen stool in the other room, I heard awed voices and celebratory clapping as the lunar lander drew closer to the Sea of Tranquility. The swinging door between living room and kitchen opened, and George crossed the kitchen to get his drink.

"Come out and watch the moon landing," he said as he poured tea from the pitcher into his glass. Ice cubes clunked, almost throwing tea out and onto the counter. "I know you're not too interested in it right now, but years down the road, you'll be glad you saw such an historic event, even if it is just in hazy black and white on a TV set."

"You're probably right, as usual."

"And, your father would not want you to be rude to his guests."

"No lectures today, if you please, Professor Knightley. I promise I'll go back in now and behave like a good girl." My stool scraped the floor.

He put a hand on my arm to stop me. "Hey, something's really bothering you, isn't it? This moping around isn't like our cheerful, lively Emma at all."

I sighed in exasperation and blinked back tears. "Today is my mother's birthday, and it's like everyone just forgot about her."

"Ah, I see."

Carol Ann had just slipped into the kitchen, so she heard the last part of my confession.

George's eyes quietly conveyed his empathy. "Is there anything I can do?"

A sudden idea seized me and my head shot up to ask if he might...

"I want to go to Hillcrest. Will you drive me?"

His brows knit together in a perplexed-looking frown, causing me to wonder what he was thinking. It was atypical for George Knightley to be unsure of himself.

"Please?" A tiny hint of a whine crept into my voice. "Nina would take me if she were here. Or Isabel would take me if she weren't away in Italy this summer. But I can't ask Daddy to leave his party." I hung my head. "I almost think he scheduled it today on purpose so he wouldn't have to think about Mama." Playing for sympathy usually didn't work with George but today it might.

After a long, considering silence, George replied. "Sure, I'll take you to Hillcrest, Emma Kate." He turned to Carol Ann with a charming smile —"Maybe your friend would like to accompany you?"

Carol Ann grimaced slightly, and I remembered that my friend really hated going to Hillcrest. But suddenly, when George asked, Carol Ann nodded and seemed to think the trip was a fine idea.

"Oh yes! I'd be happy to go with you."

I knew she wouldn't be so eager to go if it wasn't George taking us, but I would take her company any way I could find it today.

"Thank you." I gave him a warm smile, truly grateful for his kindness.

He returned my smile, but it wasn't the indulgent, teasing grin from before. It was full of comfort, an interchange between close, familiar friends.

"All right, then. Let's go watch the moon landing. The party should be winding down after that, and we'll find your father and tell him where we're going. It will be several hours before the actual moonwalk. We should be back in plenty of time to see it." He held the swinging door open and with a sweeping gesture, he ushered us back into the living room.

The lunar module touched down, and everyone's eyes were glued to the set in anticipation. I had to admit, it *was* pretty exciting. I barely heard Neil Armstrong's voice crackling over space and time and through the speakers beside the TV screen.

The Holloman twins' father shushed us all. And then I heard it:

"Houston…um…Tranquility Base here. The Eagle has landed."

The room erupted into cheers and applause. I shot George a reluctant grin. He was standing a few feet away with his hands in his pockets, smiling back at me, and immediately my mood lifted.

TWO

George sat behind the wheel of his father's Mercedes convertible, top down at the girls' request. The day was hot, sunny, and humid. That was one thing he missed about California—the agreeable Mediterranean-like climate.

"Why didn't you drive your Corvette?" Emma's little friend piped up from the back seat.

"It's a two-seater. There are three of us," he replied, making eye-contact through the rear-view mirror.

"We could have squished together," she suggested, her eyelashes fluttering in her attempt to look enticing.

So cute, their little crushes. He wondered, though, if her crush was on him or on his Vette.

"Too dangerous." His uncompromising response seemed to make her shrink back against the seat.

He stole another glance at Emma sitting beside him in the passenger seat. She was solemn but not as glum as she had been at the house. For a minute there, he thought she might cry, a sure sign that she was deeply troubled. He had rarely seen Emma cry, not even when she was little. Of course, he hadn't been around her as much in the last four years, and teenage girls had a way of softening up. Maybe she was as emotional as the rest of them, now that she was in high school. Pity, if that was the case. He'd always had a grudging respect for the little Woodhouse girl who pouted and frowned when she was hurt or punished but refused to cry in front of anyone.

Of course, this was an important day for her. One that would make even the toughest person a little emotional. George wondered at the wisdom of Mr. Woodhouse having a get-together on his wife's birthday. But as Emma said earlier, perhaps he wanted to forget. It was understandable, but he was sorely mistaken if he thought Emma would ever forget. Mistaken and inconsiderate too, especially of Emma's feelings. And what made Nina run off to Florida this week? She was usually a lot more tuned into Emma's well-being. She rarely left her niece to deal with these things on her own. Perhaps she too needed to escape the memories.

The Mercedes clung to a curve in the road, and George slowed as they approached the next hill. Beside the road, he saw a white brick sign with the word "Hillcrest" in black letters adorning the entrance.

"Turn here," Emma needlessly reminded him.

George cornered onto the long, paved, tree-lined road that led up to the place. Flowers were everywhere. It appeared the staff put a lot of effort into making everything look pleasant and welcoming.

He rolled to a stop at the end of the road, and Emma opened her car door without saying a word. Her friend looked back and forth between them, but George nodded to her. "You'd best go in with her. Do you want me to come around and get the car door for you?"

"Oh!" she said, "Oh. No, that's not necessary. I'll get it." She giggled again.

This one is quite the giggler.

Emma rolled her eyes, opened the back door, and pulled her friend out by the hand.

After parking the car, he jogged up a short flight of steps covered with green indoor-outdoor carpet and opened the painted wood and etched-glass door. George halted once he was in the foyer, letting his eyes adjust to the low light and absorbing the cool quiet. A chandelier graced the high ceiling, and little groups of soft chintz chairs and sofas were scattered about to welcome visitors. The flowers on the end tables were artificial, so instead of their perfume, he smelled the faint scent of industrial-strength cleaner. The woman at the front desk looked up and beckoned him with a warm smile.

"Can I help you, sir?"

"I'm here with Emma Woodhouse to see Barbara."

"She said you'd be along in a minute." She pointed to her left. "It's down that hallway, Room 304."

As he approached the room, he saw Emma's friend, whose name he couldn't remember to save his life, leaning against the hallway wall, arms crossed. She wrinkled her nose, and he became aware of the smell of urine, and the sickly-sweet odor of glucose IVs and tube feeding. The friend looked up, saw George, and quickly pasted on a bright smile. He braced himself—it was always a shock to see Barbara here at Hillcrest—and gestured Emma's young friend to stand in the doorway with him.

Emma was beginning to resemble her mother somewhat in appearance, and fortunately, she also seemed to have Barbara's brains and outgoing personality.

George smiled at the comparison and then grew solemn. The Woodhouses were a perfect family for a while, but when Emma was seven, Barbara suffered an aneurysm. She was unconscious for weeks, and the doctors were not sure she would make it, but then miraculously, she began to turn around. Her family was ecstatic at first, but over time, it became apparent that a complete recovery was not to be. Barbara could no longer walk or talk or feed herself. After several months of attempted rehabilitation and around the clock nurses, John made the tough decision to put her at Hillcrest Convalescent Center. He'd told George once that he wanted his daughters to have as normal a life as possible, and perhaps that was his primary motivation. But Barbara living at Hillcrest also allowed John to avoid dealing with his own heartbreak on a daily basis. When considered from that point of view, it wasn't the most altruistic decision, especially since finances weren't an issue—but George tried to never judge another man's decisions unless he had walked a mile in his shoes. He had no idea what John Woodhouse had to endure.

After Barbara went to stay at Hillcrest, her family came to see her almost every day. But as the girls began to grow up and become more involved in school and other activities, those visits became less frequent. Isabel was gone for the entire summer this year studying art in Italy.

However, Emma's devotion to her mother had yet to waver. She insisted her father take her to visit Barbara almost every Sunday and most holidays as well. Thus, mother and daughter had a relationship of sorts, and Barbara's single sister, Nina, moved into a small house across the road from the Woodhouses to perform the office of mother to the little girls. She really stepped up to the plate, in George's opinion, and he had a lot of respect and admiration for Nina Taylor.

Emma's voice carried him forth to the present, and he stepped just inside the room, not wanting to disturb the mother and daughter's precious time together.

Emma sat in the chair next to her mother's wheelchair, arranging pillows to support Barbara's flaccid right side and help her sit upright.

"I'll talk to them about this, Mama. They should check on you more often so you aren't all slumped over this way." She arranged the blanket over her mother's legs and replaced a slipper that had fallen off. "There, that's better, isn't it?"

A hoarse, unintelligible moan issued from Barbara's mouth. Emma leaned over and kissed her mother's pasty cheek. "Did you know it's your birthday today?" She reached over and pulled a card off the nightstand. "See, here's one of your birthday cards. It's from Nina. She went to Florida this week with some friends from work."

Barbara grunted.

"Yes, she needed a vacation from me, I'm sure." Emma laughed. Barbara put her left hand to her daughter's cheek and made a soft, maternal murmuring sound.

"And look." Emma stood and walked over to the table below the window sill. "These are from Daddy and Isabel and me. Don't they smell nice?"

Barbara patted her knee with her stronger hand, and Emma chuckled. "I'm too big to sit on your knee now. I'm almost grown. I'd squash you."

They sat in comfortable silence for a minute until Emma ventured another topic. "School starts in about a month." Barbara's eyes watched her intently, waiting for her to go on.

"I'm taking geometry, English, world history, biology, chorus, and Latin." She ticked the subjects off on her fingers. "Daddy said you'd approve of me taking Latin. He said you told him it was the most useful thing you'd ever learned because it helps with so many other subjects."

Barbara nodded and her lips spread into an asymmetrical smile. She groaned loudly and made a sound that was almost like a laugh.

"Oh! What am I thinking? Where's your little picture board?" Emma hunted around the room and frowned when she opened the nightstand. "This thing doesn't do you any good sitting in the drawer. I'll have to talk to them about that, too." She laid the array of pictures and simple words mounted on a piece of cardboard in her mother's lap. They proceeded to have a one-sided conversation of questions and comments from Emma and indications of "yes" and "no" from Barbara that lasted almost fifteen minutes. George joined them when Emma beckoned, and he shook Barbara's good hand. That's when he realized how much of a burden a one-sided conversation could be, but young Emma made it all look easy, introducing topics and comments in a matter-of-fact way that belied her youthful age. Her friend stood timidly at the door, waiting, but obviously ready to leave the moment Emma was willing to go.

Finally, after one more check for her mother's comfort, they made their goodbyes. Emma embraced Barbara, whose eyes shone with unshed tears.

"I'll see you on Sunday, okay?"

Barbara gave a jerky nod that required her head and most of her upper body to execute and pointed with a gnarled hand at the board in her lap.

"What?" Emma looked down. "Oh. Yes, Mama, I love you too."

They were a quiet bunch on the way back to the Woodhouse home. Emma's friend stared out the window and George felt solemn too.

Emma let out a long sigh, and he looked over at her, afraid of what miserable look he might see on her face. Instead, she smiled at him. "Thank you for driving me to see her, George. I won't forget it."

"You're welcome." He tried to keep pity out of his expression because he knew she wouldn't want it.

She turned to address her friend in the back seat. "Hey, Carol Ann." *So that's the girl's name!*

"Yes?"

"You want to call Debbie and Sheila and see if they can go to the movies tonight? Don't worry, George." She turned back to face him. "You don't have to drive us. Debbie's got her driver's license and her mother's Cadillac."

"Well now, that's a relief."

She stifled a chuckle. "Yes, yes, you can go back to doing whatever it is you big-time college graduates do."

"Filling out law school applications probably," he grumbled.

"You know, you really ought to get out more." She poked his arm as she spoke to emphasize her point. "All work and no play makes George a dull boy."

He grinned at her teasing and turned in at the big house on Hartfield Road.

THREE

OCTOBER 27, 1973

LEXINGTON, KENTUCKY

I paced the hallway in front of my father's hospital room, impatient for the doctor. I had arrived from Georgia earlier that afternoon, and after a brief stop at home to check in with Mrs. Davies, our housekeeper, I rushed straight over to Saint Luke's Hospital. What a whirlwind twenty-four hours it had been! Ever since I got the call from Nina about my father's stroke, I had been on a mission to get home. After telling the dean of students what had happened, I was granted leave to come home for a week and sort out what I could.

How am I to bear it if he doesn't recover? He's my only surviving parent since Mama passed away. A panicked feeling rose in the back of my throat and tears threatened to spill over. *No, mustn't think like this now. Have to focus. Ask the doctor my questions. Figure out what to do next. Daddy is stable. Intermittently conscious. These are good signs.* I shook my head to rid my morbid thoughts.

The floor nurse said Nina and Isabel had gone out for a quick bite to eat and would be back soon. I chewed my thumb, a bad habit from childhood that still reared its ugly head when I was overly anxious but immediately stopped when I heard the elevator ding. *Thank goodness. Nina is back. Now we can start planning what on earth we're going to do.*

But it wasn't Nina who stepped out of the elevator. It was George Knightley, followed by a pretty woman with dark hair and eyes whom I didn't know.

George was dressed in white shorts, a polo shirt, and sweat bands around his wrists. His *Woman of the Month* was dressed similarly in a pale pink tennis skort and matching top. Apparently, they had just stepped off the tennis court. *Or out of a country club advertisement,* I joked to myself, despite my anxiety.

After a frantic look around, George spied me standing in the hall. He strode over and enfolded me in a fierce embrace before taking me by the shoulders and stepping back so he could look in my eyes.

"Emma! How is he? How are you?"

"How did you know?" I was flabbergasted that George, of all people, would be the first familiar person I would see in the neuro wing of the hospital.

"Mother called the country club looking for me. We were just getting ready to go out on the courts. I would have been here earlier, but I was out of town until late this morning and didn't know what had happened."

I looked over his shoulder, reminding him of his companion. "Oh, um, Emma—this is Jeannette Eaton." He stepped back, indicating his date with a hurried gesture. "Jeanette, Emma Woodhouse. Her father is Dad's law partner and my boss."

"Oh"—Jeanette shook my hand, hers all limp-wristed and soft—"Nice to meet you. I'm sorry about your dad."

"Thank you."

"What have you found out?" George interrupted.

"Nothing much. I'm waiting on the doctor now."

"Is John…?"

"I just arrived about a half hour ago myself, but I had a chance to talk to the nurse and peek in on him. He's conscious, but he seems confused, and his left side is affected. He's having trouble moving his arm."

"Where's Isabel?"

"She and Nina just stepped out for a quick dinner. They've been here all day."

"What about you? Have you had dinner? Can I get you something? Take you somewhere?"

Jeannette stiffened and let out an exasperated sigh. *Oh, so now I'm ruining her tennis match and dinner date with Mr. Wonderful?* I smiled fondly at George and took his arm, leading him toward my father's room.

"Now, don't you worry one iota about me, George Knightley. I'll be just fine. Would you like to see Daddy? I'm sure you would be a great comfort to him." I glanced over his shoulder at Jeannette and gave her an affected smile. "We'll just be a minute, Jenny, and then you two can be on your way."

George approached the bedside, his blue eyes serious, brow furrowed in concern. "John?" he ventured in a soft voice, touching Daddy's arm. "How are you, sir?"

Daddy roused from his sleep and looked around the room for a second before settling his eyes on George.

"Who are you?" he asked. His voice was hoarse and uncontrolled.

George looked taken aback at Daddy's lack of recognition. "It's George, sir, George Knightley."

"You're not George Knightley! George would never look so unkempt. Filthy things, mustaches. So difficult to keep groomed."

I stifled a chuckle, and George looked aghast that I would find this funny. I went up and put my hand on his arm.

"I'm not laughing at him, just at you. You should see your expression." I cleared my throat and addressed my father. "It really is George, Daddy." I leaned and whispered in George's ear, "He doesn't recognize you with the mustache."

"I've had it for three months. He's seen me plenty of times with it."

"His short-term memory isn't very good. At least, that's what the nurses have told me."

"Will he recover his memory?"

The smile slipped off my face. "They don't know yet. I'm hoping the doctor can shed some light on the situation when he gets here. It's only been two days since the stroke, so I'm hopeful, but..."

"Your father's going to get well, Emma Kate," he said, squeezing my hand.

Tears stung my eyes. "Yes, I know you're right. I know he will." Looking at Daddy's now closed eyes, I whispered, "He just has to."

George put his arm around me in a show of support, and I leaned my head against him—to borrow a bit of his strength so I could deal with the days ahead.

"How's Wellington this fall?"

I shrugged. "Same. They were very kind about me taking a week to see to Daddy."

"That's good." His arm slipped from around my shoulders, and he clasped my hand in his. He looked down and fingered the charms on the bracelet around my wrist. "Is this your mother's bracelet?"

"Nina gave it to me after Mama passed away."

"And you always wear it?"

"Not always. I wear it a lot, though. I like to remember her."

"I remember her wearing this when I was a boy. It's beautiful."

"Like she was."

"Yes." He smiled and gave my fingers a squeeze.

There was a long silence during which we stood there, listening to the beep-beep of the IV and watching Daddy's eyelids flutter to and fro. A rustle came from behind us, and George let my hand go so I could turn and greet the visitor.

"Nina!" I rushed to my aunt, hugging her tightly.

"Oh, my dear girl!" she said, her hand stroking my hair and giving me an extra squeeze. "I'm so sorry about this. And so glad you're here, safe and sound."

Isabel came in behind her and the three of us clung together.

"Who's there?" Daddy called from the bed. "Is it my girls?"

"Yes sir," George replied, smiling. "All three of your girls are here to take care of you. What a lucky fellow you are!"

Isabel and I approached the bed. George led Nina to the doorway to speak privately to her. She nodded and patted his arm. "We will, and thank you." He turned to make his farewells.

"I'll check in with you tomorrow, Emma. Isabel."

"Bye, George. Thank you for coming." Isabel's voice barely carried across the room, it was so soft.

"Yes, yes," I said, teasing to lighten the atmosphere. "Your little lady in the visitor's lobby is awaiting her Prince Charming. You best get to it."

He grinned at me before spinning on his heel and exiting the room.

"Oh, and George…" I called after him.

He turned.

"Keep the mustache. I like it even if Daddy doesn't."

He shook his head, smiling and muttering to himself. "Nonsensical girl."

FOUR

DECEMBER 23, 1973

DONWELL HORSE FARM, HIGHBURY, KENTUCKY

Glasses clinked and Perry Como's voice crooned in the background. George wandered in and out of the little cliques, saying hello, playing junior host. It was more his parents' crowd, but the Donwell Christmas party was a local tradition, and he was expected to attend. Several area big shots were there: the mayor, the circuit court judge, the county attorney. There were many non-legal types on the guest list too, even though it was a business party. Knightley and Woodhouse had represented some very wealthy and powerful people over the years. Several owners of thoroughbred horse farms, most of the members of the racing commission, and the president of Keeneland Race Course were all mingling throughout the rooms.

George's appearance at the party was doubly important this Christmas. The new year would bring about some changes at Knightley and Woodhouse. George was slated to take over running the Lexington branch of the law firm. That had always been the long-term plan, but Mr. Woodhouse's stroke had sped up the event's timing considerably. The elder Mr. Knightley had already begun cutting back his involvement, replacing court cases with rounds of golf and globetrotting. He still provided guidance to the other attorneys and continued managing some of the family properties. George's younger brother, John, whom they called Jack, was fresh out of law school, newly wed to Isabel Woodhouse, and had been asked to head up the new Louisville law office.

George was happy for his brother; it was a big honor and a lot of responsibility as well, but Jack had always been serious and determined—not like the stereotypical reckless younger brother at all. If George were completely honest, though, in a hidden corner of his heart, he was envious of Jack's opportunity. It would be an exciting challenge setting up a new office in a new town. But George had his stake in Lexington, and as the elder son, he had the management of the farms to keep him busy as well.

Over by the buffet table, he saw Emma ladling some punch into a cup for her father and having an amiable chat with one of Knightley and Woodhouse's clients. She gracefully extricated herself from the conversation and rested her hand on Mr. Woodhouse's shoulder, encouraging him to take the cup. Walking closer, he heard her voice as she reassured her father.

"Just a little bit won't hurt, Daddy. It's not that sweet. And it's for toasting."

George caught her eye, and they exchanged gentle messages of amusement regarding her father's fastidious ways. George had missed talking to Emma this fall, he realized suddenly. When she was still at home, they were together at family and community gatherings, especially once his brother began to date her sister. Emma's forthright opinions and her unique way of seeing the world through what George laughingly referred to as her "Emma-colored glasses" had always diverted him. Now she was getting a glimpse of the larger world, something she sorely needed, in his opinion. It would make her a much more interesting woman in the long run.

He remembered with some nostalgia how excited he had been to go to college at eighteen—hard to believe that was eight years ago. Up until that time, George Knightley enjoyed a sheltered existence in quiet, Kentucky horse country. After high school, he was ready to see more of what life had to offer and find his place in the big, wide world.

All in all, UC was a good experience. By the time he reached his senior year, however, the Berkeley culture had started to wear a little thin. At first, he believed many of the free speech movement ideals would solve the country's problems. He whole-heartedly supported the anti-war sentiment, the Civil Rights Movement, and the defense of the First Amendment. But he had also seen the seamy underside of that culture: drug abuse, poverty, and the societal breakdowns resulting from an absence of structure and guidelines for group behavior. There was so much promise at the beginning of the "Age of Aquarius," but after a while, it seemed to go nowhere in the cold, harsh reality of the world. The United States was still in Vietnam, there was no victory in Johnson's "War on Poverty," and now there was all this Watergate mess, with Nixon smack dab in the middle of it.

George also found himself surprisingly too conservative for the "free love" movement. "God knows I love women," he was fond of saying, "but..." After the novelty wore off, casual physical encounters began to feel empty and meaningless to him. He was much more particular these days, although it was often not an issue anyway—the demands of law school and his new career cut down on his social life considerably.

His mother beckoned him to come speak to one of her friends. He winked at Emma and crossed the room to answer the parental summons.

George was glad to see John Woodhouse on the mend these days. He could walk with a cane around the house and had almost full return of his left arm. His stint at the rehabilitation hospital was over about a week ago, and Isabel and Emma were relieved to have him home at last.

The law office felt empty the last couple of months without George's boss around. John Woodhouse wasn't the sharpest man who ever passed the bar, but he was competent, and he was kind. He had thrown himself into his work after Barbara passed away, followed a few months later by Emma leaving for college—and it was hard to imagine working without him.

After the few weeks he had spent in the rehabilitation center, it became clear that John could not return to his former job. His memory for long ago events was as good as ever, but new information was often forgotten, and he was easily confused, even about daily matters such as medicines and paying bills. Subsequently, he was unable to try cases anymore. How would his girls manage now that he required constant care? Although Nina had her trust fund, she had only recently been able to pursue her dream of being a librarian and was now working full-time at the university. Isabel and Jack were moving to Louisville after the first of the year. Emma, of course, still had two and a half years of college in Georgia. They could hire nurses but that wasn't the same as having a family member around to supervise the help. It would be a lot to ask of Isabel, but she was probably the best choice, even though she was newly married, because she was older, out of school, and would be living closer than Emma. George could offer to stop by regularly—make sure the hired staff were doing their jobs and his old boss was being well cared for. He started to move toward Emma to suggest it when he was interrupted by the chime of a spoon against crystal. The senior Mr. Knightley was getting ready to make a speech.

"Can I have your attention? A moment, please." Mr. Knightley charmed everyone in the room with his gregarious smile. He always made it look so easy. "Jonesy, turn down that infernal music for a second."

The butler fiddled with the knobs on the stereo until Mr. Como had faded away completely.

"Well, here we are, at the end of another year. 1973 has been a memorable one, for good things—like a successful year at Knightley & Woodhouse"—the crowd lifted their glasses and murmured "hear, hear"—"the promotion of George to managing the local office, and marriage of my son Jack to his lovely Isabel last June." He raised his hand toward the happy couple. Jack gave one of his rare smiles, and Isabel looked up at him in total adoration.

"It's also been a year for the bittersweet—the unexpected retirement of my faithful friend and law partner, John Woodhouse." The crowd turned and raised their glasses to Mr. Woodhouse, who at Emma's urging, lifted his own glass with a shaky smile.

"I'm so glad you are well enough to join us tonight, my old friend, and wish you many peaceful years in the circle of your family. You will be missed at the offices on Surrey Street."

Mr. Woodhouse nodded his thanks.

"I also have the honor of announcing some additional news that I found out only this afternoon."

George stopped with his martini half way to his mouth. *I wasn't aware of any other news.*

"Jack and Isabel are not only taking on a marriage and a new house, but they are also taking on the supreme challenge of making doting grandparents of John, Joanne, and me. Isabel is expecting a baby in the spring."

George almost dropped his glass. His eyes snapped to his brother and saw Jack's frown. Obviously, he hadn't meant for their father to make this announcement tonight. Isabel was blushing profusely, although her smile was so bright it could have powered the entire house for an evening. People surrounded them as congratulations and the sound of clinking glasses filled the room. George sought Emma, who was smiling and clapping along with everyone else. She met his gaze and laughed at his shock. This was obviously no secret to her then. Nor was it a shock to Nina Taylor, who looked at George too, eyebrows raised and smiling broadly. He threaded through the crowd and approached Emma's aunt and her circle of friends.

"George, darling." Nina's friend Paulette slipped her arm through his and dragged her fingers up and down his bicep. *Doesn't the woman realize I'm about five years too old to play Ben Braddock to her Mrs. Robinson? There ought to be a name for women like this so single men could warn each other about them.*

"Merry Christmas, Mrs. Thomas."

"And Happy New Year to you." Her voice oozed sexual frustration and her breath smelled of vodka when she leaned up and kissed his cheek.

"Uh... Nina, may I tear you away from your little group here for a bit?" He detached himself from Paulette Thomas and took Nina's elbow, leading her to the side of the room.

Nina looked apologetic. "Sorry about Paulette. She gets a little delusional when she's had a drink or two."

"Oh, yes, well..." He waved her comment off with a shrug and a careless gesture.

"What is it?"

"Did you know about Jack and Isabel's baby?"

"The baby? Oh, yes, Isabel told us some time ago."

"And Emma knows, I presume."

"Yes, of course."

"I guess Isabel will be pretty busy this coming year."

Nina nodded and took a sip of her drink.

"It's a lot to take on: a new home, a baby, and taking care of John—now that he's returned home."

Nina's party smile slipped a bit. "That was the plan originally, but…"

"If it helps at all, I can check on him periodically, several times a week, if need be."

"That's very kind of you, but you don't need to worry. John's in good hands."

A sense of brotherly unease settled over him. "If Isabel is moving to Louisville and having a baby, and you're working full-time at the university, whose job is it to see to John Woodhouse?" he asked, already dreading the answer.

Nina looked at him, a little uncomfortably.

"Emma." He answered his own question. "Emma is quitting college to take care of her father." An unpleasant tightness crept over his expression. "Don't you think it's unwise to let her quit school?"

"Now, George, relax. She's not quitting school. She's going to go to the university and live at home."

"Nina," he said, a little exasperated. "That's not the same thing as getting an education away from home. There's a lot more to it than what she reads in textbooks. How is Emma going to gain that life experience? If she does this, she'll never get to study abroad. She won't discover how it is to live on her own. Think of all the opportunities she will miss."

"I've reminded her of all that. This move is her choice. I can't talk her out of it."

He whirled around, looking for Emma and saw her standing by the punch table with her father and a couple of his friends. He started to move in that direction when Nina put her hand on his sleeve.

"George," she said in her quiet, yet commanding librarian's voice, "I know you have good intentions, but don't upset Emma or her father with your questions and opinions. Not tonight."

He stopped short. Of course, Nina was correct, as always. This was not the right time or place. "Yes…no…yes," he stammered. "That's wise advice, and no, I don't want to ruin their evening. You're right…yes." He hoped he could keep himself from saying the words burning a hole in his tongue.

Nina searched his expression and gifted him with one of her kind, sisterly smiles. "If it makes you feel any better, I'm not thrilled with the idea myself. But it's not like she's dropping out, just transferring to a local school. And, as you know very well, Emma can be quite stubborn when she sets her mind, and she's determined to do this for John."

"Hmmph," he replied, knowing Nina knew all about her niece's single-mindedness and disappointed that she wouldn't use her motherly influence to curb it, even if it was for Emma's own good.

FIVE

The holiday party was in full swing, and congratulations flowed in from every corner about Jack and Isabel's happy news. All the excitement discombobulated Daddy, but I deflected most of the questions with ease. "Daddy is thrilled he's going to be a grandfather ... Isabel is due in early April ... Isn't it great? ... A baby will be a wonderful addition to our family ... Yes, Mama would have been ecstatic."

Isabel was beaming like the sun. Jack, on the other hand...

I watched my brother-in-law during the next few minutes and then made my way over to him. Standing at his side while we both surveyed the room, I leaned toward him and spoke out of the corner of my mouth.

"Jack Knightley, you don't look nearly happy enough to be an expectant father."

"I don't know why my dad has to announce it like this...in public, in front of God and everybody."

"So, what does it matter? Everyone thinks it's fantastic."

Jack scowled. "Everyone thinks we're idiots for starting a family so soon after getting married."

"And God forbid anyone think that Jack Knightley is an idiot for even one second!" I said, laughing softly.

"What if something goes wrong, Em? How will Isabel face them all? Have you thought about that?"

"Of course, I haven't thought about such a morbid thing! Good Lord, you can be such a spaz sometimes." A thought occurred to me, and I pointed my finger at him. "And don't you be saying things like that to Izzy either. It's not good for her or the baby to get any kind of weird negative vibes from you."

Jack rolled his eyes and snorted, but then his face took on a genuinely worried look, and my heart went out to him. He did love Isabel beyond all reason and that meant I could forgive most any fault he had.

"Don't worry, Brother John," I said with a smile, using my childhood nickname for him. "I just know that everything will work out fine."

"Do you?"

"Yes, because it must. I won't tolerate anything else."

He chuckled then, and I grinned into my wine glass.

"You're too young to drink that," he retorted.

Now it was my turn to roll my eyes. I started to return his barb, but George approached us, giving me an opportunity to deftly change the subject instead.

George held out his hand to his brother. They looked much alike, although Jack's eyes were brown, not blue, and his hair was a little darker. And George was a tad bit more handsome. In my opinion.

"Congratulations, you son-of-a-gun."

Jack shook the outstretched hand George offered, and each brother clapped the other on the shoulder.

I looked the other way to hide a smile. *Why don't they go ahead and hug each other? Men!*

"Thank you."

"You should have given me a clue. I had no idea." George turned to face me. "Did you have any idea?"

"What? Oh, yes, Izzy told me a few weeks back. Isn't it wonderful news?"

"Yes, yes, wonderful."

Isabel beckoned for Jack from across the room, and he excused himself, leaving George and me to ourselves.

"Is that when you decided to leave college?"

I blinked, looking at him in surprise. "Pardon?"

He drew the corners of his mouth in a stern frown. "When Isabel told you about the baby—is that when you decided to move back home?"

"It was the deciding factor, yes. Daddy needs someone to take care of him and run the house. It was going to be hard on Isabel to begin with, but now, with the baby coming, it would be almost impossible."

"You could hire help."

"And we will, but he still needs a family member around to ensure that he's cared for properly. He can't be left alone, at least not yet."

"What about some place like Hillcrest?"

I shook my head. "We thought about that, even discussed it briefly, but I couldn't send him there—too many memories, for all of us. It is a fine facility. There's no other place in town I'd consider for him, but Daddy needs to be at home to get well. I know it in my heart."

"But Emma," George persisted, "it means you have to leave college."

"I'm going to finish college." We took our conversation into the smallish breakfast nook off the big dining room.

"I can't believe your father would ask this of you, and I certainly can't believe this is what your mother would have wanted. I wish you'd reconsider."

"My father did not ask this of me," I said, feeling my temper rise. "And Mama could never have anticipated anything like this would happen to our family. How do you know what she would have wanted?

"And besides"—I turned back to look into the party room so I wouldn't have to see the disapproval on his face. *I swear, sometimes he can be more critical than Jack!*—"I'm getting a degree—but at the state university. I made plans back in November in case it came to this. I've already been accepted here in the College of Arts and Sciences, and I sign up for classes in just a few weeks. I'll still get my education. Don't you worry about that."

"If you were a normal young woman, I wouldn't argue with your decision at all."

I set my glass on the table and turned to face him, hands on my hips. "Now what's *that* supposed to mean?"

"It means that a local education would be fine for any other girl, but you're smarter than the typical college co-ed."

"Your faith in the competence of womankind is overwhelming. On behalf of females everywhere, I thank you for your vote of confidence, Professor Knightley."

I snuck a glance at his face to gauge his reaction to my sarcasm. He had two fingers pinching the bridge of his nose like I'd given him a headache.

"I am trying," he said through gritted teeth, "to give you some brotherly advice."

"You're not my brother, George."

"I'm the closest thing to a brother you've got, except for Jack. And I'm apparently the only one who sees this move home for the mistake it is."

I stared, almost daring him to go further. And of course, being George, he did.

"You have so much potential. I've seen it. You could do anything you set your mind to. But if you come back home—there's no challenge for you here, Emma. Your father idolizes you. Nina doesn't make you do anything you don't want to do—"

"George Bryan Knightley! Enough already! The decision is made. My father is my only parent still living. The house needs someone to run it. Nina shouldn't have to assume a role that is either my sister's or mine. She's already given up too many years of her own life for us. Isabel lives out of town, is married, and now she's going to have a baby. It's down to me. And that's final."

"But your college…"

Finally, I exploded, although I managed to keep my voice surprisingly low. "I *hate* Wellington College, alright? Is that what you wanted me to say? It's my mother's alma mater, and she always wanted me to go there, so I went, and I hate it! The girls are all either snooty or boring. The classes are outdated and tedious. There are no guys on campus because it's an all-girls school, and the guys off campus are only after a one-night stand."

George stood, blinking at me. If I hadn't been so ticked off, his expression would have been amusing. *I think he just realized for the first time that I like boys.*

After a pause to wrap his mind around that development, he went on. "There are other colleges, Emma. Money's not an issue. Why not go someplace where you'll be happy *and* challenged? Wouldn't you like to develop a career? Maybe go to law school? Join the law firm someday and follow in your father's footsteps?"

I chortled, shaking my head. "The last thing I want to be is a lawyer." I set my wine glass, half empty, on the sideboard. "I know you mean well, and I guess I should be flattered that you think I'm intelligent when you have such a low opinion of women's brains in general. That isn't very liberal-minded of you, by the way. It clashes with your beatnik Berkeley image. But don't worry, I'll keep your misogynistic little secret from the *Woman of the Month*. Not that she would care if she knew. What's her name again?"

His mouth twitched into a smile. If I could get him laughing, I knew he'd leave me alone.

"Her name's Valerie."

"Ah yes, Valerie. She's nicer than Jeannette anyway."

"Glad you approve."

"I didn't say that."

He laughed out loud.

With the tension broken, I drove my point home.

"Moving back home is my decision, George. I'm a grown woman, and I've made up my mind. I don't know how much longer I'll have with Daddy. I've experienced the loss of a parent, and it's a pain I wouldn't wish on anyone. I'm not trying to make you feel sorry for me, but I do know of what I speak. And I know that if he needs me, I can't walk away."

"I'll say this for you, your dedication to him is admirable."

"You would do the same, if it were you."

His intense blue gaze landed on me, as if I was a puzzle he couldn't quite figure out. "Perhaps," was his only response.

"You would. I know you would—because you always do what you think is right. And this is right." I turned to go back into the dining room. "I'm going over to get a club soda and check on Daddy. Can I get you something?"

"No thanks."

"I think I saw your Valerie looking for you earlier. You didn't abandon her to your mother, did you?"

"Of course not." He took the hint and wandered off. I think we were both grateful to let go of that awkward subject, my unexpected return home.

SIX

George stood at the front door of the Woodhouse residence and rang the doorbell. It clanged with an old-fashioned kind of formality, making him feel rather insignificant. The two-story Doric columns framing the house front always made him feel like a small boy, even after all these years.

Mrs. Davies, the housekeeper, opened the door and gave him a bright smile full of welcome. "Mr. Knightley! Come in. It's so good to see you! Let me fetch Miss Emma. Won't you have a seat?" She gestured to the living room on the left.

"Thank you, Mrs. D." He nodded his appreciation and stepped inside.

It had been quite some time since George had graced the Woodhouse home. Before the stroke, he saw John most every day at the office. And Emma had been, of course, away at school.

His eyes wandered to the top of the two-story foyer. The chandelier crystals sparkled in the late afternoon sun, showing a layer of dust, some of which floated in lazy patterns down to rest on the sturdy hardwood floors. The foyer had an open, graceful elegance that strongly reminded him of Barbara Taylor Woodhouse in her prime: equestrian heiress, daughter of old money—older even than his own. The Taylor farms and land were left to her half-brother Edwin, in the grand old male-inherits-land tradition, but Barbara still inherited a vast sum of money from her parents. She'd had education, opportunities, and class—a result of the union of her family's good fortune and her own good sense. It was regrettable that she was unable to pass these advantages to Emma in person.

Nina was, in many ways, a good role model for Emma. Nina Taylor didn't have to work, but she did because she enjoyed it. The library was a productive outlet for Nina's need for intellectual stimulation, a characteristic she and Emma shared. In George's opinion, however, she just didn't have the same authority that a mother would have.

And that led him to the current situation, and why he canceled a date to go horseback riding with Valerie this afternoon.

The other night at the Donwell Christmas party he'd stuck his nose in where it didn't belong, and he knew that. If Nina found out he'd chastised Emma that night—after she'd warned him off—he'd have some explaining to do. But because of the connection between their families, and now the marriage of their siblings, George harbored a specific interest in Emma's well-being. As any brother-in-law would, of course. And the "poor, motherless lamb," as his mother often called her, had no one to guide her.

It was time to let go of the college disagreement. Emma was right; she was grown up now, although she didn't always act like it, and it was her decision to make. Besides, he had a grudging admiration for her devotion to her family.

"George!" She came bounding down the stairs, rounding the newel at the foot of them and clearing the last step with a little hop. She had on blue jeans and one of those flimsy, gauzy tops you could practically see through. "Well, hello there! What are you doing here?"

"Came by to visit your dad—and you, of course. If I'm welcome."

She sauntered to him with a smile and linked her arm in his. The smell of honeysuckle drifted over him, and he relaxed.

"Handsome fellows are always welcome at Hartfield Road," she said, leading him toward the parlor.

He halted, causing her to turn around and face him. "I also wanted to make amends—for the other night."

She waved him off with her free hand. "Oh, you were just being you, Professor Knightley. I'd forgotten all about it."

Her eyes flitted downward, indicating that might not be the absolute truth, but there was also friendliness in her manner, and he knew that was genuine. She would forgive him, although forgetting might take time.

"So, to help make amends, I brought you a present—a gift of goodwill."

Her eyes lit up. "Oooh, I love presents! Although, they say 'beware of Trojans bearing gifts'— but I'm sure you wouldn't bring a wooden horse. Where is it?" She leaned around to look behind him.

"It's out on the front porch."

She bounded toward the door, laughing. "Maybe it *is* a horse, after all."

"Wait!"

"Why?"

"I need to explain first."

She crossed her arms and frowned. "Okay..."

"It is a gift, Emma Kate, but I don't want you to feel obligated to take it."

"Oh, for heaven's sake, why wouldn't I want to take it?"

"It's, well...maybe I should just show you. But remember, if you don't want to keep it, all you have to do is say so."

"The suspense is killing me! Will you just show me the present already?"

He stepped outside and returned a second later, carrying a big box. It clunked from side to side, held high enough that she couldn't see into it. He set it on the foyer floor and lifted the lid. His hands disappeared inside, and a little yelp was heard as he drew the golden bundle out of the box.

"Oh, George! A puppy! It's beautiful!"

"It's a she, actually, a golden retriever. She's nine weeks old."

Emma reached out her arms for the wriggling, tail-wagging ball of fur. "Aren't you the prettiest little thing? Oh, look! She likes me!"

He laughed as the pup leaned up and licked Emma's face. "Well, of course she does. Everyone likes Miss Emma Woodhouse."

Emma held the pup, crooning to her in soft tones, like one might use with a baby.

"She's to keep you company, when your dad is resting, or when you go outside, and he doesn't want to go with you. I know how you love the outdoors."

He waited a minute, watching while Emma played with the dog. "Do you like her, Emma? Would you like to keep her? It's not a bit of a problem to take her back, if you don't think—"

"Take her back? Absolutely not! She's adorable. Thank you, George!" She buried her nose in the soft fur. "I love her already." Emma set her down on the floor and watched her walk around in a circle before letting out a bark.

"What will you name her?"

"Hmm…" Emma's eyes opened wide. "I'm going to name her Maude."

"That's an odd name for a dog."

As if in reply to his derogatory statement regarding her new name, Maude came over and promptly wet on his wing-tips.

"It is not an odd name!" She snatched up her puppy. "Don't listen to him, Maude. He has no idea how to talk to ladies."

Mrs. Davies came hurrying in. "What was that noise? It sounded like a…" She did a double take at the dog in Emma's arms. "Mr. Knightley, you didn't!"

"He surely did, Mrs. D. Meet Maude, our newest family member. And fetch a towel, if you don't mind. Our new family member just tinkled on Mr. Knightley's shoe."

Mrs. Davies pursed her lips and frowned at George as she hurried off to get the towel, muttering something about "more work" and "shoes" and "serving you right."

"I've got all her paraphernalia in the car. Bed, leash, food, water dish. She's all scheduled for shots at the vet and for obedience training when she's old enough."

"You thought of everything."

He shook his foot. "Everything but an extra pair of shoes."

Emma laughed and gave Maude a gentle squeeze, making the pup let out an excited yelp.

1974-1975

"The real evils, indeed, of Emma's situation were the power of having rather too much her own way, and a disposition to think a little too well of herself: these were the disadvantages which threatened alloy to her many enjoyments. The danger, however, was at present so unperceived, that they did not by any means rank as misfortunes with her."

—Jane Austen, *Emma*, Volume 1, Chapter 1

SEVEN

MAY 31, 1975

LEXINGTON, KENTUCKY

I stood beside my sister in the historic Bodley-Bullock House courtyard, holding my flowers, and praying the honey bee landing on them would drink his fill and quietly fly off without causing a ruckus. I hated flying insects, especially the ones that sneak up on a person with stingers in their tails. The day was beginning to heat up, but thankfully Nina had decided on a morning wedding. However, the outdoor afternoon reception was certain to be a sticky, humid scorcher.

The ruffle covering the bodice of my bridesmaid's dress tickled my forearms, like a butterfly's wings, making me want to twitch. The dress was pretty—for a bridesmaid's dress. Lavender suited Isabel's and my coloring very well, and the gauzy Georgette fabric was light and comfortable. The dresses were full length, styled off-the-shoulder, with an eighteen-inch ruffle around the hem to match the one that was currently tormenting my arms. Nina had us wear a spray of wildflowers in our hair, the same flowers that were in our bouquets. I would have preferred to wear my hair up, because I thought it looked more elegant and it would have been cooler. But the bride wanted us to leave it down and "natural-looking," and brides should always get what they want. George commented before the ceremony that the Woodhouse sisters looked like spring wood nymphs, which made me chuckle.

Now that Isabel and I were situated in front of the crowd, I heard a toddler's voice behind me call out, "Mama!" That was followed by a few giggles and a stern shush from Jack Knightley. A smile came unbidden to my lips. Little Henry had spied Isabel and was probably squirming like crazy to get down from his father's arms and run to her.

I loved that sweet boy and doted on him like any maiden aunt should. Although I knew I wasn't objective, I was also quite certain my nephew was a genius. He could already build with blocks, and he sat looking at things like stereo schematics for twenty minutes at a time—when he wasn't terrorizing their cat or climbing up the bookshelves.

On cue, Isabel and I turned to face the back of the outdoor sanctuary. Seated in neat rows of white folding chairs was a small gathering of friends and family: people from the library where Nina worked, the rest of our family, as well as other friends and neighbors from the sleepy little community of Highbury, situated not too far from the hub of horse country. Jack continued whispering to a wiggly Henry and…

My eyes widened in surprise. *Good heavens! Is that George Knightley holding little Taylor?* Jack and Isabel's daughter was only six weeks old, and I had to admit I was mildly impressed. *Not every man has the temerity to hold a newborn during a public event, and in a tux, no less.* Taylor's tiny fist shot up toward the sky—in some kind of show of girl solidarity perhaps—and George glanced down, bouncing her gently and swaying her from side to side.

The processional began and everyone rose as the couple made their way slowly down the center aisle. They broke tradition and accompanied each other to the outdoor altar, covered in flowers. Nina had insisted that she was a thirty-six year-old woman and hardly needed to be "given away." Not that she had any male relatives left to perform such an office anyway. Her father and half-brother were both deceased. There had been some thought to Daddy walking her down the aisle, but the idea of performing in front of all those people seemed to frighten him so I declined on his behalf.

Nina had always been beautiful, graceful, and elegant, but for years afterward, people would say she radiated a happiness that had made her absolutely stunning on her wedding day. The man beside her was on cloud nine as well. I tried to hide my smug smile as I watched them stroll up the aisle to the music of a string quartet, remembering my own role in bringing them together...

Bob Weston ran a restaurant supply business that had rapidly expanded in the last several years and was now thriving. He was big and burly but a good-looking man in his mid-forties. He was not my type of course—he was far too old—but he was still quite a catch for an older woman, say over thirty. I couldn't believe I'd never thought of matching him with my aunt before then. After all, I had known him for years, having gone to high school with his son. Frank and I even dated for a short while my junior year. Frank's mother, Rosemarie Churchill and Bob divorced when Frank was only three. Ms. Churchill moved back to Alabama, taking her son with her. He stayed until he was a junior in high school, when he apparently needed a "firm hand" and moved in with the father he saw only once or twice a year.

First of all, the idea of Bob Weston giving a wayward son a firm hand was a joke to anyone who knew him. He was the most affable, easygoing man I had ever met. Needless to say, his son pretty much did as he pleased while he stayed with Bob. Frank left town for Birmingham right after graduation at the request of his mother and the promise of an athletic scholarship to the University of Alabama. The land of the Crimson Tide, and the discipline of their baseball team, helped Frank mature into a much more settled young man. Although he was only an average baseball player, Frank achieved a measure of academic success at 'Bama. Currently, he was in New York, finishing up some kind of business internship he obtained through his Churchill family connections. They were well-connected too. Frank's great-great-grandfather was a cousin of the Churchills for whom Churchill Downs was named. At any rate, the New York City internship was why he wasn't present at today's event.

As always, Bob excused his son's absence; he forgave him everything. In my opinion, it was shabby for Frank to miss his own father's wedding, but perhaps I only felt that way because Mr. Weston's new wife was my beloved Aunt Nina.

I liked to boast that I was the one who introduced the happy couple. It was quite the fortunate coincidence, made more fortunate by my subsequent gentle influence that began over a year ago.

One gorgeous spring day, Nina and I had gone to lunch at Travers Restaurant. We were talking when Bob marched in, his booming voice invading the dining room as he spoke to people at two or three tables. Bob knew almost everyone in town because of his business, and he had never met a stranger anyway. His laugh rang out a couple of times through the restaurant, and about the third time, I happened to notice that Nina was watching him.

"Earth to Nina," I teased.

"Hmm?" She startled, following that up with an embarrassed laugh. "Sorry, sweetie. I was distracted."

"I can see that." An idea began to form in my mind. A surprising, wonderful idea. I glanced at the source of Nina's distraction. "Oh, look, it's Mr. Weston. I haven't seen him in ages."

"You know him? He's quite a bit older than you, Emma."

"I went to high school with his son. You might remember him—Frank Weston?"

"Oh, yes. Dark headed boy, very handsome, but kind of wild, wasn't he? I recall being glad you didn't date him for very long." She glanced over at Bob again. "*That's* his father?"

I nodded and took a sip of tea. "Frank looks more like his mother, I think, but thankfully he has his father's personality. His mother was apparently a real shrew, and they divorced many years ago. But Mr. Weston is a nice man. I always thought he was handsome too, in a fatherly kind of way." I took another sip and pretended to consider my words a few seconds while I observed my aunt's reaction. Nina was trying unsuccessfully to not stare at him too much. That was all the encouragement I needed. "And he's loaded...and single."

Nina brought her gaze back to the table and laughed. "You never quit, do you?"

I put on my best wide-eyed, innocent expression. "Ni-na! I would *never* try to fix you up, but..."

"Yes, Em-ma?"

"Like I said, he *is* a nice man." And at just that moment, as if I had tugged on his marionette string, Bob turned and saw us. I stole a quick look at Nina's blushing cheeks and sent Bob a bright smile and wave. I knew he'd come over and say hello. He was too gregarious to stop himself.

"Emma, no..." Nina said in a frantic whisper, but it was too late. Bob was beside our table, booming out his hello and patting my shoulder.

"Well, if it isn't little Emma Woodhouse! Goodness, gal, I haven't seen you in a month of Sundays. How've you been?"

"I've been well, sir, and you?"

"Fantastic! Business is on the upswing—we've just relocated our offices onto Central Avenue. Needed more space for delivery trucks and storage."

"That's wonderful, Mr. Weston."

"What are you up to these days?"

"I'm living at home and going to college. I suppose you heard about my father's stroke."

His face fell. It was a dramatic change in expression, yet somehow it didn't look affected on such a personable man. "I did, I did. William Larkins told me the last time I was over at your dad's office. It's an awful shame, honey. How is John?"

"He's doing quite well, actually. We have some wonderful help, and I'm there to look after him, so..."

"He's a lucky man to have a daughter like you."

"Thank you, that's a kind thing to say." I paused—just a beat, to make it look spontaneous. "Oh, how rude of me! Mr. Weston, this is my aunt, Nina Taylor. Nina, Bob Weston." He turned, and I delighted in the way the air ignited between them. His eyebrows rose, and his lips curved under his mustache, and Nina's eyes sparkled. *Bingo!*

He almost stammered out his response. "Well, um...hello there." He stood unmoving for a second and then hurriedly stuck out his hand. "It's good to meet you." He enclosed her hand in both of his when he shook it. I wriggled with happiness.

"Good to meet you." Nina's voice was soft and sort of sultry-sounding. *If that's how women show their interest in men, I'll have to cultivate that skill. It seems to be working pretty well on old Bob right now!*

They chatted for a second, just small talk. Bob found out Nina worked at the university library, and I had a feeling he'd be by there in a few days. Then, he turned back to address me.

"Frank is coming into town next month."

"Oh? And how is Frank getting along?"

"He's fine, just fine. Made the Dean's List at 'Bama last semester."

"That's right, I *thought* he went to the University of Alabama. And on the Dean's List, too. Good for him. Is he still playing baseball?"

"Yes, as a matter of fact, he's playing left field. Not starting, mind you, but it's an honor to just be on the team. 'Bama's Crimson Tide is doing well this season. We're hoping for a conference championship."

"I'm sure you're very proud of him."

"Proud as punch, but us daddies are like that, aren't we?"

"Yes, but we all understand proud papas, don't we, Nina?"

Nina smiled pointedly at me, but she answered, "Yes, we do."

"I'll tell Frank he should give you a call when he gets in town. I know he likes to get together with old friends when he's here."

Cold day in hell before that *happens.* I liked Frank, I really did, and he was a cutie, but after we stopped seeing each other, he'd never made any attempt to call me when he was in town or out of it, so I doubted that would happen this time.

"I'd be glad to hear from him," I said, all politeness.

"Hey," Bob said in a rush, as if a thought had just occurred to him. "You still live in Highbury, right?"

"Yes, we do. Out Hartfield Road."

"Do you like the area? I've been looking for a new place in the country for myself. Need the fresh air."

"You should definitely take a look out there, Mr. Weston. There's still plenty of land for sale, and some fine older homes too, if you'd rather have a fixer-upper. Nina lives out there by us, and she loves it, don't you, Nina?"

"Mm-hmm, it's lovely. Not too far from town but quiet. And near family for me, which is important."

Bob looked pleased enough to burst. "Well, now, I might just take a gander out that way."

"There are some tracts of land about a quarter mile from Hartfield Road, over on Ninevah Pike. A new subdivision with split-level homes and ranch houses is going up right off Highway 28." Nina smiled. "And then there are my favorites, the older places like the Newton Estate, the farmhouse over on Box Hill, the Randalls' place. Do you know Steven Rockwell?"

I froze. Nina shouldn't be mentioning other men if she was trying to entice Bob's interest.

"Hmm…I think so. He's with Advent Realty, isn't he?"

"Yes, his wife is a friend of mine. You should call him. He knows the area very well because they live out that way too."

I breathed a sigh of relief that this Steven person was married, and it seemed that Bob did the same.

"I'll do that. Thanks for the tip," he said. His enthusiasm for the idea was obvious by the twinkle in his eyes.

"Wonderful!" Emma exclaimed.

"I'll let you two get back to your lunch. I'm supposed to see the shift manager about some tomatoes, and I'm late already. Good to see you, Emma."

"Good to see *you*, Mr. Weston."

He turned to Nina and eyed her left hand. I grinned. *No, you sweet, dear man, she's not married.*

"Very nice to meet you, Miss Taylor."

"Nina, please."

"Nina." His deep bass voice rumbled softly, like a big V8 engine.

"Goodbye."

"Advent Realty, right?"

"Right."

"I won't forget." He was backing toward the kitchen, barely missing a two-top table, and then he was gone in the same whirlwind he'd come in.

I took another sip of tea and raised my eyebrows at Nina over the rim of my glass. She was sitting there with a smile on her face. To my delight, she whispered, "Wow," and cleared her throat.

And that was how I, Emma Katherine Woodhouse, took a serendipitous event and improved the lives of two people who were quite dear to me. It felt wonderful to be so useful, so I continued to throw them together. I invited Bob to barbeques on Hartfield Road and to other neighborhood get-togethers. I suggested restaurants where I knew Bob had business ties, in the hope that he would chance upon Nina and me while we were dining there.

He started taking her out a mere two weeks after that chance meeting at Travers'. After he bought the old Randalls' place in Highbury, he no longer needed my help to develop a friendship with Nina. It turned out they shared a love of remodeling and found lots to talk about on their own—they were always together then. A few months after that, while Maude and I were out one Sunday morning at dawn, I looked over at Nina's driveway and saw him sneaking to his car. Last Christmas, they said they were getting married, and I was thrilled.

Now they were here in a garden on a beautiful spring morning, and finally, fourteen years after my beloved aunt Nina shortchanged her youth to care for her sister's family, she was making a family of her own.

EIGHT

George sat under the white canopy at the old Randalls' place, the elegant house where Bob and Nina Weston were hosting their reception and, after a brief honeymoon to Key West, would make their new home. George drummed his fingers on the bar, waiting on the martini he'd ordered. Later on, of course, he would grab some champagne for a toast or two, but for now, the martini was what he needed. The band continued setting up, and all the guests waited for the wedding party to arrive from Bodley-Bullock House. The photographer planned to take wedding pictures galore there, and George didn't envy Jack one iota. His brother had to stay, being part of Nina's immediate family, so George handed little Taylor off to her mother and left for the reception with all due haste.

He had received his drink when he spied Tim Elton waiting by the gate and scanning the crowd in search of an "important" person to attach himself to. He saw George, nodded his head in greeting and started his approach, and although George's eyes darted around seeking escape, he was trapped.

"Knightley!" Tim came up and held out his hand. When he shook hands, he turned so he was half-facing the room and smiled broadly.

Tim Elton was a relative newcomer to Highbury. He was from

Western Kentucky, and his father had gotten him a job as a public relations officer with the Legislative Research Commission in Frankfort, the state's capital. It was common knowledge that Tim's true ambition was to be elected to the State Legislature, and every time Elton shook someone's hand, it was if he was posing for a publicity shot.

"Tim, good of you to come. I'm sure it means a lot to Nina to have the Highbury neighbors here."

"I wouldn't miss it. Weston throws a great party, and I'm sure this one will be no exception. Some damned fine-looking women here this afternoon too." He winked and nudged George with his elbow.

"I'm sure."

"And more to follow with the arrival of the wedding party."

George gave him a cool stare, which made Elton backtrack, and then he reciprocated with an oily smile. "Unfortunately for men everywhere, your lovely sister-in-law is already taken."

"Yes, she is—very much so." George mentally rolled his eyes at the blatant flattery about Isabel.

Elton let out a wistful sigh. "Your brother seems to have his life well in hand. Maybe I need to take a page from his book, give up my wild bachelor ways, and settle down."

George sipped his drink and said nothing, but then Elton rarely needed any response to keep talking and this conversation was no exception.

"Father is pushing me to run for the legislature next term, and he thinks it might be good to lend some thought to the marriage question."

"The marriage question?"

"Getting hitched, jumping the broom, acquiring the old ball and chain."

"I see."

Tim nudged his shoulder again, nearly dislodging the contents of George's martini glass. "You might *see*, but you don't *do*. After all, you've managed to keep your bachelorhood intact for a long time now. Then again, your career path is already set, so you can call your own shots in that arena."

"Yes, it is, and yes, I can."

Elton sighed, an affected little wisp of air let out into the heat of the day. "I do envy you that. The Knightley dynasty is a long-standing tradition. You just step right in and simply carry it on."

"I wouldn't say it's simple."

Elton's eyes went wide, obviously worried that he had given offense. "Oh no! Not simple at all. A great deal of responsibility—didn't mean to imply otherwise."

"I'm sure you didn't."

Tim delivered an awkward laugh, as he cast around for a more neutral topic and apparently decided "acquiring the old ball and chain" was neutral enough. "Father has this friend in Frankfort with four daughters, just like stair steps, from twenty to twenty-six." He gestured the steps with his hand. "My dad keeps trying to get me an invitation to meet them."

"Does he?"

Tim leaned in and whispered. "Supposedly all very pretty, and their father is well-connected in the state Democratic party. It might be good to ally myself with one of them before embarking on a House of Representatives bid."

"How lucky for you, then, that your father knows him, and that there are four of them, just waiting for you to ride down and make your choice."

Elton grinned, completely missing the sarcasm. "We'll see. There might be something even better for me around here close. You just never know."

There was a flurry of tuxes and gauzy lavender fabric at the side of the house, and the wedding party drifted over in fits and starts, ambling under the archway of flowers near the entrance to the tent. Isabel was holding Henry's hand as she chatted amiably with the best man, Weston's older brother from St. Louis. Jack was carrying Taylor, and Emma followed him, fiddling with the flowers in her hair and smoothing her dress. At last, the bride and groom appeared, and everyone applauded. Elton stood there, clapping his hands and nodding with an ingratiating smile that George found mildly annoying. Tim turned and touched George's arm, saying, "Excuse me."

George watched him make his way over to greet Emma. She smiled and spoke to him, and he offered his arm to escort her to her father, who was now sitting comfortably at a white linen covered table. Tim's behavior struck George as suspicious but he had no time to think about it further because out of the corner of his eye, he saw a pint-sized munchkin unsteadily careening his way. He barely had a second to set down his glass before Henry ran right into his leg, throwing his chubby arms around George's knees.

"Hey, little man. Where do you think you're going?" George lifted him up past his shoulders and jostled him like he was about to pitch him above his head. Henry let out a delighted squeal.

"Doe!"

"I'm not Doe, you rascal. Say George."

"Dode!"

"Almost." George grinned up at him, teasing by not quite tossing him up in the air the way he loved. "Say George," he repeated, "Ge-or-ge."

"Doje."

"Close enough." He pitched him up gently and caught him while he laughed.

"Better do that now, before he has a bunch of cake and upchucks all over that Lord West tuxedo of yours."

"Emma." He smiled, tucking Henry under his arm like a bundle. "We're glad you made your way over here to see us, right, Henry?"

Henry giggled and squirmed in his uncle's grasp.

"I'm supposed to go and mingle, according to Daddy. Isabel's sitting with him, waiting for Rita."

"Who's Rita?"

"The new au pair."

"Ah. Is she from Europe?"

"Arkansas. She's a niece of Mrs. Goddard's."

Amusement welled up in his smile, but he managed to check it. "I'm glad Isabel and Jack will have a few hours to enjoy the reception without the curtain climbers." He tousled Henry's hair.

"Don't call *my* nephew and niece curtain climbers." She reached for Henry.

"He'll get footprints on your dress, Emma Kate," he warned.

"Oh, pooh, who cares? We've already taken the pictures." She kissed the boy's cheek and set him down. "Go find your mama, precious."

Henry took off toward Isabel and Taylor, while George and Emma watched him go. Mr. Woodhouse looked alarmed at the impending whirl-wind of a toddler, but Jack scooped him up and took him over to a pleas-ant-looking girl who must have been Rita.

"Can I get you a drink, Miss Woodhouse?" George held out his elbow and she took it. "What will you have?"

"It's a wedding, so I'm going to have champagne, of course."

He held up two fingers to the bartender. "It was a lovely ceremony."

"Oh, it really was, wasn't it? Nina looked exquisite. And the wedding was unpretentious, yet elegant, just like she is."

Handing her a champagne flute, he replied, "I thought for a minute you might cry during the vows."

"Cry?" she protested. "Certainly not! I'm happy for them..."

"But you will miss her?"

"I admit, I will."

"She's not far away."

"Yes, but her life will be different now."

He wasn't quite sure what to say. "You must be happy that she'll be well taken care of."

Emma smiled and shook her head. "She's not some poor nineteenth century governess, you know. She has a career and her own money."

"That's not what I meant, as you well know. What I meant is that West-on's a good man."

"That he is," Emma agreed. "You know"—she took a sip of champagne and leaned over to speak low in his ear—"I'm the reason they got together."

"Oh, I doubt that."

"It's true! I introduced them."

"Perhaps you were the reason they met, but that's where your influ-ence ended. They're adults. Capable of managing their own lives."

"Yes, but I did little things to throw them together, like invite him over for dinner and to the neighborhood parties—and just look at the happy result. I'm a born matchmaker. I could write a book."

"Whatever you say," he returned, his voice bored, his gaze wandering around the tent.

She scowled at him, but it was a friendly scowl. Then her countenance brightened as Isabel crossed her line of vision, carrying the baby.

"I saw you holding Taylor during the ceremony." Her voice was rich with amusement.

"Did you now?"

"It was a priceless picture. I only wish the photographer had gotten it, so the whole world could enjoy the domestic side of George Knightley that I saw today."

He smirked at her teasing. "Yes, well, Jack needed some assistance, so I filled the bill. I wonder why they didn't leave the babies with Rita during the ceremony?"

"Nina wanted them at the wedding. Anyway, I'm confident your help was appreciated."

"Glad to be of service."

He bowed his head in a formal gesture, which made her laugh.

"And you did so well with her too. You're a natural! Who knew?"

"Your praise is overwhelming."

"On second thought, it shouldn't surprise me that the decisive, commanding George Knightley can manage an infant. He sure can manage everyone else."

"Emma, are you trying to flatter me?"

"Not in the least."

They stood, side by side, observing as the crowd gathered in clumps of chattering finery.

Emma chuckled. "Look at Tim Elton, working the room. That man needs to settle down and find himself a woman."

"I noticed he singled you out first."

"Ha-ha. Aren't you a funny guy?" Emma shook her head. "No, I'm not the girl for Tim. Although, I bet I could find him one, since I'm quite the matchmaker now."

"Trust me, Tim knows his own mind on the subject—or rather, his father's mind," he continued under his breath.

"Tim Elton is very handsome, but if he continues following those political aspirations of his, he will need more than good looks to get ahead. He needs to have the right kind of woman by his side—someone as pretty as he is, but sweet-tempered, wholesome, the proverbial girl-next-door. That's where my judgment is superior to his. Men never know how to pick a woman that's good for them."

George rolled his eyes and shook his head. "Poor Tim Elton. Emma's on a mission to find him a wife."

Before she could fire back, Nina and Bob Weston stood up at their table, thanking their guests for sharing their joy. The best man rose to make his toast, which went on too long and was mighty dull.

Out of the corner of his eye, George saw the hand holding Emma's champagne glass descend slowly to her waist, a bittersweet expression on her face.

"They're so happy, and it's wonderful."

"Yes."

"But the selfish part of me can't help thinking…"

Patiently, he waited.

Her voice dropped to a whisper. "I have a sneaking suspicion my life will never be the same."

George shifted his champagne to his other hand and put his arm around her shoulders in a gesture of comfort, and as the best man finished his toast, they joined the other guests in raising their glasses to the new Mr. and Mrs. Weston.

NINE

JUNE 6, 1975

I fumbled with my boxes as I tried to open the door to the Knightley and Woodhouse offices on Surrey Street.

"Oh drat," I mumbled.

"Here, miss, let me help you." The voice at the door was sweet, a lilting twang to the vowels, but unfamiliar, which made my head snap up in surprise. I knew everyone in the law office because I brought the whole staff doughnuts on the first Friday of every month. A young woman, about my age, with reddish-brown hair and milky white skin was hurrying toward the door, almost turning her ankle on those Candie's high heels of hers.

"Thank you!" I breathed a sigh of relief as the young woman took the top two boxes.

"These smell delicious."

"Spaulding Bakery makes the best crullers in town."

"So all the paralegals tell me. They said doughnuts were arriving this morning. Where do you want to put them?"

"I'll take them to the conference room. I know my way, and I'm sure Mr. Knightley would give me a piece of his mind for asking a client to carry pastry boxes!"

The young woman giggled. "Oh, I'm not a client. I'm the new front office secretary," she announced in a voice full of pride and enthusiasm.

"Oh! My apologies. I didn't know George had hired anyone new. Let me put these in the kitchen, and I'll come introduce myself properly."

As I returned to the front office, I paused at the door to peruse the new Knightley and Woodhouse employee—just so I could tell Daddy about her later. He always wanted to keep up with the goings on at K&W Law.

She was nearly my height, and she had that pert, hourglass figure that would have been so coveted about twenty years ago but was out of fashion since the arrival of models like Twiggy and Cheryl Tiegs. Granted, the girl's figure was somewhat hidden under a badly-fitting polyester suit, but she deserved some points for at least *trying* to dress professionally. Her hair was gathered at the nape of her neck, little strands escaping the band she had tied around it. She blew one of the strands up and out of her face as she stood at the Xerox machine. Walking toward her, I held out my hand.

"I'm Emma Woodhouse."

She gasped. "You're Emma? I mean Miss Woodhouse? John Woodhouse's daughter?"

"Guilty as charged. And please call me Emma."

She pumped my hand up and down a little too enthusiastically. "Everyone around here speaks so highly of you and your father. I'm Mary Jo Smith."

"I'm please to meet you, Mary Jo. Have you been working here long?"

"Just about"—she paused, looking up and counting—"three weeks... this Friday."

"And are you from here in town?"

"Me? Oh no. I'm not from here at all. I just moved here from West Virginia. I finished my secretarial program at the community college last spring, but there's no jobs around there. So, my mother said to move away, and I came here because this is horse country and I love horses. I was so lucky I found a job right away. This is such a cool position. I just love it here." Her animated expression was contagious. I could see the wisdom of having someone so cheerful at the front desk. Kudos to George Knightley.

"That's wonderful. I'm sure they're glad to have you."

What a sweet and pretty girl she is! Much better than that last grumpy battle-ax they took on. And she's just moved here all on her own, poor little thing. Just like Mary Richards on the Mary Tyler Moore Show.

The phone on the front desk rang. Rang again. Rang a third time. I raised my eyebrows at Mary Jo, who suddenly jumped when she realized she should answer.

"Oh! That's my phone!"

"Yes…"

"Excuse me."

I tried not to smile as she hurried over to the desk.

"Knightley and Woodhouse Law Offices, how may I direct your call?"

I gestured to her that I was going back into the staff room and mouthed, "I'll be right back." Mary Jo nodded. Once in the kitchenette, I went about making the coffee and noted that they were almost out. *Perhaps I should pick some up this afternoon before I head home.* Footsteps sounded behind me, and I saw George in the doorway, looking at a fistful of papers in one hand and carrying an empty coffee mug in the other.

He looked up a mere second before he bumped into me. "Emma!" He smiled. "What a nice surprise."

"Surprise? It's the first Friday."

"What? Oh, right, first Friday. Spaulding doughnut day." He put down his papers and mug and rubbed his hands together. "Okay, let me at 'em. I'll get first pick this time."

"They're on the table."

"You don't have to do this, Emma, but we're all glad you do." He pulled a cruller from the box and sank his teeth into it. His eyes closed. "Mmm. Still warm. Good thing you only bring these once a month. I'd be round as a beach ball otherwise."

I had an extremely difficult time imagining trim and fit George round as a beach ball.

Mary Jo's voice sounded from behind him. "Did you need any help with the…? Oh, good morning again, Mr. Knightley."

"Morning, Mary Jo. Have you met Emma? Her father was the head honcho here before he retired a couple of years ago."

"Yes, we met when she brought in the doughnuts earlier, sir."

"Do help yourself." I indicated the open box. "Coffee will be ready in a minute."

"Aren't you going to have one, Emma?" Mary Jo asked as she chose one from the box.

"Oh no. Emma doesn't eat junk food like doughnuts." George took a bite and looked at Emma with a teasing smile.

"I do *occasionally* eat junk food. But I've already had my breakfast this morning, which was homemade granola, skim milk, and fruit, and it's a bad habit to snack in between meals."

"Did you and Maude run this morning?" George asked.

"Of course." I turned to Mary Jo. "Maude is my golden retriever."

"You must be one of those health nuts." Mary Jo looked at me with interest, as if she'd just met someone from a foreign country. A lot of people used the term "health nut" in a derogatory way, but somehow when Mary Jo said it, it didn't sound quite so insulting.

"I'm not a health nut. Mr. Knightley exaggerates. You will learn that he often does that to tease me. I do, however, try to stay healthy. I have to make sure Daddy eats well, and Dr. Perry says with my family history I need to be doubly careful about nutrition and exercise. It's a good thing I never took up smoking." I gave George a sharp look.

"I rarely ever smoke any more, Emma, at your insistence."

"I'm relieved to hear it. It is not good for you at all. Dr. Perry says—"

"You're absolutely right. It's not good for me. It hinders my tennis game."

Mary Jo snickered.

"Doughnuts, on the other hand, do not." He took another one and winked at her as he strode out the door, fresh coffee in hand, and papers under his arm.

"It's such a nice change, working for a gentleman like Mr. Knightley."

Goodness, what an odd thing to say! "What kind of place did you work before?"

"I was a cashier at the Piggly Wiggly grocery in Beckley. That's in West Virginia. The assistant manager kept trying to hit on me. That was one reason I left and went to secretarial school."

"Well, I can assure you no one in a position of authority will ever try to hit on you at K&W Law. Mr. Knightley will make sure of that. He is a gentleman through and through. I've known him all my life. He believes in women's liberation, and he supports the ratification of the Equal Rights Amendment." Mary Jo's expression was blank, so I changed the subject.

"Are you coming to the office breakfast tomorrow morning? They do that once or twice a year, and it's marvelous."

"Oh yes. I wouldn't miss it!"

"Do you know your way to Spindletop Hall?"

She shook her head. "Where?"

"The university alumni club? Oh, never mind. Why don't you let me swing by and pick you up on my way out there? I'm attending in my father's place. The office staff is kind enough to include him, but he's rarely up to those kinds of parties anymore."

"I wouldn't want to impose—"

"Nonsense. It's not an imposition whatsoever. You're new in town, and I'd be happy to show you how to get there."

"Well, if you insist—"

"I do insist. We'll have a wonderful time."

"Far out!"

I bit my lip to keep from laughing at Mary Jo's outdated slang.

After the office breakfast party, Mary Jo and I rapidly became fast friends. I only had a few pals from college, the result of changing schools in the middle of my sophomore year and of living at home instead of in a dorm or sorority house like most of the other girls. I decided not to join a sorority when I came back home, because really, what was the point? There were plenty of tasks to occupy me already, such as running the household and supervising my father's care. Until I met Mary Jo, I hadn't realized how lonely I was for girlfriends. Most of my high school chums had moved away; some of them, like Carol Ann, were even married already. My two constant companions, Nina and Izzy, were both married now too.

So, from my perspective, Mary Jo was a barrel of laughs and a much-needed breath of fresh air. She said the funniest things, made even funnier because she didn't realize the humor in them. And she was sweet, a genuinely kind person who thought ill of no one, and sporting that right off the farm, wide-eyed, innocent girl-next-door look. I envied her hair; it was the prettiest shade of light brown with just a touch of red. Mary Jo said that came from her Irish background on her mother's side. Her father had left the family when she was a baby, and she didn't remember him at all. I thought perhaps that was one reason Mary Jo treated Daddy so well. With some encouragement and attention, I believed Mary Jo could become an elegant and beautiful woman, so I appointed myself to the position of guiding influence. After all, what was the point of having education and knowledge if I didn't share it for the betterment of my friends? Especially with a girl who so desperately needed my help to realize her true potential. Nina and Izzy had been my guides to woman-hood, and now it was my turn to be a mentor to someone else.

One day in late July, I stopped by K&W Law right before noon to take Mary Jo to lunch, and when I entered the front office, Mary Jo was seated at her desk, as usual. Perched on the front corner of said desk, regaling her with some apparently fascinating tale, was one of George's paralegals. For the life of me, I couldn't remember the man's name. They were all "George's paralegals" in my book. This fellow *was* rather handsome: a debonair grin, curly black hair cut close to his head, and velvet brown eyes that were just a shade darker than his skin. His voice was pleasantly deep, and his speech was slow like rich, thick molasses dripping from a spoon. He was, in a word, smooth.

Mary Jo's dazzling smile, bordering on overt flirtation, was a bit worrisome.

"Mary Jo, surely, we can do better for you than one of the law firm's paralegals," I muttered under my breath.

Mary Jo spotted me then and beckoned me over. "Hi, Emma! Is it lunch time already? This morning's just flown by."

The young man stood up hurriedly, probably concerned that he was caught shirking his responsibilities, but he smiled at me anyway. He was so tall, I had to look up to meet his gaze.

"Hello, Miss Woodhouse." He inclined his head respectfully.

"Mr. ...?" I looked at Mary Jo in expectation, hoping she would get the hint that she should be making introductions, but she only sat there, looking at Mr. Paralegal and lost in her blue-eyed enchantment.

He held out his hand. "Oh, sorry, I'm Robert Martin. I knew who you were, of course, but I'm not surprised you didn't know me. I work a lot in the Louisville office these days."

I shook his hand with a quick, firm grasp. "Yes, I recall now. I've heard my father and Mr. Knightley speak of you."

He looked very pleased to be remembered. "I was just discussing books with Mary Jo here."

"I told him I usually read romance novels, but he said I should try Agatha Christie mysteries. Have you read those books, Emma? What do you think?"

"Well, sure—"

"And I just finished *The Killer Angels*," Robert said. "It was very good, but Mary Jo wasn't sure she'd enjoy a book about war. And that makes sense, given that she's such a peace-loving person." He looked at her with avid interest, and forty-seven alarm bells sounded in my head.

"Are you about ready to go to lunch, Mary Jo?"

She startled. "Oh! Yes, I'm ready."

"Not to rush you, but I need to get back for yoga class at two."

"Of course. Sorry to keep you waiting." She opened her bottom desk drawer and drew out her purse. She looked up at Robert, her eyes all dewy and her voice soft. "It was good to talk to you. I'll see you this afternoon."

He pointed at her while he blinded her with a brilliant smile. "At coffee break, right?"

She nodded, and he left the room, grinning.

―――――――――

Mary Jo sat across from me at a two-top in Duke's Café, picking at her salad.

"Don't you like your lunch? I know you prefer burgers and fries, but the vegetables are so much better for your health."

"Oh, this is fine. I do feel a lot healthier since I started eating more salad and cottage cheese for lunch, like you suggested. And I've lost a couple of pounds too."

I beamed at her. "I thought you looked slimmer. Now, we just need to get you started with some exercise, so you'll be even healthier."

Mary Jo stirred the lettuce around some more. "So, what do you think of Robert?"

"Robert? Oh, Mr. Martin." I paused, weighing my words carefully. "He's one of the paralegals, isn't he?"

"Mm-hmm. He asked me to go see *Jaws* with him this Saturday night."

"He isn't hitting on you, is he, Mary Jo? I can speak to Mr. Knightley about it if he's imposing on you."

"Oh, it's not like that at all! He's very polite and respectful. Don't tell Mr. Knightley. I don't want to get Robert in any trouble. He's really a nice guy."

"Well, if you say so." I frowned and then returned my attention to my salad.

"It's perfectly fine. Honest. I like Robert—he's a friend. He's cute too. His eyes are so dark and expressive, and he's tall. I've always liked tall men. Robert and I have really gotten to know each other lately. So, what do you think? Should I go see *Jaws*?"

"Do you want to see *Jaws*?"

"I probably wouldn't go if it was just me, but..."

"I wonder why he thought you would like a gore-fest like that." I shrugged my shoulders. "But a lot of men aren't very sensitive to women's preferences."

Mary Jo shook her head. "Oh no, Robert's definitely tuned-in to the women in his life. He talks about his mother and his sister very fondly. His birthday was last month, and he sent his mother flowers that day. He called the florist from my desk, because William Larkins was on the phone in the back."

"That was kind of him to think of his mother."

Mary Jo's dreamy expression was back. "I overheard what he put in the card, even though he said it so softly. I think he was a little self-conscious about it, but it was so sweet..."

"Do tell." Maybe this would help me figure out what Mary Jo found so fascinating about this guy.

"The card said, 'Dear Mama. Thank you for my life. Love, Robert.'" She put a hand to her heart. "Lord, it makes me tear up just to think about it."

"He seems to be supremely attached to her."

Mary Jo smiled and nodded. "So, should I go?"

I probably let a half a minute go by as I considered Mary Jo's dilemma. "Do you think it's a good idea to date someone at the office?"

"What do you mean?"

"It's just that I know how much you love your job. I would hate for your co-workers to see you as unprofessional because of some office fling."

"Would they think that? Everyone in the office likes Robert, and I don't think there's a rule against co-workers going out, is there? You don't think anyone would say anything because he's black, do you?"

"Goodness, no! No one at Knightley and Woodhouse thinks that way. It *is* the seventies after all. But sometimes people perceive interoffice friendships between men and women as romances. That's often viewed in an unfavorable light, regardless of the rules. Especially for a young woman like yourself."

Mary Jo sighed. "I hadn't thought about that."

"I would never tell you what your decision should be, of course. But it's a strange time for women in the workplace, and it pays to think these things through beforehand."

"Yes, I guess you're right."

"Perhaps, if you'd like some fun, you might consider going out with someone outside the office, somebody like...oh, I don't know. Somebody like Tim Elton perhaps?"

"Tim Elton?"

"I introduced you at Linus & Lucy's Café last month."

"Oh, I remember now. Do you think he'd ever go out with someone like me? I mean...wow, he's really a hunk."

"Yes, he really is." I put my napkin to my lips to hide a smile. "And yes, I do think he'd go out with you. He said something very flattering about you that day."

Mary Jo sank back against the booth, her eyebrows raised in surprise. "He did? What was it?"

"I don't know if I should say."

Robert Martin seemed to be forgotten within a moment. "Oh, please tell me Emma! I'll die of curiosity if you don't. Please?"

"All right. I guess it won't hurt." I leaned in toward her and whispered to lend some extra drama to the compliment. "He said you were a *fox*." I smiled at the blush that spread over Mary Jo's cheeks.

"He did?" she squeaked.

"Cross my heart." *And my fingers too, but she doesn't need to know that. Tim says that about every girl he meets, so I'm sure he said that about Mary Jo as well.*

After that, the rest of lunch sped by with giggles and discussions of Tim's various assets—both financial and physical. It was as if that paralegal Robert Martin had never existed at all.

TEN

"I'm not sure this super chummy friendship with Mary Jo Smith is such a good thing for Emma." George accepted a drink from Nina, thanked her, and walked toward the back door that led to the Westons' newly remodeled porch. He had dropped off some legal papers for Bob to sign and was waiting on him to get home so they could review them.

Nina followed him outside and indicated a seat before she settled herself on the back-porch swing. "Why do you say that?" Nina had been telling him about Emma and Mary Jo planning a long weekend shopping trip to Atlanta at the end of the month.

"I know Emma, not as well as you, but I've known her all her life, and I've had the unique opportunity to see her from outside the family looking in."

"I didn't know you were so interested in our Emma."

"I've always taken an interest in her. She was the precocious child that charmed every adult in the room. I wondered what would become of her because I knew all the things she could do if she would only apply herself with any kind of consistency. I want her to do well."

"And she is doing well—she has a straight A average."

"Exactly my point. Without any effort at all, she has a four-point average, and she's had some difficult classes: calculus, chemistry, physics. But then she goes and changes her major to psychology. What's she supposed to with a degree like that?"

"I can't believe that surprises you. You know how much she loves studying people. Perhaps she isn't sure what she wants to do yet, but she'll put the knowledge to good use."

"I hope you're right, but I can't help this vision in my head of her corralling poor unsuspecting girls like Mary Jo Smith and turning them into her personal, platonic Pygmalions."

Nina chuckled. "What a gift you have for alliteration, George. That comment's a little dramatic, don't you think?"

"Emma's too quick and clever for her own good. Unfortunately, she's also a bit spoiled and has been under her own sail since she came back from Georgia—probably even before that. She goes from project to project, never really seeing anything through to completion.

"Remember the painting phase? She spent all that time and money on paints and canvas and lessons—and just about the time she was developing some skill, she gave it up."

"Oh, I loved that little cottage she painted for my birthday present that year."

"And then there was the book group. She was going to read the classics with all the English lit majors she met in one of her classes. She lasted four months.

"After that was the interest in photography, complete with the addition of a dark room to the house. Now it sits virtually unused, the equipment collecting dust month after month."

Nina sighed. "All true."

"Plus, there were countless little things—the rose garden, the macramé, the piano lessons, and on and on. I'm afraid poor Mary Jo is but another project to be started and then discarded when the next interest comes along."

"I disagree, George"—Nina admonished him in her quiet way—"you're forgetting some of the 'fads' that Emma *has* stuck with: the health-conscious eating for her and her father, which the doctor says is helping John tremendously, the long-distance running, the yoga. And college—she could have easily quit college after her father's stroke, but she hasn't.

"And, furthermore, I disagree that helping Mary Jo is a bad thing. I think Emma could become very selfish if she focused only on self-centered 'projects', as you call them. But helping someone else, focusing outside herself—that has always brought out the best in Emma. She has such a generous heart, and she's so devoted to those she loves. I think that's a marvelous quality in her."

"I'm not suggesting that she not help people, of course, or that she not befriend Mary Jo at all. But Mary Jo idolizes Emma. She relies too heavily on her guidance, and Emma, who thinks she has the answers to everyone's problems, is too free with giving them. It's not good for Mary Jo to depend on someone else to that degree, certainly, but I'll go farther and say it's not good for Emma either. The exclusive company of Mary Jo Smith is like a steady diet of candy. Emma may like it, but it doesn't benefit her. If she surrounds herself with people who never disagree with her, I don't think she'll ever truly grow up. At the very least, she won't become the woman she could be."

"In some ways, I think Emma is very mature. She's committed to her family, very responsible. She's witty, and bright, and..."

He laughed warmly. "And she has quite a champion in you, Nina."

Nina smiled. "I love her too much to see any true fault in her, I suppose. It comes from taking care of her all those years and knowing what she went through when my sister was ill."

"You loved and cared for her well, and no one could have done better. She's fortunate she has you."

Nina nodded her acceptance of the compliment. They were both silent for a minute, and George decided he'd probably been too critical in Nina's eyes.

"Well, I guess it's better to be interested in helping others than some of the things my former girlfriends have been interested in, like which designer makes the best dresses and whose party to attend on a Saturday night."

"Are you having lady problems, George?"

"You can't have lady problems if you don't have a lady. I haven't dated much since I broke up with Marilyn."

"You two seemed quite serious for a while. You dated for how long?"

"Three months. I thought perhaps it would work, but over time I realized that although she was beautiful, she had very few interests, outside her appearance, the Junior League, and where we were seen together. A wise man wants a woman who is interested in the world around her, so he has someone to talk to after the party is over."

"And you are nothing if not a wise man," Nina teased. "It's too bad, though. Marilyn was, as you said, such a pretty girl."

He set his glass down on the wicker table and stared into it. "And that was a major part of the problem. Her beauty made her vain."

"I always thought she resembled Emma—they both have those unusual hazel eyes and a similar hair color, almost like honey."

"Emma is a little blonder, I believe. And to her credit, Emma doesn't have Marilyn's vanity with regard to her appearance. Men find that type of conceit very off-putting." He grinned up at Nina. "No, Emma's vanity is her absolute confidence that she knows what's best for all. She's so self-assured. I think perhaps a little romantic angst would do her some good. She's never had her heart bruised."

"Come now. You don't wish a broken heart on our Emma."

"A broken heart? Never. One that's a little bent? Maybe."

"Now you're just cutting up."

"You know me well, Mrs. Weston." He heard a car door slam. "Ah, the man of the house has arrived. I'll just talk with him a few minutes, and then he's all yours again."

ELEVEN

AUGUST 23, 1975

"Lordy, lordy, it's hot!" Mary Jo tried to fan herself with her visor, but it was a futile gesture.

We had gone over to the park that morning to play tennis, or rather, I was trying to teach Mary Jo tennis. She had never played before, but she'd wanted to try it ever since she saw Cheryl Tiegs model a cute tennis dress in a magazine.

We met every Saturday in August to work on the game, but I was starting to get frustrated, because it was going nowhere. Then again, it might have been my teaching as much as Mary Jo's lack of athletic prowess. I had tennis lessons, of course, but eight lessons the summer before last did not a tennis instructor make. George offered to play opposite me. He said I was athletic enough to play well if I would practice more, but when did I have time for that? I couldn't always get over to the country club on the spur of the moment, and whenever I called to reserve a court time, they kept saying I needed to call further in advance. Who could actually *plan* their recreation that way? I was a full-time student and had a household to run.

The result was that Mary Jo and I ended up at the public park courts instead. People rarely used those, especially early in the morning.

I spun my racket in my hand. "Okay, okay, you win. We'll go over to the health food store and get some iced herbal tea and have a chat."

"But it's only been fifteen minutes. Are you sure?"

"I can't play in this heat either. We'll hit the courts again next Saturday."

Mary Jo was quick to acquiesce, as usual, and we were gathering up the tennis balls scattered on the court when I heard someone calling my name.

"Emma!" Tim Elton came jogging up and raised his hand in greeting. He looked impeccable, his dark, wavy hair falling over his face in that Rock Hudson kind of way, and as he approached us, a tantalizing combination of musk and woodsy scents drifted our way. He smelled nice—which was saying a lot in the sticky, oppressive heat.

"Good morning!" I replied, giving him my most welcoming smile. "What are you doing here?"

"Me? I... uh..." he stammered, looking up, down, and all around, until his eyes landed on Mary Jo. "I was supposed to meet a friend here for a game this morning, but it looks like I've been stood up."

"Who was your friend?" I asked.

"You don't know the person," he answered after an awkward pause.

I elbowed Mary Jo in the ribs and stage whispered, "Perhaps it was one of Tim's admirers. The ladies all think he's quite the charmer."

He looked back and forth between us. "Oh no!" He laughed. "You're teasing me, Emma. You know that isn't the case. It was a co-worker—a male co-worker, I assure you. Do you ladies play tennis?"

"A little and very ill, as Elizabeth Bennet would say."

Mary Jo turned to me and whispered, "Who's that? Have I met her?"

"I'll tell you later," I muttered out of the corner of my mouth, as Tim laughed heartily at my joke. "It's actually pretty sad, Tim. I've been trying to teach Mary Jo how to play, but I'm afraid I'm not that good a tennis coach. We were about to give it up."

"Oh, I'm sure you're an excellent teacher. You're so athletic yourself. And so patient."

"I'm afraid I lack the technique though. You, on the other hand, play very well."

He ducked his head and blushed.

Genuine modesty is a good quality in a man, and Tim wears it well.

"I've just had the best idea! *You* should teach Mary Jo tennis."

They both looked at me, stunned.

"Say what?" Tim said. Then he collected himself, and after a second, he gave me a brilliant smile. "I'd be glad to give the two of you a few pointers. Since my friend didn't show, we could even start this morning."

"Great idea!" I smiled encouragingly at Mary Jo.

"But what about the health food sto—?"

"We can do that later." *Good Lord, Mary Jo! Catch up here! Can't you see I'm trying to get you and Tim to spend some time together?* I raised my eyebrows and smiled pointedly, casting a furtive look over at Tim.

I could almost hear the gears turn and the bell ring as Mary Jo caught on. "Oh yes! That would be so helpful."

I sighed in relief and shook my head. Being a young woman's guide and counsel certainly took some quick thinking at times!

We spent the next twenty minutes under the tutelage of Tim Elton, tennis extraordinaire. He was pretty good—told us nothing I hadn't heard before, of course, but the way he explained how to serve and hold the racket seemed to help Mary Jo. He was really into his new role as coach, and my ego soared when he stood behind Mary Jo and put his arm around to help her adjust her hand position on the racquet. He winked at me and a smile bubbled from inside me. Tim Elton, who always seemed so difficult to please where women were concerned, was finally showing some interest in one. The one I had chosen for him, of course.

"I think I'm going to have a little Labor Day picnic at our house." I had been considering having a party for Daddy's birthday, which was on September 4. He didn't like venturing out much, but he always enjoyed it when his friends visited with him.

"Oooh, how fun! I love picnics," Mary Jo agreed.

"I'll invite the Westons, and Mrs. Goddard, and Tim Elton, and George, of course. Mr. & Mrs. Knightley are still in Europe, so they can't come. Daddy will be disappointed about that, but I'll just have to remind him that they're traveling. And I guess I'll have to invite my aunt Delores and my cousin Helen. Thank goodness, Helen's cousin Jane is in New York."

"I've not met your aunt. Or your cousins."

"They're not necessarily the type of family members you show off, Mary Jo. Technically, Jane isn't even my cousin."

"What do you mean?" She sipped her Tab and those earnest blue eyes searched my face.

"Well, every family has at least one eccentric branch, I suppose. And it's the seventies—people don't feel embarrassed by quirky family members like they used to, but...are you sure you want to hear this?"

She nodded, and I leaned back against the ladder back chair. It gave an ominous creak as if to signal the start of a dramatic tale.

"All right then. Delores was married to my mother's older half-brother, Edwin, and they have a daughter, an unfortunate creature named Helen." I touched my temple with my forefinger. "Not quite all there, I'm afraid."

Mary Jo gasped. "Oh, how sad!"

"Delores is my aunt by marriage, of course, and she has another niece who is almost exactly my age. She's an actress in New York and while her first name is Martha, she goes by her middle name professionally. So, she's Jane Fairfax."

"Is she famous?"

"Heavens, no!" I snorted. "She does a lot of that 'Off-Broadway' stuff—writes my aunt and cousin about it all the time. You would think that anyone who had any talent at all would be *on* Broadway, but they all seem to think Off-Broadway is a big deal."

"You've never told me about Jane before. How interesting!"

"I don't think there's much to tell, really. She left home right after high school, not that I can blame her for that at all. She's always wanted to be an actress, ever since she was a little girl. I have to admit, Jane does have a lovely singing voice and plays the piano quite well. She's a sweet girl, but she's so quiet and closed off. Most of the time she seems to be off in her own world. But she had it rough growing up, so I shouldn't be so hard on her."

"Why did she have it rough?"

I shook my head in pity. "Mm-mm-mm. It's kind of a sad story."

Mary Jo reached over and patted my hand.

I looked up, surprised at her compassionate gesture. Mary Jo's eyes were kind and concerned—and interested.

"Well, you know about my mother's family. They owned an old but well-known horse farm here in the Highbury community. When my grandparents passed on, my mom and Nina became beneficiaries under a family trust, and my mother's half-brother, Edwin (from my grandfather's first marriage), inherited the farm and some money of his own. Edwin was considerably older than my mother, and he died early of a heart ailment, before I was even born. He had run the horse farm for several years though, and that ended up being a bad thing. After he died, it came to light that the farm was deeply in debt. Edwin also had some gambling 'issues,' so most of his estate was sold off to pay his creditors, both on the high and the low side of the law. All that was left afterwards was a small bit of money that my grandparents put aside for Helen. It was set up so she could draw the interest off it for living expenses, but the principal was tied up until she was married or fifty, whichever came first. At the rate she is going, Helen has an excellent shot of reaching fifty—she's healthy as a horse—but the chances of her marrying are slim to none because, to be horribly blunt, she's nuttier than a fruitcake."

"Oh my! And what about Jane? How does she fit in to the story?"

"Oh yes... Jane. Well, Helen shared her money with her mother, my aunt Delores, but there just wasn't that much to share, so they barely squeaked by. Nina and Daddy even help them out from time to time when things are tight, so they have what they need. It isn't easy, but they always got along okay. Then, when Jane was fourteen, a terrible tragedy occurred."

"What happened?"

"Jane's parents were killed in a car accident."

"Oh no!"

"So, Jane came to live with her aunt—who remember, is also my aunt by marriage—and my cousin Helen. It was a bleak time for all of them, as you can well imagine. I felt sorry for Jane, but she was so..."

I remembered how frustrated I was when I tried to reach out to Jane all those years ago. The resentment all came flooding back. Even now, it still annoyed me. "She's so aloof. I tried to be kind to her, to be friends. I really did. But she shut me right out.

"Anyway, there was very little money to support them all. So as soon as she could, Jane left to pursue her dreams of being a theater star in New York."

"How exciting." Mary Jo sighed.

"Jane had some connections, I gather, through a girlfriend of hers, Natalie Campbell. Natalie's father is a playwright, so they helped Jane get started, get auditions, whatever."

"What a story!"

"Isn't it? I've often wondered how she could leave Delores and Helen here to fend for themselves, but I suppose not everyone feels compelled to take care of family members the way I do for Daddy. Her situation is different from mine, as George reminds me periodically when we've talked about it. Helen is Jane's cousin, not her parent, and Daddy isn't able to work, whereas Aunt Delores and Helen probably could, if they had the inclination. But some people can't be resilient, after being raised to lead a life of privilege, like Aunt Delores and Helen were.

"Jane, on the other hand, has done better for herself, but then she isn't hampered by family obligations like me, or by Helen's...oh, shall we say, quirky personality."

"I can't wait to meet them," Mary Jo said with conviction.

"You're sweet to say so, but I wouldn't expect too much if I were you." For about the fourteenth time, I marveled that Mary Jo Smith was almost too good-natured to be true.

TWELVE

George was deep into reading *Shogun* when the phone rang, startling him with its clanging interruption. It was the Sunday before Labor Day, and although he had Mr. Woodhouse's birthday party to attend tomorrow, he'd eschewed all other social engagements for the weekend. He was savoring the solitude of being holed up in his townhouse, ordering takeout and catching up on his reading. No legal briefs dared enter the place this weekend.

He answered the phone hanging beside the fridge and simultaneously fetched himself a cold beer.

"Hello?"

"George, hi. How are you?" It was his brother, sounding a little more harried than usual.

"I'm fine. What's up?" Jack rarely called him on the weekends unless there was a family thing going on.

"I'm feeling a little guilty."

"This sounds serious," George quipped. Jack was always feeling a little guilty about one thing or another. It was part and parcel of his nature.

"Ha-ha. No, I mean it. I called to ask you a tiny favor."

"I'll do what I can."

"Can you go over to Hartfield Road and check on Emma?"

George set down his beer on the counter, concern sweeping over him. "What's wrong with Emma?"

"She's fine, I think. But she's watching Henry and Taylor, and it wasn't a pretty scene when I left. And the au pair went to see her family in Arkansas for a few days."

"Jack, she's trying to set up for her father's birthday party tomorrow. If you needed a babysitter, you should have hired one."

"Well, she offered, and I was kind of in a rush, so…"

George suddenly processed the background noise coming over the phone—voices on an intercom and some kind of beeping noise.

"Where are you?"

"I'm at the emergency room with Izzy."

"What?"

"We came down for the weekend, stayed at Mom and Dad's house while they're gone to Europe. We didn't stay at Hartfield because you know how the babies discombobulate John."

That was an understatement. John loved his grandchildren, but small doses were about all he could handle. "Is Izzy alright?"

"Yes, I think she's doing better, now that she has the IV fluids."

"What happened?"

"She was fine Friday when we drove down here, but she started running a fever that night, throwing up and stuff. I guess I kind of neglected her, because I was trying to keep the kids away so they wouldn't get it. I didn't realize how bad off she was. But she couldn't keep anything down, even water, and I started to worry…"

This was an unusual amount of worry, even for Jack.

"So, she has the flu or something?"

"Maybe, but it's complicated because…" Jack hesitated.

"What?"

"She might be pregnant again."

George was grateful his brother couldn't see his expression. *Good Lord, Jack. Don't you ever give the poor woman a rest?*

"I know what you're thinking, and yes, I *do* know what causes that, but this one wasn't planned."

"But Isabel is okay?" George repeated, wanting to reassure himself.

"Yes, much better. But now that the crisis is over, I'm starting to feel bad about leaving Emma to take care of my kids on her own. Taylor's been colicky, and you know, John Woodhouse can be a handful all by himself. He wouldn't leave his room for fear the children are carrying 'poor Isabel's infection.' When I left, he was fretting to Mrs. Davies about Emma catching the flu."

George could well believe it. Since his stroke, John's careful, detail-oriented ways in combination with his confined environment had made him almost pathologically afraid of illness. Emma handled him fine, but he could imagine the chaos on Hartfield Road right now. He could at least go by, ease his brother's mind, and maybe keep John out of Emma's hair.

"Sure, Jack. I'll go by and offer my services, such as they are."

"Thanks. I hate to ask, but I guess I sort of panicked about Isabel. I..." He stopped and cleared his throat, and George suspected he was trying to avoid choking up. "You know how Isabel loves babies."

"Yes, I know."

"I've got to be more careful though. This is too much. She's going to make herself really ill. The doctor says there's a chance she'll miscarry—if she's pregnant, that is."

"Don't borrow trouble, little brother. Hope for the best. I'm on my way over to Emma's. Don't worry about the kids. Just take care of your wife."

"I appreciate it, George. Really. I owe you."

"Keep us posted."

"I will."

After they hung up, George put on his shoes and took his keys off the hook. He jogged around back to the garage underneath his townhouse and pulled open the garage door. He'd traded in the Corvette for a BMW —a more grown-up car for a more grown-up man. Or so Marilyn had convinced him.

His former girlfriend had some rather specific ideas: what car he should drive, what clothes he should wear, which restaurants were the best. George appreciated a woman who paid attention to details and was organized, but Marilyn wanted to manage every facet of his life. Plus, she seemed to have no interests of her own except for how she could complement him. That rigid approach to life left no room for spontaneity. And it eventually drove him away from her, because despite his growing responsibilities, George Knightley still liked to play sometimes.

He was much better off without that kind of suffocating structure in his life. He could breathe again now that Marilyn was out of the picture, but he wondered how many times he was going to think he'd found the right girl, merely to realize later she was absolutely the wrong woman.

Maybe the only way to find the right woman is to make her yourself.

He wished he could find the kind of devotion that Jack and Isabel had for each other. They seemed to…fit somehow. He offered up a quick prayer for his sister-in-law as he sped down the empty city streets and out to the state road that would lead him to Highbury.

When George arrived at the big house on Hartfield Road, he had to ring the bell twice before a harried Mrs. Davies answered it.

"Mr. Knightley," she sighed, blowing a wisp of graying hair out of her eyes, "you picked the wrong day to come calling."

"It's not a social call, Mrs. D. Jack telephoned and asked me to check on Emma and his kids."

"Well, then, you come right in, young man, and thank the Lord, you're here. Don't know how Miss Emma does it. I been tryin' to get some of this housework done for tomorrow's party, but between her father fretting and them little ones, I can't hardly get a thing accomplished. You hear that baby squalling? Lord have mercy, that child got a set of lungs on her! She got the colic for sure."

Indeed, George could hear little Taylor screaming, interspersed with Henry's toddler yells. Poor Emma, she was probably at the end of her rope.

He went upstairs first to check on John and found a man who was nervous as a cat.

"Come in, George. Come in. This is a mess, a real mess, I tell you. Poor Isabel is mighty ill. Jack took her to the hospital. Did you know that?"

"Yes sir, I did."

"And the children are here, because he's with her, and poor Emma is taking care of them."

"So I heard."

"And tomorrow is my birthday party, and Emma has so much work to get ready for it. She's such a dear, and she worked so hard to make it nice for me. And now we'll probably have to cancel the whole thing, and she'll be so disappointed."

"Maybe not. Mrs. Davies is here to help."

Mr. Woodhouse wrung his hands. "But Emma will get Isabel's fever, because I'm sure Izzy caught it from the babies, and now Emma's taking care of the babies. And we can't have all that company tomorrow, because then they'll all catch it too."

"Oh, I wouldn't worry about it. As you see, I'm here."

Mr. Woodhouse stopped his hand-wringing and looked at George. "You are here, at that. Do you think it's wise to visit us in our time of sickness?"

"I'll be just fine."

"Why are you here?"

"To check on you, of course. I thought I'd come up here first, before I went in to help Emma—so I wouldn't bring any germs in here with me." His lips twitched, but Emma's father seemed not to notice.

"That is smart thinking, George. Very smart." Mr. Woodhouse's expression was solemn and long-suffering.

"So, do you need anything—before I go downstairs into the germ pit?"

"No, no. Well, maybe just a pitcher of water—the distilled kind, from the bottle in the refrigerator. Emma gets that for me, because it doesn't have any impurities in it."

"I'll bring it right up."

Mrs. Davies offered to take the water with her, as she was going back up the stairs. Bracing himself, George turned to face the chaos in the family room.

Taylor had settled into a rhythmic howl, and Henry was grimacing, both hands over his ears. George looked at Emma, holding Taylor in one arm and drawing Henry to her with the other. She kissed him on the head and spoke in his ear, before standing up and crossing to the stereo console. Curious as to what she had planned, George watched from the doorway.

Emma put the needle on the record as she continued to bounce Taylor gently in her arm. The introductory groove of "Superstition" filled the room, and Emma cranked up the volume to drown out Taylor's howls. Henry started bouncing up and down, keeping his hands over his ears. Emma transferred Taylor to her shoulder, patting the baby's back in time with the beat.

George grinned, leaning against the doorway with his hands in his pockets and watching in amusement as Emma and Henry danced.

He pushed off the doorframe and made his way into the room, touching Emma's elbow so as not to startle her. She half-turned in surprise and a happy smile broke over her features like the sun bursting from behind a cloud. There was a soaring feeling in his chest, and without thinking, he put his arms around the two of them from behind, joining in and moving Emma and Taylor in an easy rhythm to the song.

After a minute, she turned and handed him Taylor, whose little body was taut from screaming. He cradled their niece against his chest, letting the warmth of his singing voice and his easy movements calm her. Emma reached out both hands to Henry and the two of them danced, Emma swaying side to side and Henry still bouncing up and down.

Thus occupied, he almost missed Mrs. Davies when she came into the room as if to ask Emma a question. Her mouth agape, she watched them for a second. And yet, the moment seemed a tad too intimate, like they had been caught in a special family moment, and he wondered what the old housekeeper was thinking. He winked at her, and without saying a word, Mrs. Davies walked out, shaking her head and smiling to herself.

THIRTEEN

SEPTEMBER 4, 1975

"I heard you took care of the children yesterday," Mary Jo said, popping a grape in her mouth as we arranged fruit on a tray.

"I did. That's why we're still arranging food trays two hours after the guests arrived. Where did you find that out?"

"Your father told me. He's really worried about you getting sick."

"I'm afraid he's perseverating on that today."

Mary Jo blinked, in that way that I had come to recognize as her lack of comprehension.

"It means he keeps thinking and talking about it."

"Oh."

"It may spoil the party for him, which I hate, because he so rarely gets together with people anymore. I wanted him to have fun today."

"He seems to enjoy talking about you and Isabel being sick. I heard him tell your aunt Delores and Helen. Twice."

"I'm not sick! And I'm not getting sick either. I won't allow it." I'd been discreet regarding the real reason for Isabel's overnight stay at the hospital. She miscarried late in the evening. Isabel was devastated but physically she was okay, and Jack and the children were with her. There was no need to worry our father any further.

"Is Isabel feeling better?"

"Oh yes, she's much better today, but she and Jack thought it best to just go back to Louisville and rest."

"Oh, I'm glad..." Mary Jo's eyes widened. "Not that she went home. That she's better."

"Yes." I put the last finishing touches on the tray. "Now, I want you to go out there and put this tray right next to Tim Elton and throw him one of your million-dollar smiles while you do it, okay?"

Mary Jo squirmed uncomfortably. "Do I have to? He makes me so nervous sometimes. I'm afraid I'll drop the tray."

"Mary Jo, what am I going to do with you?"

"I don't know."

"Here. You take the ice bucket and tongs then, and I'll take the tray. How's that?"

"Much better." Mary Jo's whole countenance lightened at the suggestion.

"And offer to get Tim another drink or some more ice. You've spent most of the afternoon talking to Daddy—I appreciate you distracting him, but we need to nudge Tim a little bit. Has he asked you out yet?"

"Um...no."

"What is the matter with that man?"

"Emma..."

"Do I have to push you into his lap?"

Mary Jo looked alarmed.

"I'm joking, Mary Jo. Of course, we're not going to be so blatantly obvious."

"Oh, that's good." Relief washed over her features. "Emma..."

"We won't have to force a thing. I'm sure when Tim sees the beauty right in front of him, he'll realize you two are perfect for each other."

I walked over to the kitchen door and Mary Jo opened it for me.

"Thank you, dear."

"You're welcome," Mary Jo said softly, as she followed me out into the yard.

I sauntered over to the buffet table where Tim was standing, talking to Bob Weston. I smiled at them, placing the tray strategically, and indicating that Mary Jo should put the ice right there—next to Tim.

He turned to face us while Bob was in mid-sentence.

"Lovely spread, Miss Woodhouse."

George's gaze narrowed on Tim, and I wondered if that might be intended as a double entendre. No matter. I ignored it and responded to his literal meaning.

"I decided at the last minute to do buffet style. I know it's informal, but you'll forgive me. We're all good friends here, right?"

"Absolutely." Tim grinned. "Have you been at the tennis courts lately? I haven't seen you around."

"Oh, I think we've probably given up on it until next spring. There's so much to do in the fall, and I've started back to college. It's my senior year. Busy, busy, busy."

"What a shame," Tim said. "I have to say I've missed going *courtin'* with you ladies."

I grinned and stepped back behind Mary Jo to get a slice of cheese from the tray, nudging her ever so slightly toward Tim.

"You really helped us a lot, right, Mary Jo?"

"What? Oh, yes, you really helped... a lot." She grimaced at her lame finish.

"I have to go check on Daddy, if you'll excuse me?"

"Of course," Tim replied. "Hurry back."

"George, would you mind getting some beer for the cooler out here?"

"Sure."

I left Mary Jo and Tim to themselves. When I looked over a few minutes later, Tim was talking to her with his typical animated gestures, and she was smiling. But after a couple of minutes, they stood awkwardly silent. Mary Jo turned around to get another branch of grapes, and Tim turned back to Bob Weston.

"Busy plotting?"

I jumped at the sound of George's low voice in my ear and turned to scowl at him.

"Don't sneak up on me like that! You just took ten minutes off my life."

"Sorry." George took a sip of his beer.

"And I'm not *plotting*."

"That's good."

"Although you have to admit, they look good together."

He rolled his eyes and walked off, muttering, "Nonsensical girl," into his beer can.

"I saw you chatting with Tim. Making an effort."

Mary Jo smiled as we sat in the backyard gazebo on the swing. The party guests were all gone, Daddy was tucked safely in his bed, and we were enjoying a glass of white wine in the evening quiet.

"It was a good party."

"Yes, it was." I slouched back against the swing. "But I'm exhausted."

"Emma?"

"Yes?"

"I need your advice about something."

"Well, of course, I can be a sounding board for you, Mary Jo, but I want you to make your own decisions—not just take my advice." I was remembering George's "plotting" comment from earlier.

"I've gone out with Robert a few times—just as friends."

"Robert?"

"Robert Martin...from the Louisville office."

"Oh yes, I remember."

"We've had—I don't know, maybe four dates, and last time he said something about maybe dating each other, you know, exclusively." She looked at me, anxious for my reaction.

"Wow, it must have been tough to let him down easy. You're still going to be friends, though, aren't you?"

"You think I should tell him 'no'?"

"Oh, my goodness!" I bolted upright on the swing and set my wine on the table beside it. "I can't tell you what you should do, Mary Jo! You were talking with Tim today at the party, and I just assumed..."

"I don't know what to do. That's why I came to you. Can you advise me? You know so much about men and everything."

That's a laugh. If I know anything about men, it's only by watching them from afar. It certainly isn't from experience. Silly college boys from Georgia don't count as men.

"I wouldn't dream of deciding anything so personal for you. It's simply not my place."

Mary Jo looked miserable as she took a healthy gulp of wine.

"But...maybe I can help you sort it out for yourself. Tell me what Robert said to you—maybe exclusive dating wasn't what he meant exactly."

"Oh, I think it's what he meant. He said, 'Mary Jo, each time we get together, I discover that I like you more and more. You're sweet, and beautiful, and we have the best talks, don't you think?' And then I said, 'Yes, we do have good talks.' And then he said, 'Maybe we should think about making this...' and he gestured between us, '...a more, well...maybe we should be more than just friends. I'd like that.' Wasn't that a nice way to say it? Or was it too...short?"

"Do you mean 'blunt' perhaps? I think that's the word you want."

"Yes, was he too blunt?"

My mind was whirring. "No. It was pretty smooth, actually."

"I thought so too."

"It *was* nice. What did you tell him?"

"I just kind of hemmed and hawed around and said I'd have to think about it."

"I see. And what did he say then?"

"He looked disappointed, and I felt just awful, but then he smiled and told me to take my time."

"Here's the thing. You've come all the way from West Virginia, and you're meeting all kinds of people, learning a new job, living in a new place. There's so much to see and do. And the world's your oyster, Mary Jo. But if you think that you're going to prefer Robert Martin's company to any other man's—to the point of not getting to know any other man—then I guess you have to say 'yes.'"

"Okay."

"But if you're thinking, 'Hey, I'm still young and I value my freedom right now, and I want to see what's and who's out there for me'—then you have to say 'no.'"

Mary Jo sat a while, pondering and sipping her wine.

"I guess I'm not ready to tie myself down yet. I'm going to tell him 'no'. That's the right decision, isn't it?"

"Now that you've decided, I have to tell you I think you made exactly the right choice." I raised my glass. "Vive la femme moderne!"

Mary Jo blinked.

"Long live the modern woman!"

"Oh, yes, the modern woman." Mary Jo let out a wistful sigh. "I wish I knew how to speak Italian."

I pursed my lips to keep from smiling.

"Emma?"

"Yes?"

"Can I ask you something?"

"Sure."

"Why don't you have a boyfriend? You're smart and beautiful. I would think men would like you a lot."

"Why, thank you, Mary Jo. What a kind thing to say! But I'm just not interested in dating right now. I've got a lot on my plate—taking care of Daddy, going to school—and a boyfriend would be too much. Plus, I haven't found a man I care for that much. Maybe I never will."

"But don't you want a family? Children?"

"I haven't really thought about it, I guess. I'm only twenty-one. I have lots of time to find true love, right? And I can see Henry and Taylor any time I want. So, in all honesty, I have no reason to fall in love and get married...well, ever, if I choose not to."

"I see what you mean. I guess I just always thought that love happened when it happened, you know? That you couldn't choose *if* or *when*."

"You *always* have choices, Mary Jo. That's one of the best advantages of being a modern woman."

"Yes, I suppose it is."

Mary Jo went back into her pensive mood, and I gently turned the topic to other things as we relaxed into the late summer evening.

FOURTEEN

OCTOBER 11, 1975

George pulled up outside Emma's house and opened the car door. He sat there, changing into the running shoes that Emma bought him for an early birthday present.

It was a beautiful autumn morning. There were still some vibrant colors on the trees: crimson red, burnt orange, mustard yellow. The faint, clean smell of dampness emanated from the leaves already on the ground. The sun was barely over the horizon, and the air was crisp and cool.

As he walked toward the house, he was greeted with a bounding blur of golden fur.

"Maude, old girl, how've you been?" He bent down to scrub her behind the ears the way she loved, and she wriggled from head to tail. "You going with us today?" She barked and leaned against his leg, so he would pat her flank.

"Of course, she's going with us. If I run without her, she paces and whines and makes Mrs. D nuts."

He lifted his gaze to find Emma striding toward him. She had on a pink jogging suit with a white satin stripe down the side. *I didn't even know they made the things in pink.* Her hair was pulled back in a ponytail, and her face was scrubbed clean. Taken together, the effect made her look about eighteen.

"Good morning, Miss Woodhouse."

"Professor Knightley."

"So, tell me, how does Maude know when you're ready to go running?"

"Oh"—she shrugged—"I don't know, unless she's used to the time of day I run, or she recognizes the clothes."

"Hard to miss them," he said, gliding his eyes from her head to her toes.

She blew a raspberry at him, standing with arms akimbo. "Are you finished pestering me and ready to show off your inner Prefontaine?"

"I'm no runner, Emma. Don't expect too much."

"I'll go easy on you," she teased. "We'll just go around the streets in Hartfield Estates."

They turned out of Emma's driveway and jogged on the side of the state road about two hundred yards until they reached the entry for Hartfield Estates subdivision. Emma reached down and unhooked Maude's leash, letting her run ahead through the empty lots.

"It must be odd for you to see this suburban sprawl springing up around you."

"Sometimes. After all, it was my family's farm. Delores was unwise to sell it all in one chunk, but I guess she felt a little desperate after Edwin died. If she had subdivided it herself, she would have made a lot more money. Maybe enough that she wouldn't have to live in the old broken-down house on a shoestring budget.

"The man who bought the land originally held on to it a long time. I think he wanted to restore the farm. But when he died, his kids just wanted the money. They live out of state and have no use for a horse farm. Shame, really.

"Nothing like that will ever happen to Donwell Farms. I know, because you'd never allow it," she said, blowing out a whoosh of air.

"It won't happen while Jack and I are around anyway."

"Good for you and Jack. If everybody sold off their land, this area would lose its bucolic charm completely."

They ran in silence for several minutes before George ventured a comment.

"I wasn't going to say anything, but now I think, in all fairness, I must."

"What is it?"

"Your Pygmalion attempts with Mary Jo are having some beneficial results."

"Oh?"

"Yes. She's just as pleasant to the clients and hardworking as she ever was, but her manners and her dress are more professional than before. You've done her a great service, I believe."

Emma smiled a self-satisfied grin. It was probably unwise to feed her ego, he told himself, but George felt obliged to give credit where credit was due. Besides, it was fun to make her smile.

"I told you she was a beauty waiting to be discovered. Now if only the available gentlemen would notice."

"Not that I care anything about that, but I think some of them have. Or rather, one has."

She halted in her tracks. He stopped and turned around. "What?"

Her face was wide-eyed and hopeful, like a kid who received a new bicycle for Christmas. "You can't drop a comment like that and leave it hanging! Who is it that's interested in Mary Jo?"

He looked at her for a moment, embarrassed to be caught in idle gossip, but decided it wouldn't matter if she knew. "Robert Martin. Let's walk, and I'll tell you."

She fell in step beside him.

"Robert knocked on my office door a few weeks ago. It was one of those days he drove down from the Louisville office back in the summer. He told me he and Mary Jo had gone out a few times, more as friends really, but he wanted it to become more exclusive. Then, he asked me if I would have a problem with two employees dating."

"I couldn't have thought of a better question myself," Emma muttered.

"Yes, it was considerate of him to ask about the company policy first. Robert Martin is a man who has a great deal of common sense. He was level-headed about it, and he's in Louisville most of the time anyway, so I told him I didn't see any issues."

Emma said nothing, and George started to get an "uh-oh" kind of feeling from her silence.

"He asked if she was seeing anybody, and if I thought she would consider him. He was asking for my opinion of her, I guess."

There was still no word from her, and she wasn't out of breath.

"I said she was free as far as I could tell, and she was a pleasant and hardworking girl, and I wished him luck."

"I guess I should tell you…"

His Emma's-been-meddling sense started tingling. "Yes?" he said in a guarded tone.

"He did ask Mary Jo about dating him exclusively."

"Ah, he did. Good for him."

"She told him 'no.'"

George stopped walking. "She told him 'no'?"

"Yes—I mean, correct—that's what she told him."

"I hope you're mistaken."

"I'm not. She asked—I mean she told me about it."

"She let you influence her about who she should date, didn't she? To the point of turning down a good, decent man like Robert Martin. Unbelievable! Well, she's a bigger fool than I thought."

Emma harrumphed. "Oh, of course! If Mary Jo doesn't want to date your paralegal, she's an idiot? Because Robert Martin is the best she can possibly do for herself."

"I never said that…" Anger welled up in his chest. "And there is nothing wrong with Robert Martin. You're making it sound like he's a shiftless bum. I know he's my employee, but I'm proud to call him my friend as well. He's a bright, young man with a good future ahead of him. And he's a gentleman, which is becoming a rarity these days."

"Someone as pretty and sweet as Mary Jo ending up with a man who has reached the pinnacle of his career before he even reaches thirty? Even with all his fine qualities, Mary Jo could do so much better."

"Oh, really? Where could she find better?" He stopped mid-stride. "Wait a minute—is this about his race? His family?"

"How dare you even suggest that?" Bright red flags appeared in both her cheeks. "I am *not* a prejudiced person!"

"Well, you shouldn't be. You were taught not to be."

"Of course, I was taught right from wrong."

"Robert is a good man."

"I'm sure he is. You wouldn't hire any other kind."

"He comes from a good family. His father's a minister. His mother was head mistress of a school before she retired."

"That doesn't mean he's right for Mary Jo."

"Mary Jo, on the other hand, is uneducated and, forgive me, but she's not the sharpest tool in the shed. She's the daughter of some poor woman in West Virginia who may or may not have been married to Mary Jo's father."

"She is not illegitimate! Her parents are divorced!" Emma's voice rose with indignation. George closed his eyes and pinched the bridge of his nose in frustration. She was so headstrong, and they were getting farther and farther from the main point, which was the wrong-headedness of Emma's interference. She continued, rationalizing her prying activities.

"You're forgetting her sweet, kind disposition and her beauty. It seems to me that's all men want in a woman anyway."

It was a rarity that he was genuinely angry with Emma, but now, she was exasperating to him—a know-it-all who in truth knew almost nothing. What she had done would hurt Robert, and possibly hurt Mary Jo too. He had to try and make her see that. "I don't know what kind of psychobabble you've been reading in those magazines of yours, or what they've been teaching you in college, but sensible men aren't interested in foolish women!"

She gasped her indignation at his comment.

Who have I just insulted more—her or Mary Jo? Why does she always bring out the worst in me?

"And why should she take your advice and start dating Robert Martin?"

"If I remember correctly, I never gave her any advice, unlike some of her nosy friends."

"If you know so much about romantic relationships, why do you have this endless parade of shallow, simpering girlfriends? You don't know anything about love—although you do seem to know quite a bit about dating."

She was angry because he'd insulted her, and perhaps rightly so. He took a deep breath and tried to ignore the surprising sting of the remark. "You know, it's one thing to help someone improve herself, but this is something else entirely. Can't you see that this kind of intrusion into other people's personal lives is a gross misapplication of your time and considerable intellect?"

She rolled her eyes at him—actually rolled her eyes—like a fifteen-year-old drama queen. A sudden thought leaped into his mind, a memory of the cookout last month.

"If you're thinking about fixing her up with Tim Elton—"

"I would never—"

"I saw you trying to throw them together at your father's birthday party. But be realistic, Emma Kate, Elton will never shackle himself to a girl who can't help him politically. In fact, I've heard him mention a family of girls in Frankfort whose father is well-connected in the state-level political circles."

Emma looked at the ground, and began walking briskly. "If I were trying to fix her up, then your advice would be welcome, but—"

He cut her off with a sharp gesture and a harsh timbre in his voice. "Enough! You know my view on the matter. I don't want to talk about it anymore if you're going to persist in this silly subterfuge. I know what you're really thinking." He whistled for Maude, who came running toward them at full speed, the fur on her underside wet with dew.

"I agree we shouldn't discuss it further. We obviously have completely different opinions on this. I'm ready to head back home anyway."

They finished the outing in silence and at a hurried pace. When they returned to the house, George went up to say a quick hello to Mr. Wood-house, and then he took his leave of Emma with nothing but a curt nod.

FIFTEEN

NOVEMBER 27, 1975

Before I knew it, Thanksgiving was upon me. Because Nina was a newlywed, and Izzy was absorbed with recuperating from her miscarriage and caring for her young family, I offered to host Thanksgiving dinner at our house on Hartfield Road. I asked Mary Jo to come but she wanted to go see her mother for the holiday. I couldn't really blame her for that, but it put the quietus on my plans to get things going for her with Tim Elton. Since Mary Jo wouldn't be there, I ended up not inviting Tim either. The two of them were beginning to frustrate me; he wouldn't pony up and ask Mary Jo on a date, although he sat and talked with her whenever he saw us out walking, having lunch... whatever. And Mary Jo would hardly say a word in his presence.

When I asked her about that, she said, "He's so handsome, he makes me nervous."

"Don't you like Tim? He likes you. He's always finding us out places and coming over to talk to you."

"Oh yes!" she insisted. "I really like him. I just never know what to say when he's around. He's so much smarter than me and uses all those big words."

"Mary Jo, you have a much better vocabulary now, and you're a hip, modern girl. You have an interesting job and lots to talk about. Don't be intimidated."

"I know you're right. It's just hard for me to be myself around him. I'll try to do better though. I did see him smile at me a lot during your dad's birthday party."

Tim and Mary Jo seemed to be stuck right in that place where she was overwhelmed by him, and he wouldn't do anything but smile at her. I was weary of them always relying on me to provide the conversation. *There are people, who, the more you do for them, the less they will do for themselves.*

Thanksgiving ended up being a family gathering, which was perfectly fine with me. Nina and Bob were there, along with Izzy, Jack, Henry and Taylor, and I invited Mr. & Mrs. Knightley and George, of course. And, because they were family too, I had to invite Delores and Helen.

Thanksgiving morning arrived cloudy and cold, as I was keenly aware, because I was up at the crack of dawn. I didn't run that morning, however. There was too much to do. *What possessed me to invite all these people and feed them a three-course meal?*

"Mrs. D?" I called, striding through the dining room and into the kitchen about mid-morning. "Have you seen the cornucopia soup tureen?"

"The corn-you-what?"

"The cornucopia—the soup tureen with the vegetables and fruit on it, sitting in a basket?"

"Oh, you mean the horn of plenty?"

"Yes, the horn of plenty."

"I didn't know what corn-u-what's-it meant."

I closed my eyes, took a deep breath, reminded myself how pleasant and efficient a housekeeper Mrs. Davies was, and tried to hold the frustration I wanted to let loose.

"At any rate, do you know where it is?"

She came over and patted my cheek. "What's the matter, lamb? You look frazzled."

"I wanted to use the soup tureen for the lobster bisque, but I can't find it, and I tried to make the pie crusts myself, but they look awful, and I was up late last night polishing Mama's silver and—"

"Why you do that, child? I told Miri to polish before she left yesterday."

"Well, she didn't, and I knew you had a lot to do this morning, so you needed your rest. And I knew I wouldn't have time, because we couldn't get a nurse to take care of Daddy on a holiday, and I needed to get his meds and his clothes ready. So, I..." My voice wobbled, much to my embarrassment. "I just want everything to be nice for everyone."

Mrs. Davies laid her hand on my arm. "Now, don't you worry about a thing, Miss E. We'll find that soup tureen, and I'll get a couple of those new-fangled ready-made crusts out of the fridge so you can finish up your pies. You go take care of your daddy and get yourself ready, and you can come help me after that, alright? It will all turn out just fine." She tucked a loose piece of hair behind my ear, eliciting a grateful smile.

"Emma?" A voice came from the other room, and Daddy walked in, wearing black socks and his boxer shorts, and holding one pair of slacks in each hand. "Which ones was I supposed to wear?"

"Daddy! Why are you walking around the house in your underwear?"

He stopped, looked down, and blushed furiously. "Oh dear! Oh, I forgot I didn't have my pants on yet."

"How could you have your pants on? You're holding them in your hands."

Mrs. Davies turned away, smiling.

He stood and blinked at me for a few seconds. "So, I have. How silly of me. I apologize, Emma, Mrs. Davies." He was so contrite, I didn't have the heart to scold him.

"It's okay. No harm, no foul." I took his arm and led him back to the stairs. "I'm going to put the correct pair over your arm, and I'll take the others and put them away."

"I can put them away, honey."

I smiled at him, knowing he would forget again as soon as he reached his room. "I think these need to be washed, and I'm going up to the laundry room anyway."

"Oh, all right, then."

Maude came streaking by him as she ran in from the other room and flattened him against the wall.

He sighed and shook his head. "I know you love that animal, Emma, but she is a troublesome creature!"

I kissed his cheek. "I'll put her outside until after dinner. Try not to be too hard on us though. We troublesome creatures love you."

He smiled back at me. "I love you too, Daughter. You could never be troublesome to me. And Maude is a good dog." He paused, thinking. "We have company today?"

"Yes, it's Thanksgiving."

"I wondered why the nurse wasn't here today."

"Juanita's with her family for the holiday. And our company's coming at two o'clock. Your dearest friends and family will be here."

"Ah, good, good. I should like to see them all."

"Here you are, George. I brought you one of your martinis."

"Thank you." He nodded, taking the glass from me. It had been awkward between us since our argument about Mary Jo and Robert Martin, and I hated feeling uncomfortable with George. He was upset with me, but honestly, Mary Jo was a rare prize, not to be shuffled off to the first man who admired her. *Women should be very choosy about the men they fall in love with.* Tim Elton could broaden Mary Jo's horizons in a way that Robert Martin never could.

But in the meantime, I would make an overture of friendship. George and I had to get past this argument. *We've been friends too long to let some silly squabble come between us.*

The perfect conversation piece arrived right then in the form of Jack and Isabel and the children. I swept down upon them all with hugs and kisses and snagged the baby from her mother's arms.

"I can't believe how she's grown!" I exclaimed as I laid my cheek against the soft, little head. "Hi, sweet girl. Are you here to see Auntie Emma?"

I paraded Taylor around the room, looking out windows and talking to Daddy, slowly making my way over to George and his martini.

"Dare we speak to grumpy Uncle George, Taylor?"

He smiled, and I considered that enough of an invitation to sit beside him.

"If you understood your adult friends the way you do these babies, we might never disagree." He paused. "Perhaps, we disagree because I'm so much older than you. Do we have a generational gap, Emma Kate?"

"Surely not! Seven years is nothing. Perhaps we were very different when you were seven and playing baseball, while I sat in a playpen, but I think I've just about caught up to you now."

"I suppose we can be friends then."

My heart soared. Thank goodness, he could never stay mad at me for too long.

"Friends." I held out my hand, and he shook it. He reached his arms to Taylor and she went right to him.

"Flirt," I accused her in a jovial voice. "I know how it is—you always choose the handsome guy over poor Aunt Em."

George laughed, and I knew we were right back on track.

"For what it's worth, I'm truly sorry about Mr. Martin's feelings being hurt. But surely, he's over it by now."

He shook his head. "I don't know. He asked for a permanent transfer to Louisville. My loss, Jack's gain—he's a fine paralegal. But perhaps I can lure him back at some point with something else."

"I hope so, if he's that helpful to you."

"I'm rarely trying cases myself these days. More and more of my time is caught up in running the farms, the other properties, and so on."

"Are you happy about that?"

"It's my job, learning to run the family holdings. I like being out and about, and it gives me more free time."

"I heard you've been seen escorting Julianne Ryman around town these days."

"Hmm."

"She's not your usual well-heeled Junior League type."

"Well, she's generally too busy for parties and things. Being a resident at the hospital takes up a lot of time."

"She must be extremely smart," I said in a small voice, a touch of envy crawling into my heart. I knew many things about medicine from reading and my experience taking care of my parents, but given my family obligations, medical school would never be an option for me.

"Julianne is smart," he answered, watching my face. Then he winked at me. "But no smarter than the present company."

"Always tooting your own horn, Professor. What am I to do with you?"

He chuckled and Taylor put her chubby hands up to pat his face. He spoke to her and she leaned in to give him an open-mouthed kiss on his jaw, complete with drool. I grabbed a Kleenex from the box next to them and dabbed at his clean-shaven cheek.

"There, all better."

"Thank you, Auntie."

Mrs. Davies came in and announced that dinner was ready, and Rita stepped forward and held her arms out for Taylor. George handed off the baby and spoke to the au pair in a soft, friendly voice, evoking a fierce blush as she involuntarily let out a school-girl titter. Mentally, I rolled my eyes. *What is it about George Knightley that reduces every woman between two and eighty-two into a gooey mess of smiles and giggles? Don't they realize they shouldn't feed his ego that way?* Next time we'll give Rita the night off and I'll hire sturdy, austere Mrs. Gruetmann from down the road to babysit.

SIXTEEN

The long dining table at Emma's house was set with Wedgewood china and polished sterling silver. Autumn floral arrangements graced the sideboards and the table. Crystal sparkled in the glow from the chandelier and the late November sun. Despite the various conversations and the clink of dishes, there was a peaceful aura to the table, punctuated by the elder Mr. Knightley's deep voice, Nina's gracious laughter, and Emma's brilliant smile. George heard an intermittent staccato bark from outside and felt sorry for poor Maude. It was driving her nuts to not be in the middle of the fray; he would have to offer her a walk after dinner. Emma would hardly have had time to exercise her properly today with all the chaos of a holiday party.

Emma. He glanced up the table at her, pride rising in his chest. She did an incredible job with Thanksgiving dinner. All the traditional fare was on display: turkey, mashed potatoes, green beans, Mrs. Davies' melt-in-your-mouth butter rolls. His mother had wondered aloud on the way over to the Woodhouses' if so young a girl could pull off a big holiday meal like this, but George knew Emma would make everything run like clockwork and told his mother so.

"Mrs. Davies will do the majority of the cooking, and they hired a couple of local girls to serve and clean up." He smiled across the seat at his mother's pitying expression.

She shook her head. "There's a lot more to entertaining than slapping some food on a table. And the poor, motherless lamb had no one to show her the proper way to have guests."

"Nina taught her plenty over the years."

"I know, but she didn't actually live at Hartfield as mistress of the house. It's different." She smoothed her skirt in her lap. "Just don't expect a fine dinner party," she remarked, almost to herself.

"I'm sure I won't be disappointed," he said lightly.

He wasn't and neither, apparently, was his mother.

"Emma, dear," she piped up near the end of the main course, and Emma turned to her in mid-bite. Her fork sank back to her plate.

"Yes, ma'am?"

"What a delicious Thanksgiving feast you've set for us. And the house is just lovely too. Brava, my girl."

Emma's cheeks turned slightly pink; George's mother rarely offered compliments. "Thank you. I had some wonderful help."

John Woodhouse declared, "Emma always does everything she attempts to perfection. Yes, she certainly does! The meal is wonderful, dear. Although we don't usually eat food this rich. I wonder about all the butter in the potatoes and the dressing. Too much butter is bad for the digestion."

"Oh, it's a holiday," Jack cut in. "I'm sure we'll survive a little extra butter."

John blinked, as if trying to determine if he should argue with Jack or not.

Emma's voice rose and she leaned forward to change the subject, addressing Nina, two seats down from her.

"Tell us how Frank is doing these days."

"Oh!" Nina put her napkin to her lips and returned it to her lap. "I almost forgot. He's planning to visit at Christmas this year. He called us just last week about it."

"Wonderful! I'll look forward to seeing him again," Emma said. "I know how you and Bob wanted to spend Christmas with him in your new home. It must be difficult to share him the way you must with Frank's mother."

"A lot depends on whether she's willing to share him with us," Bob said. "She says he can come but doesn't like to be without him, so who knows?" He shrugged. "I think her mother, his grandmother Churchill, demands a lot of his time and attention when he is in Alabama as well."

"He spent the fall semester in New York on a business internship to finish up his degree, so she's been without him more than usual this year," Nina explained. "So, this may all come to nothing, but he called me and said he was coming."

Emma's cousin Helen broke into the conversation. "Oh! Speaking of prodigal sons coming home, we have had a letter from my cousin Jane too, and she says she's coming home for Christmas this year. Of course, she isn't a prodigal son, is she? She's a prodigal daughter, I suppose. No, no, that's not right…a niece. She's a prodigal niece. That doesn't have the same ring to it as prodigal son, does it?"

Emma cut her off. "So, Jane will be here for Christmas? She isn't acting in some Off-Broadway play at the moment?"

"Oh no, no. Not right now, no. She's not. And there's some other news from her as well, very exciting news, very happy."

Delores Taylor tried to give her daughter a discreet shush, but poor Helen didn't ever take hints or subtlety very well, and after a glass of wine or two, one might as well forget it.

"I'm sure it's fine, Mother. Jane would want everyone to know. It's such happy news. We're just so, so pleased for her. Even though we've known for some time, since October, or maybe it was September. Hmm… she sent a letter. When was it, Mother?"

Delores opened her mouth to answer, but Helen waved her off and plunged ahead. "Oh well, it doesn't matter anyway." She giggled and took another sip of sauvignon blanc. "Jane is engaged to be married!"

"How wonderful!" Nina exclaimed. Several congratulations flowed around the table. Helen beamed.

"And who is the lucky fellow who has stolen Jane's heart?" Mr. Knightley asked politely.

"His name is Dixon, Michael Dixon…or Mike. She calls him Mike, I think. He's in the theater too. He's a director. He directed her in that Off-Broadway production of *A Chorus Line*. She was in that earlier this year. But it's not on Off-Broadway anymore. Doesn't that sound odd—on *Off-Broadway*? At any rate, *A Chorus Line* opened on Broadway in July. Jane's not in that production. I don't know why. Maybe because she was not one of the principal players. It was a minor part she had, just a minor part. In the Off-Broadway production, I mean."

Emma gave her a not-so-patient smile. "Yes, I understand what you mean. And so, she fell in love with this Mr. Dixon while acting in that musical?"

Helen nodded. "And he asked her to marry him in September. *That's* right. It *was* September. I remember because..."

"Well, that is marvelous news, Helen."

"Oh Emma! Jane will be so delighted to tell you all about it when she gets here."

"I doubt that," Emma muttered, looking at her plate.

George tried to give her a censoring look, but he couldn't help the grin he gave her instead. For some reason, Jane Fairfax really seemed to rub Emma the wrong way. He couldn't see why; Jane was a perfectly nice girl. In fact, she was a kindred spirit—and probably more of a stimulating friend for her than K&W Law's front office secretary—but as Nina liked to point out, Emma could be unreasonably stubborn once she made up her mind about someone. And she had made up her mind about Jane Fairfax some years ago.

Delores started to speak up, but Helen interrupted her. "Jane has the lead in the Coles' Theater production of *Camelot*. It's playing locally you know, in March and April, and she's coming to spend Christmas with us, and then start rehearsals in January. Wasn't that nice of her to agree to be in a local production? She's playing Guinevere—that's the lead role...well, the lead female role, that is. Not the male lead...obviously. But of course, you would know that, wouldn't you? I didn't need to tell you."

George's parents exchanged amused looks.

"I saw Mrs. Cole in town the other day, at the supermarket...was it the supermarket or the bank? Anyway, she said to me, 'Oh, Helen, we are so pleased to have an actress from New York in our local production!' Wasn't that nice of her to say that about Jane?" Helen sighed. "The Coles are such nice people."

By this time, everyone was finished with the main course and Emma took the opportunity while Helen was finally catching her breath to offer pumpkin pie and coffee all around. The girls cleared the table and served dessert on plates with autumn leaves around the rim.

After dinner, George made good on his intention to take Maude for her walk. She saw him come outside, and she was so excited, he had to use his stern voice to keep her from leaping up on him. He had barely hooked her leash and rounded the corner of the house when he saw Emma striding toward him.

"May I join you?" she asked. "Please?"

"Of course."

She sighed in exasperation. "Thank goodness. I need a break from Helen. She's about to drive me bats."

"Now, now, Emma Kate…"

She was standing beside him, petting Maude, but then she stopped and pointed her finger at him. "No lectures, Professor. I'm wiped out, and if I have to hear about Jane Fairfax and her Off-Broadway and her Guinevere and her happy news anymore this afternoon, I'm not responsible for what comes out of my mouth."

"I know she can be a little trying, but Helen is one those people who requires some extra grace."

"I'll say. You know, I'm starting to actually feel a little sorry for Jane Fairfax having to put up with that incessant chatter for four whole months."

"So, which is it: Do you dislike Jane or do you feel sympathy for her?"

"Both, I suppose."

"Emma…"

"Actually, I never said I disliked Jane. Not once."

"Helen and Delores will be thrilled to see her again."

"No doubt."

They walked under the bare branches as the sun waned in the late afternoon sky. It had cleared up considerably since the morning, although it was still brisk. Emma's nose and cheeks were pink from the cold wind. She drew in a deep breath.

"I've made a decision."

"About?"

"I'm going to try and be *more friendly* to Jane while she's here this winter. And don't give me that look."

"What look is that?"

"That smug know-it-all look you have, like Emma's your little puppet and you're pulling her strings."

"I'm not giving you any kind of look." The smile came unbidden to his lips. "But I'm glad you're making the effort. Why the change of heart?"

"I wouldn't call this a change of heart. I've never had anything against Jane, except how everyone talked her up all the time, but that's not her fault."

"No, it isn't."

"I've been thinking that when it comes right down to it, she and I do have some things in common."

"You do."

"And we're connected by family."

"True."

"Well, maybe I was a little jealous of her. In the past."

"You're a bright and beautiful girl, Emma Kate. What would you have to be jealous about?"

"I'm no Off-Broadway actress, that's for sure."

"I've never known you to have aspirations for the theater."

"I don't. It's just…"

He waited, curious as to what she'd say.

"I don't have any aspirations, George."

"What do you mean?"

"I'm going to graduate college in six months, and I have no idea what I want to do with my life."

"I assumed you would continue to care for your father and manage the house on Hartfield Road."

"Yes, I'll have to do those things, but without school, I'll have a lot of extra time on my hands. What will I do with myself? Sometimes I just wonder..."

George let the silence hang in the air, resisting the urge to fill it with platitudes or worse, his own suggestions. Years of practicing law had taught him to offer nothing when he had nothing to contribute. Perhaps it was time to apply that concept when dealing with Emma.

Emma's voice became very small. "I want to do something that matters."

Who knew she thought this much? How interesting that, after knowing her all her life, she could still surprise him.

"You're speechless, I see. I've astonished you with my previously unimagined seriousness."

"Not at all." He reached for her elbow to point out a tree root in her path, but instead of stepping over it, she skirted around next to him.

After another moment of silence, he answered, considering his words carefully, as he intuited that his response might be a kind of turning point.

"I'm confident that, in time, you will find the sense of purpose that you seek. As you go through the process of finding it, though, I might advise you to keep two things in mind. One, I think you're in for a lifelong search. Finding a purpose isn't a finish line at which you suddenly arrive. It's an ongoing journey, shaped by your time and place in the world, by your talents, and by your obligations. You may be one of those people, Emma Kate, who is blessed and cursed with more than one life's purpose. And two..."

"Yes?"

"You do matter—to your family, to your friends."

"I do?"

"Of course you do. And"—he hesitated—"well, you matter to me."

"Aw, shucks, Mr. Knightley." She playfully punched his arm, but her smile beamed and her face flushed with pleasure.

They moved out from under the trees and he looked across the field. A bulldozer sat on the other side, glowing a garish orange in the sunlight.

"Another street in the subdivision?"

"What?" She followed his gaze. "Oh, yes. The cancer grows."

"Progress."

"So they say."

"We can turn back."

"Let's."

He turned back under the shade of the trees, toward the main house.

Emma held back a branch for George. "It looks like Nina and Bob are going to have company for Christmas too."

"Perhaps they will, and then again, maybe not."

"It seems you'll finally get to meet the elusive Frank Weston."

"Hmmph." George had no desire to meet a spoiled, overgrown schoolboy with jock for brains.

"Well, I, for one, am looking forward to seeing Frank again. I'm glad his mother's finally letting him visit with Bob. It's been years since he's been here. Rosemarie Churchill really is a bossy, frightful woman."

"And Frank Weston is a grown-up, twenty-two-year old man. If he wanted to visit his father, he would have found a way to do so already."

"That's easy for you to say, George. You answer to no one. You run the farms and the law office, preside over your *Woman of the Month* club, and steer your own life. Frank, on the other hand, is just starting out. He still relies on his parents and has to stay in their good graces. His father is more easygoing than his mother, so Frank bends to Rosemarie's will because Bob won't impose his."

"Perhaps."

They walked in silence, until some minutes later, George went on.

"I suppose I don't like the way he keeps leading Bob and Nina to believe he'll visit, and then, at the last minute, he manufactures some asinine reason not to come. It's rude."

Emma shook her head. "I don't think Bob and Nina are quite as critical of him as you are. They understand his situation and his temperament. Therefore, they understand his behavior and make allowances for it. They're showing him 'grace,' in your words. You know, a lot of people really liked Frank back in high school, including yours truly. He's a barrel of fun."

"I can't fathom why you are standing there defending him."

"Technically, I'm not standing—I'm walking."

"Smart aleck. What I mean is, people give Frank Weston the benefit of the doubt because he makes such pretty excuses. But words are cheap. Polite *behavior* is a universally admired trait, an indication of integrity, and everyone understands that when they see it. A man's actions are what show his good character."

"Yes, sir, Professor, sir," Emma said and gave him an exaggerated salute.

"I'm just saying..." George muttered, not saying much of anything else until they returned to the house.

SEVENTEEN

DECEMBER 22, 1975

The roar of the university fight song echoed through the coliseum as the basketball team returned for the second half of the game. I waived my little paper pom-pom in the air and cheered loudly, although it was hard to sing the words above the pep band. From his seat right beside me, Tim Elton showed his debonair smile and joined in the song.

Nina and Bob had bought a group of tickets, which was quite a coup; everyone around these parts was crazy about university basketball and the games were always sold out. Originally, the party had included the Westons, their friends the Coles, Jack and Isabel, Mary Jo, and me. But Mary Jo picked up some kind of virus and couldn't join the fun. At the last minute, Nina asked Tim if he'd like to go, to which he gave a resounding 'yes'. He was an alumnus and an avid basketball fan too. Helen and Aunt Delores hated the noise of basketball games, so they were to join the group at Nina's afterward for an informal Christmas party.

George Knightley was attending a hospital Christmas party with Julianne-the-doctor early in the evening, and then they were going to be at Nina's too. I was anxious to meet the new lady in George's life—actually fretted over it. He needed a special kind of woman to tolerate his quirks and his schedule, and I wasn't sure this Julianne person had what it took. He had so many responsibilities, and a doctor would be very busy with duties of her own. I didn't know how that would work out for them, and I wanted to see them together to judge for myself if Julianne would suit my friend.

At the game, Tim sat on one side of me and my sister on the other. It was quite a blowout, so no one was too worried about the outcome for the home team.

"Would you like a Coke?" Tim asked me, putting his arm around the back of my chair.

"No, thank you."

"Some popcorn, then?"

"Tim, you've already offered and, or bought me a hot dog, a pennant flag, nachos, a chocolate chip cookie, and enough soda to float me away for good."

"I like indulging you."

"Thank you"—I smiled sweetly—"but really, I'm fine."

"As you wish, my lady."

Isabel excused herself to go to the restroom, and Tim went down a few rows to talk to a friend from college. Jack moved over into Izzy's seat and leaned his head over to speak in a low voice.

"You got a thing for Elton?" he asked, nonchalant and serious at the same time. It was a trick only Jack could manage to pull off.

"What?" I stared at Jack, and then turned back to watch the mascot run around the gym floor, trying to scare up some enthusiasm from a lackadaisical crowd. "I most certainly do not have a *thing* for Elton."

"Then I suggest you stop encouraging him."

"What?"

"You heard me. You're going to find yourself in an awkward situation if you don't put the kibosh on that flirtatious banter."

"Jack Knightley, you are insane! I am not flirting with Tim Elton —at all!"

"Looks like it from over here. Probably looks like it from where he's sitting too."

"You're grossly mistaken."

Jack shrugged. "No skin off my nose. I'm just telling you, he might be reading those smiles and all those reminders about your summer tennis lessons as interest."

"Shows what you know. I'm trying to get him to ask Mary Jo Smith out, but he's dragging his feet."

Jack looked at me, dark eyes piercing my bravado. "He'll never ask her out. Not as long as he thinks he has a shot with you."

"I'm telling you, you're wrong. Tim is not interested in me. Not one iota."

"Emma!" Tim yelled from four rows down.

When I waved, he pumped his arm back and forth—a big smile on his face. "This is my old college roommate, Chuck!"

I waved again, and Tim looked at me with an even bigger grin, making a gesture like he was drinking and pointing at me.

Jack smirked. "He's asking if you want another drink."

"I know what he's asking," I hissed in annoyance. I shook my head "no" and snatched up the program Tim bought me, burying my nose in it, and pretending not to notice either Tim's attentions or Jack's smug I-told-you-so look.

I spent all of halftime weighing my conversations with Tim more carefully. Not that I really thought Tim had a thing for me. There was still hope he was interested in Mary Jo, and I tried to talk her up even more in the second half.

But I was running out of time. Now it was almost the end of the game, and the crowd was beginning to disperse early since the score wasn't even close. Nina and Bob had already made the trek back to their car, so they could prepare to receive their guests. Jack and Isabel were packing up and making noises like they were ready to go as well.

"Not much of a fan, are you?" I teased Jack. "You're not even staying till the end of the game."

"For your information, Isabel is tired and wants to go back to Nina's. And it will take forever to get out of the parking lot." He looked between Tim and me with feigned innocence. "I have a great idea. Maybe Tim would offer to stay with you until the final buzzer, since you're such a dedicated basketball fan. What do you say, Elton? Can I trust you to bring my sister-in-law safely to her aunt's house?"

I shook my head "no", but Tim's sense of chivalry had been called to the forefront.

"Of course, you can rest assured that the fair Emma will arrive safe and sound as soon as the game is over." He turned to me. "We won't leave until *you* give the word, and then your chariot awaits, my lady."

I narrowed my eyes at Jack, but there was no escaping the situation now. I just had to bear it as best I could and hope Tim would forget about it in the morning. *I probably should offer to drive. He must have had a little too much beer.*

After the game, as we walked to his car, Tim tried twice to put an arm around my shoulders and once to take my hand.

I held it out, palm up. "Keys, please."

"Pardon?"

"You've had too much to drink, Tim. I'm going to drive."

"I only had one beer during pre-game."

I began to get a sinking sensation in the pit of my stomach.

Tim took his key and unlocked my door. Once I was seated, he leaned down and asked in a syrupy voice, "All set, honey?"

Oh, good grief! "Yes, thank you."

He shut the door and jogged around to the other side, humming the fight song as he started the engine.

While we waited in line to get out of the parking lot, he reached over and tried again to snag my hand, but I leaned forward, digging in the glove box.

"Don't suppose you have a Kleenex in here, do you? I think I'm getting Mary Jo's cold." *There. That should keep him off me.*

"You were over at her place nursing her, weren't you? That's so like you, Emma." He looked at me with puppy-dog eyes and sighed, a sickening sound that made the back of my neck itch.

"You're the kindest, most generous person in the world, helping out a sick friend, but really, you need to keep yourself well. For your father's sake—and for all of us that care about you." He reached behind the seat and pulled out a box of tissues, smiling all the while, and leaving his arm up on the seat behind my shoulders.

"You know, Emma, I couldn't help but notice how nice you look tonight. That bright blue really suits you."

"Thanks." I leaned against the door, staring out into the night. "It's starting to snow."

He leaned over the steering wheel and peered up into the windshield. "Well, so it is. Kind of romantic, isn't it?"

"It's too bad Mary Jo wasn't feeling well tonight."

"Mm-hmm."

"She loves basketball, much more than me. That's something you two have in common. I know she hated to miss the game tonight."

"Yep, it's a shame."

"Maybe she can come next time."

He grinned at me and turned on the radio. "I'll be happy to escort you ladies wherever you'd like to go."

I gave up on conversation then and rode along in silence all the way out to Nina's while Tim butchered the lyrics to several love songs on the radio.

We arrived, none too soon—in my opinion—and I bolted out the car door, almost before he put the vehicle in park. Tim jogged up alongside me, humming "The Things We Do for Love," and barreled through the door with me, calling out, "Ladies and gents, the party can begin! Emma has arrived!"

I gritted my teeth and set off to find Nina, yanking off my hat and gloves as I entered. It would have been polite to offer to take Tim's coat too—I knew where the closet was—but I'd had my fill of Tim Elton for the evening. All I wanted was to find my aunt and get some bourbon-infused egg nog.

I stood at the closet, muttering to myself about my cursed luck in the man department when I heard my name.

"Hey, George." I yanked a hanger out of the closet and jabbed the ends into the sleeves of my jacket. "Well, I just had the ride from hell..." I turned and snapped my lips shut when I realized he wasn't alone.

The new *Woman of the Month* wasn't George's usual type, that's for sure. She was petite, almost exotic-looking with her olive skin and her jet-black hair, cut short in that bob that was all the rage these days. Her features were delicate, almost pixie-like, but there was an intensity that hummed around her like a swarm of honey-bees.

"Emma, I'd like you to meet Julianne Ryman. Julianne, Emma Woodhouse. Her sister, Isabel, is married to Jack."

Dark, intelligent eyes peered out of a heart-shaped face. "It's good to meet you, Emma. I've heard a lot about you."

"And I you." It wasn't exactly a lie. I had been asking around town about Julianne Ryman for several weeks. George himself had said precious little about her.

"Was that your boyfriend that came in with you?"

"No!"

Julianne started at the vehemence in my tone, and George's lips twitched.

I consciously softened my voice and let out a small laugh. "I mean, Tim is just a friend."

"Oh…okay then," Julianne said, amused.

I slipped into hostess mode. "I'm so glad you could come tonight. George tells me the schedule of a resident is pretty hectic."

Julianne nodded. "I had to work Thanksgiving weekend, so they let me have off any weekend in December I wanted. That way I got to show George off at my hospital holiday party, and then he returned the favor." She smiled up at George, laughter dancing in her eyes.

He returned the smile and turned back to me. "So, you rode over here with Tim, I take it."

"Yes." I leaned over and laid my hand briefly on his forearm, lowering my voice. "Jack, the little sneak, whisked Izzy off before I knew what was happening. You know how he is, George. He has to be the first one out the door and out of the parking lot."

"He hates being stuck in traffic, that's a fact. You remember that time he took you and Isabel to Keeneland?"

"I'll never forget it. I thought I was going to have to spend the night in the stables." I turned to Julianne. "Jack kept saying all afternoon, 'We're leaving after the sixth race. We're leaving after the sixth race. Gotta beat the crowd. Traffic's a nightmare later in the day.' Blah, blah, blah. Well, I didn't think too much about it, and I bet a long shot on the sixth race that ended up winning. I hadn't won a thing all afternoon, and I was standing in the line to collect my payoff, with Jack standing behind me complaining and hinting I should leave my winnings behind. Can you imagine? I'd waited all day for that tiny dose of instant gratification, and he wanted me to leave without it."

"Shocking."

"It was *terribly* shocking. But you have to know Jack. Luckily for me, George was there that afternoon, with some other friends, and he agreed to let me tag along with them for the rest of the day."

George cut in. "I was only giving Jack some time alone with Izzy. It wasn't any trouble at all."

Laughing, I touched his arm again. "I spent a great deal of my youth tagging along after George. He's an awfully good sport about it."

George bowed. "You're welcome."

"You two sound almost like brother and sister."

Both of us halted at Julianne's remark and stared first at her and then at each other. George was the first to break the silence. "Yes, well, we've known each other a long time." He shifted his glass to his other hand. "How were the roads, Emma Kate? I overheard your father tell Nina there might be a snowstorm."

"Daddy's here?"

"He is. He came with Delores and Helen."

"You're kidding."

"Nope."

I closed the closet door with a whoosh. "Oh, I should go check in with him right away. He always worries if I'm out when the weather's dicey. I can't believe Delores convinced him to go out on a night when there's even a chance of snow."

"I think it's good for him to get out some. See his friends."

"Oh, I agree. Definitely," I conceded. "But I have to admit, this time he surprised me. I hope we don't pay for that little impulse later on. He may lose his nerve, now that the snow is falling. See you later, George. Nice to meet you, Julianne."

"You too."

I hurried into the kitchen just in time to see my father clutching Nina's hand and speaking to her in earnest tones.

"Is everything okay, Daddy?"

"Emma! Thank goodness, you're here safe! I was ready to send someone after you. When you didn't arrive with your sister, I was so worried."

I'm going to strangle Jack Knightley. "I'm fine, as you see. You worried for nothing, Daddy. I really wish you wouldn't."

"It was my fault," Jack spoke up from behind me. "Isabel was ready to leave, so I asked Tim Elton to stay with Emma and drive her here afterward." Jack looked genuinely contrite about worrying Daddy. "She wanted to see the rest of the game."

"That was very considerate of you, Jack, to think of poor Isabel, and I know Emma loves her basketball."

"What made you decide to come to the party tonight, Daddy? I thought you were staying home."

"Delores called and asked me to accompany her and Helen. She said I could ride home with them too, but"—he leaned in to speak quietly, though his voice wasn't very soft at all—"Helen just about scared me to death with her driving. I think I'd rather go home with you and Isabel and Jack instead."

I bit my lip to keep from laughing out loud. "I'm sure we can work that out."

"But I don't know what we'll do if it snows."

Jack spoke up. "I certainly don't want to be stuck here all night. Nina and Bob would have to set up cots all over the place like army barracks."

"I listened to the weather report earlier," Tim interrupted. "It's not supposed to get bad until well after midnight. Good thing the snow didn't come earlier today. We might have had to cancel our little party." He grinned stupidly and put an arm around my shoulders.

I moved out of arm's reach. "Think I'll go get some eggnog."

"Not too much, Emma," Daddy called after me. "You know you aren't used to rich food—or bourbon whiskey."

"I'll take it easy, Daddy. I promise."

Later, Nina perched on the arm of my overstuffed chair, resting her arm along the back, and leaned over to give me a quick squeeze.

"Merry Christmas, precious girl." She rested her cheek on my hair in a maternal gesture of affection.

"Merry Christmas, Auntie." I smiled at George and Julianne, who were sitting on the sofa across from me. "Nina always gets sentimental around the holidays."

George beamed at us, and almost as an afterthought, awkwardly took Julianne's hand, fumbling with her fingers until she set her wine glass on the end table and—laughing—finally linked their hands together.

"I do," Nina admitted with wine-fortified cheerfulness. "Christmas is the best time to be sentimental about family. And we have double the reason to be thankful this year."

"Oh?" I asked, wondering if perhaps Nina had some family news of her own to share. Planning a little cousin perhaps? She was thirty-seven, but it wasn't out of the question. She'd be such a wonderful mother.

"Yes." Nina glanced around for Bob, and finding him talking with a couple over by the fireplace, her face broke into a misty, sappy smile. "It looks like Frank will be visiting very soon."

"By Christmas?"

"Perhaps. Or maybe for New Year's. Bob and I had a letter from him yesterday. Would you like to hear it, Emma?"

"Yes, please."

Nina went off to her desk to retrieve the letter, and I chuckled as George rolled his eyes, his beaming smile fading into a look of vague annoyance.

Surprised, Julianne asked, "Well, what's that look for?"

"Oh, don't mind him, Julianne. He has an attitude about Frank Weston."

"And why is that?"

"I do not have an *attitude* about Frank Weston—or anyone else for that matter."

I ignored him and addressed my reply to Julianne. "He thinks Frank is the worst sort of callous rogue because he backed out of attending Bob and Nina's wedding."

"Rogue, no. Self-centered and spoiled, yes. Callous, well, that remains to be seen, since he's yet to grace his father and stepmother with his presence."

I smiled at him patiently. "Ok, I'll grant you, he's been a bit indulged, but that's Bob's fault more than his. And he's been busy in New York with this internship. He's never been the kind of young man who divides his time well."

"Oh, so you've met him, Emma?" Julianne took a sip of wine, watching George with a forthright curiosity while he fought to suppress a scowl.

"Heavens, yes, I've met him. We dated for several months when he lived here before."

"Old flame?"

I dismissed her comment with a wave. "Ancient history. He's a cutie though—baseball player. Nice legs."

Julianne laughed as Nina arrived with the letter. She sat next to Julianne and read portions of it while I "oohed and aahed" in all the right places.

"So, what do you think, Emma? About Frank?"

"Yes, Emma," George interjected. "Tell us your thoughts."

Julianne elbowed him gently in the ribs and drew her dainty features into a disapproving frown.

"Oh, I definitely think he wants to visit."

"I agree," Nina said. "It's just a matter of whether Rosemarie Churchill will relent. She's so possessive of Frank." She leaned forward and whispered to the group. "I think she's jealous of Bob—his success, his happiness. She's so unpleasant to be around, and I think she thinks Frank will end up liking it better here than Alabama."

"It's such a shame she feels that way," I said.

"Isn't it? Life's too short for that kind of envy to rule your family."

"Too true."

"I do hope Frank gets to come to Highbury before you go back to school in January, Emma. Maybe you could show him around. Help him get re-acquainted."

I laughed. "If I remember Frank Churchill correctly, he has no difficulty getting acquainted with anyone. Ever. He's just like Bob—a charming extrovert."

George turned to Julianne. "I'm off to get another drink. Can I get you something?"

"I'll come with you." Julianne stood and reached out her hand to him. "I was thinking I'd visit the hors d'oeuvres table myself." She beamed at Nina. "Everything looks so yummy."

"Thank you. Please, help yourself."

As they walked away, Nina whispered, "What do you think of George's new gal?"

"Well, she's got more substance than his typical *Woman of the Month* club member."

"Emma, what a thing to say!"

"George Knightley is the poster child for Serial Daters Anonymous. Except he's not so anonymous these days. He's fast developing a reputation for having commitment phobia. Why, just the other day…" I stopped to look up at the man looming over us.

"I'm not interrupting, am I?" Then Tim Elton sat right down between us. "Good." He paused a beat. "Emma, is there something I can get your father?"

"I'm sure he's very comfortable."

"Are you sure? Because he sounds a bit upset."

"What?" I listened, and sure enough, I heard Daddy's strained and anxious tone coming from the other room. I'd been so engrossed in discussing George's love life, I'd tuned Daddy completely out. "Excuse me," I said, rising and handing my glass to Tim.

"Well, the snow's falling thick as blackberries in July. I must say, John, I admire your chutzpah in braving the elements this evening. Roads must be getting slick about now." Jack was standing at the window, staring out into the dark. Having his back to the room, he didn't see the alarm that bloomed over Daddy's expression.

"What's that you say, Jack? Really? Do you think the roads are slick? Isabel? Delores's car doesn't drive well in the snow. We're liable to go off the road in a ditch somewhere! Maybe we should go now before it gets too bad."

I was ready to punch Jack Knightley—right after I finished disposing of Tim Elton.

Isabel sat beside Daddy, patting his hand. "I don't know. I mean, it's snowing, but I don't know how bad the roads actually are." Her anxiety was only slightly below our father's. "Jack? Maybe we *should* think about going home. I would hate to be stuck here and have the children over at Hartfield alone with just Rita. Especially if the weather's going to get bad."

"What if the electricity goes out?" Daddy wrung his hands. Suddenly, this impulsive adventure seemed disastrous to him, even if it was a respite from the consternation and noise of his beloved grandbabies.

Nina came into the room as the voices got louder. "I'm sure it will be fine, John."

Bob Weston, seeing his wife's concern, joined in the fray. "I saw that it was snowing, but I didn't say anything, so as not to upset John."

Jack turned from the window, taken aback by all the angst in the room, especially from his father-in-law and his wife—as well as my scowl. "I'll take you all home if you like. Suits me fine to get back to Hartfield Road at a decent hour."

"But what if we slide off the road? Emma?" Daddy turned to me for solace.

I opened my mouth to soothe, to reassure, but before I could say a word, Isabel piped in.

"If we slide off the road, I'll just walk the rest of the way and bring back the truck to get you. It's not that far."

"Isabel! Walk? In the dark? And the cold?" Daddy shook his head. "You'll catch your death!"

"It's highly unlikely that Isabel's life will be at risk." Jack set his coffee on the sideboard, then added, "But it's less likely the sooner we leave."

"I think I want to go home. I'm getting very worried now. Yes, I think we should go. I really think we should."

I sighed. Daddy was starting to perseverate. Jack, not living with him since the stroke, didn't understand what he'd started with that one thoughtless comment. Safety, or rather the fear of not being safe, was Daddy's numero uno worry.

George walked in the door, coat and gloves on, snowflakes sticking to that wavy brown hair. "I've checked the weather. Taken a quick peek at the roads."

"You went out in the storm—just to check the roads?" Daddy was incredulous.

"Yes, sir. Drove up the driveway too. It's not a winter storm at all. The roads are certainly passable, and the heavy snow isn't coming till way after midnight. You'll be just fine, sir—whether you leave now or an hour from now."

"I think I want to go home. But George says the roads are fine, so the roads are fine, right, my dear?" Daddy looked at me as if I was the only one who could save him. It about broke my heart.

"George always tells you the absolute truth, Daddy. It's okay. We'll leave pretty soon. I want you to enjoy the party and don't worry about a thing. I'll take care of it." I kissed his cheek. "Just don't worry, okay?"

"Yes, you're right. It will be fine. George said so."

Nina distracted him with a new antique roll-top desk she'd found the week before, but he continued to mutter to himself. "It will be all right. It's fine."

I glanced over at George, smiled and mouthed, "Thank you."

He walked over and leaned down to murmur in my ear, smelling of delicious sandalwood and the cold outdoors. "I'm afraid he won't be at ease until all four of you are home safe and sound."

"You're probably right. I should take him home. He won't enjoy himself, and the others aren't sure how to handle him when he's like this."

"I know you'd like to stay a bit longer..."

I looked up at him and read his expression perfectly. "No! Don't you dare pity me, George."

"I—I'm not."

"He is not a burden to me. He's a gift."

"You're right, of course."

"He's my father, and it's my choice to care for him. For as long as I can."

"I know. You're a good girl, Emma Kate. I'm not feeling sorry for you."

"Good."

"Just admiring your heart. I'll get your coat."

George so rarely complimented me. It warmed my insides like the eggnog had an hour before. I turned toward the window, to collect myself, and saw the frank, assessing stare from Julianne Ryman, who had apparently watched the entire interchange from across the room.

Tim Elton insisted on driving me to Hartfield Road.

"If I bring a girl to a party, I always see her safely home," he insisted, opening my door, like we were on some kind of date. I growled under my breath and sent vile epithets to Jack Knightley, ten minutes in front of us.

My mild annoyance turned to incredulity when he turned onto a scenic overlook of the Kentucky River and stopped the car.

"What are you doing, Tim Elton?"

He grinned. "I thought we'd park for a while."

"Well, un-park and get me to my house. My father will be frantic if I'm not right behind him."

"Jack and Izzy can handle him for a few minutes."

"I don't know what you think we're going to do here, but if you think for one minute that you can...make a *move* on me—"

He pulled back. "Emma, don't be silly. I know we can't fool around in the car."

"Well, thank goodness you've got that much sense!"

"The gear shift is in the way." He leaned toward me. "I thought we'd just neck a little."

"Say what?"

"Come on, Emma." He put an arm around my shoulders and tried to draw me close.

"Back off!" I shoved at his chest. "Do you honestly think I'd make out with you in your stupid car? What kind of a girl do you think I am?"

"A fun one, I hoped."

"I could never do that to Mary Jo!"

"Mary Jo? Mary Jo Smith? What's this got to do with her? You girls have some kind of lesbian affair going on?"

"What? No!" I glared at him, then shook my head. "You're drunk. I can't believe I let you drive."

"I'm not drunk."

"You'd have to be to come on to me after the way you led on poor Mary Jo."

"What?" Now, Tim looked incredulous. "I never led Mary Jo on."

"You did! You gave her all those tennis lessons and talked to her at parties. Dropped by Nina's when we were there."

"Emma," he said patiently, "darling. I did those things because she was your friend. So I could spend time with *you*."

"You mean you never were interested in Mary Jo? At all?"

He scoffed. "Of course not. Why would I be interested in some Hicksville secretary from the boonies? She's nice—good enough for somebody or other—but *you're* the girl for me."

I put my head in my hands. "Oh, dear Lord! I've made a terrible, terrible mistake."

"It's okay, baby. We've got it all straightened out now." He leaned in again.

"Get back!" I hissed through gritted teeth. "Put your hands on the steering wheel, put it in gear, and take me home. Now!"

"But Emma," he wheedled, "we're made for each other. You, with your old family and elegant ways, and me with my ambition and charm. You and I, we could be one of Frankfort's power couples. But Mary Jo? She'd be an embarrassment. My father would never approve of me going after her. But you? You're the real deal: sexy and smart and classy, all rolled into one. He'd definitely approve of you."

"There is no way on earth I would ever..." I sputtered. "Even if I felt that way about you, which I don't, it would never work. We don't suit—not at all."

"Why ever not?"

"My father is a founding partner of Knightley and Woodhouse. My mother was a Taylor—her family owned half this county for over a hundred years! And you're a...a...a politician!"

If I hadn't been so mortified, I would have laughed myself silly. Handsome, debonair Tim Elton, who always had that slick smile on his face was now opening and closing his mouth like a fish out of water. It made him just about that attractive too.

After about a half minute of staring at me, he drew his lips together in an angry line and slammed the car into reverse. Fishtailing in the light blanket of snowflakes, he sped off down the road, driving so fast that I was thankful I made it to my driveway in one piece.

I got out and slammed the door. Tim sped off into the dark, and I— embarrassed and furious—marched into the house.

EIGHTEEN

DECEMBER 27, 1975

"Wow!" Mary Jo exclaimed, looking up at the old Victorian house. She leaned forward to take in the entire site from underneath the windshield of my coupe. "It's super-huge!"

I put the Mercedes in park, reached in the back for the muffins I'd brought with me. I got out and stood a second to take in the Taylor family's ancestral home. A mixture of sadness, anger, and pity surged through me. How I wished Helen and Aunt Delores took better care of the place! The paint was peeling, and I knew for a fact the windows were uninsulated with no storm windows in place to keep out the winter chill. Sure, Kentucky didn't have extremely harsh winters, but a little bit of repair work would save my aunt and cousin some energy costs and make them more comfortable. Why didn't they invest in it?

"It's way too much house for two older ladies, if you ask me." I knocked on the door frame and was surprised when Jane Fairfax was the one to peek out the oval glass set in the tall door.

"Hi, Emma." Jane's soft, musical voice could barely be heard over *The Price is Right* bells and applause blaring from the television set.

"Jane! I didn't know you were in town already!"

"I got in late last night. I—I came a few days early. To spend some time with Delores and Helen—before rehearsals start in January, and take some —time to relax."

"Then I should have called first. I apologize. I'm used to just dropping by unannounced." I handed Jane the box. "These are bran muffins. Mrs. D makes them for Daddy, and they're just packed with good-for-you stuff. I thought Delores and Helen might like some."

"Thanks." Jane shivered. "Gosh, it's cold. I'm sorry, won't you come in?"

"I don't want to intrude."

"It's not an intrusion at all. I know they will be glad to see you." She looked expectantly at Mary Jo, who was hanging back and studying the ceiling of the porch.

"Oh, this is my friend, Mary Jo Smith. She's George's receptionist up at the law office. Mary Jo, Jane Fairfax. Sort of my cousin."

"Yes—sort of. Hi, Mary Jo." Jane's smile was shy, unsure.

"I'm so glad to meet you at last. I've heard so much about you."

Jane tilted her head, her expression seemed vague, confused.

"Oh, you know," I said, laughing. "Helen and Delores talk you up all the time." I took Mary Jo's elbow with my free hand and guided her in the door.

We stepped in, and I had to squash the impulse to visibly wrinkle my nose. Every available horizontal surface was stacked with papers, books, and odds and ends that had been deposited there months ago—and forgotten—if the layer of dust was any indication. Delores was sitting on the couch watching Bob Barker, and Helen came in from another room to see who was at the door.

"Who could that be? And so early in the day? And two days after Christmas too?" A smile lit up her face. "Emma! What a nice surprise! What brings you here?"

And just like that, my heart softened. The old house was a pit, but Helen was always happy to see me.

Delores turned around and greeted us with a smile. She patted the sofa beside her. "Come sit by me, honey lamb. How's John this morning?"

"He's well, thank you. I'll be glad when Juanita gets back from her Christmas visit with her family. She makes the world go so much more smoothly for Daddy. I do my best, but he's used to her way of doing things and her routine."

"And here is your little friend Mary Jo." Helen moved a stack of newspapers off a chair and offered it to her. "She's always with you nowadays. How are you, dear? I'm so glad you get to meet Mary Jo, Jane. She's a great friend of Emma's." Helen sat down beside her mother on the couch. "Mother! You really need to turn off that infernal TV. It's no wonder you can't hear a thing! I can hear it all the way to the other end of the house."

Jane got up and turned the volume down before sitting in the chair juxtaposed to me.

"So, Jane," I began, "how is New York at Christmastime?"

"It's nice."

There was a pause while I waited for elaboration that never came. I tried again. "Helen tells us congratulations are in order."

"Pardon?"

"On your engagement."

"Oh, yes. Thank you."

Another pause. A poorly dressed woman on the TV spun the wheel while the audience cheered madly. I gritted my teeth.

"Have you set a date yet?"

"Um…no. We haven't." Jane looked around the room as if seeking an escape. "Mike's…well, he's really busy right now."

"I'm sure."

Helen piped in. "You missed George yesterday, Jane. He came by to bring us one of those big fruit baskets the law firm gives out at Christmas. Said he ordered one with extra apples because he knows Mama likes them. Isn't that right, Mama? George is the kindest man, don't you think? I think he is. A real gentleman."

"He certainly is," I said. "One of the best I know."

"How fortunate we still have some gentlemen around to visit with. We lost Tim Elton, you know."

"What do you mean?" I glanced sideways at Mary Jo. She had shed some tears when I told her the news about Tim's supposed Emma-infatuation, even after I explained it was an interest that wasn't at all returned, and that I suspected he was only gold-digging anyway.

Mary Jo stiffened and glanced down at her feet. Jane studied the two of us with interest.

"George said that Tim is moving to Frankfort!" Helen said. "To Frankfort! Why would he do that? Highbury is so much nicer, so much quieter. But then, maybe it was too quiet for him. He's young and handsome. I'll bet he's charming all the ladies in Frankfort now."

I folded my hands primly in my lap. "I don't think the ladies in Frankfort are any lovelier than the ones in Highbury."

"Oh no, certainly not. Certainly not. Especially now that Jane has come. She just adds to all the loveliness already here."

Delores shushed her daughter.

Helen ignored her mother and plundered on. "Oh! Jane has news. News of someone we all know. Or rather, *we* don't know him, because we haven't met him. But he's a bit famous around here. We all know of him, don't we, Jane?"

"Do tell all." I leaned toward Jane with an inviting smile.

Helen answered for her. "It's Frank Weston, Bob's son from Alabama. Frank Weston was in New York when Jane was in *A Chorus Line,* and he found out she was from Kentucky, and then he found out she was from Highbury. So, he had to meet her because his dad and his new stepmom live here."

"Then you've seen the elusive Frank Weston. I haven't seen him in years. How did he look? He always was a handsome devil."

"He's nice looking."

"Hopefully, he learned how to wheel and deal while he was up in New York."

"He seemed to know a lot about the place where he worked."

"I knew him in high school—even dated him for a time. He was never too serious about anything. I wonder if that's changed."

"Oh, I wouldn't know much about that. I just met him a few times."

"Well, I hope he comes to see his father and new stepmother soon. I'd love to catch up with him again."

Jane fidgeted in her chair. "He never said. Um…would you all like something to drink? Tea or coffee? Or…anything? To drink?"

"Oh no, please don't go to any trouble." I'd had my fill of terse, vague answers and stood abruptly. "We really can't stay very long. Daddy will be expecting me, and I've got to run Mary Jo by the garage to pick up her car."

Helen's face fell. "I wish you could stay longer."

"I'm sure Jane wants to rest…after her trip."

"I know she likes your company, don't you, Jane?"

"Of course," Jane said through a tight-lipped smile.

"Maybe next time." I turned to the chair. "Are you ready, Mary Jo?"

"Now that's weird." I put the car in gear and turned around in the gravel drive. "Put your seatbelt on, Mary Jo."

"What's weird?"

"Jane wouldn't tell me anything about Frank Weston. How annoying is that?"

"Maybe she was tired."

"Tired of all Helen's chatter, maybe. But the point is, I was being friendly and interested, and she wasn't. That superior, condescending attitude of hers is as hard to take as it ever was. Just because she is some big shot actress in New York now…mm-mm-mm." I frowned in disapproval.

Mary Jo was quiet and then, "Thank you for taking me to get my car."

"You're welcome, of course. Now, tell me again what happened to it."

"I was coming into work one day last week, and there was a patch of ice on that overpass down by Pine Street. You know the one?"

"Yes."

"Well, I hit that ice and spun around three times. Scared me to death! Then I hit that guard rail in the passenger side door."

"Oh my!"

"And I was sitting there, crying, and wondering how I was going to get my car *anywhere*, and you'll never guess who came to my rescue?"

"The modern woman does not need a rescuer, honey."

"That day I did. Guess who it was?"

"Mary Jo!" I said, exasperated. "How could I ever guess such a thing? Who was it?"

"Robert Martin."

"Oh, really?"

"He was driving into the Lexington office to work on some things, and he saw me sitting there. He flagged down a policeman, and they called a tow truck to take my car to this body shop Robert knows. He said he knew the people who owned it, and they wouldn't take advantage of me. He even got the estimate and helped me rent a car so I could go home and see my mom for Christmas."

"I wish you'd called me. I would have been glad to help."

"Oh, I know you would. You're the best friend a girl could have! But it was all okay. Robert helped me take care of everything."

"Then I'm glad he was there."

"It was awkward."

"I'm sure."

"Here he was, being so nice. I didn't expect that after I said I didn't want to date him."

"It was a gentlemanly thing to do," I conceded. "But then, I'd expect no less from one of George's employees, would you?"

"No, I guess not."

They rode on in silence before Mary Jo blurted, "When I turned Robert down, did I really do the right thi—"

"Yes!" There was only so many times I could hear that question and not lose my temper over it.

More silence filled the car.

"Well, Frank didn't make it to his father's house for Christmas. I'm holding out hope for the New Year though. Maybe after the weather lets up a bit."

"Maybe."

"I wonder if he's changed much since high school. Maybe it's because I still live at home, but sometimes I think everybody's changed except me. I don't think I've changed hardly at all."

1976

"Seldom, very seldom does complete truth belong to any human disclosure; seldom can it happen that something is not a little disguised, or a little mistaken; but where, as in this case, though the conduct is mistaken, the feelings are not, it may not be very material."

—Jane Austen, *Emma*, Volume 3, Chapter 13

NINETEEN

"I hate Valentine's Day!" Mary Jo pouted as she selected a chocolate from the box on the coffee table. "Ooh, Godiva! Where did these come from?"

"George brought them by." Nina set down a tray with tea cups and a tea service on it.

"Gosh, he's such a nice guy."

"Yes, he is." Nina poured out. "Here you go, Mary Jo. A nice cup of tea will chase those Valentine's Day blues away."

I glanced over the top of my newspaper. "I think George got chocolates for everyone he knows. I noticed a box with Jane's name on them when I was over there checking on Helen and Delores yesterday."

"Yeah, he got some for the office too, but we had to share a big box. We didn't get our own."

"Jane probably shared hers, since she's such a lovely, considerate girl, according to George. And Helen. And everyone else. Apparently."

"Emma," Nina chided.

"Or George got every lady in their house a box. That sounds about like him."

Nina waggled her eyebrows at the girls over the rim of her tea cup.

"Perhaps our George has a thing for Miss Fairfax? He certainly talked her up enough at New Year's Day brunch."

My head snapped up, and I put the paper aside. "George and Jane? Don't be ridiculous! She's engaged, remember? To Mike Dixon, the fabulous theater director in New York City."

"Yes, but Mike Dixon is far away, directing some film all the way over in Ireland, and Jane's here all alone."

Mary Jo chimed in. "Yeah, what's up with that anyway? If I were Jane, and in love with Mike Dixon, engaged to him and all, I wouldn't be here in Kentucky." She paused to take another chocolate. "I'd be in Ireland. With him."

"Helen said Jane wanted to help out the Coles with their theater venture. Drink your tea, Emma, honey, before it gets cold."

I picked up my cup. "That's what Helen *says,* but I'm with Mary Jo. I think it's weird. Don't you think it's weird? I wonder if Jane and the famous Mike Dixon are having trouble. You know those artistic types. Drama, drama, drama."

"Who knows?" Nina shrugged her shoulders.

"Besides," I continued, "George is unavailable. He's still dating Julianne Ryman, isn't he?"

"Is he? I haven't heard hide nor hair of her since the Christmas party."

"Oh, oh!" Mary Jo clinked her teacup in her saucer. "I saw them together, maybe about a month ago. She came by the office, and he took her to lunch."

"Oooh, lunch. Yep, sounds serious," Nina teased.

"No, it's not serious! Remember of whom you speak—George Knightley—and his *Woman of the Month* club." I snatched up a butter cookie and took a vicious bite.

"Maybe he just needs to find the right woman."

"Or *maybe,*" I said, "*no one* will ever be good enough to suit him."

Nina nodded. "He is particular, but then, I suppose he needs to be. He has a lot of responsibility on his shoulders with Donwell, the law practice, the other properties—not to mention all the investments. I've heard that Mr. and Mrs. Knightley might move to Florida next winter."

"Which will leave even more responsibility to George," I concluded.

"He needs help, that's for sure, but I'm not sure a wife is the right answer. Why can't Jack step up to the plate? Shoulder some of that burden?"

"Jack has the Louisville office. And a family to care for."

"Exactly!" I pointed my finger at Nina for emphasis. "And Jack should share the role of steward. For my niece and nephew. Donwell is their legacy. I don't want what happened to my family's Hartfield to happen to Donwell. I don't want that for Henry and Taylor."

"They may have to share their legacy with little cousins. George could have children of his own someday."

"Like *that* will ever happen."

"Seems like this thing with Julianne could be significant. It has been going on several months now."

"There's nothing in particular wrong with Julianne. I like her."

"I do too," Nina said. "She's very nice."

"But if we're talking spouses, she isn't right for George."

"Why not?"

"She has her own life, her own career—which is all fine. Becoming a doctor is a noble endeavor, and I applaud her for it, but that lifestyle doesn't mesh well with George's needs. Their relationship can't go anywhere...in the long term."

"Why not? I think it's romantic, the lawyer and the doctor," Mary Jo said.

"Because if Jack isn't going to help carry the load," I said patiently, "George needs someone who can help him—who can share the steward-ship of Donwell Farms, the other properties, et cetera, et cetera. That leaves him free to guide the law practice." I grinned. "Which is *my* legacy."

"Interesting perspective." Nina poured herself some more tea and added some sugar to it. "I had no idea you had thought so much about George's future."

"Our futures are sort of intertwined."

"Hmm, I suppose."

"Why are you in such a hurry to pair off George anyway?"

"I'm not, unless—"

"I think my ears are burning, ladies."

I startled and for some reason a guilty flush crept up my neck. I schooled my features into a composed smile and greeted the topic of our conversation as he walked in the door. "Hi, George."

"Didn't mean to interrupt. Bob let me in."

Nina scooted over to one end of the couch. "You are always welcome, George, dear. Have a seat. Tea?"

"No, thank you."

"What brings you to our door?"

"I heard the prettiest ladies in town were here." George walked in and settled on the couch beside Nina. "Actually, I was out this way visiting Mom and Dad and saw Emma's car when I drove by." He crossed one ankle over his knee. "Thought I'd stop in a second and say 'hello.' And then I heard my name, so now my curiosity's piqued."

"Nina was just engaged in a bit of speculation."

"Oh?" he asked mildly.

"Tell us, how long has Mr. Knightley, Esquire been dating Dr. Julianne Ryman? Inquiring minds want to know."

"Well, let's see." He picked up a Valentine cookie off Nina's tea tray and munched it. "I think we started seeing each other somewhere around early October. So that's what? Four months now. I didn't realize it had been that long. We're both so busy. We don't see each other often. Perhaps that makes the time fly by." His eyes twinkled, icy-blue, and he tossed me that I'm-a-handsome-devil smile. *Julianne Ryman better snap him up before he loses interest.*

"So. The *Woman of the Month* has become the *Woman of the Season*, and we're all wondering, how did that happen? Nina here was engaged in speculating about you getting engaged."

George looked startled, and the handsome smile disappeared. "Engaged? To Julianne? I think it's a little early to be thinking about *that*."

"I told Nina as much."

"I'm sitting right here. No need to talk as if I weren't."

I grinned at my aunt and turned back to George. "I've also heard you've been playing Cupid all over town."

"How's that?"

"Delivering Valentine chocolates everywhere you go. And here, I thought I was special."

"You are special. Perhaps you got the biggest box of all."

"I'm one of many recipients of your confectionary benevolence." I counted on my fingers. "The ladies at the law office. Here to Nina—and right under Bob's nose too, you shameless flirt."

"Well, you know, Nina is a pretty hot tamale."

"Stop, you two!" Nina blushed.

I paused for effect, darting a glance at Nina. "Chocolates have even been delivered to Jane Fairfax."

"Well, aren't you a nosy Rosie?" George gave me a smug grin. "Been keeping up with my good deeds, have you, Emma Kate?"

"Do you deny it?"

"Guilty as charged. I delivered some sweets to Jane the Fair—fax."

Nina and I exchanged a look.

"Oh, I get it now. You two have been pairing me up"—he rolled his eyes to heaven, amused—"with sweet, unsuspecting Jane. Never mind that I'm seeing someone, and she's engaged. Your faith in my romantic prowess is flattering, but," he added, "even if I were foolish enough to try and juggle two, beautiful, smart women, Jane Fairfax, notwithstanding all her talent and grace, is too reserved for me." He looked around and saw three pairs of eyes staring at him expectantly. "You know. A man wishes for a woman who's more…forthcoming."

No reply from any of us.

"Responsive, perhaps." He shifted uncomfortably.

I smoothed over his awkward moment with a light laugh. "Listen to the *man about town* wax eloquent about the perfect woman. But never fear, we comprehend the truth. You're not the marrying sort, George, and we all know it."

"Oh, really?" A little frown crept across his features.

"And that's fine with me. You couldn't stop in to say 'hi' whenever you see my car in Nina's driveway if you were married."

"And we all know Emma's word on these matters is final. I am not allowed to marry."

"It's settled then." I tossed him a brilliant smile, and our gazes held for one long breath.

"In other news," Nina said, "Frank is finally coming for a visit."

George looked from me to my aunt. "Oh? I'm sure you'll be happy to see him again."

"Again? I hardly remember him from before, and he was just a boy then. I only met him a couple of times when he was dating Em."

"Many moons ago," I said.

"But, yes, his flight arrives day after tomorrow and Emma's helping us throw a little party this weekend to celebrate. Very informal thing."

"In case he doesn't show," George muttered under his breath, earning a glare from me.

"You'll come, won't you, George?" Nina asked.

"Certainly. I can't wait to meet the mysterious Frank Weston."

"And bring Julianne. We haven't seen her since before Christmas."

"I'll see if she's free." George rose.

"Are you off already?" Nina asked.

"I came to say 'hello,' and now that I've done that... I'll let you all get back to your tête-à-tête."

"There's three of us. It's not a tête-à-tête," I called after him.

"Yes, of course, you're right. Think I'll complete the Randalls' hat trick by speaking to Bob on my way out. Have a good evening, ladies."

They sat there in silence for a few seconds, before Nina glanced back at the door. "We made him uncomfortable."

"Do you think so?" Mary Jo asked anxiously.

"George is used to me teasing him."

"I know, but that was different." Nina's gaze stayed on the doorway.

I picked up my newspaper again. "For heaven's sake, why would anything *we* say make George uncomfortable?"

TWENTY

George strode out to his car and slammed the driver's side door shut. Damn it, if they didn't make him uncomfortable! Not the marrying kind? What did that mean? How would Emma Woodhouse know anyway? Sure, she'd grown up watching him—maybe a little closer than he'd thought. They'd watched each other grow up. Their families were too entwined not to. But was that really how she saw him? A perpetual bachelor? A quirky uncle to the next generation of Knightleys, fathered by Jack?

And did she see herself the same way? A single woman, caring for an infirmed and aging father. The stereotypical spinster aunt to Izzy's brood of chicks? Like, like...heaven forbid, like Helen? Who would be left for her after John passed, far off in the future, God willing? He chased away the thought of her in her older years, alone and lonely. She would find someone. Some guy would snap her up in a heartbeat. He was sure of it. He was surprised it hadn't happened already. As for himself...?

George had always assumed that he would marry someday. Perhaps. It was most likely expected of him. Wasn't it? And yet, his mother had stopped dropping hints after Henry and Taylor came along.

Actually, he'd never really given marriage much thought at all.

He would be thirty this year. His younger brother was married with two rug-runners already. Perhaps it was time to complete the process of growing up—all the way.

If only the right woman would magically appear.

TWENTY-ONE

The next morning, three hours before my ten o'clock class, I dragged myself out of bed for a run with Maude.

"If I can live through February, I can live through anything," I groused to a quiet house. Daddy was still asleep, as was his habit. Juanita didn't arrive to take care of him until eight thirty, and Mrs. Davies had the morning off for a dentist appointment.

Maude nearly bowled me over when I stepped into the kitchen. Her tail and hind quarters wagged with fierce intensity, trying to weave in and out of my legs as I stepped to the sink. I filled my own glass and then filled Maude's bowl. We both stood there, drinking; the sound of Maude's lapping echoing through the room.

I set my empty glass in the sink and looked out on the sunless dawn. The days were still short and cold, the clouds low and gray, and the air was heavy with moisture. The cold February rain was supposed to hold off until afternoon, according to the forecast. I took Maude's leash off the peg by the back door, earning a gleeful yelp and more tail wagging for my trouble.

"Come on, girl. Let's try and infuse some energy into this lifeless day."

My favorite route took me into Highbury and right by the Westons'. I noticed—with some curiosity—a rental car parked in the driveway.

Resolving to call Nina when I returned home, I made a turn down the lane and saw a man approaching on foot.

Nice form. I admired the long, lean look of him as he came toward me, decked out in special running gear and a bright red toboggan. If he was a new neighbor, I definitely wanted to meet him. As he drew near, I squinted and then a cry of recognition burst out.

"Frank Weston!"

He stopped, stunned for a second, and then, waving, he continued his jog toward me until we were only a few feet apart.

"Hello there!"

"It's Emma. Emma Woodhouse."

"Well, of course, it's Emma!" Still, he looked relieved that he hadn't had to recall my name on his own. "How the hell are ya?"

"I'm good. Nina said you weren't supposed to be here until tomorrow."

"I caught an earlier flight, got in about nine thirty last night, rented a car, and surprised the folks."

"I'm sure it was a surprise."

"Yeah, I wouldn't do that to just anyone, but I figured family would forgive, you know?"

"So, what do you think of Kentucky? Has it changed since you left? You haven't been here in what, four years?"

"Almost five. I left right after my senior year of high school." He grinned at me. "It looks a lot like I remember, but there are differences. The countryside is still beautiful—and green. You miss that in the city. I just finished spending five months in the Big Apple, and gawd! I was hankering for a little foliage."

I couldn't help the smile that crept over my expression. I'd forgotten how funny Frank could be.

"I love Dad and Nina's house. Man, they really made that old place into something. I saw the before pictures, and"—he gestured with his hands, mimicking his mind being blown—"Wow! And Nina's amazing! Dad really lucked out with her. I remember her some from when we were kids. I can admit it now, I kinda had a crush on her. She's still a fox, but she's really cool, you know? And Dad is totally gone over her, so I'm happy for him."

A little over the top, but as the praise is for Nina, I guess family will forgive.
"I didn't know you were a runner."

"Me? Oh, yeah. They made us run for baseball conditioning, but I got to where I enjoy it. I'll even run in the cold. Like you."

"Oh, I'm not a die-hard runner. I just try to stay fit."

"Which you do very well."

"So, you just came from town?"

"Right you are. Wanted a quiet run around a charming Southern town, and Highbury fits the bill. Made me feel right at home. After spending some of my time in Manhattan lately, in the city that never sleeps, this is nice and peaceful, like running in Central Park."

"I'd heard you were working up there."

"Just an internship. Now I'm doing some interning with my dad, and starting to look for something permanent. The New York firm I worked for is supposedly expanding next fall. They said to interview, that they were pleased with my work so..." He trailed off. "But that's enough about me. What have you been up to?"

"Nothing too exciting. Finishing up my degree in psychology this spring."

"And then?"

"Then? Well, no plans yet. You know, I'm taking care of my father since he had his stroke."

"I'd heard about that. I'm sorry he's been ill."

"It's okay. He's doing a lot better, but he still needs care."

"So, what do people our age do around here for fun?"

"Well, there's not much. Go to dinner, and hiking—"

"I dig hiking."

"And the Keeneland Spring Meet is coming, if you like horse racing. And of course, the Derby parties in May."

"All sounds good. Hey, I met someone from here when I was in New York. Gal by the name of Jane Fairfax. You know her?"

"Sure, I do. We're related, by marriage. She's staying with my aunt Delores and my cousin Helen."

"She said I should look her up, say 'hi' when I was in town. So, I'll have to do that."

"She's a lovely girl." I eyed him with speculation.

He smiled at me, friendly and easy. His eyes were a deep brown to go with the dark brown hair that curled out from under his toboggan. Dimples winked in both cheeks. *Tall, dark, and handsome.*

"Oh, it's not what you think. She's engaged or something, isn't she?"

"Yes. But still, you'll have to make an effort to drop in and say 'hi'. I'm sure she'd appreciate it. It's pretty provincial here. She'll be glad to have some news of New York. She's an actress, you know."

"I did know. I thought the name sounded familiar, but I didn't actually meet Jane in person until we ran into each other at the Weymouth Theater. Dad told me she was doing some kind of local theater thing here?"

"Yes. *Camelot* at the Coles' Theater in Lexington."

"Guess it's an *off* Off-Broadway thing." He grinned mischievously.

"Theater is a rough business. Although from what I understand, Jane is very talented in both acting and singing."

"Yes," he said quietly.

Perhaps he disagreed with my assessment of Jane's talent. "I guess we'll see in April."

He looked at me, confused.

"When *Camelot*'s on the stage."

"Oh. Yeah." He nodded. "Hey, you want some company on your run?"

"I don't want to make you run back the way you came."

"I don't mind. Not at all. I'll be the mysterious new man in Highbury running around with the town's pretty girl-next-door."

"You're still an incorrigible flirt."

"Guilty. Come on, Emma. Make me look good in front of Highbury."

"I'm sure you can run circles around me. Just look at you." I couldn't help but look at him. He was built like a Mack truck: broad shouldered, tall, lean without that muscle-bound look I detested—and, I noticed as he cut in front of me to lead us back to Hartfield Road, past Delores and Helen's house, he had a fine rear-end.

He spun around, jogging backwards in front of me. "So, you never answered me, where's all the action around here?"

"Around here? There's nothing. You'll have to go to Lexington for nightlife, but it's only twenty minutes away."

"I'm going to start making the rounds with Dad tomorrow—visiting the restaurants he supplies. That should help me get the lay of the land in my old hometown. I've got to start looking for a place too." He glanced over at the old Taylor house. "Well, look who it is! The talented Miss Fairfax, coming in from a morning walk of her own."

By the time I had turned to speak to Jane, the door was closed, and no one was there.

"Guess she wasn't feeling too friendly."

I shrugged. "Guess not."

TWENTY-TWO

George rang the bell at Julianne's apartment twice before she answered, fingers fiddling with a silver hoop at her ear.

"George, you're early!"

"By five minutes." He brushed her lips with a kiss.

"I didn't get out of the hospital until after six." She stopped and looked him up and down. "And you're dressed up. You didn't tell me I was supposed to dress up."

"You look fine."

"Aargh!" She rolled her eyes and strode down the hall to her bedroom. "Give me three minutes!"

"Three minutes. I'm timing you, J.R."

She called from behind the door. "Fix yourself a drink. And don't call me J.R.!"

He laughed as he picked up a crystal decanter from the sideboard and poured a splash of Maker's Mark into her cut glassware. As he sipped, he glanced around the room. Nice furniture, covered in dust because she had no time to clean and no money to hire in. Books and papers stacked precariously on the coffee table. Shoes in front of the couch. Except for those touches of mess, the room looked like she was hardly home. Because she wasn't, he realized. Her life was at the hospital.

"Who is this party for again?"

Irritation surfaced in his voice. "Frank Weston, the prodigal son of Highbury."

She poked her head around the door. "Well, *that* sounded snotty."

"Spoiled, frat boy jocks annoy me, I guess."

"Hmm." She stepped out of her bedroom, wearing a wrap dress with a large pointed collar. "Pot, meet kettle."

He lowered his glass and glared at her.

She laughed as she donned her khaki-colored trench coat. "Don't look so offended, honey. You *were* a frat boy, and you *do* play a lot of tennis and golf." She slipped her arms around his neck. "And you don't act spoiled"— she stood on tiptoes and kissed him—"but really, you pretty much are. In the most charming of ways." She took the bourbon from his hand and set it on the coffee table. "So, if you don't like this Frank guy, why are we going to his party? We could stay in, order Chinese." She swayed sinuously against him. "Have our own party."

"Tempting, but I said I'd make an appearance." He picked up the glass and set it on a magazine. "You really need a coaster or two."

"I've got some in a drawer somewhere." She stepped back from him. "So, we're going to see this Frank person because…?"

"For Nina and Bob, I guess."

"Oh, I like them! Wait, they haven't been married long enough to…"

"Remember? Frank Weston is Bob's son from his first marriage. He's visiting for a few months. Working with his father."

"I see. Who else is coming?"

"Oh, I don't know—friends of Bob's, some of Frank's old pals from high school that are still around. The Highbury crowd. Emma, of course."

"Why 'of course'?"

"I think the Westons would like Frank to hook back up with Emma now that he's in town."

"Hmm, interesting."

"They dated for a short time in high school. Then Frank left to live with his mother. Nina didn't care for him then, but I guess she thinks now that he's grown up, and well-traveled, and has good prospects, he would be good for Emma."

"That's nice. I've heard you talk about how Emma has been too sheltered."

"And her life experience is so...unvarying. She's made the best of what life handed her, but..."

"Maybe Frank can open up the world for her."

"I think Bob and Nina are making a mistake. It's not a good idea to try and fix people up."

"It doesn't usually work."

"Exactly right, and Emma doesn't need a Frank Weston. He's just another needy man-child for her to take care of. I mean, I love John Woodhouse like a second father, and I know he needs care... but Emma... What she needs is..." He stopped when he noticed Julianne's raised eyebrows. "Good grief! I'm gossiping like a teen-aged girl. Let's go already."

"Let's. You've sparked my curiosity," she murmured, as she picked up her keys, "about a lot of things."

TWENTY-THREE

"Nina!" I walked to my aunt and took both her hands as I kissed her cheek. "I'm so sorry I'm late. I had to settle Daddy down for the evening."

"I'm glad you could make it." Nina gave me a hug. "Let me take your coat. How's your father handling being on his own this evening?"

"He's fine because he's not alone. Delores offered to sit with him until I got back." I looked around the room. "Quite a crowd."

"Oh, you know how Bob is. He knows just about everyone in town. And the ones he didn't know, it seems Frank did."

"Frank Weston can cultivate friends faster than anyone I've ever met." I scanned the room again. "No Jane and Helen?"

"Jane has play practice. Helen's here though—over there, talking to Frank."

"Must go rescue him then."

"Now, Emma." Nina studied her stepson engaged in an animated conversation with Helen. "He doesn't seem to mind her, actually." She winked at me. "Although I'm sure he'd love *your* company."

I had been looking forward to seeing Frank again all week. Partly because he was handsome, but that morning on our run, I'd also found him less goofy than he was in high school and still a lot of fun. He was less elitist than I'd expected too, given that he'd been living with Bob's ex-wife, Rosemarie, and the stern matriarch of the family, Mrs. Churchill. Frank was often at the elder lady's beck and call, according to what Bob had told Nina, and Frank's grandmother held his inheritance in an iron fist. She was a formidable woman, Nina said, and used to getting her way. I wanted to see how Frank would behave in the presence of his father and new stepmother. *That* would tell me about his real qualities.

Frank waved me over.

As I suspected, in need of a rescue from the loquacious Helen, aren't you, Frank?

"Hey Emma!" He gave me a look once up and down. "You look good."

"Thanks. So do you."

"Listen, Helen here was just telling me, among other things, about a place in town where they used to have parties. You know, community get-togethers—"

"Out by the old distillery," Helen interrupted. "Bromley Crossing. Do you remember it?"

"Yes, I remember. Gosh, I don't think I've been out there in years."

"Dad and I were looking for a place to have a Derby party this year."

"He doesn't want to have it here?"

"You know, this place is great, almost perfect in every way. But I think we need something bigger. A place where Dad could entertain business colleagues and clients and not worry about having them traipsing through his house and having to clean up after them. Bromley Crossing seems perfect—unless you have another opinion?"

"My opinion isn't worth that much. I love parties, but I rarely give them."

"But I thought you were the socialite of the county."

I tried to decide if he was serious or teasing me.

Helen exclaimed, "Oh, but she is! Our Emma's company is sought all over Highbury. And now that Jane is here, we have even more talent and culture. She isn't here today, unfortunately. She has play practice, as I told you when you asked me earlier, Frank. Yes indeed, she and Emma are the definition of talent and culture. I'm going to get another glass of wine. Do you want me to get you one, Emma?"

"No, thank you. I'll get something shortly."

Helen nodded. "You want to look at all the choices first. I don't blame you. That sounds like a good plan. Always get what you like because that makes a party so much more fun, don't you think?"

Frank looked at me with raised eyebrows and a secret smile.

"Yes, of course."

"Of course," Helen said as she set off for the kitchen.

"Oh, Helen." I sighed.

"She's a hoot. She sure does love her cousins."

"Particularly the talented Jane Fairfax."

"She is the definition of talent, apparently. Or perhaps, you were the definition of talent, and Jane the definition of culture?"

"Did you go visit Jane like you said you would?"

"I did, I did. Stayed there almost an hour before I realized it. Hardly got a word in edgewise."

"That sounds about like Helen. So how was Jane?"

"She looked pale. I thought being in the South and in the country, she might have picked up a little color."

"Well it is winter, after all. And she is naturally pale."

"I like the tanned look, I suppose. Makes a woman look healthy."

"I'm somewhat pale myself, but I've decided to embrace it. Too much sun is bad for the skin."

Frank backtracked. "But even though you're pale, you have that wholesome look. Jane just looked sickly. But then I always thought she looked unwell, every time I saw her."

"So, you two ran in the same circles?"

"Ah...um...kind of. I had some friends who were part of the theater crowd, so Jane and I would see each other from time to time."

"And you saw her perform?"

"More than once." He cleared his throat. "I'm out of beer. Walk over to the bar with me and get something to drink."

"Then there's no disputing her talent? We hear about her all the time from Helen and Delores."

"Yes."

"I just wondered if she lived up to the hype."

"I guess Mike Dixon thought so. He directed her in *A Chorus Line*, and then before anyone knew what was going on, he asked her to marry him."

"Yes, do tell me about that. It was all so sudden and mysterious, and now he's gone and she's here, and no one seems to know a thing about it."

His expression clouded. "I wouldn't know anything about Jane and Mike, not how things really were behind the scenes." He handed me a glass of wine. "Have you tried this pinot? It's exceptional."

"Well, aren't you discreet—almost as discreet as Jane herself." I sighed as I took the drink. "And here I thought you'd tell me more in a ten-minute conversation than I've gotten in three entire visits at Helen's. But gossiping is unattractive, as George Knightley often reminds me." I gave him a teasing grin. "Ah, well. I guess I'll never know anything about Jane's love life."

"So, you know her pretty well then?"

"I've known her most of my life, more since she came to live with Helen and Delores. We're cousins by marriage, and about the same age, so I'm sure people think we would have become fast friends, but we never did."

"Why is that?"

"I'm sure part of the reason is that she went to public school and I to private. She was into music and drama exclusively, and I had more—"

"Eclectic taste in activities?"

"That's a kind way of putting it." *Much nicer than George's: "Emma, why don't you ever finish anything?"* "But the truth is, it was probably my fault. It was hard to like her when she was the recipient of everyone's sympathy and so idolized in my family. That makes me sound petty and mean, doesn't it?"

"Hey, I get it. Why should she get all the attention, when you were here first?"

"When you put it that way, it does sound petty. Thanks, Frank!" I said laughing.

"I didn't mean it that way. People see others from the outside looking in, and they respond to what they observe. But it isn't always fair or accurate, to judge someone by what is visible on the surface."

"Yes, I agree, and Jane herself is so hard to get to know. I guess I was never in want of friends enough to break through that ice," I said, musing aloud.

"She's an ice queen, which I'm sure serves its own purpose, but isn't a very attractive quality."

"I like her fine, except for that tendency to keep her opinions close to her vest. It makes it seem like she's hiding something."

"I can see that in her." He smiled at me: all white teeth, and mischievous looks, and two gorgeous dimples. "Anyway, I prefer a little more openness in my friends. I read somewhere that women who are outgoing are much more interesting." He took a sip of his beer. "Hey, have you met my friend Chip? He says he knows you from a class or something."

As he led me over to a group of his friends, I considered who Frank Weston had become. Nina was right—he'd grown up, matured, although there was still a youthful quality about him that surprisingly, even a stint in New York City hadn't erased. It was amazing how much of Bob showed in his manner, given the limited time they'd spent together. I thought that warmth and personality would serve Frank well. He'd become a fine young man.

I turned at the sound of voices at the door and smiled as my eyes met George's across the room. He waved at me and turned to help Julianne off with her jacket. Breath backed up in my lungs and was expelled when the sound of a hyena-like laugh assaulted my ears.

"What on earth is that unholy sound?"

Frank nearly spit his beer out. "Damn it, Emma! You nearly made me choke!" He laughed, shaking spilled beer off his hand.

"It wasn't my fault. It was that... Where did it...?" Tim Elton walked in the door behind George with a young woman on his arm. Anger and embarrassment rushed through me, and I turned my back on the door. My first thought was gratitude that Mary Jo wasn't around to see this.

Helen took my elbow. "You see that young woman with Tim Elton?"

"I certainly can't avoid hearing her," I said under my breath.

"Her name is Edith Rawlings Bitti. She's from Frankfort—her mother is Doreen Rawlings, you know, of the Frankfort Rawlings, and her father is I-talian, from New York, I think. He owns all those dry cleaner shops—

there are a great many of them around here. As you know. Anyway, she's Tim's new girl—Edith, I mean. It's quite serious."

"He sure didn't waste any time."

Helen gave me a puzzled smile and nodded. "I guess not."

"Her name is Edith, you say?"

"Edie, I think he calls her Edie."

"Edie Bitti?" My lips twitched in amusement.

"Mm-hmm. Mama saw him in the grocery store over the weekend, and he told her—told Mama, I mean—all about her. He's smitten. Every other word was, 'Edie, this' and 'Edie that.' It's so sweet. Sad for all the young, single girls that had their eyes on Tim, I suppose."

I raised a second round of thanks, praising every higher power I knew, that Mary Jo wasn't here. The annoying bray of laughter sprayed over the room again.

"My god," I whispered. "What has he done?"

TWENTY-FOUR

"My god," George whispered to Julianne, "What has Elton done?"
Julianne pursed her lips together in an attempt to keep from laughing as Tim approached them, beaming. "Stop it," she whispered fiercely.

Tim nudged Edie toward them and held out his hand, turning to face the room, eyes everywhere but on the man whose hand he shook. "Knightley! Great to see you! I guess, it's been since Christmas, hasn't it? What have you two been up to?"

"Oh, about the same." George glanced toward the woman at Tim's elbow, which was all the encouragement Tim needed to introduce her.

"This is Edie, Edie Rawlings Bitti. Her uncle is Judge Rawlings."

"Yes," George said. "I remember the judge. He was still hearing cases when I first started practicing law. It's good to meet you, Edie."

"George Knightley! I certainly know the name! Tim, you sly dog! You never told me you hobnobbed with George Knightley." An abbreviated version of her annoying bray punctured the air. "So, you know my uncle. Well, that's something I've heard lots of times before. I guess about everybody around these parts knows *The Judge.*"

"Yes, I'm sure." George put an arm around his date. "This is Julianne Ryman."

"Julianne!" Edie patted George's elbow like they were lifelong friends. "Why, Knightley, she's so dainty and petite!"

"Thank you?" Julianne answered.

"What do you do with yourself when you're not keeping company with this fine specimen of man?"

Julianne smiled politely. "I'm a resident."

"A resident of where?"

"No, a resident, at the hospital. I'm a doctor."

"Oh, silly me. Of course. A resident."

Tim beamed. "Let's go greet our hosts, Edie."

"Lead the way."

"Holy smokes, I can't believe he did it," George whispered.

"Did what?" Julianne took his hand and led him toward the bar.

"Found some poor marionette of a girl to use as a political stepping stone. Judge Rawlings is a mover and a shaker in the state Democratic party."

"Perhaps that isn't the only reason he likes her. She's pretty." Julianne looked over the wine selection. "Chardonnay, please." She handed one glass to George. "The laugh is unfortunate, but I guess he overlooks it."

George stared at her. "How?"

TWENTY-FIVE

"How on earth can he stand that awful sound?"

"Oh, come on, Emma." Frank tugged at my arm. "Walk over there with me. I'm dying to meet her. It'll be a hoot."

"Frank, I don't think…" It was too late; I was face to face with Elton for the first time since I'd spurned him. Tim's smile hardened as he made the introductions.

Edie tapped her lips, pondering. "Woodhouse, Woodhouse…hmm, I know that name from somewhere."

"My father was an attorney."

"Oh yes, Knightley and Woodhouse. He worked for Knightley over there?"

"No," I replied, tight-lipped. "*Knightley* worked for my father. Daddy and Mr. Knightley—the elder one—were the firm's founding partners."

"I remember now. My mother told me. She knows everything about the law practices in this area. She worked for my uncle as a paralegal for twenty years. If you want to know anything about the lawyers in this town, you just ask my mother. She knows it all."

"I'm sure."

"Your father must be the poor man who had the stroke. How is he doing? I heard he doesn't practice law anymore."

"Yes, my father has retired."

"At what facility does he reside now?"

"I care for him at home."

"At home? My goodness, what a lot of work that must be! And Timmy tells me you're still in college. How ever do you have time for it? Have you heard of Stone Point? It's very new, very state of the art—a convalescent home off Tates Creek Pike. They do wonderful things there. You simply must look into it."

"He went to a rehab hospital right after the stroke, but his progress plateaued so…"

"Oh no!" Edie insisted. "Stone Point will do him good. I'm sure of it. I know some of the administrators in charge. A word from me and you could get him moved right in, maybe within a week. Bless his heart!"

"That's not possible. He wouldn't want to go, and I could never turn my father from his home."

"Oh. Well." Edie sniffed.

An awkward silence ensued.

"Emma," Tim announced, "Edie enjoys tennis as much as you do. She was on Transylvania's college team."

"You play tennis?"

I opened my mouth to speak, but Edie's words kept rolling out of her mouth like barrels down a hillside.

"It's been a while since I was truly in top tennis form. It requires constant practice, you know, and life just seems to get in the way these days. I would love to get back into it, I mean, *really* get back into it properly. I was in the best shape of my life when I played tennis, and if Timmy keeps spoiling me the way he has with trips and dinners out, you'll have to roll me out the door." Her snorting laugh filled the room as she leaned over and patted my arm, nearly spilling her drink. "I know! You and I should start a tennis club!"

"A what?"

"A tennis club. I'm sure you're a member at the country club. We could petition them to start a ladies' tennis team. What a fabulous way to have fun and stay in shape."

"I'm more of a runner these days. If you'll excuse me." I turned away, barely hearing Edie's "Well!" and Elton's soothing response as I fled the scene.

TWENTY-SIX

The cold abated, and the mercurial range of weather that defined March in Kentucky arrived in the roar of a thunderstorm, the traditional "in like a lion." When the weather was warm enough, and the rain was confined to a vague, misty veil over the trees, Frank continued to join me on my morning runs. We had a certain route he favored, always passing the old Victorian Taylor family house on Hartfield Road. More than once, I thought I saw an upstairs curtain yanked closed as we ran by.

Finally, one morning I couldn't hold in my snicker any more.

"What?" Frank asked. "Do these shorts make my butt look big?"

"Nothing could make your butt look big, Mr. Baseball."

He grinned at me over his shoulder.

"No, I just think I saw Helen watch us from her upstairs window for the umpteenth time this month. Nosey, nosey, nosey."

"Oh, really?" he drawled, slowing to look up at the window. He saluted the now closed curtain and turned to face forward again. "That reminds me, are you going to the big birthday bash tomorrow?"

"You mean the party Helen is throwing for Jane's birthday?" I took in a breath and let it out in a rush. "Of course, I'm going. It's only polite."

"Yeah, me too. Dad and Nina are going, so no getting out of it for me."

"Poor, pitiful Frank."

"Life is rough."

"Is that why you cut short your golf trip?"

"Yes, dammit!"

I shook my head and clucked my tongue in a mock scold.

"I know. I'm a brat, but that's just the way I am, I'm afraid. When something catches my attention, I run with it. Terrible quirk."

"Oh, I don't know. Sometimes it's better to take a chance first, ask questions later. I've been known to do that myself," I said.

"We're very much alike in that, aren't we?"

I didn't respond, doubting the veracity of that rhetorical question. It was highly unlikely I would ever get to leave town for an impulsive weekend jaunt the way Frank had.

"Have you seen the exalted Jane Fairfax in the Coles' production of *Camelot*?" he asked.

"No, but I'm sure she does a lovely job. How about you? Have you seen it?"

"Oh, I saw it opening night."

I stopped running, surprised. "Really?"

Frank paused and turned back to me. "What?" Then he looked away, almost flustered. "Um, one of the suppliers had season tickets he wasn't using. So, I took Delores and Helen. I thought they might like it."

"Well now, that was very gentlemanly of you, Frank."

"I have my moments." He turned back and continued down the path at a walk. "You really ought to see the show before next month's fundraiser."

"Fundraiser?"

"Yeah, some kind of swanky, cocktail party thing. Nina and Bob got a card about it. Check your mail—I'm sure you got one too."

"Hmm."

"Hey, I have a great idea. Since you haven't seen *Camelot* yet, why don't I take you?"

"You? Take me?"

"Sure! We'll make an evening of it—dinner and the theater. What do you say?"

He's finally asking me out. Frank Weston, you certainly take your time!

I had a moment's indecision: Should I lead him on when I wasn't yet sure if I wanted this to go anywhere? Nina and Bob had sort of been hinting this could happen, but could we really rekindle a relationship—revive what had been a tepid high school interest at best and make it more? I certainly liked him enough to go out with him a time or two. And he was pretty much a hunk. And I had nothing better to do.

No harm in finding out.

"Thank you, Frank. I'd love to go. It sounds like fun."

"I'm all about fun, Miss Woodhouse."

I laughed and took off running ahead of him, making him chase me all the way to my driveway.

A chorus of "Happy Birthday to You" rose above the din in the Taylor house. Jane's face glowed in the light of the birthday candles, looking pleased but vaguely uncomfortable with all the attention. Encouraged by her three glasses of champagne, Helen clapped her hands and gave her young cousin a tearful, smiling hug.

I nibbled on a Benedictine sandwich with Frank Weston by my side. "Isn't it an odd thing for a Broadway actress—who until recently made her living parading about in a skimpy chorus line costume—to look that awkward as the guest of honor at a little neighborhood party?"

"Artistic types are odd, I'm told." He eyed my sandwich and wrinkled his nose. "Yuck, Emma, how do you eat that stuff?"

"I like cucumbers. I like cream cheese. And Benedictine is a Southern tradition."

"I've never seen it anywhere but here in Kentucky, and I've been all over the South."

I shrugged.

Mrs. Cole joined us, a Budweiser can grasped firmly in her hand. "Great party!"

"Yes, lovely party." I glanced around at the old but sturdy furniture that had been there ever since I could remember. The usual layer of dust on the end tables was missing though.

I'm glad Helen asked me for that cleaning lady recommendation. I don't know if it was in her budget, but it was worth it.

Mrs. Cole swept her baby-blue chiffon scarf over her shoulder, just barely missing one of the candles Helen had set on the sideboard. "Jane certainly scored a great birthday gift this year." Mrs. Cole blinked, showing off her sky-blue eyeshadow.

"Oh, she did? What was it?" I draped the loose scarf end over Mrs. Cole's other shoulder and let out a sigh of relief that the poor woman hadn't caught herself on fire.

"The piano. You haven't heard about the piano?"

I shook my head. "Do tell."

"It's sitting in the room right behind you. Arrived yesterday."

I stepped into the tiny parlor and realized Mrs. Cole was right. The furniture had been crowded together on one side of the room, and a baby grand filled the space: sleek and shiny—the glaring contrast of white keys and black case trumpeting its presence.

Mrs. Cole leaned over and whispered dramatically in my ear. "No one knows who Jane's benefactor is."

"It's obvious to me—Mike Dixon sent it. He's her fiancé after all," I replied.

"She says it's not from him. We wondered if a fan of the theater sent it."

"Well, that's a little creepy."

"Jane doesn't seem creeped out. She said it was probably a surprise from Natalie Campbell's family. They're terribly wealthy."

"Could be."

"I suppose we'll know soon enough. I'm twelve ounces light. Can I get you one?"

"No thank you, Mrs. Cole."

"You don't drink beer?"

"More of a wine girl." I held up my glass.

After Mrs. Cole stepped away, I stood beside the piano, staring at it, as if I could make it tell me where it came from. I felt, rather than saw Frank sidle up beside me, heard his smile traveling across the air between us.

"Why are you grinning like the Cheshire Cat, Frank?"

"Who me? No reason. Just wondering about the mysterious piano, like everyone else."

"The Campbells were very generous to send her such an expensive gift."

"Do you really think it was them?"

"Who else? Jane says Mike Dixon didn't send it."

"Maybe another admirer. Someone she knew in New York, someone who didn't want her to forget him. Perhaps our Jane has a deep, dark secret, hmm?"

"Perhaps." The idea of sweet, revered Jane Fairfax embroiled in a romantic scandal intrigued me.

He turned to look behind him and stepped back abruptly from our tête-à-tête. Jane's eyes were on us, her expression unreadable. Frank looked down at his hand resting on the piano and then saluted Jane with his glass. She turned away.

Helen clinked a spoon against her glass until the room grew quiet. "Jane, dear, would you be so kind as to entertain us with a song?"

There were several murmurs of agreement. Jane stood for a moment like a deer caught in headlights, but then she smiled graciously at her cousin. "If it would please you, I'd be happy to start us off." Jane eased into the room around Frank and me and sat at the piano bench.

"What would you all like to hear?"

Frank spoke up. "How about something from *A Chorus Line*?"

"As you wish, Mr. Weston."

"Mr. Weston? Who are you talking to? My father's way over there."

She only smiled and began to noodle up and down the keyboard. The noodling faded into a progression of chords as the party guests began to squeeze into the parlor. Jane opened her mouth to sing, and the room fell silent as she launched into a rendition of "What I Did for Love."

I looked from one rapt expression to the next as Jane's voice filled the tiny space. *Well of course her voice is lovely—it should be, as many voice lessons as she took.* Bob Weston was actually listening, instead of chatting up the people next to him. Nina exchanged glances with me, a happy grin on her face. She raised her eyebrows and nodded toward the piano, mouthing,

"Wow!" Frank stood absolutely still, as if bewitched. Even George had a smile of approval on his face, and I was suddenly, inexplicably, annoyed.

Jane ended the song, and even though several people asked her to sing another, she handed off the piano to one of her *Camelot* cast mates with a smooth elegance I begrudgingly admired. Jane Fairfax had gone on to bigger and better things in New York, and she had learned them well.

I joined George and Julianne as the next piano tune filled the air. "Not going to grace us with a song, Em?" George asked.

"Not in the presence of the cast of *Camelot*."

"I didn't know you played the piano," Julianne asked, surprised.

"I don't. At least not very well—a fact of which George is quite aware. A few lessons in the distant past do not a virtuoso make."

"Two years of childhood piano lessons produced a decent amount of competence," George said, smiling gently. "You have some natural talent. I've heard you play many times, and you could hold your own, even among the 'cast of *Camelot*'."

George and I held each other's gaze for a moment. "Thank you," I said in a soft voice.

"I took lessons as a child too," Julianne piped in. "My mother insisted, but I never practiced enough to become really accomplished."

I turned to her. "How long did you study the piano?"

"Ten years."

My wine went sour in my mouth, but I was saved from having to formulate a response when Jane, Frank, Nina, and Bob joined us.

Bob's booming voice overtook the music coming from the parlor. "It's just amazing to have so much talent in one room! You have a lovely voice, Jane. I can't wait to hear you play at the theater fundraiser next month."

"Thank you, Mr. Weston."

"Call me Bob, please. Yes, you've got quite a talent there. The scuttle-butt was not the least bit exaggerated."

"I've heard that *Camelot* is doing very well," Nina added.

"I think the Coles are pleased," Jane answered.

"I'm looking forward to seeing it myself. I've heard such good things," I said.

"You and Mary Jo on a girls' night at the theater? Look out, Lexington!" George took a sip of his beer, grinning around the neck of the bottle.

"Oh no. I'm not going with Mary Jo. Frank said he'd take me."

George made a little strangling noise that caught Julianne's attention. She patted his back. "Okay there, honey?"

"Yes, fine. Beer went down the wrong way."

"I'm not sure how many shows still have tickets available." Jane's lips barely moved, and she looked away from Frank.

"I'm sure I can find some somewhere," he said. "There were plenty last week. Or so I heard."

I gave his shoulder a friendly nudge. "Then you should have gotten your tickets last week, before you asked me to go. Oh, that's right. You weren't in town last week. You were soaking up the Florida sunshine."

"I wouldn't trade my trip for all the tea in China. I love to travel, and I needed some fun in the sun. In fact, I'm going back in a couple of weeks— for work, of course. You should go with me, Emma. Don't you have a spring break coming up?"

I laughed at him. "I can't just take off on a trip like that."

"Why not?"

"Well..." I counted on my fingers. "I've got a paper to write. And I have a meeting with a landscape architect. We're re-doing the herb and flower garden on the east end of the house. There's an issue with the pool plumbing that needs to be addressed. Daddy has an appointment with the eye doctor, and—"

"Well, everyone deserves to escape the daily grind sometime." Frank glanced around the circle, ignoring Jane's and George's stoic faces, and reveling in his father's and stepmother's indulgent smiles. "If spring break isn't an option, maybe you can tag along when I go up to New York in a couple of months, and I can show you around. Sort of a graduation gift."

"We'll see." I cast a nervous look around the circle, intuiting some odd undercurrents in the group. Frank *could* be uncomfortably familiar sometimes.

Thankfully, Julianne saved the moment with an anecdote about a colleague who was from New York, and I excused myself to get another glass of wine.

I stood at the counter, looking at the wine labels, and turned when I heard footsteps behind me.

"Oh hey, Professor Knightley. I thought you were drinking beer tonight."

"Emma, you aren't seriously considering going on a vacation with Frank Weston, are you?"

I blinked up at him in surprise. "Oh that? That was just Frank being Frank. That's all that was."

"I'm relieved you didn't take his silly school-boy drivel seriously. Makes everyone uncomfortable. I can't believe the audacity, suggesting such a thing in front of your aunt Nina."

"I don't think she thought a thing of it. She knows how he is. Speaks first, thinks later. It's part of his charm."

"Yes. Charming." He snorted and shook his head.

I knew I should keep quiet, but curiosity was getting the best of me. Frank's suggestion that an admirer had sent Jane the piano, and Nina's idea that George was enamored with Jane kept bugging me. "Wasn't that nice of the Campbells to give Jane a piano of her own?"

"It was badly done, in my opinion."

"Oh?"

"The parlor is stuffed full with that overgrown monstrosity now. An upright or console would have sounded just fine, given Jane an instrument to practice on, and not inconvenienced Helen and Delores nearly so much. Very impractical. I'm surprised the Campbells would do such a thing. They must not know Jane's situation very well."

I grinned and poured myself a half a glass of wine. I stepped over to the side of the room and beckoned George to follow me. He leaned one hand against the wall and inclined his head to hear me whisper better.

"Did you get an invitation to this fundraiser at the Coles?"

"I did."

"Oh. And are you going?"

"Probably. It's for the Actors' Guild, and my mother has given them lots of support over the years."

"Yes, of course. I'd forgotten. That makes sense, then—that you got an invite, I mean."

"So, I take it you haven't received one. You've never been a big theater fan," he reminded me. "Maybe Mr. and Mrs. Cole didn't think you were interested."

"Maybe. A little short-sighted on their part though. The Woodhouse and Taylor families have always been generous to local charities. You think the Coles might remember that, given that they're acquainted with us, even though we're not close friends."

"Yes, of course."

"Nina and Bob received an invitation." I shrugged. "It doesn't matter. I'm not sure I could go to their fundraiser at any rate." I paused to sip my wine. "Daddy—you know. And don't give me that poor, pitiful Emma look."

"I wouldn't dare."

"I'm not sure I even want to go."

"All right. No problem then."

"Jane plays very well, doesn't she?"

"She's a gifted musician. Found her calling early. In some ways, that's easier, but it doesn't come without its own burdens."

I snorted. "What burden does Jane carry? She's beautiful, talented, having great success in New York—"

"That's true enough." He leaned his back against the wall, arms crossed, and I leaned back beside him so we were elbow to elbow studying the room.

George frowned. "But if that's the case, why is she here—in quiet Highbury, away from all that success and her fiancé—looking pale and unhappy? I'm concerned about her, Emma Kate. Her spirits seem low. In a high-pressure career, with no strong family support, no real relaxation when she comes back home—her so-called success doesn't seem to have the same benefits as it would for someone else...like you, for instance."

"Like me?"

"Yes. Think about it for a minute, and you'll see what I mean."

I observed Jane, a thin smile on her face as she talked to Frank and Nina. "I suppose you mean that I still have Daddy, and Nina, and Izzy and Jack and the children, and Jane only has Delores and Helen—and they're so far away from her. I got to stay in college. I never had to worry about money."

"It's not only those external factors. Your personality is different too. Jane is sensitive, timid—the stereotypical artist. She needs to be treated with kid gloves. You dive in, make a situation your own. Have a lot of confidence." He grinned. "Sometimes too much."

"Ha-ha."

"I don't know anything about Jane's fiancé, this Mike Dixon, but I can't help but wonder why he's across the pond while she's here, in what looks to me like some kind of distress."

"Funny you should say that."

"Why?"

"It's exactly what Mary Jo said."

"Really? Maybe my receptionist has more intuition than I gave her credit for."

"High praise from Professor Knightley."

"I mean, what kind of man runs off and leaves the woman he loves when she's down?"

"Certainly not the one in front of me," I replied lightly, brushing lint off his jacket lapel. "You are too gentlemanly for such a stunt. And speaking of women, you should probably get back to yours. She's standing all alone over there."

"Pardon?"

"Julianne," I whispered and jerked my head toward the doorway. "She's standing over there by herself with that funny look on her face. Come on, George, pay attention."

"Oh." He stepped away, glancing from the woman at the door to the one standing next to him. "So she is. Thanks." He picked up a second glass of wine and joined Julianne. She took the glass with a "thank you" and smiled wistfully at me.

I felt wistful myself at the sight of the two of them, standing together. A night out with the ebullient Frank Weston was just what I needed to break out of this March funk. I was lonely; that had to be it. For some reason, I wanted to cry—and Emma Katherine Woodhouse *never* cried.

TWENTY-SEVEN

I entered the Carriage House restaurant bar and stood, unsure, in the doorway while Frank left his car with the valet. I could count on one hand the number of times I'd set foot in a bar since I'd turned twenty-one last year.

My hair, which Frank said looked like spun honey, hung in large, loose ringlets, and I self-consciously flipped one curl behind my bare shoulder. The sales girl at Embry's had tried to talk me into a strapless Halston dress that tied at the bust, insisting I had the willowy figure that was perfect for it, but I didn't want to spend my one evening out constantly tugging up my dress. I opted for the one-shouldered red jersey instead. I hadn't considered height when I bought the platform shoes, but fortunately, Frank was still taller than me.

The bar was almost dark and on the cool side, making me shiver. Frank stepped up beside me and pulled my wrap up over my arms.

"Cold?" he asked.

"A little."

"We'll just get a drink here while we wait for our table. I made the reservation for six thirty instead of six, apparently, but we'll still have plenty of time before curtain." There was a quiet table in the corner, but instead, he led me to the bar. As we settled on the bar stools, Frank called out to the bartender.

"Bart, my man!"

"Weston! What can I get you?"

"Makers and Coke."

"Sure thing. And for the lovely lady?"

"What'll you have, Emma?" Frank asked, smiling at me.

"Brandy old-fashioned."

"Not your usual glass of wine?"

"I'm celebrating a night on the town."

"Damn straight, you are!" Frank leaned on the bar and tapped it with two fingers. "Brandy old-fashioned—and make it snappy!" he joked.

"Big plans this evening?" The bartender made small talk as he retrieved glasses and poured shots into them.

"We're going to see *Camelot* over at Coles' Theater, after we have some dinner."

"I'm sure the lady will enjoy that." He garnished my glass with an orange and a maraschino cherry and pushed it slowly across the bar. "Try this, darlin'—and then tell me it ain't the best you ever tasted." He put both hands on the bar and smiled at me expectantly.

The dual edge of sweet and bitter traveled over my tongue. "It's very good."

"Best you ever had?"

"I believe it is."

Frank laughed. "That's high praise from Emma Woodhouse."

"Good enough, then." The bartender grinned and pushed Frank's drink across the bar. "You coming by this week? We'll need citrus fruit, and the kitchen needs some kind of special potato for a dish the chef is itching to make."

"I'll be here on Tuesday, like usual. If you guys would call ahead, I could get a jump on those orders."

"I'll talk to the manager."

I slid off the bar stool. "Excuse me. Where's the ladies' room?"

I walked off in the direction the bartender pointed, careful in my platforms, and curious about the murmurs behind me at the bar. I've learned over the years, it's better to not look behind you.

TWENTY-EIGHT

He had had better evenings, that was for sure. George hadn't seen or scarcely thought of Julianne in almost a week and was annoyed with himself that he hadn't realized it until she called him. She wasn't upset. She wasn't ever upset with him, for any reason, and that was annoying too. Still, they'd made plans to have drinks and dinner at the Carriage House. She said she had big news to share, so they found a quiet corner in the bar, and over scotch and soda, he asked her, "How are things at the hospital?"

"Going well." She breathed a sigh of relief, as if he'd given her an opening, and she took a drink as if to fortify her resolve. "I've been applying for attending positions for the last few months."

"I know. You said that there were just a couple of slots open at UK hospital." His eyebrows shot up and he leaned toward her. "You got the position here in Lexington?"

"Um, well, yeah, I did."

He kissed her cheek. "Julianne! That's great! Congratulations. Why are we drinking scotch when we should be drinking champagne?" He held up a hand to signal the cocktail waitress, but she pulled it back down.

"Wait, George." She laughed. "Just…wait."

He settled back in his chair. "Okay."

"I did get an offer from the University of Kentucky, but I also got two other offers. One is in Chicago, and the other is in Arizona."

"I see." He sipped his drink and studied her. "You're thinking about accepting one of the others."

"I'm looking at the pros and cons of each one. It isn't a simple decision. The position in Chicago is in the pediatric oncology department, and there's some interesting research going on there. Plus, you know... Chicago—it's exciting. Big city—and it's closer to my family. But it's expensive to live in Chicago, and the pay isn't as good as Arizona. In Arizona, the cost of living is less, and the job isn't as prestigious—or as stressful. It's still in the city, but there will be an American Indian population to serve, and you know that's near and dear to my heart."

"And what about here?" he asked quietly.

"Here is...familiar. I know the department, the staff, the buildings, but the pay isn't very good."

"The pay doesn't matter."

Julianne gave him a rueful smile. "It wouldn't matter to you, George, but I have a lot of medical school debt. It actually is an important factor."

He looked almost offended, but she plunged ahead with her list of pros and cons. "If I stayed here, I wouldn't have to move..."

"You have friends here." He paused. "I'm here."

"Yes," she answered. "You are." They sat quietly for a minute, both absorbed in their own thoughts before she went on. "I never expected to have such good choices. I'd planned to stay here, but I knew the positions were few and far between, so I hedged my bets and applied several places, and, well, here I am—with a pretty complicated knot to untangle. George?" She followed the direction of his gaze.

"What the hell is she doing in a bar by herself?" he muttered under his breath.

"Isn't that Emma Woodhouse?"

"It is at that." The red dress had caught his eye. He always appreciated a beautiful woman well-dressed, but when he recognized who was *in* the dress, his heart damn near stopped. It started pounding again when Frank Weston stepped in, took her elbow, and escorted her to the bar.

Julianne poked him in the ribs. "Don't look so shocked, honey. She is over twenty-one, you know."

"What?"

"Emma is not a wayward teenager sneaking into a bar. She's an adult."

"I know that. I'm just surprised, that's all. She doesn't go out much."

"You heard her say she and Frank were going to see *Camelot*. I guess they decided to have dinner too."

"Mm-hmm."

"George?"

"Hmm?"

"About the attending position?"

"Yes, of course." He forced his attention from the bar, but it was no good. Julianne's words were just buzzing in his head. "Excuse me. I'm going to get another drink. Would you like one?"

Julianne sat back against the booth, resigned. "No thanks."

He reached the bar just in time to hear Frank say to the bartender, "I dated her in high school." By the time the bartender said, "Go for it," his pulse was pounding in his temple.

"I might do just that." Frank's frat boy arrogance crawled all over him. George didn't bump him *on purpose*, not exactly, but he didn't much care if Frank spilled bourbon all over that half-buttoned polyester shirt.

"Glenlivet on the rocks," he blurted out.

"Knightley! How's it going?"

"Fine. Was that Emma I saw come in with you?"

"Yep. Taking her to see her cousin in *Camelot*."

"Aren't you generous?"

"I like to think so." He turned to Julianne and sent her a wave. "Well, there's the lovely doctor. Mind if I walk over and say 'hello'?"

"We're waiting on a table."

"Really? Us too. You want to join us?"

George started to refuse, considered, and finally pasted on a smile, surprised at the grim satisfaction he got out of this chance to supervise Emma's date. "Now that sounds like a good idea."

"Great, I'll see if they can change the reservation. Emma and I will come over and join you in a minute."

TWENTY-NINE

APRIL 17, 1976

I sat in the gazebo watching spring rain fall all around me while Maude napped at my feet. I took a sip of the iced tea in my hand. I considered wine, decided it was too early for it. A modern woman didn't depend on wine to get through a Saturday afternoon rut. It was a bad habit to get into.

But lordy, I felt so alone.

I'm not alone, I reminded myself, channeling George Knightley in my head. *I have my father, my sister, my aunt, my friends.* Although I hadn't seen so much of Izzy lately. She was pregnant again. Henry and Taylor were running her ragged, she said. She rarely left Louisville these days, except for family get-togethers.

Nina was still close by, but Bob had her hopping most of the time too —business meetings couched as social functions, weekend getaways, antiquing. When she was home, they worked on the old Randalls' place together.

And Mary Jo? Well, it was a little odd. She hadn't been around my house in quite a while. Mary Jo Smith had suddenly become very engrossed in her career. Then again, I had been busy preparing for graduation—term papers and exams and such. Maybe we'd just missed each other.

Graduation loomed like a specter over my days now. Daddy was doing reasonably well. Unless he took a turn for the worse, caring for him wasn't going to take all my time, but I wasn't sure what else to do. Charity work? Sure, I would do some of that; it was a Taylor-Woodhouse family tradition. It was expected. Should I get a job? Perhaps, but where, in tiny little Highbury? Even in Lexington, what could a young woman with a bachelor's degree in psychology but no work experience *do*? The only thing I knew how to do was to take care of things, of people. The problem was, my people were doing a reasonable job of caring for themselves these days.

I sat on the sturdy wooden rail and held my hand under the rain dripping from the roof. The pale green of new leaves and the purple of redbud trees surrounded me with shouts of "New life! New beginnings!" And here I sat, inside my well-built gazebo cocoon, insulated from the life teeming all around me. Not on the outside looking in, but on the inside looking out.

My thoughts turned to Frank, as I reached down and absently scratched Maude behind the ears.

Frank Weston. Funny, outgoing, cute hunk of man. We had a great time at dinner the other night, but he was broody after the theater. I was impressed by Jane's performance and said so, to which he replied, "Yeah, she'll be outta here and back to New York as soon as she can get away."

Then he, himself, got away—or rather was taken away a few days later when his grandmother had a stroke. He was gone to Alabama for who knows how long. He'd probably miss Derby, and the big Derby party, and my graduation too.

He acted odd that day he said goodbye to me at Nina and Bob's house. We were sitting in the living room, just the two of us, when he suddenly turned to me.

"Emma, I..."

He stopped, frowned into his beer, took a drink. I waited patiently.

"You must have seen...well, sure, you must have. You, who see it all. It's almost impossible for me to hide my feelings, and that night we went to the theater..."

He was interrupted by the arrival of his father. "Well, Emma, this is a sad business, isn't it? Poor Frank will be leaving us and under such circumstances." He shook his head. "You'll tell your mother I'm sorry about Mrs. Churchill, won't you Frank?"

"Sure, Dad. I will, just like I said I would." Frank looked at me with a sigh and a smile. The moment—and whatever he was trying to reveal about his feelings for me—was gone.

He left with promises to give me a call and let me know how he was doing. But of course, there had been no call.

I, of all people, knew how helping to care for a sick relative ate up one's time, although I doubted Frank realized how it was going to be.

Thing was, I wasn't really that disappointed. At the end of our date, Frank walked me to the door, gave me a distracted peck on the lips, and he was gone. It was how I imagined I might feel about kissing my brother, if I had a brother, that is. Well, I have Jack, but kissing Jack would be gross.

So much for Frank's offer of a graduation weekend in New York, if he was ever even serious. I braced myself for a wave of discouragement but the feeling never came. A New York getaway with Frank didn't seem like the exciting adventure I envisioned at first, and that spoke volumes. I liked Frank, but his mercurial moods and his impulsiveness did tend to wear on me. He would always rely on me to rein him in, and where was the fun in that? I could never really relax. I could never be myself.

I might as well face facts. I have no real future with Handsome Frank. I sat down on the bench, sipped my tea, and wondered who might be the right girl for Frank Weston.

Maude's tail thumped against the gazebo deck floor, as she raised her head and let out a joyful bark. A black umbrella appeared at the edge of the garden, bobbing along in the rain. I recognized the gait, the way he moved, and unbidden, a smile spread across my features. The wind kicked up and almost turned the umbrella inside out, but George reached up and took command of it once again.

"Hello there!" I called out. "Nice day for a walk."

He laughed as he stepped into my gazebo world and filled the space. "Sure it is. That's why you're out here in the middle of it."

"I like the rain. It matches my mood."

"And what mood might that be?"

"I'm bored, Professor Knightley. Have you come to entertain me?"

"I'm not sure I'm up to the challenge. You're so easily distracted."

"True enough."

He wrapped the fastening strap around his umbrella, watching it rather than me as he talked. "I heard Frat Boy left town."

"His grandmother took ill suddenly. They think she had a stroke."

"Oh, I didn't know why he left. I'm genuinely sorry to hear about Mrs. Churchill. I know she hasn't always been the most pleasant woman, at least to Bob Weston, but I'm sure Frank is fond of her. When is he planning to return?"

I shrugged. "Who knows? He may miss Bob's big Derby party, and that would be a shame."

George leaned the umbrella up against one of the benches and sat down in the gazebo's center. "Were you all planning to go together?"

"Maybe. It was implied, I guess, but we never made definite plans. Frank isn't a *definite plans* kind of guy."

"No, I suppose he isn't."

A robin landed on the bird feeder a few yards away, and I watched as he hopped around the ledge, helping himself to the seed inside.

George cleared his throat. "So, what are your plans for graduation?"

"What?"

"Your graduation—how are you celebrating the big day?"

"I have no idea."

"It's coming up fast."

"It is."

"It's a big milestone."

The surge of irritation came through in my exasperated sigh. "Is it really, George?"

"What do you mean?"

"How will things be any different than they are now? Except I won't have classes to attend, of course."

"Perhaps they won't be very different right away, but it's still an important event. I thought Nina might throw you a party."

"Graduation is the day after Derby. She and Bob will be busy preparing for that. Jack and Izzy are driving down and won't want to stay for the weekend."

"Yes, they will. We've already discussed it. They're staying at Donwell."

"Well, I wish they'd talked to me first. I'm considering not attending graduation at all."

"What? Why not?"

"It will be so hard for Daddy. University commencement is huge. Thousands of people milling around everywhere, and the parking is a nightmare, plus all the walking. It will make him so anxious and fretful. It's almost not worth it."

"It is worth it, Emma Kate. I know your father wants you to walk through commencement, just like I know your mother would have wanted it. Nina will be heartbroken if you don't."

"But..."

"Jack and Izzy and I will handle John."

"But the children..."

"Rita will watch the children. Leave the rest to me." He looked off into the garden and grumbled. "Not go through commencement! Of all the silly, foolish notions."

"If you insist, I guess."

"I do insist. And not only that, I insist you let me throw you a get-together in celebration."

"Oh, George, no one will want another party the day after Derby. It's too much."

"We won't do a big, splashy party then. We'll do...brunch. At the country club. A brunch with eggs Benedict and fresh strawberries and mimosas and whatever else you ladies like. And some manly food for the other half."

"You're going to throw a brunch?"

"I have a juris doctorate degree and run a law practice. I can organize a small gathering of friends."

"You mean hire it done."

"Hired help is a given. After all, I was well-trained by my mother. Hiring good help is a time-honored family tradition."

"Maybe Julianne can help you with the girly stuff."

"Probably not."

"Is she working?"

"Not sure. She and I…um, well. We're not seeing each other anymore." He picked up the umbrella, fiddled with the strap again. "She's off to Arizona at the beginning of July for her new attending position. And we broke up."

This is a surprise! I eyed him carefully. "I'm sorry, George. Do you want to talk about it?"

"Not really."

"Still painful?"

He shook his head, laughed a little. "No, it really isn't. That's bad, isn't it?"

I thought of my feelings about Frank Weston. "No, I get it."

"You do?"

"Sure. She was a good one, just not *The One.*"

"You do get it. I'm surprised."

"Don't stroke my ego like that, George. My self-worth is inflated enough already."

He ignored the sarcasm. "I mean, I liked Julianne, respected her."

"She was a step up from your *Woman of the Month.*"

"Yes." His gaze slid back to me. "I guess I'm getting serious in my old age."

"You're just hitting your stride, Professor." I reached over and patted his arm. "You'll be back at it in no time." It was a tease, and he surprised me when he covered my hand with his.

"I don't think I'll be doing things the way I did before Julianne. She had a lot to say to me, a lot that made sense. She said I needed to sort out my priorities, be honest with myself."

"That sounds like it was a deep conversation, one that makes me a little envious."

"She gave me some good advice, and I'm going to take it. I won't jump right back into the dating pool. I need some time to figure out what I'm looking for." He turned my hand over in his and squeezed my fingers gently before letting me go. I had a childish impulse to grab his hand and hold it against my cheek—my dear friend George, stoic in the face of his loss, and trying to figure out what was to come. I understood that perfectly, because I was in the same boat with my own life. Suddenly, the rain didn't seem so cold, and I didn't feel so alone.

THIRTY

MAY 1, 1976

I smiled at George as he handed me out of the passenger side of his car. One valet helped Mary Jo out of the back, and the other plopped behind the wheel of the Mercedes and ran his hands over the steering wheel in admiration.

"Thank you for bringing us to the party a bit early."

"It was Bob's request, was it not?" George stepped between Mary Jo and me and offered us each an elbow.

"Yes, I think he needed some extra help setting up, so he asked us to come before the actual start time." I frowned looking around at the steady stream of people filing into Bromley Crossing. "Looks like plenty of people are here to help though."

"That's Bob for you," George said good-naturedly. "He loves his friends around him."

"Enough to invite all his nearest and dearest to lend a hand. It seems to me if everyone's a close friend, no one is—if you get my drift."

"I suppose you have a point there, Emma Kate."

"Kindness, without succumbing to indiscriminate friendships with everyone he meets is an admirable quality in a man, don't you agree, Mary Jo?"

"Wow!" Mary Jo's eyes were wide as saucers as she paused to take in the white bunting around the gazebos and the tents strewn about the yard. The big building at Bromley Crossing, an old restored train station, was decorated to match, with planters full of red roses set all along the front entrance. "It's beautiful!"

"Well, ladies, shall we?"

"We shall." I squeezed his arm and beamed up at him. "I'm glad you let us tag along. You could have brought a date, or made an entrance, swaggering in alone. You would have drawn every female eye in the place, Mr. Handsome."

"Escorting two lovely ladies draws every eye, female or not, so that's even better, isn't it?"

I chuckled. "I guess it is."

"Oh, look," Mary Jo said, "here comes Frank Weston."

He was striding toward us, that same old cocky grin on his face. "There you are, Emma! I've been looking all over for you." He spoke like he was glad to see us, although his eyes still roamed the crowd as if looking for someone. He leaned down and kissed my cheek. "The three of you look like the Mod Squad coming up the path. Here, Knightley, let me steal this gal for a minute." He stepped to my other side, taking my hand, and dragging me forward.

"It looks just grand, Frank," I said. "I don't think I'd change a thing."

"Yep, it came together well. Not that I had that much to do with it. I just got back from Alabama last night."

I heard George snort from behind me and ignored it.

"But," Frank continued, "Dad and Nina had lots of help, so it turned out they didn't need me anyway."

"Yes, help is all around, in every nook and cranny." I smiled sweetly. "How's your grandmother doing?"

"Not so good, but Mom's going to send her to some rehab place...oh, she told me, but I can't remember." His fingers mimicked ideas fleeing from his mind. "Somewhere. Thanks for asking. Hey, let me get you a drink."

I glanced over my shoulder. George smiled at me once our eyes met, but his expression was subdued, and I wondered briefly if he thought I was encouraging Frank too much.

But Frank and I are friends. And George doesn't have double standards like that. How could he, when he charms every woman he meets?

The band started to play, and Frank took my hand, announcing, "Drinks can wait!" and pulled me onto the dance floor, where he whirled and twirled me around to the sounds of a watered-down version of "Get Up and Boogie."

"Look, it's Elton and Edie." Frank pointed to the couple posed at the entry, as if to wait for everyone's attention.

"Oh, bother."

"They sure do like to make an entrance, don't they?"

"Hmm." I was impressed that such a noncommittal response could convey my very real disapproval.

"And yet, there they are, all alone—not a friend in sight to greet them." He grinned at me and brushed a lock of my hair behind my ear to whisper, "Their reputation precedes them. Or maybe it's her horsey laugh, although that should fit right in at a Derby party." I held in my snicker, keeping my back to the new arrivals. He craned his neck to see around me. "I thought they were bringing Jane and Helen."

"They are?"

"But I don't see them. There's Dad. Let's eavesdrop, shall we?" He moved us closer while Tim and Edie smiled and sent coy waves and greetings to various people in the crowd.

"Where are Jane and Helen?" Bob asked, shaking Tim's hand and looking behind Edie.

Tim froze, toothy smile still in place. "Ah…"

Edie's head whipped around as she glared at Tim. "What? Oh my goodness! We were supposed to pick them up? Tim! You didn't tell me that!"

"I could have sworn I told you, honey, but it must have slipped my mind."

"How could my dear friend Jane slip your mind? I'm so embarrassed! You have to go straight back to Hartfield Road and get them."

"Of course. I'll go right now. You stay and enjoy the party. Back in a flash."

After Tim made a hurried exit, Edie finally moved away from the entry, letting more people through, and latched herself onto the host.

I raised my eyebrows and gave Frank a knowing look.

He was frowning, but seeing my expression, he pulled me into a dancing embrace. "She leads Elton around by the nose and seems about as genuine as the rhinestones on her dress."

I finally gave in to my giggle.

Several other couples began to join us on the dance floor. We were still dancing when I glanced through the window and saw Tim Elton's car barreling up the drive.

"Let's go greet them," Frank said. "We wouldn't want Elton to have to escort two lovely ladies in all by himself."

It occurred to me that Frank hadn't cared so much when it was George escorting Mary Jo and me, but I let that go and told him I was going to speak to Nina.

As we parted ways, I overheard Edie say to Bob, in a voice for everyone close, including Frank, to hear, "Your son is so handsome!"

"Thank you," Bob said.

"He just has that presence about him—you know, that 'je ne sais quoi' that young men don't seem to have anymore. My father is always chasing off those worthless young men my sisters bring around. Frank is so far above that, I can just tell." Her braying laugh ripped the elegant fabric of the music and conversation around them. "Maybe you should send Frank over to Frankfort."

"Maybe I should. Well, I've got to check on the bar real quick. Can I get you anything?"

"I should wait for Tim, I guess…"

"Okay then." Bob gave her a big grin. "Thanks for coming, Edie. Have a great time." And he was gone, leaving Edie looking around before heading toward Tim, Jane, and Helen standing just inside the door. Soon, Edie found her words, even her unique laugh drowned out by Helen's excitement.

"Tim! Thank you so much for the ride! Even though it's a beautiful day, isn't it? Just beautiful. We could have walked. It's so nice outside. You know, sometimes Derby Day is cold and rainy. I remember one year it even snowed! Of course, we were at home. We weren't out in…" She stopped and looked around the room. "My goodness! This is marvelous! I haven't been out here in years, but it doesn't look anything like I remember. So much nicer! So elegant! Bob and Nina did a fantastic job!"

"Thank you, Helen. You're very kind," Nina replied, giving her a hug and a kiss on each cheek.

"I'm just so happy to be here. It's marvelous, Nina. How did you ever manage it? You're so busy all the time. I just don't know how you… Why, hello, Edie! It's good to see you! I didn't know you were here already. It was good of Tim to come by and fetch us in his BMW. What a nice ride! We felt just like royalty. We did! It was nice of Nina to offer a ride too, but Jane said she would be much too busy to fool with the likes of us, and we were spoiled for choices—it's so wonderful to have such thoughtful friends and family. Two offers from two wonderful friends! How were we to choose? I was just telling Mother this morning… Pardon?" Helen leaned toward Nina before shifting gears to answer her question. "Oh, Mother is doing very well, very well. She insisted on staying with John today, so she took the car over there. She decided not to come with us, but she dressed up, just like she was going to a party. A party of two—well, three, I guess, if you count Juanita who stays with John. Mother wore that lovely brooch that Mike Dixon got her. Mike is Jane's fiancé, you know. He sent that brooch to Mother for Christmas, all the way from Ireland. So kind of him. Come on in, Jane, honey—don't stand out there in the wind. Oh, thank you, Frank, for escorting her in. You're always so attentive to Jane. And to us. It was so nice of you to come over and fix that screen door at the house. It was almost completely off its hinges, and he fixed it in one afternoon while Mother and I were at the store. So fortunate that Jane was home to let him in." Helen spotted Emma. "Hello, honey! Oh, you look so pretty. That dress is so becoming on you."

"Thanks, Helen."

"And I love the way you've done your hair. Gorgeous! How do you like Jane's hair?"

I stole a jealous glance at Jane's long, luscious brunette curls. "Beautiful as always."

"Isn't it?" Helen gushed as Jane's cheeks flushed pink. "She did it herself. She made great friends of the makeup and hair people in New York. And it shows. They taught her everything they know. Oh! Dr. and Mrs. Perry are here! I must go and say hello." She began to wander off. "Mrs. Weatherly, how do you do? And Norma Henderson! It's been an age! Is that your son Richard? The last time I saw him he was knee-high to a grasshopper! Just look at him now! Oh no, Norma, don't interrupt him —he's much better off talking to that pretty young woman than a broken-down old relic like me! Very well, how are you doing, Richard? Oh, excuse me. I need to move away from the door. People are trying to get in and here I stand. Mimosa? I don't believe so, thank you, Nina. I'm going to hold off for a little bit. Did I tell you how lovely everything looks? I did? I'm so happy to be here!" Helen's face beamed like a lamp without a lamp-shade to diffuse the light.

Frank moved to my side, and now that Helen had moved off, I could overhear the conversation between Edie and Jane.

"You do look especially lovely, Jane. Is that a Halston dress? I expect you have all kinds of wonderful gifts like that from your Mike. He must be a generous man. You always look top notch. Nothing like this old dress off the rack at Embry's."

"Your dress is...very striking," Jane said politely. "Embry's is where everyone here goes for formal wear."

"Do you think? I wasn't sure about this hat. You know, I'm just not much into fashion myself, but this is a big to-do. Lots of important people here, and I wanted to do the Westons' party justice. Derby only comes once a year, you know. It was a great occasion to wear my pearls. I don't see many pearls like mine here."

There was an awkward silence.

"That Frank Weston is a wonderful dancer. Most athletes are, I imagine." Edie leaned in close to Jane's ear, but didn't lower her voice at all. "And you know what they say about men who are good dancers, don't you? I've always heard they are good in b—"

"So, Emma!" Frank almost yelled to drown out Edie's innuendo. Typically, nothing embarrassed Frank Weston, but Edie Bitti had a special knack for vulgarity.

Tim had joined Edie and Jane, and Edie took his arm on one side and dragged Jane's elbow with the other. "You found us, Timmy. Interrupted me and my best pal in our girl talk."

"Best pal?" Frank whispered to me. "That was fast. But I guess Jane's all right with it."

"I wouldn't read too much into it. You know how Edie is."

"Old windbag-in-training, if you ask me."

"Well, aren't you rude?" I looked up to see Frank scowling into the crowd. "Not that I really disagree, but it's ungenerous to say it out loud. What's up with you today, Frank?"

"What do you mean?"

"You're acting peculiar. Like you're ticked off."

"I'm fine, I'm fine." He schooled his features into his trademark cocky grin. "Better?"

"Much. You're one of the hosts after all."

"You're absolutely right." He tossed a glance over his shoulder. "You're always keeping me on the straight and narrow, aren't you? Let's mingle."

Grateful that Frank was determined to be in a better humor, I dug into the pleasantries of party-going. I'd always loved talking with people and was good at it, if I do say so myself. George used to say, "Emma can get a wall to talk." Whether that was a compliment to my social skills or a commentary on my ability to find out everything about everybody, I wasn't sure.

George. I looked around for him and caught him looking right at me. He had moved across the room to speak to an attorney, leaving Mary Jo in the very capable company of Nina. Sometimes, he baffled me. Elegantly dressed, in an understated suit and tie, he really did draw every female eye in the place, and he didn't need fads and fashion to make a statement. Talk about *je ne se quoi*! George Knightley had it in spades. His genuine smile and the way he moved through the crowd, without looking like Tim Elton working the room, was compelling. My heart swelled with pride as I followed him from speaking with Dr. Perry to old Mrs. McKinney with... well, masculine grace—there was no other phrase so apt. Our eyes met again for one long second, and I smiled, gesturing with my head toward the dance floor, but he only returned my smile and shook his head.

What was going on with all these silly men today? First Frank, and then George, and now, I realized, Mary Jo hadn't had a man ask her to dance yet. I exchanged glances with Nina, who led Mary Jo close to a group of men standing near the bar. When that didn't elicit an invitation, I saw Nina heading toward Tim and Edie, whispering together at the side of the room, and thought, *No, no, no! He'll never ask Mary Jo to dance with that shrew standing right there!* I expected he would escape into the other room, but he left Edie talking to a judge she knew and crossed paths with Nina and Mary Jo. I wasn't quite close enough to hear, but a few steps brought me within earshot. It soon became apparent that Tim had no intention of escaping the room. His plan was much more nefarious.

"Tim," Nina began, "why aren't you dancing? We need to find you a partner."

"I had to get permission from my gal." He gestured with his thumb toward Edie. "But she's given me the go ahead, so I'll be glad to take you to the floor, Nina."

"Me? Oh. I've got no time to dance. I've got to check on about ten things with the bar and catering staff. But Mary Jo is free."

"Mary Jo? Oh, you mean Knightley's secretary?" His face turned stony cold acknowledging Mary Jo at Nina's side with a curt nod. "Oh, I didn't see her there. She blends right in with the wait staff. Think I'll forego dancing for now. Any other chore you need me to do, I'm happy to help, but... Excuse me."

Nina stood with abject shock on her face. I was enraged. This was Tim Elton, who had always seemed so friendly and nice! Shallow perhaps, but this? Plain meanness! And here I'd thought he was above such things and even considered him worthy of a sweet girl like Mary Jo.

Tim had stepped over to settle into a conversation with George, who stood there with a grim expression, a muscle ticking in his cheek. Tim and Edie exchanged looks of malicious glee. Mary Jo looked down into the drink the bartender handed her, her cheeks flushed, shoulders stooped in embarrassment.

That horse's ass! I wanted to march over straight away and give Tim a piece of my mind, but I knew that would only embarrass Mary Jo further. Heat and righteous indignation bubbled under my skin as I realized I was powerless to help her.

George took one glance at my fuming expression and left Tim in mid-sentence. He walked straight to Mary Jo, took her wineglass, handed it to the bartender, and leaned close to speak in her ear. Her up-turned face changed from red mortification to white shock to a glowing peachy pink, as she smiled and nodded. George led her to the floor as the band began to play.

I didn't think it was possible to be more proud of George than I was earlier, but I was wrong. Such chivalry was rare these days. How lucky Mary Jo was to work for such a gentleman! How lucky I was to have him as a friend. My heart filled to bursting as he turned Mary Jo so he faced me, his perfect eyebrow raised and a jaunty grin on his face.

"Thank you," I mouthed silently.

It was as if we were the only two people in the room.

THIRTY-ONE

Long after Bold Forbes had won the Run for the Roses, and deep into the revelry of the evening, George walked the perimeter of the party. He was itching for home, the quiet, the dark, the ability to hear his own thoughts, but he wasn't leaving without Emma, and she was still having the time of her life. She got few chances to attend parties and enjoy herself, and he didn't have the heart to suggest she end it and head home.

And he'd be damned if he'd leave her to the clutches of Frank Weston after what he saw in the men's room about an hour ago.

Frank was talking with Michael Otway, the bourbon king's heir with too much money and a nose for cocaine, and George became suspicious when they looked around before heading into the restroom one after the other. When they didn't return after about five minutes, he followed them. Michael stared at himself in the mirror, eyes bright and red. Frank brushed something off the mirror shelf and slipped a plastic bag in the pocket of his vest.

Otway took one look at George and made for the restroom exit. Frank acknowledged him in the mirror with a nod and splashed some water on his face like aftershave.

"Having a good time, Frank?" George asked quietly, as he straightened his tie.

"The best. Love Derby. I could party all night."

"I'm sure you could. Just make sure you make it someplace safe by morning."

Frank laughed. "I certainly will." He clapped George on the shoulder. "You too, old man. You too."

After that, George kept one eye on Frank, the other on Emma. She danced with those who asked her, nursed a glass of wine while she chatted with old schoolmates, earned some lustful stares from young men that made his blood boil. Still, he couldn't fault their taste. He was used to seeing Emma in running clothes, jeans and peasant tops, the occasional dress for some event. But that royal blue halter number she was wearing stunned him: the slope of her shoulders, the curve of her back displayed to perfection in that dress, the way her hair floated around her and settled like spun honey about her face, and those legs that ran right up to her neck. No, he couldn't blame the young men in the crowd for following her around the room. He even admired her restraint given all that male attention. One thing about Emma, admiration for her looks alone didn't turn her head; the poor fellow also had to flatter her brains and her sparkling personality to stir *her* vanity. She was going easy on the drinks too, which was wise, in his opinion, and when he complimented her temperance, she looked at him like he was an eight-year-old who had tugged her pigtail.

"Of course, I'm taking it easy on the alcohol—in case you've forgotten, and I do hope you haven't, since you've planned a brunch at the country club—I have graduation tomorrow."

"I know, Em. I just..."

"I'm not a child."

"I know." Boy, did he ever. Tonight's events had been a constant series of reminders.

"Just because I'm not standing in the corner half the night doesn't mean I'm being irresponsible."

"That's not what I—"

"You really ought to take the opportunity to enjoy yourself, instead of loitering about with the older generation. The only time I saw you out there was when you rescued poor Mary Jo. Good job, by the way."

"Thanks." He felt sheepish. "I don't know if it was the right thing or not, but Tim really ticked me off."

"It was absolutely the right thing to do! Tim is a jerk."

"It was incredibly rude on his part, almost vicious. Not his typical M.O."

"I know it." Emma bit her lip.

"Must be a little Edie Bitti snobbery sneaking in."

"Perhaps."

"It's almost like they aimed the snub at more than just Mary Jo. What's with that, Emma? Why would Tim and Edie have anything against you? And why take it out on Mary Jo?"

"Well…" She seemed shy now, and he narrowed his eyes at her, his penetrating look accompanied by a small smile.

"I'd guess he might have been discouraged after last year's Christmas party?"

She looked away, refusing to answer.

"Water under the bridge, though. That's none of Edie's business, nor mine, for that matter. You wanted to pair him up with Mary Jo, right? Fess up. Is that what fed this meanness tonight?"

"Oh, you're right, as usual, and they'll never forgive me for it."

"I won't say I told you so. I'm sure you've chastised yourself enough."

"I'm a know-it-all sometimes, George. Will I never learn?"

He put an arm around her shoulders, then took it back abruptly. "When you reflect on it, you do learn, honey."

"I learned more than I wanted about Tim Elton, I can tell you that. He's a self-absorbed social climber. You saw that in him before. But I didn't, not until it was too late to keep Mary Jo from being hurt."

"Well, I have to say, you chose for him better than he has chosen for himself. Mary Jo has a sweet brand of charm that Edie definitely lacks. While we danced, I had a pleasant conversation with my front office help."

"Was that your only turn around the dance floor this evening?"

"I'm not much of a dancer."

"I disagree. Besides, you're young, George, you should be dancing, meeting people, breaking hearts—being the charming, handsome devil you are."

"What?"

"It's late in the evening, and it looks like I've missed my chance to be charmed by Lexington's best-looking man-about-town." She grinned. "Or perhaps you're a bit rusty."

He stood, agog, as a slow, sultry Clapton number began. Emma flipped her hair over her shoulder and tossed some young stud a winning smile. The kid started over, but George stepped in between the two, took Emma's elbow and leaned into her, speaking low in her ear, "Whom are you going to dance with?"

She hesitated a moment, a brief, almost star-struck expression traveled over her features. "Um…" Then her lips curved. "With you, if you will ask me."

His hand slid down her arm to grasp her fingers. "Let's dance a slow one, Emma Kate. What do you say?"

"You've sweet-talked me into it. I saw you on the dance floor earlier with Mary Jo, and your secret is out. You're quite the dancer. According to Edie Bitti, that's a…fine and useful quality in a man."

He laughed as he led her to the floor, turned her under his arm, and pulled her against him in one fluid motion.

She gasped a little as he held her close. "And besides, we're in-laws, not siblings, so it won't look weird. It's not like we're brother and sister."

"Brother and sister?" Strange, that idea hadn't occurred to him in months. "No, that's one thing we certainly are not."

THIRTY-TWO

MAY 2, 1976

I stood in front of the mirror, humming as I primped in the country club ladies' lounge. Guests were assembling downstairs, and I had to admit George (or whoever he hired to do these things) had done a fine job arranging the brunch. He made me feel accomplished and celebrated. I felt happier and easier than I had in a while. First of all, a comment from Mary Jo last night led me to believe she was finally over Tim Elton. After the near disaster on the dance floor, Mary Jo barely spared Tim a glance the rest of the night, and from all outward appearances, she enjoyed the party. Amazing, really, after Tim put her down like that. I so admired Mary Jo's ability to bounce back from disappointment. Perhaps she'd had a lot of practice in that area. Regardless, it was good to see her heart on the mend.

Second, the Derby party had been a smashing success; there were even pictures in this morning's Sunday paper, which pleased Bob to no end.

Frank was still partying the night away at 2 a.m. when I turned to George and said with a yawn, "I've had the best time."

"I'm glad, Emma Kate."

"I'm ready to go home though. It's a big day tomorrow."

"We can leave anytime."

"Let me get Mary Jo, and we'll head out."

I found her in conversation with Nina, and after getting her purse, we stopped at the bar to tell Frank goodnight.

"Miss Woodhouse!" His voice was a little too loud, his eyes unbelievably sharp for so late in the evening. "Leaving so soon?"

"I am."

"Aww!"

Looking around, I said. "I believe the party's over. You're one of the last holdouts, Frank."

"At least you didn't turn into a pumpkin at midnight, like the Fair Jane Fax."

"Don't be too hard on her. She had Helen in tow."

"Right, right." He took a sip of something amber-colored in a lowball glass and gave me a speculative glance. "If y'all want to stay, I'll give you a ride home."

"I've got it covered." George cut in. "No problem."

Frank pointed to George and flashed a sly smile. "Hey, man, you're the best."

"How are you getting home, Frank?" I asked.

"Who cares?" George muttered. I narrowed my eyes at him.

"I'll catch a ride in Otway's limo. Or ride home with Dad and Nina. Don't you worry about me."

"Okay, then. Goodnight, Frank."

"See you at the thingy. Tomorrow."

I had no illusions that I would see anything of Frank Weston tomorrow. He would most likely be nursing the mother of all hangovers. That was fine with me.

So, Mary Jo's heart was on the mend. Frank didn't seem any more interested in me than I was in him, so that gave me some peace of mind. Finally, for the first time in a while, I didn't feel like I was at odds with George Knightley.

George...

His image took my imagination into flight—impeccably dressed in his suit, his blue eyes twinkling with humor, the warmth of his hand on my back when we danced last night.

A shout from downstairs snapped me back from my daydream. I ran to the balcony overlooking the front entryway, and saw of all people, Frank, with his arm around a limping Mary Jo.

"Oh my goodness!" I cried, racing down the stairs. "Whatever happened?"

"I was driving out here," Frank began, "when some jerk comes out of nowhere, passing me and every other car in a line of them, then scooting back in the lane at the last minute. Just barely missed having a head-on with a box truck. I thought, well, that's just some asshole in a hurry, but then I saw a car up ahead of me veer into the ditch. Not a person stopped to help. Can you believe that? So, when I got up there, I pulled off the side of the road, and there was Mary Jo getting out of her car."

Mary Jo took a step, then winced as her ankle gave way. "I feel so stupid. I overcorrected when that guy passed me and ran into the ditch, and then right when Frank pulled over, I got out and turned my ankle on a rock. Landed right on my rear-end. How embarrassing is that?"

"I'm just glad you aren't seriously hurt." I grasped Frank's hand. "Thank you so much for stopping to help!"

"It was no problem at all." Frank stood back, letting me close to fuss over my friend.

"Mary Jo, do you need to go to the hospital?"

"Oh, heavens, no! I just turned my ankle. I can move it and everything. See?" She winced again.

"Let's get Dr. Perry over here to take a look at it, at least. It would make me feel better."

After applying some ice and some tape to wrap the injury, I motioned for Frank, already half-way through a Bloody Mary.

"What's up, Miss Woodhouse?"

"What about Mary Jo's car? Do we need to have it towed or something?"

"Oh, I don't think so," Frank replied. "Didn't seem to be damaged." He paused, sipped. Then, as if it had just occurred to him, he added, "If someone can run me back down there, I think I can drive it right out."

I turned around, looking for George, and saw him speaking to one of the valets on staff. He pointed over to Frank, and the boy nodded. It seems as if Mr. Knightley and I had the same thought. We exchanged looks, and I sighed a breath of relief before sending Frank off with the valet.

"You and your car troubles, Mary Jo..." I shook my head.

Cringing, Mary Jo looked around, seeing the staring faces for the first time. "I'm so sorry to ruin your party."

"It's hardly ruined. As soon as we get your car up here—"

"Do you think I'll be able to drive?" Mary Jo's forehead creased with worry, glancing toward George. "It's a standard shift."

"Let's just see how you feel after brunch." I handed her a glass of water brought over by the waitress. "We'll decide then."

Later, as I sat at the big round table, watching Mary Jo and Frank telling the tale of their adventure, I was struck by how they laughed, exchanged glances, finished each other's sentences. At first, Mary Jo spoke of her fright, but in response to Frank's expression of quietly amused relief, followed by outrage at the recklessness of the other driver, she began to perk up considerably.

The revelation hit me like a ton of bricks. *Mary Jo and Frank! Holy cow, they are perfect for each other! Why did I not see it before? She, on the rebound from ghastly Tim Elton—he, sort of aimless and in need of a steadying influence. And look how they interact, how they smile and speak to one another. They've been thrown together by this accident. It's kismet. It's fate. It's...*

I glanced across the table and discovered George gazing at me, like I was his pride and joy.

No, no, no. I won't interfere. It's their business, not mine. I'll wish and hope, but no...more...matchmaking. People just don't behave the way I want them to, and it ends up being a disaster. I smiled into my iced tea. *Wouldn't George be proud of me, if he knew?*

I had my resolutions vindicated later, as Mary Jo and I sat together on the country club veranda, champagne in hand, moving the glider back and forth in perfect unison. The noise from the crowd downstairs gave us a veil of privacy.

A gentle breeze blew over Mary Jo's delicate features, and she tucked a wayward chestnut colored curl behind her ear. "Did you have a good time at the Derby party?"

"Yes." I paused, debating with myself on whether to pry or leave well enough alone. "How about you?"

"You know, I did have a good time—mostly."

I waited with bated breath, sensing the weight of a conversation looming.

"I have a confession to make." Mary Jo swirled her drink in her cup, looking in it as if to find something fascinating.

"That sounds serious."

"I suppose it is, a little. I just want it out of my head, so I can get over it and move on." She turned so she faced me, one knee on the swing. "I cannot believe I *ever* liked Tim Elton. After last night, I don't care if I *ever* see him again. But I know I probably will. I overheard Edie telling someone she expects Tim to ask her to marry him this summer."

"Oh, Mary Jo! I am sorry!"

"No, no, I don't care. Really. I don't envy her one jot. I suppose Tim is handsome in that pretty-boy way, but he's mean underneath, and that makes him ugly to me."

"I completely agree, and I think it shows excellent judgment on your part."

"You do? Oh, what a relief! I know he's your friend—"

"He is not my friend anymore, Mary Jo. He might have been, once, but too much has happened for us to be friends now. I suspect we will just fade into mere acquaintances, and that's fine with me—especially now that he's with Edie."

"I don't like her."

"Me neither."

"I think she brings out the worst in Tim. She's pretty, and she has that connected family, which makes people give her the benefit of the doubt. But she really isn't a nice person at all."

"No, she's not. As for Tim Elton, I wish I'd never introduced you to the man, and I should have never pushed you at him. I'm ashamed of myself."

"Oh no! You mustn't blame yourself. I know you only wanted the best for me."

"I did, but I should have stayed out of it."

"I don't wish Tim and Edie ill, and I'm sure they'll be very happy together."

"You're kinder than I would be." I leaned over and laid my hand on hers.

"But last night, after I got home, I hunted up a couple of things I'd kept. Things that belonged to Tim."

"Really?"

Mary Jo nodded. "I'm so embarrassed, but I'm going to tell you anyway."

"What on earth could you have kept that belonged to Tim Elton?"

"Well, one thing was a sweat band he wore around his wrist when he gave us tennis lessons. Do you remember?"

"No, I don't think I…"

"He gave us a lesson, and before we started, he took off those wrist bands and laid them on the bench. Then, he couldn't find one when we were done. Surely you remember? You made a big show of looking for it, sending us all over that tennis court to find it."

"And my shame deepens. I can't believe my audacity."

"I never told you, never told anyone, but I took the sweat band."

"You what?"

"I nicked it and put it in my bag, and I kept it all this time."

"That's kind of gross, Mary Jo." I wrinkled my nose. "So, what was the other thing you kept?"

"Oh, it was a napkin he used at the Labor Day party."

"That's even worse."

Mary Jo nodded, her eyes round and solemn. "I know. It was wrong to keep those things, especially after he started dating someone else. Then, last night after I got home, I was so angry at him, I put them in the sink and lit them on fire."

"My goodness!"

"I did. Burnt 'em right up. Had to open the window and let the smoke out and everything."

"It's a wonder no one called the fire department," I said under my breath.

"So now I'm done with Tim Elton."

"Thank heavens. Now you can move on with your life, and find someone new, if you like."

Mary Jo glanced off into the distance. "Oh, I doubt I'll date anymore—not for a long time, if ever."

"Please don't let Tim Elton ruin other men for you. They aren't all like him."

"Oh, I know that," Mary Jo answered, a dreamy smile on her face. "But I think I've been ruined for all other men anyway." Her voice faded to a whisper. "By someone else."

I couldn't help it; I just stared at her. Could she have changed her feelings so fast? Just this afternoon, when Frank rescued her after she'd been run off the road? Should I say anything, acknowledge my suspicions? No, probably not. But then, Mary Jo might think me uninterested, and that might result in hurt feelings. It would be unpardonable to interfere, believe it or not, I had learned that much, but maybe I could encourage Mary Jo, without directing her. Merely say what I could to support and encourage but not push her specifically. Yes, it was best to keep the lines of communication open between friends.

I cleared my throat. "I think I know what, or rather whom, you mean by that."

Mary Jo's eyes were round with surprise, and her cheeks colored. "Oh my goodness! I had no idea I was being obvious."

"You aren't, but then I know you both quite well."

"I would never presume he would be interested in me. Never! It's so complicated, and because he's so far above someone like Tim, I've resigned myself to spending my days admiring him from afar. He's the kindest, most gentlemanly...not to mention handsome. Just so good, you know?"

"It's no wonder really, that you feel that way about him. What he did was so thoughtful, so chivalrous."

"Oh my! Yes! When he came to my rescue, I was overwhelmed. I didn't know what I was going to do, and then—there he was. It was like magic."

"No more. We won't discuss it now, because I am done with fixing people up. So, we'll just let things take their natural course. But I would advise you, think carefully, and watch him for any signs that he feels for you what you feel for him. I don't want you to get hurt again. Perhaps it seems to you like an unlikely match, given his personality, his position, and his family, but stranger things have happened."

Mary Jo leaned over and enclosed me in an embrace. "You're the best friend a girl could ask for. Truly."

"Aww, thank you!"

"Happy graduation, Emma!"

THIRTY-THREE

MAY 29, 1976

George had always heard that a young man's thoughts turn to love in the spring. Unless that young man happened to be Frank Weston. According to Emma, he had told her that a young man's mind turned to baseball, not love. However, Tim Elton was a young man who certainly had love on his mind. Unable to sell his house, he had left an apartment in Frankfort and returned to Highbury. He and Edie announced their engagement the week after Derby, which had the effect of placing Edie Bitti at the center of every conversation in that tight-knit community. The happy couple were planning a Christmas wedding, and discussions about the event were lengthy and varied: Should Edie pick sleek satin or georgette for her wedding gown? Wedding flowers should reflect the Christmas season, but she simply couldn't stand those blasted poinsettias. Perhaps lilies?

Edie told anyone who asked (and many who didn't) that she was anticipating a visit from her sister sometime in June. Last year, Ima had married into an old Southern family, the Sucklings, so she would surely have some good wedding advice. Ima's own wedding had fifteen hundred guests in the First Baptist Church in downtown Atlanta, and the reception was spectacular enough to earn a half-page write up in the *Atlanta Journal-Constitution*.

George Knightley's thoughts had also turned to love, but not concerning his own prospects. Any thoughts along those lines, he kept private. His recent musings about love concerned someone he never thought he'd give a flying fig about. Lord knows, he'd never been a fan of Frank Weston's, but lately, he noticed Frank paying an inordinate amount of attention—behind Emma's back, of course—to Jane Fairfax. Knowing he was hardly objective where Emma was concerned, George tried to reason it away, yet it niggled at his mind.

It started at a picnic hosted by the Westons. Emma wasn't there when George first began to suspect this...familiarity existed between Jane and Frank.

Juanita had asked for the day off. John Woodhouse woke disoriented that morning, and the change in his caregiver's routine only discombobulated him more. Therefore, Emma was late to the picnic, and she missed the frequent stares full of admiration that Frank beamed at Jane as she sat and chatted with Nina. What was the man doing? Jane was engaged, and even though Mike Dixon's filming schedule had delayed his return from Ireland until August, it didn't change the fact that she was unavailable. Even more alarming was that the attention appeared to turn Jane's head. George could have sworn he saw not just one, but several secret looks and smiles, exchanged between the two of them. Was he imagining it? Or, he joked to himself, had he spent enough time with Emma that he was seeing attraction that wasn't really there?

After Emma arrived, he cornered her as she sat alone with a glass of wine and a plate of cheese and fruit at Nina's picnic table.

"Where's Frank?" he asked, glancing around the yard.

Her eyebrows shot up in surprise. "I do believe that's the first time you ever expressed any interest in the whereabouts of 'Frat Boy' as you call him."

"Hush, Emma Kate." George took a guilty glance around the yard. "Not that I care what he thinks, but I wouldn't hurt Bob's feelings for the world."

Emma stabbed a strawberry with her fork and waved it as if waving George's concerns away. "Of course you wouldn't." She grinned. "You already own the world. But you don't have to worry. Bob isn't anywhere close enough to hear you. He, Jane, Frank, and Helen went for a walk in the woods over that way." She pointed with her now empty fork. "That little wilderness adjoins Randalls' property, and Bob's thinking about buying it. So, being Bob, he wanted to show it off." She turned at the sound of voices. "And, they're back. Well, some of them."

Bob and Helen joined them at the table, as Nina came out of the house toting a tray full of tall glasses and sweet tea. Helen chattered incessantly to Bob about the "lovely woods" and what a great addition they would make to the already fabulous Randalls' house. Jane and Frank weren't with them, and it was a full ten minutes before they came walking around the side of the house, deep in conversation. Emma was chatting with her aunt and missed the whole puzzling chain of arrivals. George seemed to be the only one interested, and the only one who noticed.

The group sat around under the pergola with ice cold tea, making small talk. Frank crossed his ankle over his other knee, resting his glass there. "Hey, Nina, whatever happened with Dr. Perry and his wife going on that Mediterranean cruise? Did they do it?"

Bob cut in. "The Perrys are going on a cruise?"

"I don't know. This is the first I've heard of it," Nina answered.

"First you've heard of it? You told me." Frank sat up and put his glass on the table.

Nina face was blank.

"Oh, you remember. You told me when I called you from Alabama last month. It was supposed to be a surprise for their anniversary. Mrs. Perry wanted to go for a month but wasn't sure she could get him to stay away from his patients that long."

"I don't know who told you, but I didn't," she answered.

"Sure you did," Frank insisted. "You said how romantic it would be to vacation in Venice and Rome."

Nina shook her head laughing. "It certainly does sound romantic, but I promise, you didn't hear it from me, because I had no earthly idea."

"You didn't?" Frank scratched his head, then chuckled. "I could've sworn I... hmm." He stole a glance at Jane, who was staring at the table. "Guess I dreamed it."

"Sounds like a lovely dream," Helen piped in, holding out her glass to

Nina's offered pitcher for a refill. "Don't mind if I do. Thank you, Nina. You must be a mind-reader, Frank Weston. Yes indeed. Because Mrs. Perry said something to me last month about a cruise to the Mediterranean. She did. I thought she said Caribbean"—Helen gestured with her glass and the tea she spilled dripped down her hand, unnoticed—"because I asked her if she was going to Aruba. But then she said, 'No, Helen, a *Mediterranean* cruise, like Italy and Greece,' and I said, 'Oh! A *Mediterranean* cruise!' And she told us it was supposed to be a big secret. It was that day we ran into her at the post office, wasn't it, Jane?" Helen looked around. "Oh bother, she's gone inside. Jane told Mrs. Perry how glamorous a trip it would be. Mrs. Perry swore us to secrecy, so I never said a word about it until today. You must be clairvoyant, Frank. You dreamed all about it." Helen giggled. "I know I have the strangest dreams sometimes, but they never come true. Well, hardly ever."

"Emma," Bob asked, "you're a vivid dreamer as well, aren't you? Just like Frank?"

Jane came out with a napkin and handed it to Helen, who wrapped it around her glass. "Thank you, Jane, dear! You're so thoughtful!"

George watched Frank and Jane exchange glances over Helen's head. Jane blushed and averted her eyes, trying to hide a smile, and Frank winked at her.

"You know," Helen went on, "I won't swear that I didn't say anything before today, because sometimes—well, you know me—sometimes I let things slip. Maybe you did hear it from me. You know how I am sometimes."

Emma lifted her eyes heavenward, as if praying for patience.

They dawdled around the picnic table until an afternoon squall forced the party indoors to Bob and Nina's family room. Frank fetched a beer out of the refrigerator and plopped down between Mary Jo and Helen, who were discussing the virtues of *The Price is Right* versus *Match Game*.

"You know what game show I really miss?" he asked.

Mary Jo shook her head.

"*Password.* Any of y'all ever play the home version of *Password?*"

"Can't say that I have," Emma said.

"Grandmother bought it for Christmas one year. Pretty cheesy, but it would be a fun way to kill time on a stormy afternoon."

"We don't have it here," Nina said.

"Well, I guess we could make our own version."

"How?" Mary Jo asked.

Index cards and pens were fetched, and Frank made himself the impromptu game show host.

"All-righty then!" He clapped his hands together. "Team One?"

"I'll play."

"Excellent! Do we have a partner for the lovely Mary Jo? How about our local celebrity, Jane the Fairfax?"

Jane shrugged a delicate shoulder.

"Team Two must have the sharp mind of Emma Woodhouse, and we'll team her up with my favorite stepmother. I, as your host, will choose a word to start us off. Knightley, can I borrow your watch? I think it's the only one with a second hand on it. Oooh, Rolex. Nice. Now, Jane, remember, only one word clues or you'll be disqualified."

Mary Jo wiggled in her seat. "I'm ready!"

"And let's…" Frank looked around the group and spotted the band around Helen's straw hat. After showing the card to Mary Jo, he bounded over beside Helen and stuck the card in the ribbon band. "There! Now everyone can read the answer. Don't turn your head, Helen."

"Oh, I won't!"

Emma let Jane give Mary Jo the first clue. "Mistake." Mary Jo shook her head, and after five seconds passed, Emma gave Nina a second clue.

"Error."

Nina shook her head. "I'm not very good at this."

Jane's face got even pinker. "Um…Oversight."

Mary Jo shut her eyes. "I should know it."

"Gaffe," Emma returned.

"Is it…blunder?" Nina asked.

"Ding, ding, ding! We have a winner! Let's switch players around for this next one. We need to split up Emma and Nina. They practically read each other's minds. Jane, you can play across from Emma. And Nina and

Mary Jo, right over there. Perfect." He wrote out another card and showed it to Emma, who laughed out loud.

"I can't believe you," she whispered to him.

George leaned over and read the word Frank had handed her.

Emma began. "Entanglement," she said, barely containing a smirk. Jane looked confused.

"Next," Frank said.

Nina piped up. "Dalliance."

Mary Jo thought, but then just shook her head. "I don't know."

"Infidelity," said Emma.

Nina tried again. "Liaison."

A look of recognition, followed by a cool stare at Frank, swept across Jane's features. "I thought foreign language phrases weren't allowed in *Password*."

"They're not?" Frank rubbed his chin. "Well, I'll be damned. Sorry about that."

"*Affaire de coeur*? What does that mean?" Mary Jo stared at the index card, shaking her head. "I never would have guessed that."

"Well, Jane," Frank said, turning from her to face Emma, "I guess you missed out this time, huh?"

"If y'all will excuse me, I'm just going to..." Jane stood and went into the kitchen.

George watched Jane slip out of the room, and while Frank stood talking with Nina and Mary Jo, he pulled up a chair next to Emma.

"What's so funny about *affaire de coeur*?" he asked quietly.

"What do you mean?"

"The phrase seemed to upset Jane. Why it would amuse you baffles me."

Emma's cheeks reddened. "Oh that. That was nothing, just a little joke."

"Between you and Frank."

"Mm-hmm." She turned to pour herself a glass of tea, trying to end the conversation.

"At Jane's expense?"

"It was nothing, George. Gee whiz, lighten up a little."

He sat back, lost in his thoughts. Private jokes indicated some affection on Emma's side. On the other hand, he couldn't read Frank at all—the spoiled, double-dealing, frat boy! Nor could he understand Jane's about-face from warm, shy flirting to cool, aloof exit in the space of a half hour. Should he say something? Pull an 'Emma' and interfere? Or simply let it play out?

Emma sipped her tea, gazing at Frank and Mary Jo laughing together. She wore a slightly dreamy smile, and George's heart gave a painful lurch. He rubbed his hand across his chest. An intense wave of protectiveness washed over him, an older brother-like feeling, but more fierce, zealous... was it yearning? He loved Emma—obviously he loved her—but this was different. It felt new and raw. It made him want to punch Frank Weston. The thought of Emma being played, being hurt—was too much to bear in silence. He had to do what he could to warn her, to inform her to the best of his ability. He owed it to her after all—his brother's sister-in-law, his former boss's daughter, his own dear friend. His...?

"Emma Kate?"

"Yes?"

"Have you considered the possibility that there might be a thing between Jane and Frank?" he asked softly.

"What do you mean?"

"I mean, have you ever seen anything that would indicate to you that they had some sort of relationship besides a casual friendship?"

"Not for a moment," was her brisk reply. "Jane's engaged, after all, to Mike Dixon."

"I know, but—"

"So why would *you* think such a thing? I know you don't care much for Frank, but you always seemed to think highly of Jane."

"I do."

"Why would *you* question her loyalty to Mike?"

"Do you question it?"

Emma hid behind her glass, gave a little shrug, but no answer.

George brought his hand to his chest again, then lowered it. "I've thought...just recently...that perhaps I saw some...private glances, some interest between Jane and Frank...when they thought others weren't looking."

"Well, look who's matchmaking now? How funny, after all the grief you've given me—and rightfully so, in some instances." When he opened his mouth to contradict her, she laughed and poked him in the arm. "I'm teasing you. But no. Absolutely not. I don't know what you saw to make you imagine such a thing, but I can assure you, it isn't what you're thinking. I know for a fact, that he…well, it's hard to explain, but Frank isn't interested in Jane. At all."

She was so confident. She must know the inner workings of Frat Boy's mind. George's surge of protectiveness devolved into a wave of emotion more vehement and bitter—something that felt very much like jealousy.

"Hey, George! The rain stopped. How 'bout a game of badminton?" Bob called.

George gave Emma one last look. She smiled up at him, wide eyed and innocent…beautiful.

"Sure, I guess." Before he could make an ass of himself, George gathered up his newfound envy and joined his affable neighbor in the back yard.

THIRTY-FOUR

"**B**ob did what?" I asked, horrified.

"Well, what was he supposed to do? Edie spent thirty minutes complaining about how disappointed she was that her sister wasn't going to make the trip up here from Georgia until the fall. She wanted to give them the full treatment: bourbon distillery tour, Churchill Downs, and hiking down at Cumberland Falls." Nina fanned herself with a magazine. "Apparently, the brother-in-law is a big hiker." Nina set the magazine on the coffee table and put a hand to her midriff. "Phew, my stomach's off or something." She took a sip of ice water.

At the Derby party, I mentioned to Bob that I'd never been to the Derby, never even been to Churchill Downs, and he told me he'd drive me up there during the summer. He had a client who knew someone on the board and could get us a special tour, complete with lunch and drinks. Now, I discovered that Bob had also invited Edie and Tim to go along. It turned into a nightmarish prospect, all because two particular people were added to the group. I felt sure Nina had mentioned my dislike of Edie to Bob, and yet he invited the two vipers anyway! There was nothing I could say without sounding mean-spirited and hurting Bob and Nina's feelings; I was roped into going. Spending the day at Churchill Downs with Edie Bitti and her minion, Tim Elton. Yuck.

"Hi, my love." Bob bent over the back of the couch and kissed Nina on the cheek. "What are you two discussing so intently?"

Nina patted his hand. "Nothing. Just the trip up to Churchill Downs."

"Oh. I hope you don't mind, Emma. I invited Edie and Tim to come along. I know it makes our party less cozy, but she was so disappointed about not going up there until the fall. It's always so rainy that time of year. I couldn't go and not take her too. Actually, I think I'm going to rent out a space, invite some more people, and kind of make a business event out of it. Kill two birds with one stone."

I pasted a smile on my face. "Sounds...lively."

"Lively is always better, isn't it?" He patted Nina's shoulder and got himself a beer out of the refrigerator. I nodded in outward agreement and seethed in private. Sometimes, Bob was so open-hearted, he had no discernment. Instead of a cozy outing, I was now just another guest at another business soiree of Bob's.

The hee-haw of Edie's laugh sounded from outside the front door, fanning the flames of my frustration.

Nina rose, slowly. "Looks like the Dynamic Duo is here."

Edie was all left-handed compliments as usual, to Nina, to me, but saved her most dubious praise for Jane: "So very talented, such a waste she's doing local theater when she could be someplace big, like Louisville." For George, she was much more generous: "Such a handsome devil, and so suave, must be that old family gentility." And most especially for Bob Weston: "I'm *so* excited about the Churchill Downs day trip! What a wonderful idea! I'll learn all about the place, and then I can be an accomplished tour guide when my sister and brother-in-law are here. Ima has been to the Derby, of course, but her husband hasn't, and what a time we'll show him when he gets here, won't we, Tim? I just can't thank you enough, Mr. Weston... Why yes, I can call you Bob. We're great friends, after all."

"About the Downs, Edie—I called my friend, and the track has a closed event scheduled for next Saturday. We'll have to move it to the third week in June."

"Oh?" Edie deflated like a balloon and made a similar sound as air escaped her. "Oh, that's a shame. I was really looking forward to going next week. Well, we'll find something to do, I suppose."

"If you're looking for an outing, you could come to Donwell next weekend."

My head whipped around, and George looked as if he wasn't quite sure where those words had come from, but there they were, out in the open. So, with elegant composure, he smiled at the group and said, "Yes, the more I think on it, the more it sounds like a good idea. You should all come to Donwell Farm, tour the barns, eat the strawberries. We're famous for our strawberries."

"To Donwell Farm? Really?" Edie's voice squeaked with excitement. "What a fabulous idea! Just fabulous. I'm so honored—well, we're honored. Tim and me. Right, honey?"

Tim started to answer, but his reply was lost in Edie's raptures. "It will be marvelous, just marvelous! We'll do everything outside, so as not to tromp all over your house. Your mother won't care?"

"I'm thirty years old. I think that's old enough to throw a little party at my ancestral home without my mommy's permission. Besides, Mother won't be there," George answered. "My parents are in Europe until July, when they will spend a week or two with Jack and Izzy and the kids down in Florida."

"Well, I can certainly help out since there's no woman to guide you. Women are natural party designers. You can count on me! You'll let me bring Jane Fairfax, won't you? So, you said next weekend, do we want to have people over on Saturday or Sunday?"

"I'll have to get back to you on which day. I want to check with some friends first—see which day will work best for them."

"Oh, don't worry about having enough people! I'll bring some of my friends, and we'll have a great time."

"I hope you'll bring Tim, of course, but you can leave the remainder of the guest list to me."

She horsey-laughed. "I see right through you, George Knightley! But you don't have to worry about my taste in friends. I'll bring the best sort of people, only the best. Quality people, I promise you. Just leave it all to me, and you'll have a party to remember."

"No," he said, calm but firm. "There's only one woman who will arrange guest lists and party details at Donwell."

"Oh. Your mother, of course."

"When she is in residence, yes. But I was speaking of a younger Mrs. Knightley."

Edie's brow knit as she tried to figure out who he meant. "Isabel?"

George sat back in his chair, crossing an ankle over his knee. "No. I'm speaking of Mrs. *George* Knightley. And until she exists, I'll arrange my own parties, thank you."

"Well, aren't you droll? I'll just bring Jane and Helen then, and Tim. You can decide on the rest. I know the Woodhouses will come, and the Westons, because you're so fond of them."

He nodded. "You're absolutely right, and if I can talk John Woodhouse into coming, I most certainly will. And I'll call Helen's house tonight and invite her, along with Jane and Delores."

"As you wish. A Knightley will always be used to having things his way." She clapped her hands. "Oh, this is exciting! A day at Donwell! We should dine al fresco, don't you think? Goodness, what am I going to wear? It has to be suitable for a day outside but still stylish enough for Donwell."

"Wear what you like, but don't worry about being outside all day. We'll put the food inside, to keep it cool, and away from the six-legged creatures. So, eat strawberries, catch some sun, and then, when you're ready for something more substantial, you can sit in the cool comfort of the house."

"If you need anything, any help at all, you let me know. Promise?"

"Thank you, but I assure you it will all be taken care of."

"What about parking? Will you have enough parking?"

George gave Edie a bland stare. "Of course."

I hid a smile. It had been a while since I'd been to Donwell, but Edie had obviously never been there, if she had to ask such a question. George met my gaze and held it until I blushed and looked away. Fighting an uncharacteristic shyness, I forced myself to look him straight in the eye and announced, "I'm looking forward to this outing of yours, George. Donwell is beautiful this time of year."

"Thank you."

Then, almost as an afterthought, he said, "I hope you'll come too, Mary Jo. I'd like for you to see Donwell."

"I can check with Frank. Make sure he can be there," Bob volunteered.

"Ah...um...yes, that would be...good, Bob." George got up and crossed the room to meet me at the sideboard where I was pouring myself a glass of water.

He picked up a glass and held it out to me to fill for him. Then he leaned near and spoke in my ear. "I'll put a buffet in the dining room because I want people to feel free to stay indoors if the weather's too hot. I was thinking particularly of John. Do you think he'll come? Even if Mom and Dad aren't there?"

"I do. Because I'll talk him into it. It's kind of you to consider him, George. Not everybody would."

"John is important to me. He is my parents' good friend, and my first real boss. And he's your father." He searched her face. "So, he will always be welcome in my home, wherever that might be."

THIRTY-FIVE

JUNE 5, 1976

T he last time I had visited Donwell Farm was the Christmas party
where Jack and Izzy had announced she was expecting Henry. To
my shame, it had been that long ago. George was always stopping by the
house on Hartfield Road, or the Randalls' place if he saw I was there, and
yet I hadn't visited with him at his townhouse or his family home in a very
long time. We were friends, close enough to not need formal invitations,
but I was always so busy, with school, with Daddy, with my sillier activities. I hadn't made time for him, even to check on how he was doing since
his break up with Julianne. And that negligence had to change.

"I have such fond memories of Donwell." Daddy's eyes met mine in the
rearview mirror. "I thought it might be a rather lonely place with Gary
and Joanne being gone, but..." He leaned over to look out between Mary
Jo and me, sitting in the front seats. "Today, it looks busy and happy. I'm
glad I came with you."

His words made me pay attention to the front grounds as we drove
The Lane (and it was officially called "The Lane," marked with a street
sign and everything). Fruit orchards lay about the grounds to each side;
the drive itself was lined with cedars, oaks, and maples in a way that
suggested they'd been there forever. Closer to the house, the landscaping
became more formal, well-trimmed boxwoods outlined the circular drive.

In the center of that circle, now filled with parked cars, there was a carefully tended rose garden. The house itself looked as if it had grown there of its own volition over the generations. Our house on Hartfield Road was a two-story Georgian-style, almost antebellum-looking, with its tall Doric columns and porches on both floors. In contrast, Donwell Farms mansion was rambling and massive: rich, red brick with white trim and green shutters; long, generous windows and a decorative spire—much like the ones that adorned Churchill Downs. It was a stark reminder that George's family wasn't just rich or steeped in tradition, like my own—the Knightleys combined money, family, and tradition into a genteel sort of wealth that was becoming more and more rare. Jack Knightley had his faults, I mused, but they were minor in comparison to what he brought to the Woodhouse family. He was good to Izzy and the children, and he had generations of class and elegance behind him that would give Henry and Taylor, and any new Knightleys that might come along, a legacy to be proud of.

I pulled up in the circle and saw George Knightley, Esquire, *Master of All He Surveyed,* standing at the door, waiting for us. Butterflies floated from my stomach into my chest and up into my throat. What can I say? He was a compelling sight. I'd have to be blind not to notice. He wore khaki pants and a polo shirt in a sky-blue that I knew would bring out the blue in his eyes. I stopped the car and got out to get Daddy's wheelchair from the trunk, and George pushed off the door frame, walking down the steps with a big smile.

I waved at him. "Good morrow, Professor! Don't worry about our carriage here. I'll move it as soon as I get Daddy inside."

"Leave it, Emma Kate," he said. "The others can drive around it, or I'll get Benton to move it, if need be." He lifted the wheelchair out of the trunk and expertly opened it.

"I brought the chair in case he got tired or wanted to explore the grounds some more. He's been doing really well with the cane for short distances though." I shut the trunk.

"Good thinking. Good morning, John."

"Hello, my boy, hello. Beautiful day for a picnic. Perfect for young people to scamper around outside."

"Indeed, it is." George wheeled the chair to the open car door, where Mary Jo was helping Daddy stand. "Hello, Mary Jo, how are you this fine morning?"

"I'm well, Mr. Knightley, thank you."

"Oh, we're not at the office today. I think you can call me George, won't you please?"

"Of—of course." She blushed. "You have a lovely home. George."

"Thank you. Let's go in this way." He led them around to the side entrance and muscled the wheelchair up and over the lower door threshold. "Almost everyone is here. They're out in the back yard, walking toward the strawberry patch. Except for Nina. She's on the veranda. I've got a place set up for you there too, John, or you can go inside, if you'd rather."

"I'll sit with my sister-in-law. We can catch up. I don't get to see Nina nearly as much as I used to when the girls were smaller. Before she married."

"Good enough," George said.

Nina was relaxing in a chaise lounge, eyes closed, a glass of lemonade in her hand.

"I've brought you some company," I announced.

Nina's eyes opened, and she smiled. "Hello, my lovelies! I thought you might be Frank. He hasn't made an appearance yet. Makes me worry a little."

"Oh, I'm sure he's fine." George locked John's wheels while I helped him into a deck chair.

"It's that sports car of his. I don't think it's very reliable."

"Every young man thinks he needs a sports car, right, George?" I asked. "If I remember, you had one yourself once upon a time."

"I did, and I may again, at some point. You never know."

"Men do love their playthings," I joked.

"Frank worries me though." Nina sat up on the side of her chaise. "He drives too fast sometimes."

"Maybe something held him up. How's his grandmother doing?"

"Up and down, he says. She's at home now. The rehab hospital discharged her with home health services. That could be why he's late, I guess. His mother seems to call him most every day now with some complaint or other. I think she wants him to go back to Alabama."

I poured my father some lemonade from the pitcher left on the table.

"Do you think I should have all this sugar, Emma?" he asked in an anxious voice.

I squatted down so I was eye level with him. "Here's what I think. I'll bet this lemonade is made with wholesome ingredients, because nothing but the best would be served at Donwell, right, George?"

"Absolutely. Made from scratch this morning."

"And I think this is a party, and you should enjoy yourself," I said. "I know you love lemonade, Daddy. So, you should have a glass and share some conversation with my amazing aunt Nina."

"Okay. You always know what's best, Daughter."

"I do—and don't forget it." I kissed him on the head and left him in Nina's care.

Mary Jo and I wandered back through the yard. Beyond the kitchen herb garden and the ornamental plants lay the strawberry patch, where the others were clustered in groups, picking berries, and snacking on a few. The lull of relaxed conversation rested on the breeze.

Edie's shrill laugh rang out, and I braced myself for the verbal onslaught I knew was to come.

"Isn't this the best, Emma? Just the very best! Strawberries are like manna from heaven! And the day is just beautiful! All this glorious sunshine!"

I tossed Edie a pasted-on smile and retrieved my berry basket from Mary Jo. We worked down from the others, but my gaze alternated between the rolling fields beyond the berry patch and George, who was busy helping Helen and Delores pick berries. I lifted my face to the sun, letting its warmth sift through me, right down to my toes.

"When you decide to get married," I said to Mary Jo, "don't do like Edie and marry in the dead of winter. Marry in June—it's a tradition for a reason—and then you get to have strawberries in season for your wedding."

Mary Jo ducked her head and reached under a plant to pluck a berry or two. "I doubt I'll ever marry."

I stopped short. "Why not?"

Mary Jo shrugged. "It's complicated."

"I had no idea you were thinking along these lines already, Mary Jo."

"I have been thinking about it lately." She shook her head. "I mean, like I told you, there is a man, and I...I've come to admire him, so much. He's everything a woman could want: handsome, friendly, kind."

That same rush I felt when I introduced Nina and Bob coursed through my veins. "Yes, I know. So, what's the problem?"

"Honestly? He's so far...above me. I think the chances of him feeling about me the way I feel about him? Well, the chances just aren't very good."

Edie stood up, her hand at her lower back. "Lordy, bending over like this is hard on a person who isn't used to farm labor. Oh look, there's Frank Weston—hello, Frank! We're over here!" she called, waving. He acknowledged her with a nod and started toward them.

I watched Mary Jo watch Frank's approach. Tamping down my excitement, I weighed my words carefully so as not to raise hopes but still encourage her. "You know, Mary Jo, times are changing. Even in the so-called old families, people don't put the same emphasis on a person's background the way they used to. It's one of the best things about being a modern woman—the freedom to rise through the socio-economic strata and chart your own path, based on who you are, not what your family has. That freedom extends to men as well, meaning that the object of your affection may surprise you."

"But he's..."

"No, don't even tell me who he is. But I will say"—I nudged Mary Jo with my elbow—"your taste is impeccable."

Mary Jo giggled.

"But seriously, you're right to be cautious. Just let his words, his actions be your guide. If he acts interested, you'll know what to do."

Mary Jo sat back, munched a berry and considered. "Okay. I'll do that. Who knows what could happen?"

"Exactly."

"Lordy, it's hot," Edie complained from the other end of the strawberry patch. "This sun is brutal! I love strawberries but picking them is tedious. Cherry picking is much better—because you're working in the shade."

"Or apples would be best of all," said Helen. "Because you have shade and autumn weather. Best of everything. Except if it rains. Rain would put a damper on things, wouldn't it? Get it? Damp-er." She giggled at her own joke.

"I'm going to have a seat in the shade while you all finish up. Come on, Jane," Edie demanded.

"Oh yes, Jane, we can't let you get too much sun." Helen turned to her mother. "Jane is so fair. She burns so easily. Maybe you should go with Jane and Edie, and sit in the shade too, Mother."

I saw Jane's shoulders stiffen at Edie's command, but she went along, with Helen and Delores following behind her, Helen chattering all the way.

"Mary Jo," George called. "You like horses, don't you?"

"I love them."

"I thought I'd heard that. Come over here. They're out in the field behind the barn this morning. Come see." He put one foot on the fence slat and beckoned her. They stood together, watching the foals with their mamas, engaged in what looked to me like a deep conversation. He glanced over at me and grinned sheepishly. I waved at him, remembering that there was a time he would hardly talk to Mary Jo about anything outside of work, and now, look at him. Conversing easily with an employee with whom he had almost nothing in common.

By the time I finished filling my basket and joined the group in the shade, talk had turned to Jane's plans, now that *Camelot* was finished.

"I really think you need an agent," Edie was saying. "The Coles' Theater is all well and good, but there's no reason for you to waste your summer in local productions when you could get work elsewhere that would really build your résumé. My brother-in-law in Atlanta has a college friend who hires talent for cruise ships. I could get you in touch with him."

"I don't think I'd like working on a cruise ship. I might get sea sick."

"Nonsense! The cruise ships of today are so big, you can hardly feel them move at all. That's what Ima says, and she's been on several cruises.

The ships hire all those singers and dancers to do shows now. It's the latest thing. It would be perfect for you. You'd be a shoe-in with your Broadway experience."

"I appreciate you thinking of me, but I'm really not looking for any long-term commitments right now."

"I know Mike isn't coming back to the States until August. That's two months away! What do you plan to do with yourself all summer, Jane?"

"I'm not worried. I'm sure something will turn up."

An awkward silence settled over the group.

"So, who's ready for some lunch?" George asked, redirecting everyone's attention.

He and Mary Jo walked on ahead of the rest, as he pointed off to the right at the barns, then to the left toward the creek. "That's the main farm. There are other parcels of land for crops: soybeans, corn, and of course, tobacco. It's a big responsibility, seeing to all of it. My manager is retiring as of September 1, and I'll need to fill that position right away, because I rely heavily on the farms' manager to help me run things efficiently. He lives right here on-site, in that guest house at the end of The Lane. You passed it on your way in."

"Will he stay at the house after he retires?"

"No, he's going to live with his daughter in Texas." George glanced back at me, hesitated, but then went on. "So, uh, the guest house will have a new tenant soon."

"It's a sweet little house," Mary Jo answered.

I put myself toward the middle of the group, letting the conversations wash over me and eavesdropping on the lot of them. While George seemed to be giving Bob Weston a run for his money in familiarity and oversharing, Edie continued her insensitive barrage on Jane's summer schedule. Helen nattered on to her mother about nothing in particular. Delores, in turn, ignored her, and Frank seemed to be getting more and more agitated by the minute. *All this intrigue, these social currents winding one way and then another. Good gravy, I could write a book!*

I spent lunchtime talking with Nina and Mary Jo and fussing over Daddy's plate. Guests came and went, snacking, talking, wandering about the common rooms before heading back outside. There was some talk about a stroll down by the creek. I watched Mary Jo and Frank's interactions and had to admit, her confidence had increased ten-fold from when we first met and I tried to foist icky Tim Elton on her. Mary Jo didn't seem to be tongue-tied like before nor were her feelings too obvious. Perfect.

I turned to my aunt. "Nina, why don't you go with the others? You've been in here all day, and the weather's beautiful outside. Go enjoy the sunshine."

"Are you sure?" Nina glanced over at Daddy, looking through a photo album.

"I'll keep him company," I said.

"Thank you, honey. You're a sweetheart."

"Look Emma!" Daddy called out from across the room. "Did you see Gary and Joanne's pictures from Japan? I didn't know they went to Japan. When was this? How long did they stay? All that rice can't be good for you."

I gave Nina an indulgent smile and squeezed her hand. Then, I settled in next to Daddy to look at photo albums until he dropped off to sleep with his feet up.

Walking into the kitchen with Daddy's plate and a couple of glasses, I nearly dropped them when Jane Fairfax came blowing through the back door, slamming it behind her with a show of uncharacteristic temper. She stopped short, and we stared at each other, both of us startled.

I recovered first. "You okay? I thought you went with the others down to the creek."

"I did. I did go. I—I—I'm glad I found you, Emma."

"Pardon?" I asked, genuinely surprised.

"Yes, when the others come back and ask after me, could you tell them I went home with...with...a headache? Please? And give Helen and Aunt Delores a ride home? Because I'll have the car."

"I don't understand, Jane."

"I just need to get home, I think."

"Okay, but if you're not feeling well, let me find someone to drive you."

"No! No, thank you. I can drive myself, honest. I'm used to taking care of myself—I lived all alone in New York after all."

"You're all flushed. Shouldn't you sit? Or let me get you some water or something. You don't look well at all."

"I'm not. I'm not well." Tears filled Jane's eyes, but she gasped out a laugh, not of humor but a release of emotion. "It sounds crazy, but I'm just exhausted, not physically but... All I need is some time and space to put myself back together. I'll be fine, but I need to get..."

I got it then. The one-two punch of Edie Bitti trying to get her an unwanted job, on top of Helen's constant drivel, had finally pushed Jane to her limits. Honestly, I didn't know how she had stood it even this long. I myself would have blown my stack weeks ago with the lot of them.

"Sure, no problem. We've got Helen and Delores, and I'll tell them you were feeling sick and you left. Don't worry about a thing."

Jane leaned forward and put a hand on my arm. "Thank you. Thank you so much." She looked at me with this unusually earnest expression— and here I thought nothing ever got under her skin.

In a blink of an eye, she was out the front door.

Not five minutes later, Frank also stormed in and slammed the door. Annoyed, I stepped into the foyer, pulling the French doors closed behind me.

"Shh, Frank. My father's sleeping."

"What? Oh, sorry." He didn't sound sorry though. "Christ on a crutch, it's hot."

"I thought you walked to the creek."

"I did. Damned nuisance. Nothing to see down there. Did I mention it's blasted hot?"

I didn't bother with a reply, and he began to pace the foyer. "Wanted to get my sunglasses out of my car. Hiked up that hill from the creek. Pretty much missed the whole party anyway because my mother called again this morning about Grandmother. Drove like a mad man to get here, just to have the fun stuff already over with. All I got to do was walk down by the creek. Probably got ticks and chiggers all over me."

"I don't think George allows ticks and chiggers at Donwell Farms," I teased, trying to lighten his mood.

Frank shot me a foul look and kept pacing.

"Come on, Frank. Calm down." I turned to go back into the sitting room toward Daddy's gentle snores. "And quit your pacing. You're just making yourself more hot and miserable."

"Maybe I'll just leave. I should have stayed home, but Dad and Nina made such a fuss about me coming over here. Looks like the party's over. At least from your dad's point of view. And I saw *Jane the Plain* leaving the premises like a bat out of hell."

"Frank," I admonished.

He shrugged.

"There's a lunch buffet in the dining room."

"Not hungry."

"Maybe you'll feel better if you eat something."

"Too hot to be hungry."

"Suit yourself then." I sat down on the sofa opposite Daddy and picked up the latest issue of *Southern Living* magazine.

After a couple of minutes, he followed me in with a plate of sandwiches and fruit. I raised an eyebrow, and he grinned sheepishly.

"Guess I was hungry after all. Is there Heineken?"

"In the fridge."

"What a whiner!" I mumbled to Daddy's sleeping form. *That moodiness would drive me bats. Good thing Mary Jo is so even tempered.*

Frank came in and sat beside me, putting his beer on the coffee table in front of us and picking up the album Daddy had been perusing before his nap.

"Where's this?" He pointed at the photo of Mr. And Mrs. Knightley in Italy.

"Lake Como."

"Nice." He took another bite and flipped the pages of the album. "I should go to Italy. That's what I should do. Backpack through Europe. I've never done that. Every guy ought to do that at least once."

I laughed. "You never will. Your mom and grandmother would never allow it."

"You never know." He smiled, more like himself. "Maybe I'll take them with me."

"I'll believe it when I see it."

"Maybe I'll take you with me."

"We'd get lost or distracted and never make it back."

"Are you going to Dad's Churchill Downs thing on the nineteenth?"

"I suppose." I sighed. "It's not Italy."

"No, but it's somewhere that's not Highbury."

"I thought you loved Highbury."

"It has its attractions. Is your friend Mary Jo going along? To Churchill Downs, I mean."

"Yes, I think everyone that's here today will also be there at Churchill Downs."

"I've seen the Downs. It was named for some great-uncles' cousins, twice removed or something. I'll be bored and grumpy."

"We'll get you a mint julep, and you'll be fine."

"No, I'll hang out with you girls. You'll be my mint juleps. I'll go, because I'll be even more grumpy if I know you're there having fun without me."

"Well, pick your poison then. Grumpy here or grumpy there. Makes no difference to me."

Voices on the veranda signaled that the others had returned.

"If it will make you happy, I'll go to Churchill Downs," Frank told me as he took hold of my hand and swung it back and forth.

"I'm glad. You'll enjoy yourself. I know it. I won't allow you to do otherwise."

THIRTY-SIX

The day of the Churchill Downs outing arrived with an ominous array of clouds, gray and purple, like a gigantic bruise hovering over the Earth. The group gathered at the old Randalls' place and split off into cars. George offered to drive Helen, who couldn't stop talking about how treacherous the weather had turned, and Jane, who lived in the city, and didn't do much driving at all. Frank then stepped in and said he would drive Mary Jo and me.

"But Frank," I said, "you drive a two-seater, and counting you, there are three of us." I thought perhaps he would relegate me to George's car. It would mean traveling with Helen, God help me, but I thought I could take one for the *Mary Jo and Frank team* so they could be alone together. Before I could suggest it, however, Frank offered to drive my car instead.

"I can drive my own car," I protested, but he wouldn't be swayed.

"If I let you drive in this weather, and in downtown Louisville—now, what kind of gentleman would I be?"

"A modern one that gives me a little credit for driving my own car?" I whispered to myself. No one heard me but George; his lips twitched in amusement.

Bob was already in Louisville, having driven up that morning to make sure all was ready. Tim and Edie announced if they had known about the carpooling, they could have carried a passenger, but they were in his sports car and had no room. There were no comments as no one wanted to ride with them anyway.

Frank held his hand open. "Give me your keys, Emma Kate. I'll bring your car around." I scowled at him and dropped them in his hand. I might not have relented, but he threw me off when he called me by my nickname. It was like nails on a chalkboard. No one ever called me Emma Kate, except for George Knightley. He made it sound more elegant, like Anne Marie from *That Girl* and less like Billie Jo from *Petticoat Junction*.

Frank was back in a couple of minutes. "Your chariot, my lady." He opened the passenger side door with a sweep of his arm. After I was inside, he opened the door for Mary Jo, casting a look over his shoulder at the crew in George's new Volvo. As soon as he got in the car, however, and he had no audience but the two of us, all that chivalrous charm faded away. I didn't think I'd ever seen him so glum, not even the day of the strawberry party.

About half way to the city, the skies opened, and lightning sprayed across the sky like fingers, followed by the crash of thunder, and a torrent of rain.

"We sure picked a good day for the racetrack," I said, hoping to get some conversation out of either one of my companions. Mary Jo stared out the window, saying nothing. I turned to Frank.

"Huh?" he answered.

"Never mind." I reached over and turned on the radio.

The fissures in our group persisted once we reached Churchill Downs. Bob tried to mix and mingle, include us all in one tour, but he had other guests to attend to, and the Highbury crowd never really coalesced. I was disappointed in the entire outing. Instead of a charming tour of the racetrack in glorious sunlight with good company, and steeped in the ambiance of wealth and tradition, I was stuck inside, sitting with a vapid Mary Jo and a Frank who kept sighing and scowling and fidgeting.

Bob did have us all together at a big round table for lunch, and Frank perked right up, enough to flirt with me, almost shamelessly. Enough for

Edie and Tim to exchange sneering looks, and for George to look somber by comparison. Enough for Jane to just stare at her plate.

I smiled and laughed, not because I was really enjoying myself, but because flirting was the best substitute I had for the real fun I had anticipated. It was all surface buffoonery, all shallow interchanges, and while my vanity was pleased, I myself was not.

"You did right, persuading me to come along today," Frank said to me as we sat after lunch, drinking coffee. "I really would have missed out. Last Sunday, I was ready to hit the road for Alabama."

"You were a grouch last weekend," I answered. "I'm not sure what your problem was, but I was nicer to you than I should have been. You certainly worked hard enough to make me beg you to join us."

"I was not a grouch," he pouted. "I was hot and tired."

"Then Alabama would not have been a good solution. It's even hotter down there."

"Then where should I have landed? Tell me, oh wise one, for I'm at your command." He winked at me.

"Well, that's for you to decide. I have no hand in it."

"You might have more of a hand than you realize."

I laughed, a bitter sound, even to my own ears. "Such flattery. If I had so much influence on you, you wouldn't have been so cross last weekend at Donwell."

"Oh, sweet Emma, you influence all things around you, including me, from the moment you cast your attention upon me. I saw you first on a winter day that was as dreary as this summer one, and you brightened everything around you."

I glanced around, aware for the first time that no one else was laughing or joining in the banter. "Hush, you're being ridiculous," I whispered to him. "And the rest of the table is not amused."

"Well, why not?" Frank raised his voice and infused it with a mocking tone. "I saw you on a cold, gray February morning, and I remember it as if it were yesterday." He leaned over and poured some cream in my fresh cup of coffee. "May I?"

I nodded, and he whispered as he poured. "What will liven up this party, do you think? Any kind of silly small talk is preferable to this silence." Louder, he announced to the table. "My friends, this quiet has gone on long enough. Emma, who as we know is mistress of us all, demands to know what you all are thinking. Speak up, now!"

Helen laughed. Mary Jo smiled. Edie scowled. But George spoke up first.

"At this moment, I'm not so sure Emma would want to know what we're thinking."

His words made me squirm, but I tried to laugh it off. "I'm not sure I would want to know what you all think either. Well, maybe one or two of you might be kind to me." I glanced over at Bob and Mary Jo.

Edie turned to her fiancé. "My mother always taught us to respect other people's privacy. As far as their thoughts go. Yes. But she was from another generation. Perhaps that kind of discretion is perceived as old-fashioned these days."

"Your mother was quite right, I think." Tim leaned toward her. "Some young women in this *Me Generation* will say most anything. Best to just gloss over it as if it were a joke."

"She has thrown down the gauntlet," Frank whispered as he handed me a sugar packet. "So, I'll up the challenge." To the table he said, "Very well, then. Emma waives her right to know your most intimate thoughts, and instead, will settle for some clever contribution to our table's discussion. Doesn't matter what it is, as long as you can entertain Emma, at least as well as she says I entertain her. One golden nugget of sparkling conversation. Or two moderately interesting ones." He laughed. "Or three mediocre topics will do, in a pinch."

Helen giggled. "Oh, I could do that. Three mediocre topics. No problem for me. Not at all."

My temper finally escaped, disguised under the cover of flippant, careless words. "Oh, I don't know, Helen. Do you think you could limit yourself to only three?" I grinned without humor at Frank and Mary Jo. Frank was staring across the table, not paying attention. Mary Jo smiled uncertainly. Helen sat, speechless for once, mouth open. After several seconds, she closed her lips, her face turning beet red.

"Oh, yes. I'm sure. I often talk about mediocre things, don't I, Jane?" Helen didn't wait for an answer. "I must stomp on everyone's last nerve, or she wouldn't have said…. Well…"

"Sparkling conversation topics," Bob cut in. "Emma would be the perfect person to start one."

Some of table laughed nervously, and George, wearing a stern expression, spoke up. "Well, that relieves the rest of us of the burden of conversation. Perfection, apparently, has already been discovered."

"Well, this is all well and good, but I can't think of a thing, sparkling or otherwise to add." Edie stood up and laid her napkin beside her plate. "Oh, look. It's stopped raining. Let's go out and walk around a bit, Tim."

"Of course, honey. I know I wouldn't have anything to say that Emma would like to hear. We'll go enjoy the sunshine."

"Come with us, Jane." Edie reached out her hand.

"No, thanks. I think I'll finish my coffee." But she didn't touch it after they left.

"There goes the happy couple," Frank said. "How long have they known each other anyway?"

"Since January 10," Mary Jo answered.

"Not long, then. A whirlwind romance. How lucky for them, that it worked out. Whirlwind romances, you know, don't always have such happy endings. After some time, when people really start to know each other, they discover little habits and quirks that maybe aren't quite as appealing as the qualities they saw in that first blinding rush of attraction. Many a man has made a commitment based on a quick infatuation, and then lived to regret it."

Jane surprised the table by speaking up. "It happens. I've seen it all the time in the theater crowd. Both men and women can succumb to infatuation, overwhelmed by the emotion and drama of the theater. I guess it could happen in a variety of places—at an ocean resort, on a cruise ship, during a semester abroad." She looked around the table, finally resting her gaze on Frank.

"Go on," he said softly.

"Oh, nothing really." She shrugged. "Just that people rarely regret those affairs over the long term. There's usually time for the lovers to come to their senses before they do anything permanent. Then they put the infatuation in its proper place—an affaire de coeur, a passing phase, a fling— nothing more. And then, they each go on with their lives, sadder but wiser."

I stared at her, not sure whether I had ever heard that many words come out of her mouth at one time. Frank stared at her too, a cool assessment, before turning back to me.

"Well then, in order to avoid that depressing scenario, I'll ask someone sensible to choose when it's time for me to settle down." He put his elbows on the table and leaned toward me. "How about you?"

"How about I what?"

"You pick the perfect girl for me. After all, you did the job for Dad— and a splendid job it was. I'm sure I'll love the gal, whomever you pick. Find her. Train her up. Make her over."

"In my own image, I suppose?"

"Exactly. I'll go backpack through Europe, then fly back to New York and find the perfect job. When I return in a year or two, you can present me with the perfect woman."

"I accept the challenge."

"I like 'em lively. And blonde, too, if you can manage it."

"I'll keep that in mind." I wondered if Mary Jo had ever considered going blonde.

Jane stood. "Helen, let's go outside and get some air. Would you come with me?"

"I'd be happy to, honey. I was going before, but this is better. We'll catch up with Tim and Edie. There they are." She pointed out the window. "Oh no, that's not them. Goodness, she doesn't look anything like Edie. Bless me."

George followed them after a minute, and I remained at the table with Bob, Frank, and Mary Jo, until even I grew tired of Frank's flattery. It was an almost manic level of ingratiation that soured my stomach. I excused myself and wandered aimlessly out by the stables, in the cool quiet left by the rain. The stable smell soon returned with the heat, and I turned back, preparing myself for the ride home with Frank and wondering which Frank would be my companion on the return trip: flirty, nuisance Frank, bad-tempered, sullen Frank, or hopefully, Southern-charmer Frank would magically reappear.

I saw him, waiting for my car alongside Mary Jo, and quickened my pace, when a hand caught mine from behind. It was George Knightley.

"Emma," he said in a low voice, leading me slightly off the path and out of sight of the others, "can I talk to you for a minute?"

"Sure, Professor. What's up?"

"We've known each other forever, all your life, in fact, and that connection brings with it a familiarity that you've probably endured rather than enjoyed all these years. But when I see a wrong, I have to try and make it right."

"Whatever are you talking about?"

"That dig you took on Helen. How could you be so mean to her? I didn't think you had that kind of malice in you."

I stopped, and I felt the red flush of shame creep up my cheeks. I tried to dismiss it. "Oh that? It was just a joke."

"I've heard you say that phrase 'just a joke' more than once recently—in situations I didn't think were all that funny."

"Good gravy! Helen is so harebrained sometimes! How could I help saying it? Besides, it wasn't that bad. She probably didn't even catch my meaning."

"Oh, she caught it all right. She's talked about it non-stop ever since she and Jane left the table. Talked about how patient you must have been with her all these years when she annoyed you so."

"Come on, George. I know she has a good heart, but as good as she is, she can be pretty ridiculous."

"That's another word I've heard you say more than once recently. Look, I know Helen has her issues. But no matter how she tries your patience, she doesn't deserve to have you embarrass her—laugh at her—in front of people that might be influenced by your treatment of her."

"I—I..."

"I don't know what put you in such a mood today but lack of kindness and grace for a woman not as capable or as fortunate as you are? That's beneath you, Emma, the real you, the Emma that I know and lo—I could hardly believe what I saw today. It was like watching a polite society train wreck. I don't even want to imagine what your parents would think if they had heard you."

Tears began to well up behind my eyes. "George—"

"Look, I hate this…this…lecturing you, as if you were still a little girl. But you need to hear this, and it seems I'm the only one who has the gumption to tell you: you are not a girl anymore. You are a young woman, an adult, blessed by Providence with beauty, intelligence, and grace—and your actions should reflect those qualities." He put his hands in his pockets and looked off into the distance. "And now, I know you're angry with me, but I speak only out of lo— As your friend, Emma Kate." Car doors slammed and voices called from the entrance. "I've been your friend forever and a day, and friends tell each other the truth. Even when it hurts or angers. I hope…" He hesitated. "Someday, you might remember that." He didn't look back at me. "Let's go home."

I followed him in silence, my own emotions rioting just below the surface and threatening to boil over—not in anger, but in embarrassment, followed closely by soul-bruising remorse. He walked me to the car and handed me in without a word. Mary Jo and Frank chatted all the way home, but I didn't chime in, didn't even listen. My feelings consumed my thoughts.

George was mistaken about me, that's all. I wasn't a mean person! I loved my family, my friends. I looked out for them. I helped them. I wasn't cruel. Was I? Maybe not cruel. That was too harsh. But selfish? Yes, as I thought back over the last several hours, I could admit I'd been selfish and vain all day. Or, maybe all my life.

I was half-way home before I realized I hadn't even told George goodbye or thanked Bob for the outing. The opportunity for thanking Bob came easily enough. I found him before I left Randalls' for home. But George went straight to his car and left with only a brief word to Bob. I tried—twice—to call his townhouse and attempt to explain, apologize, something.

But there was no answer.

On Monday, I stopped by Knightley and Woodhouse. Mary Jo was cagey, which was completely unlike her. No, George wasn't in the office today. No, she wasn't sure why not. No, she wasn't sure when he would be back. Or why he wasn't answering his home phone. I left after five minutes, feeling uneasy and annoyed. What right did *she* have to keep George's whereabouts from *me*?

By Thursday, I was at my wits' end with unanswered phone calls. I even inquired after him at Donwell, but the staff hadn't seen him all week. In a panic, I took a third trip in as many days by his townhouse and was relieved to see his Volvo in the driveway.

I knocked, but there was no answer. Music blared from inside the house. Concerned, I tried the door and found it unlocked. I made a mental note to fuss at him about the danger of leaving his house open. He lived downtown after all. I pushed the door open.

"George?" I called, shutting the door behind me with a soft click. The foyer was completely dark, but I could see the waning evening light coming from the living room window. An orange glowing ember at the side of the sofa drew my attention. That was when I saw the wisp of smoke.

"George!" I gasped, hurrying forward, but he couldn't hear me for the loud music. I rounded the end of the couch and there he sat. The lit cigarette was in the ashtray and his head was in his hands, obscuring his face.

Sensing movement, his head snapped up. Somehow, he recognized me in that almost dark room. I reached over, turned off the stereo and turned on a lamp by the chair. When I faced him again, we just stared at each other for several seconds. Then, he smiled.

"Hello, Emma."

"I've been trying to call you for four days. Where have you been? I was worried sick."

"Sorry. I've been in Ocala, checking on a new client for the firm—a pair of brothers who have a farm there in addition to one they own around here." He picked up the cigarette, leaned back and took a drag off it, leaving it between his fingers when he was done.

He rubbed his chin thoughtfully with the other hand. "I didn't know anyone would be checking up on me, or I would have left a clearer message about my whereabouts. The client wanted to remain anonymous until they met with us, so I told Mary Jo to just say I was out of the office."

"Well, that explains that."

"She didn't give me up?"

"No, but I kept looking until I found you."

He chuckled. "Miss Woodhouse always finds her man."

"Yes, she does." I walked over to him, lifted the cigarette out of his hand, and stubbed it out in the ashtray. Part of me wanted to chide him for smoking, but I judged this wasn't the time. I sank down on the couch beside him. He stiffened and turned his back to the corner, so he faced me head on.

"So, why are you here, Emma Kate?"

"A couple of reasons. One was being worried, of course."

"I'm fine, as you see."

I gave him a dubious once over. "Mm-hmm, I see. I also wanted to apologize to you for my behavior at Churchill Downs last weekend."

He shook his head and started to speak.

"No, let me finish." I didn't want to be interrupted. Saying sorry was hard enough; admitting I had been mean to someone was a new, uncomfortable experience—uncharted territory and nigh impossible to travel. "You were right to tell me off. I should never have said those things to Helen. It was wrong of me. I have apologized to her, even though I'm sure after last weekend, you think I don't have a kind bone in my body—"

"You're wrong, Em. I think you're capable of great kindness. I'm glad you're making amends with Helen. She's nuts about you."

"Well, personally, I think she's just nuts—"

"Emma," he drawled, but there was an undertone of amusement to it.

"But she's family, and I do love her. I told her that too. It may take some time to earn her forgiveness, but God love her, she'll forgive pretty darn near anything. We should all take that particular page out of her book, I guess."

He reached over and put his hand on mine, then retrieved it quickly. He stood up and went over to the sideboard, poured himself a glass of Woodford Reserve. He tilted the bottle at me. "Drink?"

I shook my head. He had never offered me whiskey before.

Looking down into the glass, he said, "I'm glad you're here, actually. I wanted to talk to you before I left."

"You're leaving again?"

He nodded, then took a drink and closed his eyes. Never had I seen him look so distressed, and I found it distressed *me* to no end.

"I'm going back to Ocala. I'll be gone for a few weeks. These men are important clients and they need to be handled personally. We were going to send William Cox, but I told Jack I'd go instead. I'm on a red eye tonight, in fact. While I'm there, I'm going to drive over and visit Jack and Isabel at their beach house on the Gulf."

"Oh."

"Do you have anything to send Izzy and the children? Except for your love, of course, which nobody carries."

He was hiding something. Now that I was paying attention to him, I could see the tension written all over him. "Is something the matter, George?"

He took another drink. "No. I...no."

"I'm your friend. You can tell me. I won't tell a soul if you don't want me to."

"You're a good friend Emma, and I appreciate that." He stood there a minute, swirling the amber liquid in his glass. "You know, I think I owe you an apology too, maybe more than you owe me one."

I sat up straighter and frowned in confusion. "Whatever for?"

"I think perhaps, these last couple of years, I've been awfully hard on you, starting with when you returned home after your father's stroke. It just all sort of came to a head that day at Churchill Downs."

I waited, not able to trace his line of thought.

"Don't you want to know why?"

"Only if you want to tell me."

He crossed the room and sat in the chair next to the lamp I'd turned on a minute ago. "I didn't realize it at first, but I think it's because sometimes, you remind me of someone I knew in California."

"Oh. Annoying tag-along co-ed?"

He chuckled. "You don't annoy me, honey. Not at all." His face grew somber, and he took a gulp of whiskey, as if fortifying himself for something unpleasant. "No, the girl's name was Dorothy. She was from Kansas, if you can believe the irony of that."

"Sometimes I think a person's name is bound to their fate. Like George means farmer—which you are after a fashion, and Knightley reflects your chivalrous nature." I smiled at him, trying to lighten his mood. The smile he returned made me feel sad instead, so I tried again. "If you tell me her last name was Gale, I'm going to laugh and not believe a word you say."

"No, her last name wasn't Gale. Her father was a doctor, and she grew up in a small town and lived in a beautiful two-story house with a beautiful yard and a white picket fence. She had a beautiful mother and three beautiful sisters."

"Did you visit her there?" My curiosity about this mysterious woman was overwhelming. Who was this girl who affected George so much he was smoking cigarettes and drinking liquor when he thought about her? Suddenly, out of nowhere, my heart constricted into a painful knot.

"No, I never did. I just heard her speak of them all so often that I could picture exactly what they were like."

"Was she beautiful too?"

"She was a pretty girl—I always thought she looked a little like Linda Ronstadt—but more than that, she was a smart girl, a girl with convictions."

"And you fell in love with her." My chest still felt tight; it was an extremely unpleasant feeling and I wiggled around and tried to take deep breaths. George seemed not to notice.

"I didn't, but I might have, if we had known each other longer." He settled back in his chair, cleared his throat and went on. "You have to understand the time and place, Emma Kate, in order to understand the story."

"Then tell me. Make me understand." I stayed perched on the edge of the couch, every nerve on alert. George rarely spoke about his college days.

"It will seem odd to you. You grew up sheltered and safe, and so did Dorothy. But then you went to a small women's college in the South, before you came back home at nineteen, and she went far away—where big things were happening that no one had any control over. It was freedom without limits, without cost—or so we thought.

"I met Dorothy in a political science class my junior year. She was no shrinking violet, that's for sure. She had strong opinions on many things —interpretation of the First Amendment, the McCarthy hearings, the blacklisting of actors, Vietnam, the women's lib movement.

"I'd never met a woman quite like her, beautiful and articulate, passionate and intense. She was so self-assured, so confident, so sure that she knew how things should be, and yet, there was a soft, kind side to her too, an almost child-like fascination with all the world had to offer. I guess infatuated is the right word for how I felt about her. Women like that—their intelligence stirs men's intellect, their beauty stirs the libido, and their innocence—real or imagined, stirs the protective instinct. It's a powerful combination.

"I wouldn't say we dated, because she didn't date in the traditional sense. We 'hung around' together. We partied together." George looked away, as if pained to say the next words. "We slept together."

"I see."

"Like I said, it was 1968 at UC-Berkeley. Casual relationships were the order of the day—free love."

"What happened?" I was anxious to get away from this part of the story.

He laughed, but it wasn't George's laugh. It had a harsh, ugly sound to it. "I found out that free love meant that she was free to love other men too. I also found out I'm not good at sharing women, so I gave her an ultimatum—me or her *freedom*. She didn't choose me, so we stopped … seeing each other? Is that a good euphemism for it?"

"I don't know."

"Anyway, we lost touch after that. The fall of my senior year, I was walking in downtown San Francisco with some friends, and this girl walked up to me, dressed almost in rags, tried to put a flower in my hand, to sell it to me I suppose. She reeked of marijuana smoke and unwashed person.

"It was her, Emma. I couldn't believe it. It was Dorothy. I invited her to go with me into the bar, and we talked for over two hours. She told me about quitting school, about living 'on the road,' about getting to what was real, what was important, but the sparkle was gone from her eyes. I tried to get her to come with me, but she refused, saying she had the life she wanted with her friends and her new experiences. I gave her my phone number and said if she ever changed her mind and needed a hand, I would help her.

"A few weeks later, I got a call in the middle of the night from the San Francisco Police Department. Apparently, she'd been picked up for carrying drugs and drug paraphernalia, and she asked me if I would come and bail her out.

"She stayed at my place that night, crashed on the couch in a drug-induced stupor. When I woke up the next morning, she was gone.

"A couple of weeks later, she called again. I went, took her to a coffee shop, tried to sober her up, and get her to go back home to Kansas—go anywhere but back to the self-destructive life she was living. She said she'd think about it. Said she probably would if she had the money. So, I gave her some cash. Looking back, I realize I should have bought her the ticket instead, but what can I say? I was younger then, and a lot more naïve.

"The third time she called, I got angry. I told her she was using me and I wasn't going to help her if she wouldn't help herself. She yelled at me for being part of the problem with society, and then she cried and said she was sorry. And then she offered to *thank* me with her body—if I came and got her out of jail. I hung up."

He shuddered. "The next day, your chivalrous Knightley changed his phone number. It's hard to admit—that I was that angry, bitter...unfeeling."

I sat in silence, waiting. Then—

"Whatever became of her?"

He looked at me, as if seeing me for the first time since he began his tale. "I have no idea." He drained his glass. "From the look on your face, I'll bet you're offended that you remind me of this girl."

"I have to admit, yeah, I am a little offended."

"I certainly don't think you would run off and get all strung out and sleep around for bail money."

"Flatterer."

His lips quirked up for a second. "It's the way she was when I first met her that reminds me of you. She had your same wit, your tenacity when you believe you're right, and she shared your innocent view of the world. What happened to her later was the drugs, not her. But she was so sure she could handle everything that she didn't even realize when she was into things she couldn't handle. If I think I see you heading down a path that might be over your head, even in a small way, it makes me a little crazy, because I lo—" He stopped and shook his head, as if to clear it.

"What are you trying to say?" My voice was gentle, inviting him to tell me everything that was on his mind, just lay it all out there, once and for all.

"Be careful of Frank Weston, Emma."

I sat back, surprised. "Frank? Whatever for?"

"I know he's not a hippie pothead at Haight-Ashbury, and he's an old flame of yours, and he's Bob Weston's son, but something about him doesn't sit right these days. There are many ways a man can lead a woman astray. Will you take care, based solely on your trust in me?"

"Of course. There is no need to worry, but yes, I promise to take care, alright?" I walked over and plucked his glass off the end table and took it to the sink. His eyes followed me from the kitchen back into the living room. I stood before him, hands on my hips.

"Good old Frank has raced off to Alabama again anyway."

"His grandmother took a turn for the worse?"

"She's fine, or so he says. I don't know what he's about, running down there at his mother's and grandmother's every whim. Why would he do that when he has a father and stepmother right here in Highbury, who would let him be exactly who he is, and not demand that bizarre supplication of him? Nina told me, his grandmother constantly threatens to cut him off, whenever he commits what she considers an infraction." I paced in front of the couch. "Everybody's off to somewhere, it seems. Jane Fairfax took off for Manhattan."

"Really?"

"She said she was going to get an apartment, wait tables, and start auditioning again. I called to see if she wanted to go to lunch, or wanted help packing, or help arranging transportation for that monstrosity of a piano in the parlor."

"What did she say?"

"No, no, and no." I sighed. "If I didn't know better, I'd think she was avoiding me." The sarcasm dripped from my voice. "Helen says she's heartbroken to be leaving. I'm actually a little concerned about Jane's well-being, but she's made it quite clear she wants no help or kind gestures from me, so I guess I have to accept her refusal and hope she takes care of herself."

"I thought for sure she would have waited until Mike Dixon returned to go back to New York."

"Yes, me too. But there's no figuring out Jane Fairfax."

"I guess not."

"Now, what time is your flight? Why don't you let me drive you to the airport instead of trying to call a cab? They're almost like phantoms in this town, virtually nonexistent. And you're in no shape to be driving a car after chugging that bourbon. How many did you have before I got here?"

"Just one or two, Miss Woodhouse, but I'll take you up on your kind offer. Before I go, though"—he got up and opened a drawer in the sideboard—"sit back down a second. I got you a present."

"Oooh, I love presents."

"I know." He handed me a little square velvet box.

I opened it and looked up at him, surprised and delighted. "It's a charm for my bracelet." I ran my finger over the silver trinket. "A key?"

"Yes. I debated with myself about what to choose. You've already added a few, like the graduation cap, a piano, a heart—"

"Daddy gave Mama the heart. So, why a key?"

He squirmed a little and cleared his throat. "The thing about you, Emma Kate, is that one symbol doesn't cover all the things you do or all the things you are. That's why this fits you so well." He reached over and touched the bracelet on my wrist. "The artist's palette charm is for your painting phase. The house represents the household you run. The camera is from your stint as a photographer. And so on. I got you the key because…well, to remind you…"

"Yes?"

"You have the key to your own life, to your future. You can open any door you choose, do the things that matter to you, be the person you aspire to be. You have that power—just because you're Emma Katherine Woodhouse. I don't want you to ever forget that, so that's why a key."

I was stunned that he knew how much words like that would mean, and happy that he spent time thinking of me. And I was so proud that I could call George Knightley my friend.

"I just wanted you to always remember."

"I will, George. I promise." This felt like a goodbye. Why was he telling me goodbye?

"Let me get my bag and load it in your car." He started to get up and move toward the door.

"George?"

"Yes?" He turned back, a world-weary look in his eyes.

"I'm sorry about your friend."

"Thanks, Em."

"It was a tragic waste of a life."

"Yes, it was."

"George?"

"Yes?"

I stepped close to him, so he could read the truth in my eyes. My hand rested on his arm. "Whatever happened to Dorothy wasn't your fault. You know that, don't you?"

"My head knows that, but there are times when my heart wonders if I could have done…I don't know, something else for her."

"Well, my heart is sure that you are not to blame for any of it, including your outrage when she used you." My voice shimmered with indignant, protective anger.

"You're a good girl, Emma." He paused. "No, I take that back. You're a damned fine woman, and I'm glad I know you."

My heart filled to the brim with warmth. He stroked my cheek with the back of his fingers and caressed my jawline with his thumb. He brought his face next to mine. I caught the faint scent of tobacco, smothered under the bourbon whiskey. Then, he did the strangest thing…

With soft, warm lips, accompanied by the gentle brush of his mustache, he kissed my cheek.

George turned and picked up his bag. "Let's go, ma jeune et jolie chauffeuse," he said, and he was out the door.

THIRTY-SEVEN

June dragged into July, and my life settled into what I presumed would become my own version of normal life, post-college. Daddy's health remained stable, so I pondered what to do with myself, now that I had fulfilled my parents' wishes and finished my education. No job really appealed to me, at least not one I could get with my credentials. I thought about graduate school—a law degree? Counseling? Business? In a fit of boredom, I decided to renovate the guest house beside the pool. Then, I re-landscaped the pool area and ordered new patio furniture.

Word came from Nina that Frank's grandmother Churchill had passed away. Nina and Bob became more forgiving of Rosemarie Churchill for constantly badgering Frank during his visits to Highbury. It seemed less and less like Rosemarie was jealous of Frank visiting Bob, and more and more like Mrs. Churchill's health had been worse than anyone realized. Frank planned to remain with his mother for some unspecified length of time, helping her settle the estate, although I figured the lawyers would carry out the bulk of that task. The old matriarch was gone, and Nina expressed some relief that Frank would no longer be subject to the whims of a woman who was not in her right mind— most likely from her illness, bless her heart—who threatened to cut poor Frank out of her will and then welcomed him back into the fold just as impulsively.

Nina's other news was more joyful. She was expecting a baby, and she and Bob were over the moon about it. I was thrilled for them and anticipated the arrival of my little girl cousin—I just knew the baby would be a girl—in February.

July Fourth was the two-hundredth birthday of the nation, but there seemed to be no real Bicentennial celebrations anywhere. I watched Highbury's annual fireworks display from my back veranda, my father by my side. He spent the half-hour beforehand grieving that he would be exhausted tomorrow but that he might as well stay up because there would be no escape from the noise.

"I hope Juanita doesn't go to Lexington to watch the fireworks, like she talked about. It's bad enough that Nina and Bob went, and Nina in her condition too. Fireworks are so dangerous."

A shower of red, white and blue burst open, arcing over the night sky. "Oooh," he exclaimed. "Look how pretty!"

I felt the let-down of a lackluster Bicentennial season. I'd enjoyed the build-up to July Fourth: the Bicentennial minutes on TV, even the history and government *School House Rock* on Henry and Taylor's Saturday morning cartoon shows. But the Bicentennial reality, like so many realities these days, was anticlimactic.

All that boredom came to a crashing halt at 10 a.m. on July sixth with a call from Bob Weston.

"Emma? Can you come over?"

"Sure I can. I'll be right over. What's up?"

"Oh, no, don't drive yourself. I'll come and get you."

Alarm bells went off in my head. "What's wrong, Bob?" My heart began to pound. "Is it Nina? The baby?" Then, "No, you wouldn't leave her to come and get me if it were the baby."

"No, no. No. Nina and the baby are fine."

"Then what is it?"

"I promised I would let her tell you. She wants to break it to you. I promised."

Fear threatened to steal the air from my lungs. "Something's happened to Izzy? Or the children?"

"Oh, no, honey! Nothing like that, I promise! It's just…well, it's unfortunate, is what it is. Just unfortunate. But don't fret. It's nothing so tragic. No, not tragic. I guess it could be a good thing. It could."

"Bob, you're still scaring me." I racked my brain to think what could rattle him so. "Is Frank all right?"

"Hmm? Oh, yes, he's fine. Better than fine, but...I just talked to him on the phone. Not half an hour ago."

Perplexed, I waited for Bob to arrive, but try as I might, I couldn't get a sensible word out of him. He ushered me through the house and into the sunroom where Nina sat with a cup of herbal tea. The morning was humid, the sun hot, and the only sound was the rise and fall of cicadas in the woods next to Randalls'.

"Here she is, Nina. I've brought her to you, so you can be at ease now. I'll just leave you to it then. I'll be right in the kitchen if you want me." He leaned down and kissed his wife's cheek and said in a low voice. "I didn't say anything. Just as I promised. I've left it all to you. Women are better at this sort of thing."

He left, and I sat down next to her. "Are you okay? Bob said you and the baby were fine, but you look pale. Did you call the doctor?"

"No, I'm fine. I guess he really didn't tell you." She gave me a wan smile. "I'm surprised he didn't blurt it out. I guess I should have more faith in him."

"It must be about Frank, but given that Bob says he's fine, I can't imagine what it could be."

"Yes, it is Frank. He called us this morning."

"Well, that in itself is a surprise. Frank is no morning person, from what I can tell."

"Even more so, as where he is right now, he's three hours behind us—in Las Vegas."

I started to make a joke about debauchery in Las Vegas, but Nina was looking at me with such anxiety, I held my tongue.

"Frank called us this morning to tell us that he went to Las Vegas to—Emma, he got married!"

"Frank eloped?"

"Yes, and it's even more bizarre than any of us could imagine."

I could imagine some pretty bizarre stuff: a truck stop waitress, a show girl, maybe even a transvestite.

Nina covered my hand, squeezed it gently. "He ran off with Jane Fairfax!"

I bolted to my feet. "He did what?" I began to pace back and forth, the refrain of "Not again! Not again!" racing through my mind as I thought of poor Mary Jo. "You're kidding!"

"I wish I were, honey. I know you're shocked. Bob and I certainly were."

"But Jane is engaged…to Mike Dixon! And has been for several months."

"Frank confessed he and Jane had an affair last fall when they were both in New York, right about the time Mike left for Ireland. They kept it secret from everyone—for obvious reasons, I guess. Neither their friends nor their families had any idea at all. Frank told Bob that the affair was the real reason she came home last winter. She wanted some perspective, to help her decide what to do—and whether or not she wanted to break it off with Mike."

"The piano," I whispered. "A secret admirer." Then louder, "So that's why he appeared so suddenly in Highbury after putting off his visit for so long."

"Emma," Nina admonished me.

"It wasn't to see his father and stepmother but to pursue his illicit love affair. What a piece of work!"

"We were surprised, of course, and a little disappointed in her—that she didn't break off her engagement beforehand. That would have been more proper."

"Huh, well, yeah, you're right about that."

"But Jane is a lovely girl, and we like her, so his choice of wife isn't really the problem. We were mostly concerned about who else might be hurt by this turn of events."

"What?" My mind was on Mary Jo, so I was confused, wondering if Nina had guessed Mary Jo's feelings. Then I saw the compassion, the pain in Nina's eyes. I knelt at her feet. "Oh, Nina! Please don't fret! I know you might have thought perhaps Frank and I had something going. But I promise you, even though we went out a time or two, I never thought it would go anywhere."

"Really, Emma?"

"Honest. When he first came back, well, I was a little interested, I guess. He's a cutie pie. And there's not too much to choose from around here."

Nina laughed. "Not for you anyway."

"But that was only at first. Rest assured, Frank and I are friends, nothing more."

"You have no idea how relieved I am to hear that. Bob will be too. I must confess, we secretly entertained the idea that you all might work something out. It would have been lovely to have two people so important to both of us, always in our lives, part of our family."

"I am just fine, so don't give my feelings another thought." I stood up and started pacing again. "But really, Nina, there's no excuse for his behavior. Coming here after avoiding you all for so long and then flirting with me in front of everybody the way he did. Sure, I didn't read too much into it, but I might have. He didn't know if he was leading me on or not. Shameful, really!" I stopped pacing, my eyes widening in horrific realization. "And Jane! To have to sit around here and watch him behave that way toward another woman after they had that affair! And have nowhere to go—stuck here playing Guinevere...and I even went to the theater with him to see it! Went out with him, right in front of her." I covered my eyes. "No wonder she wouldn't even see me before she left. I can't blame her!"

"Frank told Bob that Jane had broken it off with him. He came here to find her because he wanted another chance. It's really quite romantic, when you think about it."

I turned and stared at my aunt, agape. "Romantic? Nina, he treated her without any respect. Flaunted another woman in front of her to try and make her jealous. He used me to do that!" That thought rankled more than any other. "Made her miserable to the point she left her family and went back to New York alone!"

"He didn't know she'd gone back. He told his father he didn't know, and when he found out—"

"How?"

"Pardon?"

"How did he find out?"

"Oh, I don't know. A letter or something. A call maybe? Anyway, sometime after his grandmother's funeral, he went after Jane. He told her he loved her and asked her to marry him straight away. They left for Vegas the next day."

My head stopped spinning, so I sat down. "Of all the crazy, stupid stunts. Married in Vegas. Probably by an Elvis impersonator. Strip joints everywhere around. Without her family or his or any of their friends. Just crazy."

"He seemed so contrite about what had happened. He wanted to make it right—wanted to marry her—as soon as possible. I felt a bit sorry for him, Emma. He's suffered the past few months. That much was obvious to Bob."

"*He's* suffered? What about *her*? She's the one I feel sorry for. Everything seems to be just fine for him now. What did his mom say?"

"She seems okay with it. She's taken a vacation. I guess her mother's death took quite a toll on her, and Bob says she's kind of an emotional person. Frank said his mother didn't seem to mind one way or another."

"So, no one knew about the affair back in New York? Do you think poor Mike Dixon had a clue?"

"None, as far as I know. And for what it's worth, the gossip is that he's taken up with an Irish girl starring in the movie he's directing now."

"Theater types." I rolled my eyes. "Drama, drama, drama. Well, I guess we'll all get used to it eventually. I still say they should have been upfront with everyone and had a decent length of engagement and a discreet wedding either here or in Alabama. I can't believe I'm saying this, but even Tim Elton and Edie Bitti did a better job of this engagement business. And when I think back on things I said to Frank, to Jane—me and my big mouth! But then again, how was I supposed to know they were harboring this big secret?"

"I've thought back on the things I said myself, wondering if I've said anything that would hurt them, but I can't think of anything I said to either of them that both Frank and Jane might not have wanted to hear."

"Lucky you. Your only blunder was telling me that George had a thing for her. I've stuck my foot in it countless times—with both of them."

Bob peeked in the door, and Nina beckoned him forward, whispering to me, "Put him at ease, honey. He's been so worried about you."

I turned, pasted on a bright smile, shook Bob's hand and then embraced him. "Congratulations! Jane will be a lovely daughter-in-law. Frank is a lucky, lucky man!" *The jerk.* Of course, I left that last remark in my head, and after many assurances of my best wishes while Bob drove me home, I flopped down on the couch in my quiet, peaceful living room.

How on earth was I going to break this news to Mary Jo!

Breaking the news ended up being easier than I ever anticipated. Thinking it might be best to tell Mary Jo when others weren't around, I invited her for lunch on Saturday, and fretted for the rest of the week how I might broach the subject. Poor Mary Jo had been the innocent victim of my matchmaking schemes twice now, and it brought to mind how George had once told me, "Emma, everything you do does not help Mary Jo, just because you wish it would." True, I hadn't planted the idea of Frank Weston myself; Mary Jo came to her feelings about him all on her own, but I *had* encouraged her, and what a disastrous result! I should have known better, and now that I really thought it through, Frank and Mary Jo were almost certainly a match made in hell.

My own, unintentional role in the whole debacle made me angry, mostly at Frank, but also at myself. At least I could let go of my guilt about Jane. Miss Fairfax had her happily-ever-after—or at least a happy-for-now. Jane's behavior before she went back to New York made perfect sense. She saw me as the other woman being thrown in her face. My offer to help pack appeared to be gloating, my gifts of muffins and herbal tea like poison. But there was nothing I could do about the past. I could only move forward, and moving forward meant helping Mary Jo.

It struck me as ironic that I was playing the same part that Nina had played with me earlier in the week. If only this conversation would have the same outcome! I was heartsick on Mary Jo's behalf.

The doorbell rang, and I called to Mrs. Davies, "I'll get it."

I opened the door to Mary Jo's smiling face. "Hi, Emma!"

"Hi."

"It doesn't seem like I've been out here in forever. How's your dad doing?"

"He's fine. We can go see him in a minute, but let's just have a seat first. I have some news."

"News?" Mary Jo's brow wrinkled. "Oh! I guess you mean the news about Jane Fairfax. Don't that just beat all? Her and Frank, I mean. In love all this time, and no one knew! Well, you probably did. You read people so well."

This is bizarre! She doesn't seem the least bit upset. I spoke slowly, as if to let the words sink in. "Jane Fairfax and Frank Weston ran off to Vegas."

Mary Jo nodded. "Crazy, huh? I'm starving. What's for lunch?"

"And got married."

"I know. Bob came in the office yesterday and told me the whole story. He said it was kind of a secret, but I could talk to you about it because you already knew. Did you know about them dating before they came here to Highbury?"

"I think 'dating' is quite the euphemism for it. Of course, I didn't know! I'm your friend! If I had known, I would have warned you."

"Warned me? Whatever for?"

"I never would have encouraged you if I knew Frank was in love with someone else."

"Why would I care about...? Oh! You thought I was interested in Frank Weston?"

"Aren't you? I mean, weren't you?"

Mary Jo laughed. "No way! I've never been interested in him. Not one bit. The man I was talking about, well you said I shouldn't tell you who he is, but you talked like you knew. He's much more than Frank Weston ever thought about being. So much more—gentlemanly, perfect, educated, handsome..." She sighed, a dreamy sound that was eerie in its familiarity and flashed me back to adolescence in a terrifying moment of clarity. I swallowed loudly around the lump in my throat.

"Mary Jo, are you talking about"—I swallowed again—"George Knightley?"

"Of course." My face must have shown my horror, because Mary Jo continued in uncertain tones. "At first I thought Mr. Knightley would never consider me as dating material. He's my boss after all, and I know what you said about dating men in the office. But then you said I had such good taste, and I know how close he is to your family, so I thought that meant you thought it possible. Even probable."

"But you said the man came to your rescue. Frank was the one who helped you!"

"When?"

"At the graduation brunch, when that guy ran you off the road on the way to the country club."

"Oooh! I see what you were thinking, but no, I meant when Mr. Knightley—I mean George, I'm supposed to call him George outside the office—when George asked me to dance after Tim embarrassed me at the Derby party. That was when I realized what a true gentleman he is. That was when I fell for him."

"Oh, dear Lord, what is to be done about this?"

"Done about it? Something has to be done about it? I don't get it. If I liked Frank, it was okay, but if I like George, it's not?"

I tried to keep my voice calm. "It's just that you and George are so different...in—in personality. And he's your boss. And—"

"But you said I had wonderful taste. You said that stranger things had happened. Oh dear, I hope people won't try to keep us apart! If George doesn't mind the differences in our ages, in our backgrounds, or that he's my boss, then why should anyone else?"

Deep breaths, Emma! I purposefully steadied my voice. "Do you think George...feels the way you do?" I cleared my throat to keep my voice from squeaking. "Returns your feelings? Has he told you so?"

"Not in those exact words, but yes, in little ways, I do think he has let me know that he likes me. And he took the time to show me all around Donwell, as if he hoped..." Mary Jo blushed. "You know, maybe it might be my home too, someday."

My heart stopped. And the truth, the entire delirious, heart-wrenching, maddening, soul-weakening truth buried me in a landslide of sadness and loss. Mary Jo couldn't marry George and live at Donwell! That was simply impossible, because it was now painfully obvious that the only woman who should marry George Bryan Knightley was...Emma Katherine Woodhouse!

I listened as Mary Jo told me how George had been kinder to her recently. He was more interested in what she thought about the inner workings of the office and had taken her suggestions. He'd even discussed a case with her on the phone and trusted her to call a client and get information he needed, not just sit there and direct calls to the attorneys and paralegals. The last time he was in town, he'd brought her coffee, just the way she liked it, for no reason at all!

As I thought back over the last couple of months, I realized I had also noticed George's softening opinions toward Mary Jo. Stupid me! I had even rejoiced in them as evidence of his broadening horizons, being more accepting of my friend. After all, he had commented on the pleasant conversation he shared with Mary Jo at the Derby party.

"That night was the first time I'd ever thought of Mr. Knightley, you know, in *that* way, but I would never have held out hope for him—never would have thought it possible—except for you. I remember at your graduation party, you said to let his actions guide my feelings, and I have taken your advice. I've watched and waited and hoped, and now, I think he might feel the same way about me that I do about him."

I know not how I got through lunch. It was torture to listen to Mary Jo talk incessantly about George, as if now that the topic was opened, the floodgates had burst. After the meal, Mary Jo suggested we take a walk around Hartfield Estates "like we used to," but I put her off, saying the bulldozers had destroyed our favorite path in order to put in a clubhouse for the subdivision. It was partly true. Another route could have been found, but I wanted out, away from everyone, but especially away from Mary Jo.

As she left, Mary Jo turned to me and asked in all earnestness, eyes wide and uncertain, "Do you really, honestly think I have a chance with him?"

I paused, took in her pleading expression, and felt my heart beating in my throat. This was the day for terrifying epiphanies, and the next one came rolling on in. I knew nothing about anyone, not really, because you never know someone until...well, you know them. I'd been wrong so many times—about Tim, about Frank and Jane, about Mary Jo—why would I know anything about George's heart and mind? He gave out nuggets of his thoughts and feelings like the chocolates he passed out at Valentine's Day (and just as infrequently). I'd unwittingly played a role in his reluctance to share with me, I knew that. With my schemes and opinions, and my arrogant self-assuredness that I knew what was best, I had effectively shut him out. He didn't share personal thoughts with me because there was no point. If we disagreed, I ignored him or stomped all over his advice, and then did what I wanted anyway.

Mary Jo's hopeful face brought me back to the present. How could I, not knowing George's true heart, treat Mary Jo with the respect due a friend and still be truthful? How could I be a friend and answer? Perhaps the way George would, if he were in this position? What was a truth I could tell Mary Jo, something I knew, for a fact, about George Knightley?

"Well," I began, "I don't know the answer to your question, not really."

"Oh." Mary Jo's shoulders slumped and a sigh escaped her.

"But I've known George Knightley all my life, and one thing I know for sure is that he is the last man in the world who would intentionally lead a woman to believe he cared for her more than he really does."

"Oh!" Mary Jo's smile bloomed. "Oh, well then." She threw her arms around me in an embrace I did not return, but the lack of enthusiasm didn't dampen Mary Jo's happiness one iota. "Thank you, Emma! Thank you for lunch, and thank you for everything!"

Mrs. Davies came up behind me as I watched Mary Jo's car drive away.

"You want I should clean up them dishes, Miss Emma?"

"What? Oh, yes please. Clean them up, toss them out, I don't care."

Mrs. Davies frowned at me. "You okay, child? You're all flushed."

"I'm fine." Panic stole over me as I realized I was about to lose it all in front of the housekeeper. "I—I—I'm taking the dog for a walk."

"In this heat? Why don't you wait until evening, when it cools off some?"

I shut the door and hurried to the back to retrieve the leash. "Will you tell Daddy?" I called back.

"Sure, honey, but..."

"Where is it? Where is it?" I opened two kitchen drawers and checked the mud room hooks for Maude's leash. "Screw it! We'll go without the stupid thing." I slammed a drawer shut. "Maude! Come here, girl! How about a walk?" Paws clattered over the floor as Maude raced toward me, joyful barks punching through the air. I buried my face in her fur, starting to feel the tears behind my eyes. Emma Katherine Woodhouse never cried, *never!* Except for today.

For a while, I wandered aimlessly, through the Hartfield Estates, looking at the Tudor-style mini-mansions, the mountains of earth where split-levels would grow, the empty lots where Maude ran free, chasing after moles and squirrels, and Lord knows what else.

Okay, first things first. I rubbed my pounding temples. *Well, as unlikely as it seems, the Earth has just tilted on its axis, and I'm in love with George Knightley. When and how did this happen? And how did it happen without me even realizing it?*

I had entertained the thought of dating Frank back in the winter, when he first reappeared in Highbury. And he used me to make Jane jealous—the horse's ass—but I wouldn't think about that right now. It was too embarrassing. I remembered all the subtle comparisons I'd made between George and Frank, some voiced and some only in my head. So, it seemed, perhaps, that Frank Weston had been the catalyst, the key that turned the lock on my heart. It was Frank's many foibles and impulsive, immature qualities that made me begin to discern what I wanted in a man—and what I didn't. In holding Frank up against George, I'd unintentionally made my choice. I just never saw him as my choice before, for a lot of reasons. His brother was married to my sister. For years, he had that *Woman of the Month* club. Then there was Julianne Ryman, whom I liked, even though I envied her. I thought it was her ambition, her drive I envied, but now, of course, I knew it for what it really was: base jealousy. I envied her because, for a time, she had George.

By every quality I could think of, George Bryan Knightley was the gold standard of men. In my mind's eye, I saw his sky-blue eyes crinkling when he smiled, felt the warmth of him holding me as we danced. *Oh, that was heavenly!* I heard his honey smooth voice singing to baby Taylor as she cried. Etched in my memory was the way he stood at the door of Donwell to greet me: confident, elegant, powerful, but also kind and gentle as he helped me with my father's wheelchair. A dreamy sigh escaped me, and in spite of my torment, I giggled at myself. How many times had I heard that same George-inspired sigh float out of some girl's mouth in my younger years?

In fact, I'd heard it only today—from silly, stupid Mary Jo Smith!

No, that isn't fair. Poor Mary Jo—her heart will be broken if he doesn't care for her that way, as she says. But, could he care for her that way? She has that open temper he says he likes, sure, and she's pretty, I guess, but Lord! So much inequality of mind! They have nothing—nothing—in common! His intellect runs circles around her. They'd never be able to have a decent conversation. And she has no knowledge of what it takes to manage Donwell Farms. She'd be no help to him at all.

But honestly, would that matter? George could find sparkling conversation with his friends. He could hire someone to help him manage the farms and the other properties. He could hire any damn thing he wanted—he was George Knightley after all. Men in his circumstances fell in love with their secretaries all the time—so many times—it was a laughable cliché. Was it possible he just plain loved Mary Jo?

This is my fault, all of it! Through my arrogance, my hard-headedness, I have done a terrible thing! And if he loves her, I have no one but myself to blame. I am responsible for the demise of my own happiness. What I did was worse than doing nothing, because in trying to help, I've done harm instead. If I had left Mary Jo to her own devices, she'd probably be dating Robert Martin right now and feeling happy as a clam about it. But no, I had to shove her into my society, put her with people that made her uncomfortable, all for my own vanity—so everyone could see my precious charity case. Befriending her wasn't wrong in and of itself, if we had had any real hobbies or interests in common. But I tried to make her someone she's not, and now look what has happened! I've let this awful, unequal affection bloom right under my nose. Mary Jo in love with George! Or worse, George in love with Mary Jo! Little, chestnut-headed, simple-minded half-Knightleys running Donwell Farms into the next generation? And probably running it in the ground! What will become of it? What about Henry and Taylor?

The tears came in a flood as I kept walking and turned down the state road. Sweat poured off me now, and my head hurt from squinting in the sun. *Why didn't I think to grab my sunglasses?*

I knew I was dear to George. How could I not be? Our histories had intertwined again and again since childhood: Daddy and Mr. Knightley starting the law practice, the marriage of Jack and Isabel, the children who were so precious to both of us. I had grown accustomed to a close friendship with George, one where he stopped in at my house or Nina's—just to say hello. We shared this small Highbury community, and he was one of the few people anywhere who understood my world. He had gone away and seen what was "out there," lived in another state, traveled many places —and yet, he had come back. He had returned to Highbury, to Knightley and Woodhouse, to Donwell, his legacy. He had returned to his roots, but they were only roots—there was so much more to him—and George's roots were as big as my whole world.

What did I think would happen? Did I think George would never marry? Never have children? He himself had recently hinted that it was time to settle down. Could he ever settle down with me? And even if he wanted me, could I ever settle into any marriage? The new Mrs. Knightley would have so much to do, just being Mrs. Knightley. As long as my father lived, which hopefully would be for many years yet, he would need my care. I couldn't leave him—he was my charge, as I had been his. My father might have married again, had a whole new family, but he had devoted himself to Izzy and me, and to his work. How could I now leave him for a husband, children, and replace him as my main priority?

Okay, so I probably couldn't marry George anyway. But why can we not all go on, just as we are? Maybe he doesn't love Mary Jo, and it's only wishful thinking on her part. When he comes back—and goodness, he's been gone a long time—but when he comes back, I'll go into the office on Doughnut Friday, and I'll watch the two of them and see how it is. With objective eyes. I can do that.

Images of George and Mary Jo smiling at each other over doughnuts and coffee grabbed my attention with psychedelic surreal clarity. The tears started again, and I realized I had walked through Highbury clear to the other side of town, and stood at the entry to Randalls'. Maude ran up the driveway, barking as if to announce us, and Nina appeared on the porch, waving.

"Hi, honey!" she called. "What are you doing over here on foot? Did you walk all this way?"

I broke into a run, my tears blurring my vision. There were times when a girl just needed her mother, and this was one of those times. My mother was gone, but Nina had loved me as unconditionally as a mother would, and Nina would love me still, even after I confessed all my faults and mistakes.

"Emma?"

I sobbed as I clung to her.

"My sweet darling, what's the matter? Is your father okay?"

I nodded, still not able to speak.

"Then what has upset you so?" She stroked a hand down my hair. "Come in. I can't believe you walked here in this heat. Let's get you some ice water and you can tell me what happened. What happened, Emma, honey?"

"It—it's my heart."

"Your heart?"

"Nina, my—my h—heart is bro—" I hiccupped. "My heart is broken!"

The water, followed by tea and cookies and a nap in Nina's guest room, restored me somewhat. As did pouring out my heart and soul. Nina listened, that patient act of love that raising two nieces had taught her.

"Let me see if I've got this straight: you thought you might have liked Frank when he first came back to town, but that went by the wayside pretty quickly—which was fortunate, as it turned out. After Tim told you he'd never be interested in Mary Jo and gave up on you for himself, he started dating Edie. You thought Mary Jo was interested in Frank, and you encouraged her, but you never said who you meant, because—"

"Because I didn't want to influence her again. It was such a disaster the first time."

"Right. So, today you asked her over to break the news about Frank and Jane, only to discover that it wasn't Frank that Mary Jo liked, it was—"

"George. And when I thought about George with Mary Jo, it almost made me ill, because—"

"You think you're in love with George."

"I am, Nina. There's no 'I think' to it, and it's more than some adolescent crush. I love George Knightley. I've probably loved him for years. Why are you smiling?"

"I'm smiling because I'm happy, Emma. I wasn't sure I'd ever hear you say that you loved someone." Her eyes shone with a hint of tears. "My darling, my tough little bird, you saw too much, way too soon, of the sorrow loving someone could bring and not enough of the joy it gives. It was similar for me when Barbara was ill. I was young, about your age, when she had her aneurysm, so it was similar—but still, it was not the same. I loved her so much, but she wasn't my mama, and for you I know it's been so much harder. Love is a risk, and it took me years to finally take that risk myself, after all that had happened. I wasn't sure you'd ever take the chance."

"I didn't take the chance, Nina. It hit me like a branch in the face."

Nina's soft laugh drifted out. "Sometimes, that's the way it happens." She tucked my hair behind my ear. "And now, not only do you have a chance for love, but the man you love is someone good and kind, a man who is worthy of you. It's wonderful."

"It's a train wreck."

"Hmm." Nina reached down and stroked my hair in a gesture of comfort. "Let me tell you what I hear. I hear that Mary Jo is enamored of George—and who wouldn't be?"

I scowled at her. "You're not helping."

"So, we know her feelings, but—and this is an important but—we don't know his. When he comes back from Florida, watch and listen, and let his actions be your guide on what to do next."

"That's exactly what I told Mary Jo—before I knew she had her sights set on George."

"And it was the right advice. Trust your judgment. You're smart enough to know what you're seeing."

"You overestimate my ability to read people."

"I don't think I do. You're quite good at reading people, once you let go of your own agenda and look with your eyes open."

"Oh Nina! I've made such a mess of things!"

"That's your youth talking, honey, not the facts. By the way, you're certainly not alone in that feeling. I talked to the newest Mrs. Weston today."

"Jane?"

"Yes. I thought we should wait to call them, at least until they got back from their honeymoon, but Bob wanted to extend an olive branch, let them know we didn't hold any of this elopement business against them, and welcome her to our family. My half sister-in-law's niece is now my step daughter-in-law. How weird is that? Had you even thought about it?"

"It so confusing, it makes my head hurt."

"Only in Highbury." Nina shrugged.

"So, how is Jane?"

"Happy, I think. She's so private, it's hard to tell. Unlike Frank, who shouts his happiness from the mountain tops and sings Jane's praises all day long. He could give Helen a run for her money in that department."

"Did Jane say anything about what happened?"

"She doesn't mention Mike specifically, although she did say she wishes things had begun differently between her and Frank. She wished she hadn't felt as if she should keep their affection for each other such a secret. I do think it's been a very trying time for her, deciding if she should stay with Mike or follow her heart."

"She must love him then."

"I think she does."

"When I think on how I acted when Jane, Frank, and I were in the same room, I'm mortified. My actions must have hurt her so much."

"Oh Emma, how were you to know? You had no idea what had happened, nor what was happening between them after he arrived. You didn't mean to hurt her."

"Nevertheless, I think she must hate me."

"On the contrary, she asked after you in particular."

"Really?"

"She asked me to thank you for your kindness that day at Donwell. She said you'd know what that meant. And for offering to help her pack when she moved back to New York. She says she has no excuse for not answering you when you called. She was just not herself right then."

"If I'd made those sorts of gestures earlier, worked on developing a friendship with Jane the way I ought, I might have seen that she was struggling with a decision. She might have even told me, and I could have been a real help to her, instead of a menace. Not fix it for her but been a good listener, a friend."

"It's not too late."

"Oh, I think maybe it is—at least for a close friendship. Some things you just can't take back. Anyway, there won't be much opportunity for it. I'm assuming she and Frank will be settling far from Highbury."

"New York, most likely. He's going to look for a job there."

I sat up. "I'd better get home. Daddy will start to fret."

"I called him and said you were here and assured him I'd drive you home."

"You don't have to do that."

"I certainly do. So, round up that animal of yours, if you're ready."

"I love you, Nina."

"And I love you. Don't worry, honey. Life is too short for worry. Have faith that what's meant to be will happen."

"You're going to be a wonderful mama."

"Thank you." She gave me a squeeze. "I had the best girls to practice on."

Daddy was pacing the room by the time I got home. The weatherman on TV was talking about a tornado watch into the evening. After settling him down, I distracted him with a game of checkers while I wondered what the future would bring. The excitement of the past year was fading, and now days stretched out before me. Frank, who had at least kept things stirred up around Highbury, was gone. Jane, who might have been a good friend, was gone. Tim and Edie would marry in a few months, but I didn't like being with them anyway. Spending time with Mary Jo wasn't the least bit appealing now. Nina's baby would be a welcome addition to the family but would also supersede anything else as the focus of Nina's and Bob's lives, which was as it should be.

I longed for George's company—to sit and talk with him, be with him. But he was gone, and I didn't know when he was to return.

THIRTY-EIGHT

George walked barefoot by the shore at Jack and Izzy's vacation house on the Gulf. The sun had set while he was out, and the evening stars began to shimmer into a deepening violet sky. Waves washed up the sand and back to the ocean in a soothing rhythm that calmed his mind. The salty breeze, ever a constant at the beach, ruffled his hair, turning his barely tamed waves into curls that went whichever way they wanted. Much like his thoughts were these days.

He had finished last week in Ocala, but he couldn't bring himself to go back home yet. To watch Emma's deepening infatuation with that man-child, Frank Weston. And see Nina and Bob's indulgent, happy smiles every time Frank paid Emma the slightest bit of attention? Revolting.

So, he'd come to spend July Fourth with his brother's family. Play golf with his parents. Build sandcastles with the children. Soak up the sun. But...

He climbed the wooden steps to the back deck of the house. Maybe he'd stay another week after the family left for Kentucky. Take himself on vacation. No one would miss him anyway. The staff attorneys and paralegals could handle whatever came in the office. He needed to start interviewing for the Donwell Farms manager position, but he had until September, after all. It wasn't that urgent. He plopped into a deck chair and leaned back, closing his eyes and listening to the ocean come close and recede, come close and recede—the analogy between that ancient push and pull and his story with Emma Woodhouse didn't escape him. They were children whose fathers worked and played together, and Emma followed him around the yard as he scampered about with his friends. He went to college; she grew up while he was gone. She left for college; he finished law school and began practicing law and learning his role as steward of the Donwell legacy. She returned to take care of her father; he was dating...who was he dating then? He couldn't remember. While she finished college, busy with her studies and John Woodhouse, he tried to force a serious relationship with Julianne Ryman. Then Julianne was gone. He looked around, and there was his Emma Kate: beautiful, elegant, sharp (if sometimes misguided), and more than anyone else, she *understood* him. He'd always neatly managed the women in his life, but there was no manipulating Emma Woodhouse—and wasn't that fascinating? She steered her own ship. And yet, in part because of their shared history, his soul was at home with hers, simple as that. No pretenses, no expectations. At the end of the day, if he dropped in to say hi, it was just the two of them, talking, bantering, laughing. They thought enough alike to get along and were different enough to challenge each other and keep things interesting. Friends with sparks.

Of all the things he admired about Emma, at the top of the list was her enormous capacity for love. Nina had that pegged, all right. *Was there ever a daughter who loved her family as deeply? What she's done for John is priceless. Isabel is his daughter too, but she didn't take on responsibility for an invalid while she tried to finish college. And Emma did it all with a cheerful nonchalance, as if to say "Of course, I did it. Why wouldn't I?"*

A light flashed on in the kitchen, and Izzy picked up the telephone. George watched her sit at the counter, laughing with whoever was on the other end of the line. She and Emma shared that smile, but to that surface charm, Emma added a depth of understanding. The loss of their parents: one to death, the other to debilitation, had shaped Izzy into a kind but dependent woman. Emma, however, had fought to build her strength and independence, and her steadfast loyalty shone through it all. If you were lucky enough to be one of her people, she'd overlook your foibles and love you with a warrior-like fierceness.

He knew this because he had been one of her people, her close friend, and he'd blown it. That discussion at Churchill Downs had been the final nail in the coffin. He'd just realized he wanted her, and then he lost her. Hadn't Julianne warned him? She said he needed to bring his feelings about Emma to the surface, really take an honest look at them—and address them before he blundered—before it was too late.

Now, it was too late.

He closed his eyes again and startled when the door opened. Light flooded the deck and Isabel stood silhouetted in the doorway.

"George! There you are. I was just coming out to find you. That was Nina on the phone."

He sat up, all senses on alert. "Everyone okay at home?"

"Yes, everyone is fine, but you will never guess what she told me."

"If I can't guess, then you'll have to spill the beans, honey."

"Everyone in Highbury is all in a state."

"Why?"

"Jane Fairfax and Frank Weston eloped last weekend."

It was as if Izzy had whisked his chair out from under him. "What?"

"Jane and Frank—they ran off to Vegas and got married!"

When George arrived at the house on Hartfield Road, Mrs. Davies told him Emma was out in the gazebo, where she'd spent a lot of her time the last few days.

I wish I'd known everything about Jane and Frank from the moment it happened. My Emma Kate, all alone with her broken heart! If I ever see that rat-bastard again, I'll pound his head into the sidewalk.

Sprung from his memory with a painful jolt was a conversation he had with Nina, months ago now, when he said Emma needed a bruised heart. Asinine, cruel thing to say! Now that she had one, his own heart ached for her.

He tried not to presume too much, but the refrain kept repeating in his head: *Emma is free! Free for me to sweep in and pick up the pieces. But...no. Wait...I don't want to be her rebound affair, the transition to the next man.*

Oh hell, who am I kidding? I'd happily be a rebound if it meant I had a chance. His worry about how his love for her would affect their friendship seemed trivial now. If she couldn't love him, he had only himself to blame. He willfully turned from her, and when he did, she slipped away.

I could still be her friend, though. I'm here to comfort, not demand. To think of her, not be self-serving. Maybe there's hope for us to be an "us" someday. Right now, I'll have to be happy with only possibilities.

The gazebo was several yards from the back deck, in the midst of a few shade trees. He heard her music coming from the inside, suggesting she must have brought her portable record player out with her. He didn't see her when he first approached because she was lying on the porch swing, her head propped up against the arm rest with pillows. One long leg was bent up so her foot rested on the seat; the other rested on the wooden floor and moved the swing back and forth. She looked so peaceful, reclining there with her eyes closed, holding a glass of wine loosely in her fingers. He stood for a few seconds in silence—admiring, loving, breathing her in. Finally, he called softly to her.

"Emma Kate?"

She leaped up, startled, wine sloshing out of the glass.

"George!" she gasped, clutching her heart. Then she laughed. "Goodness, you scared me! You shouldn't sneak up on people like that." She transferred the glass to her other hand and shook off the one wet with wine.

"Sorry."

She sat back on the swing, leaning over to lift the record needle off the 45. He walked up the steps and sat beside her.

"I didn't know you were back from Florida."

"Flew in this morning. I'm surprised Mary Jo didn't tell you. She made my flight reservation."

She stiffened, but her only response was, "I haven't talked to her for the last couple of days."

They sat for a minute in silence, listening to the crickets chirping their evening song.

"Would you like to stay for dinner? We're having lasagna," she asked, looking off in the distance toward the house.

"Hmm? Oh… dinner. Yes, thank you. Lasagna sounds good."

A heavy sigh escaped her, and George eyed her carefully. *If she cries, I'll push Frank Weston's face in the pavement and break his fingers.*

"Oh"—she began, as if suddenly remembering something—"you just got in town, so you don't know the news."

"The news?"

"Jane and Frank have eloped. They flew to Las Vegas and got married last week. It's been quite the uproar around here."

"Um… yeah. I'd heard that…Nina called Izzy while I was with them in Florida."

"We were all surprised out of our socks, but I bet you weren't. You said all along Frank was hiding something. You saw the secret looks between them, and you were right. I was shocked to find out they'd been carrying on, even last fall—and while she was engaged to Mike Dixon too. Unbelievable."

George reached over and took her hand. "I know you're disappointed in him."

"I have to admit I am."

He brought the slender fingers to his lips and kissed them. She stared at him and then at her hand, but he didn't care. "Time is the great healer, Emma."

"Healer?"

"I can't believe he did this after he made such a big show of pursuing you. And all the while he was secretly trying to convince Jane to leave her fiancé. It's shameful—the way he treated her, the way he led you on. Ungentlemanly."

"Led me on…?" Her brow furrowed in confusion. Then her eyes opened wide. "You thought I had a thing for Frank. Nina thought so too." She covered her eyes with her free hand. "I can't imagine how inappropriately I must have acted to make both of you think that."

He squeezed her hand and smiled at her bravado. She'd never admit that Weston had hurt her or wounded her pride. He rubbed his thumb over her knuckles, trying not to remember how it felt to hold her that night they danced. He really wanted to hold her now.

"You're sweet to be concerned, but, honestly, there's no need."

He paused, holding her hand in mid-air. "Pardon?"

"I've known Frank for years, well enough to see that he will lead people down a primrose path, and let them think whatever they want—as long as it serves his best interests. He's funny and nice enough, not to mention handsome, but he doesn't have your honesty, George. He doesn't have your integrity or your respect for people, especially for women. I told you before you left, you didn't need to worry about Frank messing with my head. That was the truth. I know you think I'm naïve, and perhaps I am, but I watch people, and I learn. I'm sheltered, but I'm not stupid. And there's no way I would let someone as unworthy as Frank Weston break my heart." She laughed, a rueful sound. "Frank—now there's a man whose name is bound up in his fate. His name is Frank, but he's not frank at all, the little sneak."

"How like you to crack a joke at a time like this." He smiled at her.

"Perhaps it's karma," she went on. "The challenge of his life will be to live up to his name."

George sank back against the swing, and his smile dimmed. "I guess he got everything he wanted, without hard feelings from anyone."

"What do you mean?"

"Think about it. He has a fling with a beautiful, young actress while he's in New York. She's engaged to someone else, but she falls victim to his charm. In a fit of remorse, or indecision, she retreats to her family. He follows her, and proceeds to treat her poorly. Flaunts another woman in front of her. If he had searched the world, he could not have found another woman who suited him so well. His grandmother continually threatens to cut him off if he doesn't do exactly what she wants. Then, the grandmother dies. He runs back to his girl and persuades her to elope. His family is happy for him. He has used everyone, and they all forgive him at the drop of a hat. Hmmph. Lucky man."

"Yeah, Nina and Bob forgave him the instant they realized I didn't have any hopes for him, maybe even before that. The only person he really hurt was Jane, and she forgave him too."

"I feel sorry for her, to be saddled with such a husband. I hope she didn't give up a chance at real happiness with Mike Dixon, all for some fling."

Emma shrugged. "Who's to say? It seems like they really love each other. Frank followed her here, after all. He must be crazy about her, because he made more of an effort to get her than he's made for anything else, ever. She came home to Highbury to get some distance from him and her fiancé too—to get some perspective and make some decisions. Mike Dixon was too busy to follow up, or maybe he was giving her the space she asked for, who knows. Frank was arrogant enough—or cared enough—to pursue her, and I guess eventually, he changed her mind. Poor Jane. I feel bad for her, carrying that secret all alone. If I'd been nicer to her, she might have turned to me."

"Frank Weston is a selfish, pushy, bratty child. He doesn't deserve her."

"Well, we shall see."

"I guess we shall." George's heart started pounding in his chest, as it came to him what this meant. Emma was not in love with Frank! He'd just been given a second chance, and he didn't want to blow it. "In a way, I kind of envy him, settling down. I've thought about it myself." He let out an embarrassed chuckle. "Hell, I sound like Tim Elton. Unbelievable." He shook his head, amused.

Emma was silent.

"I'm surprised you won't ask about that comment, being the consummate matchmaker that you are." He was trying to tease her, but she didn't even crack a smile.

"My matchmaking days are over." She got up, poured the rest of her wine out over the rail, and set the glass down.

"Emma," he said, more seriously this time, "I have to tell you... I can't keep my feelings to myself any longer—"

She turned around, putting her hands over her ears. "Just...don't. Don't say it. I can't bear it." Her eyes filled with tears.

George stopped, shocked. After all that animosity he harbored for Frank, and *he* was the one bringing on the tears? With his declaration of love for her? "You're right. I shouldn't have said anything. I've overstepped our friendship. I'm sorry." He started toward the gazebo archway, desperate to get away and collect his thoughts. He'd taken maybe two or three steps before he felt her hand on his arm.

"George, please...wait. That was selfish of me, and I hurt your feelings. I am your friend, and I care about you. You can say anything you like, and I'll listen."

He shook his head. "I—I don't want to be friends anymore."

"Please don't take your friendship from me. Then I'll have nothing." Her lower lip trembled. "It would be unbearable. I know I've lowered your opinion of me lately—the way I treated Jane, and Helen, and the way I let Frank flatter my vanity. But please, George! Please say you can learn to overlook my flaws. Please say you can still be my friend."

"I want to be more than friends!" He hadn't meant to blurt it out like that, but he'd lost complete control over the words coming out of his mouth. Emma often had that effect on him. He stalked to the other side of the gazebo, then stood there, glaring at her. "Damn it, Emma!"

Her mouth closed, and she just stared as if he'd lost his mind. Maybe he had.

In three more steps, he crossed the gazebo and yanked her into his arms, his lips descending on hers in a rage of emotion. He kissed her, hard. "Say something, damn it!" His voice lowered, deep. "Emma. Please..." The next kiss was soft, lingering, careful, and gentle. She didn't pull away, or slap him, or run screaming into the house, so he slid her into his embrace and kissed her again. When he pulled away, her eyes were round with surprise. *One more*, he thought, and he kissed her again, before resting his forehead on hers.

"Have you never wondered why I didn't like Frank Weston, even before he got here? I said it was because he didn't treat Bob and Nina right, but mostly it was because I knew they wanted him to be with you. It was agony to watch him flirt with you all spring and summer. And when you were snotty with Helen, I thought that showed how his callousness was rubbing off on you.

"I love you, Emma Kate. Not as a friend. But as a man loves a woman. I think I've loved you for a long time, but I thought... well, first I thought I was too old for you, and then I thought you and Frank..."

Emma finally found her voice. "But Frank and I dated years ago—it meant nothing, just a high school thing."

"Then why are you out in the gazebo all by yourself, drinking wine and listening to 'Color My World'?"

"I'm certainly not here because I'm in love with Frank Weston." She stepped back and gesticulated with her hands in obvious frustration. "I'm moping around out here because I thought I'd lost you."

Every sound in the world ceased, except the pounding of blood through his body. "Emma? Is this true?"

"Yes, it's true." Her voice started to rise as if in panic. "It's true. I love you, and I didn't even realize it until you went away. After Churchill Downs, I thought I'd finally killed your affection for me, that you were gone from my life, even as my friend, and it broke my heart, George, because I depend on you so."

"You—you do?"

"You're the best friend I've ever had. You understand me, and I understand you like no one else possibly could. No other woman should be with you but me. No Junior League *Woman of the Month*. No brilliant, noble pediatrician. I'm the one who's right for you, and"—she sniffed, her eyes filling with tears—"I'm yours, George. If you'll have me."

And just like that, every thought, every proper feeling lay there between them—honest, open, and right. She held out her arms, and in half a second, he filled them.

"Emma." He laughed and lifted her feet off the ground. "Emma!" He set her down and took her face in his hands, thumbs tracing her cheeks, her lips. His eyes roamed her face, stopping where his thumbs had last landed.

"I'm nervous," he said, smiling. "Are you nervous?"

"George Bryan Knightley, I know you've kissed plenty of women before."

"But I've just had my last first kiss. I think I'll take the next one."

Then his mouth met hers, and all cares dropped away. The world outside the gazebo buzzed and barked and brayed, teeming with life, but inside there was only George, and his darling Emma.

THIRTY-NINE

I couldn't believe how shy I felt around George since our declaration in the gazebo. We caught ourselves looking at each other about forty times during the evening, then we'd both turn away with a smile. It amazed me that Daddy didn't catch on at dinner. But then, he did spend about half the meal wondering if the lasagna had too much cheese in it to be healthy. In some cases, his tendency toward perseveration came in handy!

After Daddy went to bed, we walked out under the moonlight and stars, holding hands. George leaned back against his Volvo and drew me into his embrace. Clouds drifted across the moon, obscuring his expression, though I had already begun the process of reading his moods and memorizing him in the dark.

"Are you working at the office tomorrow?" I asked, linking my hands behind his neck, then running them down his shoulders and back behind him again.

"Um…no, actually. I'll be out at Donwell in the morning. Did I tell you our manager is retiring in September?"

"I heard it somewhere. He's been there a long time."

"He has. He'll be hard to replace."

I fell silent again, not wanting him to go, yet not knowing how to get him to stay. It was so bright, so new, this band of light between us. I couldn't let it disappear into the night. I looked up at the stars and breathed in the smell of magnolias as the breeze stirred around us. George's embrace tightened, his lips caressing my cheek, then my ear as he tucked my hair behind it, then down to my neck. His hands roamed my back and finally settled on my hips.

"You are beautifully made, my darling."

"So are you," I answered.

I heard his low chuckle and felt the heat of it travel between us and settle low in my belly, making me giddy and feverish. As I was about to ask him to kiss me again, he did just that, gently at first, then rougher, faster. It was glorious, like riding lightning. As my body seemed to melt against him, his grew more tense and unyielding.

I wanted him. No telling how long this had been building inside me, this wanting, this desire that felt new but wasn't. Now I had set it free, given it words and actions, and I realized I wanted him very much. I must have said "please" because I heard him say, "Please what, honey?"

"I—I just want you to stay."

Possibilities hung in the air between us. Then he sighed, a long-suffering sound.

"I can't stay, Emma Kate. Not like this. Not in your father's house."

"It's my house too." My voice was soft, but it picked up volume and determination when I repeated, "It's my house too."

He wound a strand of hair around his fingers, rubbing circles on my back as if to gentle a wild filly. It had the opposite effect.

Frustration edged my voice. "Don't you want to stay?"

"Yes," he said simply, but I knew him well enough to hear the determination behind it. "But…"

"Not in my father's house."

"I can't help it. It doesn't feel right to me, not until we're…" His fingers brushed my cheek. "Besides, I don't want to rush you."

"Rush me? George Knightley, I've waited for you all my life." I held his palm against my cheek, feeling the warmth and the strength there. "I guess I understand, but…" I stepped back, tugging on his hand. "Come on."

"Emma," he protested. "Don't tease me like this."

"Teasing's half the fun, isn't it?" I led him around the side of the house and opened the gate. "Not the house." I turned and walked backwards so I could gauge his expression in the lights flickering from under the water in the swimming pool. I saw the realization in his eyes just before I stopped at the box and turned the lights off.

"It's not the house."

"No."

"Take a midnight swim, George? It'll cool you off."

"Maybe." His voice wavered as I began to peel off my shirt and shorts. "It's just a swim, right?"

"Right." I reached behind me to unhook my bra, but he stayed my hand.

"Wait."

I shivered at the husky notes in his voice. "Wait?"

"Let me do it." He undid the hooks with one smooth move, caressing my shoulders as he slid my bra off and dropped it beside my clothes. Warm hands traced my collar bones, my breast bone, and then held my breasts, thumbs rubbing across my nipples. It was a little comforting to realize through my fiery haze that his hands shook as he slid them down my waist and over the flesh under my panties. He drew them down, and obediently I stepped out of them, before backing away and turning toward the pool.

I stopped on the first step, the water lapping at my ankles. Moonlight burst down on us from behind a cloud.

"Dive right in, George." I forced my attention to the water as I descended into it—night air filling my lungs, and the feel of cool water swirling around my body.

I'd always found swimming naked—the few times I tried it—to be luxurious and indulgent, like gliding through silk. I bent my torso to go under the water, took a couple of strokes, then surfaced and rolled over on my back as I approached the other end. "Aren't you coming in?" I called softly.

He stood still, silhouetted in the night, one fine specimen of man. In a sudden flurry of movement, he doffed his clothes and jumped in. We met in the middle of the pool, laughing, before lips and bodies fused. He pushed me up against the side, cradling my head in one hand and holding me to him in the other.

"Easy, easy," he whispered, but I didn't know if he was talking to me or to himself. He settled me over him and pushed in. I gasped at the contrast of cool water and hot man against my most sensitive parts. It wasn't my first time, but it might as well have been, it had been so long.

"I don't want to hurt you."

"You've always behaved like a gentleman, George Knightley."

"Yes?" He moved a lock of wet hair over my shoulder.

"This time, I really wish you wouldn't."

He stopped and stared at me, and then his hands were everywhere, and my back was against the side of the pool again. I'd never seen the savage side of him before, and it occurred to me that it was a fascinating display, and then, suddenly, I couldn't think at all.

"This wasn't what I had in mind for our first time," he said, holding me from behind and letting his hands roam over me under the water. "I'd like to think I have more finesse than that. You make me impulsive."

"We have lots of times ahead of us." I let my legs float up so I laid on top of the water, my wet hair brushing his chest. "You didn't like it?"

"I didn't say *that*." He ran his fingers over my belly.

"I think it was perfect." My hands reached back and slid down his body, finding him warm and firm underneath the water. "But if you're so inclined, there's always the guest house."

He pulled me toward him, turning me so we were face to face with our limbs intertwined, a symbol of how our entire lives had been, and hopefully would be from now on.

"My bones feel like rubber bands. I'm surprised I didn't drown," I said, combing my fingers through his hair.

He laughed and pulled the two of us under the water's surface where our lips collided. I thought my heart would burst.

I read somewhere that there is no such thing as complete truth in any human exchange. That may be true, but with George and me, two souls so disposed to loving each other, I figured that fact matters very little anyway.

The gray light of pre-dawn seeped into the guest house bedroom, where I lay sprawled across the bed.

"I don't want to know where you learned to do that, but I'm glad you did."

The early morning stubble on his jaw abraded my inner thigh as George turned his head to brush his lips there.

"The dangers of loving a woman who's known you all your life. She knows your life." He moved up to rest his head on my belly. "Is it a problem?"

I shook my head. "No. It's not something I want to dwell on, mind you, but it isn't a problem. I want all of you, George. Your past is part of the package."

"I don't know about your past or if you even have one."

"There isn't much to know and what there is...? Well, it's...unremarkable. Do you want me to tell you?"

He considered. "No, I don't think I do." He slithered up my body and pinned my wrists above my head. "It doesn't matter. You're mine now."

The delicate tissues groaned a little as he parted them, but I welcomed him back. "I'm yours."

"Mine," he chanted in rhythm with long, excruciatingly slow strokes. My body arched off the bed as I cried out, and he emptied into me, calling my name.

Later, when he got up to leave for home, in that magical time between the dark of night and the dawn of day, he left me sated and loose, tangled in the sheets of the guest house bed.

He ran a hand from my shoulder to my hip and whispered, "I love you so, Emma Kate."

I could only smile over the lump of joy in my throat.

FORTY

LATE AUGUST, 1976

"Hello, George." My father set his cane beside his dining room chair and shifted into it with my help. "Are you here for dinner again? We've certainly seen a lot of you lately."

My lips twitched. "Daddy…"

"Oh, we're glad to have you, my boy. Always glad to have you."

"Thank you, sir."

I sat down between George and Daddy. As I put my napkin in my lap, George leaned over and said quietly, "We need to tell him."

"Soon, I promise."

George slid his hand over my knee and up my thigh. "He'll have a helluva shock if he comes downstairs one morning and sees me sitting at the kitchen counter in my boxers and bathrobe." He smiled at Daddy, who was tucking into his chicken pot pie with oblivious abandon.

I shivered with barely controlled pleasure. "I'm going to tell him. After his birthday."

We had already been together six weeks, and we hadn't told anyone, although Nina knew. She'd caught us kissing by the side of the house after one of her family cookouts. She'd just smiled and shook her head, then put a finger to her lips, and backed around the corner out of sight. She knew we'd tell everyone eventually. When we were ready.

Sneaking around hadn't been our original plan, but now I almost hated to give it up. It gave the passion of new love a hot, sexy kick. To appear in public as friends, knowing we'd have our hands all over each other the first chance we got...? Delicious. I told George I was starting to understand the irresistible pull of clandestine meetings. "This has made me a more understanding person."

"Huh?"

"Yes. I think I understand Jane and Frank much better now."

"Nonsensical girl." But, in all honesty, he had to agree with me.

An added benefit of hiding our budding romance was the ability to keep everyone else out of it in its fragile, infant state. In a small, tight-knit community like Highbury, and with two people whose histories crossed and separated and meshed time and again, there would have been a tendency for everyone to put their two cents in. By insulating ourselves in a tiny love nest for two, we could explore whole new sides of each other unprovoked, uninfluenced, and undisturbed. No Daddy bemoaning the loss of his beloved daughter, even if the man I chose was his beloved protégé. No Delores and Helen fawning over us with congratulations. No Jack and Izzy, sitting in shock with their babies in a whirling dervish around them.

No Mary Jo crying tears of disappointment—again.

I kept Mary Jo's secret crush on George to myself, deciding it would serve no one's interests to let that cat out of the bag. I dreaded the day I would have to tell Mary Jo about my love for George and his for me, but our sneaking around ended up solving that problem too.

Sometime in the middle of August, I came home to a phone message from Mary Jo. When I returned the call, she sheepishly confessed she was dating Robert Martin. It was a recent development, but she thought it might get serious pretty quickly.

Apparently, when George offered Robert the job of managing Donwell Farms, the day of the strawberry party had come up in conversation. He'd told Robert about showing Mary Jo around and how impressed she was. That led to a discussion about women, and family, and Mary Jo in particular. George encouraged Robert to try again for her, if that was what he truly wanted. According to Robert, that encouragement, coupled with the newfound confidence he gained from the promotion, spurred him on to try his chances.

"I realized Mr. Knightley most likely wasn't interested in me, given that he'd encouraged another man to ask me out. But even more, I realized how much I'd missed Robert: our talks, his smile, his voice. I do love his voice."

"He does have a great voice."

"Emma, accepting his invitation to dinner was the best thing I ever did. We just...fit, you know? I'm so happy. I'm not nervous around him the way I was around men like Tim Elton. Robert is such a caring, gentle person. I always feel at ease around him."

I knew now how precious and rare and compelling that quality was in a man. When a woman found it, it shouldn't be ignored. "I'm glad, so glad that you've found someone who will value you and care for you the way you deserve. It's what every modern woman wants, isn't it?"

Later, when George and I were out walking Maude, I said, "They're so good together. Why did I not see it before?"

"Perhaps you chose not to see."

"Do you think I let race influence me?"

"Only you know the answer to that, Emma."

"Sometimes I don't think I'll ever know for sure. I would feel such shame, if that were true. My mother marched alongside Civil Rights workers. My father taught me to see the person inside the shell of color. I cried like a baby when Dr. King died. Could I, without even realizing it, let something that superficial affect me, and through me, Mary Jo?"

"Mary Jo found her way regardless. Such is the nature of love."

"Don't tease, George. I'm being serious."

He reached for my hand. "Society often changes slowly. I know it's the seventies, and we think we're so enlightened now. We hope the issues surrounding color are all behind us, but I would be very surprised if that were so. Human beings are notoriously fickle and short-sighted. But this I do know: people like Robert and Mary Jo are the ones who bring us real change, real justice. They, and ordinary people like them, show us all another path, and each time that path is taken, it becomes wider and wider until one day, it's a road traveled by many, without any thought at all as to how it came to be."

"It's quite brave, isn't it?"

"I think so."

"I'm happy for them."

"Me too."

Mary Jo and Robert were busy updating the cottage at the end of The Lane, preparing it for his move at the end of September. By the time George and I finally began seeing each other publicly, Mary Jo's infatuation with her boss was a faded memory. Even years later, Mary Jo Martin was convinced that I had waited until she began dating Robert to date George. I heard from several other people that she said, "Emma Knightley is not only a good friend but a woman with real class." What higher praise is there than that?

<hr/>

For George and me, keeping our relationship secret had also given us time to wrestle with some particularly thorny practicalities about merging our lives, like what to do about my father.

A frantic morning of angina, followed by a trip to the ER and an overnight hospital stay resulted in me standing on the doorstep of George's townhouse in tears.

I, Emma Katherine Woodhouse, the girl who *never* cried, was at it again for the second time in a month.

"How can I marry you? How can I leave him, even in the care of the best nurses, so I can share your life?" I broke down, sobbing. "It just won't work, George."

"We can make it work. It's not like we don't have options and resources."

"But he needs family. He needs me. It's not the same to have someone else take care of him. And I can't ask you to wait, not like that."

George held me in his lap as he considered.

"You can't leave him."

I shook my head. "And I can't uproot him either. It's an impossible situation."

"There's one other possibility you haven't considered."

"What do you mean?"

"After we marry, I can move in with you."

"What?"

"I can sell my townhouse and move in with you and your father."

"But…"

"Donwell Farms is but a mile or two from Hartfield Road, and the law office is a twenty-five minute drive. If John needs you to stay in your home, let me call it home too."

If anything convinced me that I had chosen the right man, it was that one statement. I threw my arms around him. "I don't know what to say, except I love you so much! I can't believe I had the good fortune to win you."

"If I say I'll move to Hartfield Road when we get married, will that shorten our engagement?" George asked, smiling.

I laid my head on his shoulder. "It will still be a respectable nine months. Like my sister and my mother, I want to be a traditional June bride. I want to eat strawberries at my wedding."

"I think that can be arranged."

EPILOGUE

MAY 21, 2017

GEORGE

Emma and I enjoyed that season of young love all to ourselves, but all things must come to an end, and by the last of September, we told our friends and families that we planned to marry the next June.

It was a beautiful wedding. I thought my heart would stop when Emma walked toward me from the back of the church. John joined her when she reached his seat in the front pew, and there was hardly a dry eye in the place, including his, when his voice wavered as he gave her away.

Emma's eyes though were dry and clear. She knew how it would be, how right we were together, and nothing less than a happily-ever-after would do.

We had our reception at Bromley Crossing. It held fond memories for us: Bob and Nina's first Derby party, nullifying Tim Elton's slight on Mary Jo, that dance we shared. There were some issues at first— some changes that Emma wanted to make that the owners were reluctant about.

So, I bought the place. Even today, it's a favorite venue for community get-togethers of all kinds: weddings, political rallies, bar—and bat mitz-vahs, and of course, Derby parties.

Life has brought ups and downs to the people of Highbury; no one can escape them. Frank and Jane were married until 1982. They divorced, as quickly as they married, and Frank, after marriages to two more Jane Fairfax-lookalikes, ended up single and selling real estate in Phoenix, Arizona. Jane continued to do some theater, but then she landed a role on a daytime soap opera that carried her through the rest of her career.

Helen is still living—if you can believe that—eighty-nine years young. After a fall a couple of years ago, Emma arranged assisted living for her, and she loves it. Some people find that situation confining and long for home, but Helen finds the company much to her liking and regales the residents with tales from her long life, told in her unique, rambling style.

Tim and Edie's marriage also fell victim to the societal tide of divorce. After ten years, two children, and a term in the state legislature, Tim came out of the closet—unfortunately, in a very public way—after being caught in a liaison with his college-aged intern one night in the Capitol offices.

Robert and Mary Jo's brood of four grew up tall and strong, and each one went on to achieve true success: a doctor, a musician, a plumber running a successful business in Lexington, and a lawyer, who works for me, in fact. She's a real go-getter.

John Woodhouse passed away after another stroke in 1981, so he only met the elder of our two daughters. Nina and Bob's daughter, Anna, grew up alongside our Melissa and Amanda, and the girls played and ran around the yard at Randalls' place or at the house on Hartfield Road, the younger ones toddling after the older ones. We lived in Emma's house until several years after my father passed on, and we had to move into Donwell to take care of my mother. By then, Taylor had married, so she and her new husband stayed in the old Woodhouse home while they saved for a house of their own.

Emma once said to me that the events of Highbury reminded her of one of those great novels of small places. "So much *life* happens here, and you'd never know."

"*You'd* know, Emma. You know everything about everyone."

She laughed. "I do. I could write a book."

"Well, why don't you?"

So, she did. Eight romance novels, four young adult stories, and a cozy mystery series of seven books set in Kentucky flew from her pen, and later, from her computer. She's still at it, although historical fiction has become her new passion.

As I predicted, Emma never found her one true calling. Instead, she found many, and this, along with a deep well of love for those around her, has made for a life steeped in wealth that can't be inherited, that I couldn't give her, and that can't be earned—only accepted.

Emma and I married in 1977, when divorces seemed as trendy as polyester suits and disco music. Thank goodness, some trends die permanently. Divorce, however, is a social trend that has continued through the decades. Sometimes a parting of the ways is the best thing for everyone involved. I know that—have witnessed that fact in my law practice, and sometimes in my colleagues and my friends.

Usually, divorce makes at least one person unhappy, and there's almost always some collateral damage on both sides. I suppose it's inevitable when people are troubled about their own relationships to ask how I've managed to stay married to the same woman for such a long time. When they do ask, I simply tell them the truth—or at least, I tell them what's been my truth:

I, George Bryan Knightley, married my best friend.

Occasionally, I get odd looks when I say it. And boorish comments, like, "Where's the passion in that? The romance? The spark?"

Although I know passion and friendship may not always coexist, my own experience also tells me that neither are they mutually exclusive.

It took me a while to believe but eventually it did sink in, and that realization allowed me to seize my chance with a woman who was my intellectual equal but not exactly like me. A woman who understood my past and still wanted to share my future. She intrigued and amused me but expected nothing less of me than the development of my best self. And, to top it off, she was—and is—stunningly beautiful, inside and out.

It's hard to believe, but we'll be celebrating our fortieth anniversary next month. What anniversary gift goes with year number forty? Marble or emeralds or some such thing? I'm not sure.

That's the kind of little factoid my wife would know. All those little details are organized and filed in that brain of hers, in tidy, little neuron drawers. I'm no slouch in the brains department myself, but I believe my wife may be the most...*competent* woman I've ever known.

Not that she never makes mistakes. When she was young, she made some real humdingers. But then, as I look back, so did I. And I continued to make mistakes a lot longer into my adulthood than she did. A few of those mistakes almost cost me the love of my life. I'm thankful every day that I caught on before it was too late.

I don't mean to sound smug, because I know, without a doubt, that fortune played a significant role in our happiness. It's hard for an analytical guy like me to admit it, but luck was one of the ingredients in the recipe that made life-long lovers out of the best of friends.

And that key I gave her for her charm bracelet? Well, I didn't actually lie about what it meant, but I didn't tell her the whole truth either. It *was* to remind her that she held the key to her own future, but it also meant something more to me. I gave it to her after I finally realized she would forever hold the key to my heart.

QUESTIONS FOR BOOK CLUBS, HAPPY HOURS, OR SPIRITED DISCUSSIONS

1. Austen wrote, "I am going to take a heroine whom no one but myself will much like." In comparing Austen's "Emma" to your "Emma," why do you think this modern Emma might be more likable to a modern reader?

A lot of readers, even those who love Austen as a writer and *Emma* as a novel, don't care for the main character. I, myself, have always loved Emma—I've known too many women like her over the years to *not* like her. So, one of my goals for *I Could Write a Book* was to write an Emma that readers could relate to and, hopefully, could like—even as they watched her struggle, falter, and ultimately grow. I did this by giving more background and exploring the dynamics in the Woodhouse family. By modern standards, Emma's been through a lot in her short life, and she deserves some kudos for it. I also wrote from Emma's first person point of view so readers could really get inside her head and see what makes her do the things she does.

2. When was the moment you think George started to fall for Emma?

I think he takes that first baby step when they have the argument at the

Christmas Party about her return home from college. It's when he says, "Perhaps." But the point of no return is when he believes he has some real competition for her in the form of Frank Weston. George Knightley is an almost perfect gentleman, but he's also a man with the very common foible of not knowing what he wants until he thinks someone else wants it.

3. How do you think the charm bracelet symbolizes both Austen's Emma and this modern Emma?

The charm bracelet itself was a relatively late addition to the story. I needed something that represented Emma, but what one thing could convey the complexity of her outer life and inner mind? That's when the idea of a charm bracelet occurred to me. It symbolizes both the original Emma and this modern one because it represents all the different facets of her life—the arts and projects she dabbles in, but never quite becomes proficient at, and the many roles she assumes in her young life: daughter, sister, aunt, homemaker, friend. In *I Could Write a Book* she's also a niece, cousin, and a student. Like many women, she wears a lot of hats.

4. Why did you choose to keep many of the original names yet chose to change Harriet's to Mary Jo?

I thought with our twenty-first century colored glasses, looking back on the 1970s and the South, that the name Mary Jo conveyed a lot about the character right away. Even Emma makes some pretty big assumptions about her at the beginning. Harriet seemed just a tad bit too old-fashioned in a way that Emma, Frank, George and Jane did not. I also changed the Miss Bates character's name from Hetty to Helen, for much the same reason.

5. It has been suggested that Emma is the female equivalent of Darcy. If she is, why do we more easily forgive Darcy for his pride and officious ways?

In my opinion, there are two reasons. One is that gender bias, though in the process of changing, is still alive and well in our culture. Emma has some characteristics that aren't stereotypically feminine, especially for her time in the Regency. She's not reserved; she speaks her mind. She isn't retiring; she directs people, or tries to. These qualities in a female still carry undercurrents of social rejection. So, when we read *Pride and Prejudice*, we're much easier on Darcy. He says, "I was given good principles, but was left to follow them in pride and conceit" somewhere near the end of the book, and we rush to forgive him. But when Emma is left to follow *her* principles in pride and conceit, she's often seen as a snob and a shrew. They aren't behaviors that are changeable, like Darcy's. They are part of her personality, static and stable faults that will endure. Or so many readers believe.

The second reason is that I believe Austen almost wrote Emma *too* well for female readers. What I mean by that is we see a little of ourselves in her—our foibles, our snap judgments, our selfishness when we think we're being selfless—these are characteristics we might not want to face in the person we see in the mirror each day. It's excruciating to watch Emma screw up because we can relate to it, a little too well for comfort. Austen was all about growth in her characters, and she wrote Emma with a no-holds-barred bluntness that forces us to look at her main character's faults, and sometimes it feels icky. But when you dig into *Emma*, the novel, you also see her admit her mistakes, accept the consequences, and try to do better. In the end, what better role model is there? That Miss Austen— she knew what she was doing.

ABOUT THE AUTHOR

Karen M Cox is an award-winning author of novels accented with romance and history including *1932, Find Wonder in All Things, Undeceived*, and an ebook novella, *The Journey Home*. She also contributed a short story, "Northanger Revisited 2015", to the anthology, *Sun-Kissed: Effusions of Summer*, and a story titled "I, Darcy" to *The Darcy Monologues*.

Karen was born in Everett WA, which was the result of coming into the world as the daughter of a United States Air Force Officer. She had a nomadic childhood, with stints in North Dakota, Tennessee and New York State before finally settling in her family's home state of Kentucky at the age of eleven. She lives in a quiet little town with her husband, where she works as a pediatric speech pathologist, encourages her children, and spoils her granddaughter.

Channeling Jane Austen's Emma, Karen has let a plethora of interests lead her to begin many hobbies and projects she doesn't quite finish, but she aspires to be a great reader and an excellent walker—like Elizabeth Bennet.

Connect with Karen:
    Website: www.karenmcox.com
    Amazon Author Page: www.amazon.com/author/karenmcox

Visit with Karen on several of the usual social media haunts such as Facebook, (karenmcox1932), Twitter (@karenmcox1932), Pinterest (karenmc1932), Instagram (karenmcox1932), and Tumblr (karenmcox).

Thank you for reading! If you enjoyed *I Could Write a Book,* please consider leaving a review on Amazon and/or Goodreads. Reviews help other readers decide if they, too, would like a story.

If you would like bits of authorly goodness in your inbox each month (updates, sales, book recommendations, etc.) sign up for News & Muse Letter - http://eepurl.com/csG1kD (distributed by MailChimp, with addresses kept strictly confidential). Karen loves to hear from readers, so don't be shy. Contact her through social media, her website, or online sites like Amazon and Goodreads—it truly makes her day.

Happy Reading!